YOURS AFTER DARK

GANSETT ISLAND BOOK SERIES, BOOK 20

MARIE FORCE

Yours After Dark
Gansett Island Series, Book 20

By: Marie Force
Published by HTJB, Inc.
Copyright 2019. HTJB, Inc.
Cover Design: Diane Luger
E-book Layout by E-book Formatting Fairies
ISBN: 978-1946136688

View the McCarthy Family Tree*marieforce.com/gansett/familytree/*

View the list of Who's Who on Gansett Island here *marieforce.com/whoswhogansett/*

View a map of Gansett Island *marieforce.com/mapofgansett/*

The Gansett Island Series

Book 1: Maid for Love (*Mac & Maddie*)
Book 2: Fool for Love (*Joe & Janey*)
Book 3: Ready for Love (*Luke & Sydney*)
Book 4: Falling for Love (*Grant & Stephanie*)
Book 5: Hoping for Love (*Evan & Grace*)
Book 6: Season for Love (*Owen & Laura*)
Book 7: Longing for Love (*Blaine & Tiffany*)
Book 8: Waiting for Love (*Adam & Abby*)
Book 9: Time for Love (*David & Daisy*)
Book 10: Meant for Love (*Jenny & Alex*)
Book 10.5: Chance for Love, *A Gansett Island Novella* (*Jared & Lizzie*)
Book 11: Gansett After Dark (*Owen & Laura*)
Book 12: Kisses After Dark (*Shane & Katie*)
Book 13: Love After Dark (*Paul & Hope*)
Book 14: Celebration After Dark (*Big Mac & Linda*)
Book 15: Desire After Dark (*Slim & Erin*)
Book 16: Light After Dark (*Mallory & Quinn*)
Book 17: Victoria & Shannon (Episode 1)
Book 18: Kevin & Chelsea (Episode 2)
A Gansett Island Christmas Novella
Book 19: Mine After Dark (*Riley & Nikki*)
Book 20: Yours After Dark (*Finn McCarthy*)
Book 21: Trouble After Dark (*Deacon & Julia*)
Book 22: Rescue After Dark (*Mason & Jordan*)
Book 23: Blackout After Dark

More new books are always in the works. For the most up-to-date list of what's available from the Gansett Island Series as well as series extras, go to *marieforce.com/gansett*

CHAPTER 1

"**W**hat in the name of *hell* is on your head?"

Arriving to work slightly hungover and in bad need of coffee, Finn McCarthy ignored the question from his brother, Riley. Finn had forgotten to buy coffee—again—and had gone without this morning. Living alone sucked. Before his dad and Riley moved out, one of them had bought the coffee. Now he had to do it, and he never remembered it until he woke up late and realized he'd forgotten. Again.

Riley wasn't giving up. "Hello?"

"What is what?" Finn choked back a yawn and tried to remember if he'd brushed his teeth before he left the house. He had, hadn't he?

Riley stepped closer to him, boasting the freshly fucked look that had made Finn want to stab him more than once in the months since his brother moved in with Nikki. "*That.*" Riley pointed to the top of Finn's head. "What is *that?*"

Finn had no idea what he was talking about until he reached up and encountered the lump of hair he'd secured with a rubber band to keep it out of his face.

Their cousin Shane joined them. "It's a man bun, and it looks ridiculous."

Riley, that asshole, busted up laughing. "What the hell is a man bun?"

"That." Shane pointed to Finn's head. "Is a man bun. They're all the rage."

Riley couldn't stop laughing. He laughed so hard, he howled, while Finn prayed that his cousin Mac would bring coffee the way he did most days.

Thankfully, Mac walked into the Wayfarer a minute later with his business partner, Luke Harris, right behind him. And was that a tray of coffee Mac was carrying? *Yes!* "What's so funny?"

"Finn has a man bun," Shane said.

"And it looks ridiculous," Riley added.

Finn stole one of the coffees and took a big sip. *Ahhh*, pure bliss. "There's nowhere to get it cut out here."

"Go see Chloe at the Curl Up and Dye," Mac said.

"I don't get my hair cut in *salons*," Finn said disdainfully. "I go to barber shops, and there isn't one on this island."

"The way I see it," Riley said, "if it's a choice between a man bun or a salon, I'm choosing the salon every time."

"The way I see it," Finn said, "no one asked you."

"Wait till Dad, Uncle Mac and Uncle Frank see the man bun." Riley started laughing again. "I gotta get a picture so we can show them in case they miss it." The bastard whipped his phone out and had the picture before Finn could react or turn away. That picture would haunt him for the rest of his life.

Maybe the guys were right—a salon was preferable to putting up with this bullshit. His hair had gotten so long, it was either restrain it or wear a hat to keep it out of his face. Hats annoyed him when he was working, so he'd grabbed a rubber band to contain it without a thought to what it might look like. Apparently, that had been a mistake.

Today, they were finishing up the shingling on the exterior of the Wayfarer, which was due to open in a couple of weeks. They were on track to meet the aggressive deadline Mac had set for the project and had turned the interior over to Nikki, the general manager. She and the team she'd hired over the last few months would be loading in furniture this week, setting up hotel rooms and the dining room, hanging wall art and making finishing touches ahead of the grand opening on Memorial Day weekend.

On Saturday of that weekend, the Wayfarer would host its first major event—the wedding reception of Shane and his fiancée, Katie Lawry. They'd joked that they were the guinea pigs to test out whether the McCarthy family's latest Gansett Island business venture was ready for prime time. The day after the wedding, Finn's famous cousin Evan McCarthy would headline the outdoor stage at the grand opening to the public.

So far, the Wayfarer was a huge hit, with Nikki reporting that the hotel was sold out for the summer and ten other weddings were already booked. That was what they wanted to hear. Each family member had a stake in the business—some bigger than others—but everyone had put something into his uncle Big Mac's latest venture so they could all be owners. Finn was proud of the work they'd done to bring the old place back to life and even prouder of being part of something the family had done together.

Before going outside to get to work, Finn slathered sunscreen all over his face, neck and arms, gathered his nail gun and a ladder and followed the others to the scaffolding that was set up on the north side of the huge building they'd spent the winter renovating. They'd done a damned good job, if he said so himself.

With the end in sight, Finn was making plans to move to the mainland after almost two years on Gansett Island. It'd been fun to hang with the family for a couple of years, to see his father and brother fall in love with women Finn liked and respected and to be part of Mac's construction company. But it was time to get back to his real life, and that wasn't going to happen on a tiny island located off the southern coast of mainland Rhode Island.

He looked forward to skiing in the winter, driving the vintage Mustang he kept garaged at home and spending time with the friends he'd left behind. Not to mention taking his career to the next level with the large construction company he'd worked for in Stamford,

Connecticut. There, he'd put his degree in civil engineering to good use. Here, he was banging nails. Not that he didn't enjoy the work, but he hadn't spent four excruciating years in college to end up a glorified carpenter.

Missy—or *Melissa* as she preferred to be called these days—his on-again-off-again girlfriend at home, was threatening to come fetch him if he wasn't home by June, and he would save her the trip to Gansett by heading home right after the grand opening. After going round and round in his mind about how he felt about her during the time he'd been gone, he was actually looking forward to seeing her. Despite the tumultuous aspects of their five-year relationship, they'd had a lot of fun together, most of the time anyway. Since they'd been broken up during the time he was gone, he'd indulged in a few one-night stands here and there, but nothing of any consequence.

It was definitely time to go home and figure out whether they had what it took to go the distance together. His dad and Riley said absolutely not. They'd never liked Missy for him, but Finn was determined to make up his own mind about her after seeing what remained after the long time apart.

He would miss his brother, father, aunt, uncles and cousins, and he would really miss working with Riley, Mac, Shane and Luke. He'd miss the family gatherings, the fishing trips Big Mac liked to organize and the time with his favorite men in the world. He'd miss Riley's girlfriend, Nikki, whom he called Nicholas while she called him Finnbar. The three of them had spent a lot of time together over the winter, and she'd become a good friend to him.

He liked being able to regularly see his cousins Janey and Laura and their kids, as well as Mac's brood and now Adam's little guy, Liam, too. Mac's wife, Maddie, was expecting another baby, and he'd heard rumblings that his cousin Grant's wife, Stephanie, might be pregnant, too. In addition, his cousin Mallory and her fiancé, Quinn, were talking about tying the knot at some point this summer.

Life on Gansett was rarely boring with the McCarthy family and their friends around to keep things interesting. It wasn't like Finn was dying to get out of there, especially with the summer coming. That was the best time of year to be on the island. But he'd promised himself over the winter that once the Wayfarer was finished, he'd make a move.

The Wayfarer was almost done, and the lease at the house was up at the end of the month. It seemed like the universe was conspiring to tell him it was time to get back to reality.

Nikki had offered him the garage apartment at Eastward Look, her family's home, if he wanted it. He was tempted to stay for the summer, but that would only prolong the inevitable.

No, he was going home at the end of the month. Tonight, he'd text his old boss in Stamford to let him know he'd be available in June, and he'd touch base with Missy, too. As he applied the nail gun to a row of shingles, he felt a sense of calm come over him. For so many months, the stay-or-go tug-of-war had raged in his mind while his family had pressured him to stay with them. He'd be the only member of the McCarthy family not living on Gansett, and while it was tempting to give in to the pressure from his family, he had goals and aspirations that couldn't be achieved on the island.

Someday, he'd like to own his own company the way Mac did. Finn considered self-employment the holy grail, accountable to no one but yourself and your employees. Mac worked his ass off, but it seemed nice to be the boss. Finn thought he would like that—someday in the far-off future that would be much farther off if he stayed here than it would be if he went home to Connecticut.

The workday dragged. Shingling was boring, monotonous work that gave him too much time to think. He wanted out of his own thoughts for a while. "What're you guys doing tonight?" he asked Riley as they helped the others clean up and shut down for the day.

"Not sure yet. Nik might be working late again."

"I want to go out."

"I'd be up for that. What do you feel like doing?"

"Drinking, raising hell, the usual."

Riley smiled. "That's your usual. Not mine anymore."

"Oh, shut up. You're not married yet."

"Nope, but I'd like to be. Sooner rather than later."

5

Finn stopped and took a closer look at his brother. "You're serious."

"Dead serious. In fact, I was going to ask if you'd help me pick out a ring."

"Wow. This is huge." While Finn was thrilled for his brother and Nikki, he couldn't ignore the nagging ache that came with losing his best friend. As soon as he had that thought, he felt stupid. Riley was getting married, not dying, for Christ's sake.

"You okay?" Riley gave him an odd look that had Finn pulling himself together.

"I'm happy for you, Ri. Nicholas is a great girl."

"I love her."

The stark simplicity of his brother's statement stayed with Finn on the ride home. Riley had promised to text him after he caught up with Nikki about the plans for the evening. *I love her.* He puzzled over his brother's heartfelt words while showering, and then while drinking a beer and eating his favorite after-work snack of corn chips and Cheez Whiz. *I love her.*

What must it be like to be so certain?

Had he ever said that about any woman, even Missy? Nope, and he wasn't sure whether what he'd felt for Missy was love or lust or some weird combination of the two. One thing he knew for certain—he hadn't had with her what Riley had with Nikki. The realization made him uneasy as he ran fingers through his unruly mop of hair, recalling that he'd planned to get a haircut.

He searched for the Curl Up and Dye salon's number on his phone and put through a call.

A female voice answered. "Curl Up and Dye."

"Hi there. What time do you close tonight?"

"Seven."

"Can you take a walk-in?"

"If you get here soon."

"I'll be right over."

"What's your name?"

"Finn McCarthy."

"Got it. See you soon."

He downed the rest of the beer and put the Cheez Whiz in the fridge next to the beer that was the only other thing in there. The meager contents of his fridge were further proof that he needed to get a life.

Since the salon was in town, he decided to walk rather than drive. As the season started to pick up steam with Gansett Island Race Week underway, parking in town could be hard to come by. A block from the salon, he noticed the dark purple paint and the sign with the catchy name painted in gold leaf. Two smiling, laughing women were leaving as he reached the door, and he held it for them.

One of them gave him the once-over as she went by. "Thank you."

"My pleasure." She was old enough to be his mother.

Inside the salon, the first thing he noticed was the rich scent of shampoo and the décor that consisted of golden wood floors, black leather chairs, chrome accents and mirrors all over the place.

"I'll be right out." The same distinctive voice he'd spoken to on the phone.

"Take your time." Finn looked around at the glass shelves of products that promised shine, body, vibrancy and a variety of other things he never gave much thought to.

"You don't need that."

Finn looked up from the bottle he was studying to find the sexiest woman he'd ever laid eyes on looking at him in amusement. Shoulder-length dark hair streaked with dark purple, ears pierced multiple times each, her left arm boasting a colorful sleeve tattoo, a sparkling diamond stud in her nose and violet eyes that riveted him. He'd never seen eyes that color before. She wore a black sleeveless top over black skinny jeans that clung to curves that made his mouth go dry.

"You must be Finn?"

"Ah, yeah. That's me." He put the bottle on the shelf and managed to knock two others to the floor. As he bent to retrieve them, his head connected with hers in a painful smack that made him see stars. *Fucking hell, that hurt!* When he looked up, he found her rubbing the side of her head.

7

"Ow."

"Sorry about that." He picked up the bottles and returned them to the shelf.

"You've got a hard head." Her face flushed when she realized the double meaning behind her words.

A surge of heat to his groin caught him by surprise. It'd been so long since any woman had interested him, and he'd nearly given this one a concussion. "May I please request a do-over of the last minute?" He held out his hand. "I'm Finn McCarthy."

She eyed his hand before she reached out to take it. "Chloe Dennis."

The brush of her skin against his made his entire system go haywire. What the hell was that about? Stunned and unnerved by his reaction to her, he quickly retrieved his hand. "Do you have time for a quick haircut?"

"Sure, but with all that hair, it's not going to be quick."

"I can come back another time."

"No, it's fine." She gestured to one of three black chairs positioned in front of a row of mirrors. "Have a seat."

Finn headed for the chair she pointed to and sat, feeling out of sorts and off his game after the head bump. He wasn't usually so clumsy or awkward around women, but he'd rarely encountered one like Chloe.

Goddess was the word that came to mind. She projected a cool, aloof aura of self-confidence, which he found incredibly sexy. He stared at her in the mirror as she approached the chair, and when she ran her fingers through his hair, he felt her touch in every corner of his body. Even the bottoms of his feet tingled with awareness.

Holy crap.

"What're you thinking?"

He didn't dare answer that question.

"Short or on the longer side?"

God, she was talking about his hair, and his imagination had run away with him.

"Um, short enough that it's not in my face at work, but not super short."

"What do you do for work?"

"Construction for my cousin Mac."

"Ahh, gotcha. He's insane. In the best way, of course."

Finn laughed. "That he is. He keeps us well entertained." Finn would miss the older cousin he'd always looked up to. The ten years between them had all but disappeared in the time Finn had lived on Gansett Island. These days, Mac treated him more like a peer than a pesky baby cousin. Finn had learned a lot from Mac, both professionally and personally.

"You McCarthy men sure were blessed with great hair."

Watching her run her fingers through his hair was one of the most erotic things Finn had ever experienced.

"I cut your dad, your uncles, your cousins. You guys could be shampoo models."

Finn cleared a huge lump from his throat. "You think so?"

She met his gaze in the mirror. "I really do."

Was it his imagination or did she look at him much longer than necessary? No, definitely not his imagination. He shifted in the seat, hoping she wouldn't notice his embarrassing reaction to her. The movement startled her, and she looked away.

Nothing like this had *ever* happened in a barber shop.

CHAPTER 2

oly hotness, Batman. The McCarthy men had gotten far more than their fair share of good looks, but this McCarthy was in a class by himself.

Chloe told herself to quit being a nitwit as she cut his gorgeous, silky dark hair, the same McDreamy hair his father, uncles and cousins had. But none of them had turned her into a stuttering fool the way he had. What the hell was wrong with her? She didn't go silly in the head over men, but she would have to be dead and buried not to notice Finn McCarthy.

Like his older cousins, he had McCarthy blue eyes, dark wavy hair, prominent cheekbones and a mouth made for sin. In addition to those attributes, Finn was also built like a man who worked hard for a living, with muscles bulging under a formfitting Henley and perfectly faded jeans that left very little to the imagination.

Yum.

She took her time cutting his hair, while trying to process the odd hum of attraction that simmered between them. Every time she caught his eye in the mirror, he was looking at her.

Chloe tried to think of something she could say to break the tension, but everything she came up with sounded stupid, which was so ridiculous. In addition to cutting hair, she made small talk for a living. So why was her brain totally blank when it came to chatting with him?

He solved the problem for her. "This is my first time at a salon."

"Really?"

"Uh-huh. I've always been more of a barber shop kind of guy, but I'm seeing that I've been missing out."

There was that look again, the one that told her she wasn't the only one who was attracted. Too bad he was off-limits to her. The McCarthys were one of the island's most prominent families, many of them regular customers. Indulging in a flirtation or whatever this was with one of them wasn't in the best interest of her business.

Better to keep things professional, even if a romp with the sexy Finn McCarthy would be a great way to break the longest dry spell in history.

Don't think about romping or anything else with him. Just cut his damned hair. Sometimes she deeply resented the voice inside her head that made her act like an adult when she really wanted to bust loose and do something fun and reckless. When was the last time she'd been reckless? Never. She hadn't had the luxury of being reckless. She'd been far more concerned with supporting herself when other people her age were off partying and doing what twenty-somethings did.

She'd risked everything to buy the salon five years ago, and since then, she had been so focused on work and growing the business that she'd barely had time for anything resembling a social life. Of course, she had much bigger reasons for staying focused on her business rather than her personal life, but she tried not to think about those things. When she did think about them, she ran the risk of sinking so deeply into the abyss of depression, she might never find her way out. So she didn't allow herself to go there.

"Have you been working on the Wayfarer?"

"Yep. My home away from home for the last six months."

"It looks incredible from the outside."

"The inside is even better. You should come by and check it out sometime. I'd be happy to show you around."

"I'd love to see it. Everyone is so curious."

"When is your next day off?"

"Monday."

"Come over at lunchtime. I'll give you a tour and buy you lunch."

Curiosity about the Wayfarer had her wavering. The thought of seeing him again tipped her toward saying yes. She forced herself to meet that intense blue-eyed gaze in the mirror. "That sounds like fun."

"Great." His smile lit up his face, and it was all she could do not to sigh. He was just too damned sexy for his own good—and hers.

She ran a comb through his hair and then shaved his neck. "How does that look?"

"Might be the best haircut I've ever gotten."

Amused, she rolled her eyes. "Sure it is."

"I mean it. It looks really good. A thousand times better than Joe the Barber in Stamford. Thank you."

"You're welcome."

She rang him up and watched him head for the door, her gaze fixed on the way his jeans hugged his awesome ass. Then he spun around and caught her looking.

"Do you want to get a drink?"

I do. I really, really do. But I can't. "Thanks, but I have plans. Another time, maybe."

"Sure, that'd be great." Once again, his smile lit up his impossibly handsome face. "See you Monday, if not before."

After the door closed behind him, Chloe stood there staring at it for a full minute, calling herself ten kinds of crazy for lying to him about having plans. The only plan she had was another night completely alone with her yellow Lab, Ranger. At thirteen, he was getting so old, he had trouble getting around, but Chloe refused to acknowledge the inevitability that was looming in the near future.

Life without Ranger was inconceivable.

Though her hands, hips, knees and ankles ached fiercely after the long day, Chloe gave the salon a thorough cleaning, as she did every night, and locked up an hour after Finn left. Why was she still thinking about him? He was a customer like all the others who frequented her salon, the only place to get a haircut on Gansett Island. Everyone who was anyone came through her doors from one week to the next. Why should he be any different from all the others?

She'd cut his brother's hair a couple of weeks ago and hadn't had any reaction whatsoever to Riley, who was equally handsome and charming. What was so special about Finn that had her body still tingling with awareness of him more than an hour after he left? Chloe was trying to reconcile her unusual reaction to him when she stopped at the island's only grocery store to pick up a few things on the way home, including a rotisserie chicken for Ranger. He'd lived long enough to deserve chicken with every meal.

In the produce aisle, she picked out vegetables for a salad to go with some of Ranger's chicken—he was good about sharing with her —and was turning toward the register when she ran smack into the chest of the man next to her, who happened to be Finn McCarthy.

Of course it was him, and of course her entire body went haywire all over again.

"Fancy meeting you here," he said.

That smile. That freaking panty-melting smile. It was, without a doubt, the best smile she'd ever seen on a guy—sexy, sincere, friendly, unguarded perfection.

"Chloe?" His brows furrowed as he studied her with those piercing blue eyes that made her want to sigh. "Are you all right? That's twice in two hours that I've nearly injured you."

"I-I'm fine." She hated that hitch in her voice that told him he made her nervous. Men didn't make her nervous. *She* made *them* nervous, and she much preferred that to this.

"You're sure?"

Thanks to the haircut she'd given him, he was even more devastatingly handsome than he'd been the first time she'd laid eyes on him. Had that really been only two hours ago? It seemed longer than that.

"Excuse me." A woman behind her needed to get to the tomatoes, which snapped Chloe out of her Finn-coma.

She moved to let her in. "Sorry about that."

"What's for dinner?"

He's talking to you. Stop being so weird! "Ah, salad and chicken that I'll share with my dog."

"You have a dog? Boy or girl?"

"A boy named Ranger."

"I love dogs."

That clicking noise was the sound of him going up a few notches in her estimation. Men who loved dogs were the only ones worth bothering with.

He gestured to his handheld basket. "I've got pasta, sauce and garlic bread. I make the best garlic bread around. Ask anyone. If you let me meet your dog, I'll make some for you to go with your salad."

Dear God. Every hormone in her body was on full alert and screaming *YES* at the top of their lungs. Did hormones have lungs? Hers did, and they were screaming.

Then he made a little pout face. "I haven't seen my dog in months. He lives on the mainland with my mom. I sure do miss him."

A stronger woman would be able to resist this handsome, sexy man who also loved dogs and garlic bread. Apparently, he was her kryptonite, because she was incapable of saying no to him. "I'll let you meet him in exchange for the garlic bread."

Again with that lethal, panty-melting smile. It ought to come with a warning: May cause panties to spontaneously combust in the produce aisle. "Deal. Lead the way."

She walked toward the checkout counter, aware of him behind her, probably watching her every move because that's what she'd be doing if she were following him. Chloe didn't make a habit of inviting men she'd just met home with her, but she knew his family and respected the fact that he had gracefully taken no for an answer when he asked her out.

Plus, she was trained in Krav Maga and wasn't afraid of any man. If anything, they ought to be afraid of her, not that they ever realized that until it was far too late. The foster father who had raised her had been an instructor and had taught her to defend herself. Her skills had come in handy more than once with men who didn't understand the word *no.* Instinct told her that wouldn't be an issue with this man, but in a world in which she was almost completely alone, she'd learned to be wary of all men until they proved themselves worthy of her trust.

Chloe paid for her groceries and then waited for Finn to pay for his.

On the way out of the store, he stepped aside for her to go ahead of him. "Did you really turn me down for a drink because you had plans with a dog?"

"What if I did?"

"That's one lucky dog."

Oh, she liked him. So many guys would be offended that she'd chosen her dog over them, but Finn found it amusing and had turned it into an opportunity to compliment her. He was racking up the points, and she hadn't even tasted his garlic bread yet.

"Should I follow you?"

Chloe nodded while trying to think about how she'd left her house that morning. Messy but clean. It would do, provided Ranger hadn't left any surprises for her. He had the run of the place during the day, and she left the dog door open for him to get in and out. She'd even built a ramp to help him down into the yard from the deck since stairs were difficult for him these days. Whatever he needed was fine with her.

She got into her battered Toyota sedan and waited for Finn to follow her.

He drove a big dark-colored pickup truck that suited him. She couldn't picture a big guy like him in a small car like hers. No, he needed a big truck, which led her to wonder what the hell she was thinking. He *needs* a big truck? Who *needs* a truck? *I've taken leave of my senses since he came strolling into my salon.* That was the only possible explanation for the ridiculousness circulating through her mind as she led him to the house she rented on the island's west side where he would be treated to her stupendous view of the sunset.

Sometimes Chloe couldn't believe she paid only seven hundred dollars a month in rent, because the sunsets made her little house worth a million times that. The saltbox house was more of a home to her than anywhere she'd ever lived, and she loved it. In fact, she dreamed about someday saving enough money to buy it, but that was more of a pipe dream than anything. Real estate on the island started in the hundreds of thousands, and she'd have to cut a lot of hair to be able to afford a fraction of that.

She pulled into her usual spot and heard barking from inside. Ranger welcomed her home every night—and every night, she exhaled with relief when she heard that bark. She feared coming home to silence one day.

Finn parked next to her and waited to help with her bags.

He followed her inside, where Ranger greeted her with his usual enthusiasm until he spotted Finn lurking behind her. Then he went into protector mode, barking and growling.

"Easy, boy. He's a friend." *At least I think he is...*

Finn squatted and held out his hand for Ranger to sniff. "Hey, Ranger. I'm Finn. It's nice to meet you."

Swoon.

Ranger cozied up to Finn, sniffing and kissing him. Lucky bastard.

Jealous of a dog. That was what it'd come to. Amused by her thoughts, Chloe went into the kitchen and reached for the medication she took every night at this time to alleviate the pain in her joints after a long day at work. Today had been a relatively good day. She'd learned to appreciate the good days and dread the days when the pain took over, drowning out everything else. She subtly took the pills while he continued to chat with Ranger. She'd kill for a glass of wine, but alcohol didn't mix well with the powerful meds she took, so she avoided it. "What can I get you to drink?"

"I stopped to pick up beer before the grocery store. Hope that's okay."

"Sure. Whatever you want."

From his perch on Ranger's level, Finn looked up at her, brow crooked. "Is that right?"

"You must've gotten an A-plus in flirting when you were in school. You're rather accomplished at it."

"Am I?" He stood to his full, imposing six-foot-something height.

She rolled her eyes. "You know you are, because women have been falling at your feet from the minute your voice changed."

"It was actually before that."

Chloe laughed, and Ranger started barking, as if he thought Finn's comment was funny, too.

For a long, charged moment, she and Finn stared at each other, and Chloe wondered if he felt as off-balance as she'd been since he walked into the salon. She'd heard of these sorts of things happening to other people but had never experienced it herself. And, to be honest, she'd always been skeptical about the idea of instant attraction. In the course of one evening, he was changing her thinking on the subject.

Desperate to find her missing equilibrium, she got busy preparing Ranger's dinner, cutting up enough chicken for him and a salad for two. As she worked, Finn leaned around her to grab a knife from the butcher block on the counter, his arm brushing against hers as he backed away.

She felt that subtle touch everywhere and then immediately dismissed it as a side effect of the dry spell. What else could it be? She didn't do foolish when it came to men. Out of necessity, she'd been forced to be practical when other girls were frivolous. That practicality had followed her into adulthood, and this was no time to start acting like a silly, simpering girl just because a ridiculously sexy man had paid her some attention.

He would move on to the next willing female as soon as he realized she was going to be far too much work. It'd happened before, and she'd learned not to get invested. She'd been on her own so long, she didn't know it any other way. Looking out for herself, first and foremost, was second nature because she hadn't had anyone else to do it for her.

While her high school friends had been actively—and successfully—trying to land husbands, Chloe started a business and nurtured it into a modest success that allowed her to live in her favorite place year-round, far away from the madness of her childhood. She avoided drama like the plague and kept to herself most of the time. Sure, she

17

had friends she enjoyed spending time with, but she was happiest at home with Ranger.

Chloe put his bowl down and watched him drag himself across the tile floor, her anxiety spiking. His struggles tugged at her heart and filled her with panic. What would she do without him? He was all the family she had left.

CHAPTER 3

$\mathcal{C}$hloe was unlike any woman Finn had ever known. Quiet, self-contained, unimpressed with his flirting game and more focused on her dog than she was on him. Finn was officially intrigued. He'd grown tired of women who threw themselves at him simply because they found him attractive. Sure, he'd enjoyed the attention at one point in his life, but he was past that now.

Seeing Riley madly in love with Nikki had stirred something in him, a restlessness he'd never experienced before. That restlessness had led him to the conclusion that it was time to go home and figure out the rest of his life. But he didn't need to think about leaving tonight when he had the intriguing Chloe to dine with.

He loved her small, colorful, eclectically decorated home that combined old and new pieces to create a cozy, comfortable atmosphere. Whereas he simply existed in the rental home he'd once shared with his father and brother, her house was truly a home. "Have you lived here long?"

"More than five years. I came out for my friend's bachelorette party and fell in love with the island."

"Was that your first time here?"

"Uh-huh. What about you?"

"I was here all the time as a kid, visiting my aunt, uncle and cousins. This time, I've been here almost two years. Came out for my cousin Laura's wedding and got bamboozled into staying to work for Mac. My parents had just split, and my dad was in a bad place, so after he decided to stay for a while, my brother and I did, too."

"That was nice of you."

He shrugged off the praise. "We like him. He's a good guy, and he got kind of a raw deal from my mom."

"How so?"

"After thirty years of marriage, she left him for another guy. He'd tell you now she did them both a favor, but at the time… It was ugly."

"That's shitty. Why couldn't she just ask for a divorce?"

"That was our feeling, too, but we've moved on. He got remarried last Christmas, and his wife is expecting a baby soon."

"Wow. How do you feel about a new sibling?"

"I'm excited." That was the one major downside to his plan to move back to the mainland. He would miss out on seeing his younger brother or sister grow up. But he planned to be a frequent visitor. "My dad is really happy with Chelsea. That's all that matters to me and Riley."

"Chelsea is an amazing person. I love her." Chloe cut the vegetables for salad while he prepared the garlic bread. "She's crazy about your dad."

"Yes, she is and vice versa. I suppose you know everyone on this island as the only one who cuts hair."

"Not *everyone*. I didn't know you before today."

Finn laughed. "That's true. I got my hair cut the last time I was home, which was about six months ago. I was long overdue."

"I do know most of the women, though. They keep me busy."

"Do you work by yourself?"

"I have one stylist who comes out for the summer. She likes it out here but can't do the winters. That works out well because I'm much busier in the summer anyway. She'll be here in June."

"It's cool how you managed to corner the market on something the island needed."

"As soon as I realized they didn't have a salon, I started making plans to open one."

"That's really amazing. I dream of owning my own business, and you made it happen at twenty-something. Very admirable." He opened a box of pasta. "Do you have a couple of pots I could borrow?"

"Yep."

While Ranger and his full belly lay off to the side, watching their every move, Chloe and Finn worked together to prepare dinner. When it was ready, they took their plates to the small kitchen table.

Finn opened a second beer while she refilled her water glass.

"This is nice. Thanks for inviting me over."

"It was the garlic bread." She took a bite, and her beautiful violet eyes lit up with delight. "Damn, that's good."

"Told you so."

"Where'd you learn to cook?"

"Um, well, calling me a cook is being really, *really* generous. I know enough to survive, but I learned how to make garlic bread when I worked in an Italian restaurant in high school."

"You learned well. Cut me another piece."

Smiling, Finn did as directed.

"So much for my low-carb diet."

"The low-carb diet goes against everything I believe in. Do you think anyone lies on their deathbed thinking 'I'm so glad I stayed away from bread, pasta, potatoes, beer or my aunt Linda's doughnuts'? I say no. No one wishes they had less of any of those things."

"You've given this some significant thought."

"Yes, I have. I don't believe in deprivation. Moderation, sure. But deprivation—no."

"Easy for you to say when you're not carrying a single extra pound."

"Neither are you."

"Whatever you say." Her tone dripped with disdain that delighted him.

"It's true. Contrary to what popular culture wants us to believe, it's actually quite sexy to have a little flesh on your bones."

"Is that so?"

"Uh-huh. I've never been attracted to super-thin women, especially if they are super thin because they starve themselves. Life is too short. We need to eat, drink and be merry." He cut another piece of garlic bread and nudged it in her direction.

"Easy, Satan. I've already had two pieces."

"Awww, you gave me a nickname. Does that mean we're going to be friends?"

She rolled her eyes. "I'm sure you have plenty of *friends*."

Finn loved her sarcasm, her dry wit, the way her eyes sparkled. He liked the purple streaks in her dark hair, her amazing tattoo, the sparkling stud in her nose and her sassiness. "Tell me about your ink." The last thing he wanted to talk about with this woman was *other* women.

She looked down at her colorful arm. "I've always loved to draw and paint."

"Wait, you drew all that?" There was everything from birds to angels to demons and landscapes folded into a mosaic of color and conflict.

"Yes." She seemed embarrassed to acknowledge her significant talent.

"That's incredible. I'm truly impressed. I can't draw a straight line with a ruler."

"Yes, you can."

"No, I really can't." He leaned in for a closer look and extended his hand. "May I?"

She eyed his hand warily. "Sure."

He took hold of her left wrist and moved her arm so he could see the full sequence of images that depicted an angel running from a demon and prevailing after an epic battle. "This," he said, trailing a light fingertip over her biceps, "is amazing. What inspired you to draw that?"

"Life."

Finn wanted to unpack the baggage that came with the one-word answer, but he didn't have the right to ask. Not yet anyway. "You're very talented."

"Thank you. I'm hoping to get the other arm done when I can afford it." She withdrew her arm from his hold, got up to clear the table and began handwashing the dishes. "Check out the sunset."

Finn stood to look out the kitchen window. The sky had exploded in a riot of pinks, oranges and purples. "Wow."

"My favorite time of day on Gansett Island."

He picked up a dish towel and began drying the dishes after she washed them. "Have you drawn it?"

"Many times, but I never seem to be able to capture the full beauty of it."

"I'd love to see your drawings. I bet they're fantastic."

"They're okay."

Finn's phone rang. He retrieved it from his pocket and saw Riley's name on the caller ID. "Excuse me for one minute."

"Go ahead."

"Hey, what's up?"

"What're you doing? We're all at the Beachcomber. Niall is playing. Come on over."

"I've got some other stuff going on tonight." Finn glanced at Chloe, who was focused on the dishes. "I'll see you in the morning."

"I thought you wanted to go out? What other stuff do you have to do?"

"Night, Ri." Finn ended the call before his brother could get pushier. "Sorry about that."

"Don't be. If you got a better offer, don't decline on my behalf."

"I got the better offer a couple of hours ago. I can hang out with my family any time."

She used a dish towel to dry her hands, wincing.

"Are you okay?"

"My hands ache after a busy day at the salon."

After noticing her swollen knuckles over dinner, Finn sensed there was more to it than that, but he didn't ask. He wanted to, though. He really wanted to.

23

"Look, you seem like a nice guy, and this was fun—"

"But?"

She looked him dead in the eye. "I'm not interested."

Stunned by her blunt comment, Finn could only stare at her for the longest time. In that moment, he realized he was very interested. Figured, right?

"I don't mean to be rude."

"Nah, it's fine. I'll, ah, just get going, then." Finn grabbed his jacket from where he'd dropped it over a chair.

"Let me pack up your leftovers."

"You can have them. No worries. Thanks for a fun dinner. I'll see you around." After giving Ranger a pat on the head, he went out into the cool air, zipping his coat as he walked to the truck. As he drove into town, he replayed everything that'd happened from the minute he walked into the salon until the second he exited her home. This had been one of the more interesting and exhilarating evenings he'd ever spent with a woman, which was telling.

He was twenty-seven and had never experienced "chemistry" with a woman like he'd had with her from the first minute his head bounced off hers. His thoughts were a jumbled mess of confusion and disappointment. Women weren't usually much of a mystery to him. Missy was the only real "girlfriend" he'd had. Since he'd been on the island, they had been off-again, but she'd always been there in the background, making it clear that he was the one she wanted when the time came to settle down—not that he'd encouraged that line of thinking in any way. These days, he thought of her more as a good friend than anything more significant.

His family didn't care for her, and his brother and father had gone so far as to come right out and tell him he could do better than Missy. Sure, she could be a bit clingy and needy at times. But he'd never met anyone he liked better than her. After one night with Chloe, he felt like he'd gotten a firsthand look at everything that was missing with Missy.

Dynamic conversation, sizzling attraction, a desire to know more about her. There'd never been any mystery to Missy. Whereas she was the proverbial open book, Chloe was closed off, contained, reserved, cautious. Finn hadn't known those things would appeal to him until he'd met her.

Whatever. She wasn't interested, and he wasn't about to let a couple of hours with an intriguing woman upend his plans. He was almost to his house when he decided to go to the Beachcomber. A beer with his dad and brother would be just what he needed after a strange day. Because of Race Week, the Beachcomber parking lot was nearly full. He squeezed the truck into the last available space and headed inside, bending his head against the chilly breeze coming in off the water. It took until about mid-June to really warm up on Gansett, and even then, the evenings were cool for much of the summer.

The first thing he saw when he walked into the bar was Riley's back. Though Finn couldn't see through his brother, he had no doubt that Nikki occupied the stool that Riley stood guard over. The two of them were inseparable, the way he and Riley had been before his brother fell for Nikki. In the last few months, Finn had settled into the new normal of having to share Riley with someone else for the first time in their lives.

He nudged his brother, who looked at him with surprise.

"Hey! You made it!"

Chelsea sat on the stool next to Nikki, his dad on the other side of Chelsea.

Riley signaled to the bartender and ordered a beer for Finn. "Thought you had other plans?"

"Plans change." Finn took a sip of the beer. "What goes on around here?"

"Chelsea is having weird contractions."

Finn glanced at her. He still found it strange to think of her as his stepmother. "Is that normal?"

Chelsea shrugged. "Victoria says it is."

Nikki placed a hand on Chelsea's baby belly. "It's so cool how you can feel her moving around in there."

Finn raised a brow. "*Her?* Do you guys know something I don't?"

"Nik is psychic." Riley smiled all the time when she was around. "She has a feeling."

Kevin took hold of Chelsea's hand and brought it to his lips. "A little girl would be fine with us. As long as she is healthy."

Standing in a room full of people, surrounded by loved ones, Finn was lonelier than he had ever been. His dad and Riley would do anything for him. He knew that, but Nikki and Chelsea came first with them, as they should. That left him the odd man out in his own family.

"I wanted to tell you guys that I'm going home after the Wayfarer's opening." Finn hadn't planned to tell them until closer to his departure so they couldn't talk him out of it. But the words were out before he could consider whether the timing was right.

"You won't be here when the baby arrives," Chelsea said, looking sad.

"I'll come visit."

His dad eyed him with the laser-sharp intellect that had made it impossible to get away with anything when he and Riley were younger. "What's so pressing at home?"

"I talked to Clint. He needs a foreman and offered me the job as long as I can be there by June first. Since the lease on the house is up on May thirty-first, I told him I'd be there."

Nikki made a playful pout face. "I was excited about you living in the garage apartment for the summer. I've got it all fixed up for you."

"You didn't have to do that."

"I didn't mind."

Finn felt Riley staring at him. "What?"

"Have you told Mac yet?"

"I was going to talk to him at Janey's." Their cousin was hosting a celebration for the crew that had renovated the Wayfarer, a family effort that had involved some family more than others, thus Janey's desire to feed everyone who'd done the heavy lifting for the rest of them.

"He's going to be bummed. I think he's counting on you for the summer and then the hotel reno."

Mac and the crew would be doing a refresh of McCarthy's Gansett Island Inn in North Harbor after the summer. There was no shortage of construction work on the island to keep them busy year-round, and Mac had cultivated a sterling reputation that had them turning down more work than they could take on.

"Enough with the guilt trip. It's time to go. I never signed on to be a lifer when I came to Laura's wedding." To his own ears, Finn sounded like a petulant child. The subtle lift of his father's brow confirmed that he sounded that way to them, too. "I'm sorry. I don't mean to let everyone down. I just want to go home."

"Because of Missy?"

His brother's question infuriated Finn. It was none of his business.

Riley nodded in response to his own question. "It is because of her."

"Shut up, Riley."

Nikki squeezed Riley's forearm. "Leave him alone, Ri."

Finn sent Nikki a grateful glance. "It's not about Missy. It's about me and what I want that can't be found here."

"What's that?" Riley sounded genuinely baffled, probably because he'd found everything he could want or need in Nikki. He could no longer understand how anyone wouldn't want to live on a remote island for the rest of their lives.

"You wouldn't get it."

"Try me."

"*More.* I want more than what can be found here. Since when is that a crime?"

"It's not a crime, but I thought you liked it here."

"I do. I *did.*" Finn shook his head. The restless, edgy feelings that were so much a part of him lately arose once again to remind him of why he wanted a change. But how could he explain the reasons to the others when he didn't understand them himself? "Forget I said anything." He downed the rest of his beer and put a ten on the bar. "I'll see you."

"Finn—"

Finn heard Nikki say something to Riley but didn't stick around to

27

find out what. He thought he'd made a clean getaway when he heard his dad calling him. Rolling his eyes, he expelled a deep breath and turned to find out what the good doctor had to say. He *always* had something to say. "What's up, Dad?"

"I was going to ask you the same thing. You're out of sorts tonight."

"Maybe a little. It happens to all of us, right?"

"Everything okay?"

"Yep. Sorry if I upset Chelsea by saying I'm leaving."

"You didn't. She's disappointed you won't be here when the baby is born. We both are."

"I don't mean to disappoint you."

"We'll get over it. What can I do for you?"

The question and the concern were quintessential Kevin McCarthy, who'd always been there for his sons. "Nothing. I'm fine. I'm just ready to get back to normal."

"I'll miss you. We all will. Won't be the same here without you."

"Don't guilt-trip me."

"I don't mean to. I'm just telling you how I feel. I got used to having you around again and seeing you every day. I'll miss you when you're gone."

"You'll be so busy with Chelsea and the baby that you won't even notice."

"You're right. I'll be busy, but I *will* notice you're not here. Trust me on that."

"Look, I appreciate that you guys like having me around. I like having you around, too, but this place isn't real life, at least not for me."

"Fair enough. I hope that no matter where you go, you'll find what you're looking for."

"So do I."

"I'm always here for you. I hope you know that."

"Of course I do. I'll talk to you tomorrow, okay?"

"Sounds good. Sleep well."

"You, too." Finn walked away from his father feeling unsettled and uncertain about the plan that had made perfect sense to him only a few hours ago. The push-pull of Chloe's rejection coupled with his family's dismay about his pending departure had him questioning everything.

Maybe he should stay until the baby was born. But the baby wasn't due until mid-June, and he'd promised Clint he'd be back by the first. If he stayed for June, he would end up staying for the summer to finish whatever Mac had lined up for them next. And the cycle would continue.

No, it was time to go.

CHAPTER 4

Over the next few days, Finn dedicated himself to working long hours to help finish the final punch list at the Wayfarer. To celebrate the finish line and as a thank-you to the family members who'd done most of the work, his cousin Janey was having everyone over for dinner, which would be fun.

As he hung stall doors in the women's restroom, Finn was looking forward to the gathering and some family fun after working through the weekend to get everything done. Although, he was also dreading having to tell Mac he was leaving.

He was hanging the last of six doors when he heard Riley calling for him.

"In here."

"Hey, there's someone here for you. Chloe?"

Finn was so surprised, he nearly dropped the heavy door on his foot.

Riley leaned against the wall. "Something you want to tell me?"

"Nope."

"You're sure?"

"Yep. Don't you have stuff to do?" Finn put down the door, leaning it carefully against the wall.

"Want me to finish that for you?"

"No need. I can do it when I get back."

"From where?"

"Chloe wanted to see the Wayfarer. I'm going to show it to her. End of story."

"That sounds like the start of a new story."

"It's not like that."

Riley studied him intently. "You've been acting weird lately. What's up with you?"

"Nothing is up with me. Move so I can get by, will you?"

Riley stepped aside, but Finn felt his brother watching as he went out to the main part of the building to find Chloe. Today she wore a denim jacket that covered her colorful arm and black jeans that hugged her sexy curves. Her hair was in a ponytail, and her head was tipped back as she studied the complex set of beams that secured the structure from the inside.

"What do you think?" Finn asked when he joined her.

"I'm trying to figure out how you did that."

"Carefully. It took four freezing days in February, two cherry pickers and seven men to make the building hurricane-proof. Those were some good times."

A smile lit up her extraordinary violet eyes. He found himself staring at the face he'd tried—and failed—to forget after she gave him the brush-off.

"How did you get cherry pickers in here?"

"See those walls of windows over there?" He pointed to the beach side of the building. "They open like garage doors to bring the outdoors inside in the summer."

"That's very cool." She shifted her gaze from the windows to him. "I was impossibly rude to you the other night, and I apologize. I've felt bad about it ever since."

"You weren't rude. You were honest."

"I wasn't, actually."

Was it his imagination or was she blushing? The idea of this badass woman blushing did funny things to his insides. "What do you mean?"

"I'm not uninterested."

"Oh." Finn couldn't think of a single other thing to say, because his brain had gone completely blank.

"So not only was I rude, I'm also a liar."

He laughed at the self-deprecating face she made. "Most true liars don't confess their sins, so you should probably cut yourself a break."

"I'm sorry if I hurt your feelings. We had a nice evening, and I was a jerk."

"You weren't a jerk, and you can make it up to my hurt feelings by coming to a party with me tonight."

"Oh, um…"

"Unless you don't want to—and I wouldn't blame you. The entire McCarthy family will be there along with various friends, so it's not your average party but somewhat of a family blowout. Feel free to say no if that's not your speed."

"You make it hard to resist such an enticing offer."

Finn laughed at her witty reply. "One thing I can promise is you won't be bored."

"It sounds like fun. I'd love to go."

"There's just one thing…" Finn knew he had to warn her. It wouldn't be fair not to.

"What's that?"

"If we show up there together, they'll have us married with children before the night is over. That's how my family rolls."

"Marriage and children, huh? That's an awfully big commitment for a first date."

"That's what I'm saying. Maybe we should do something else."

"I wouldn't want you to miss your family thing on my account. I know most of them already, so I'm not afraid to wander into the snake pit. If you aren't…"

"I'm not afraid." The heated zing of attraction that'd been so present the other night arced between them even more intensely than before, making his mouth dry and other parts of him tingle with interest. "Want to see the rest?" He needed to do something besides stare at her, or he'd have an obvious problem on his hands before too much longer.

"I'd love to."

"Right this way." He led her into the huge, state-of-the-art kitchen, where they encountered Nikki, consulting with the executive chef she'd hired. Finn hadn't met him yet, but he'd heard great things about him from Nikki.

"Hey, Finn, come meet Anthony. Anthony, this is Finn McCarthy, another of the partners."

Anthony, who had a full head of light brown hair and blue eyes, shook Finn's hand. "Nice to meet you. There sure are a lot of you McCarthys."

Finn laughed. "Yes, there are. This is Chloe Dennis, owner of the Curl Up and Dye salon, the best place to get your hair cut on Gansett Island."

"The *only* place," Chloe said, sounding amused.

Anthony shook hands with Chloe, who flinched subtly, but Finn noticed. "That makes you a good person to know around here."

Finn glanced at Chloe, concerned about the flinch, but not wanting to embarrass her. "You know Nicholas, right?"

Nikki scowled at him. "Don't call me that at work, Finnbar. And it's nice to see you, Chloe."

"You, too, Nicholas." Chloe laughed. "Sorry, but that's funny."

"I think so, too." Finn liked her more by the minute. "The McCarthys are great givers of nicknames that stick like glue."

"Good to know. I'll have to watch my back. Is Finnbar your real name?"

Nikki snorted with laughter. "No, that's my name for him."

Chloe laughed along with her. "I love it."

"You going to Janey's later, Nik?" Finn asked.

"That's the plan. See you there?"

"We'll be there."

She raised a brow. "*We* will?"

Finn realized his strategic error after he'd already made it—giving

Nikki a heads-up that he planned to bring Chloe. "No need to call the scoop into the *Gansett Gazette*."

"I'd never do that, but I hope you told poor Chloe what she's in for."

"I warned her, and she still wants to come."

"You're a brave girl."

"Don't scare her off. I like her." He curled a hand around Chloe's arm, like that was the most natural thing he'd ever done, and gave a gentle tug to get her away from Nikki before Nik talked her out of going with him to Janey's. "Come on, let's go see the rest."

"See you later," Chloe called over her shoulder to Nikki and Anthony. "She seems really cool."

"She is. My brother is nuts about her."

"I've seen them around town. They're cute together."

"So cute I want to barf half the time."

"Awww, are you jealous that your brother has a girlfriend?"

He led her past the reception desk, upstairs to the hotel. "I was— and I haven't admitted that to anyone, by the way. But I'm getting used to it now. They're really happy, and if he's happy, I'm happy. I do miss having him to run around with."

"You guys are close?"

"Very. Always have been."

"That's very sweet. I can see how it would be an adjustment to have him move on."

"It was, but I'm over it. She's perfect for him, and I like her a lot. They put up with having me underfoot as a regular third wheel, so it's not like he's forgotten he has a brother or anything." He opened the doors to one of the eight hotel rooms, where Shane was touching up the paint.

Shane turned to greet them. "Hey, what's up?"

"I'm showing Chloe around."

Chloe waved to Shane. "How's it going?"

"Good. I thought you were having lunch with Katie today?"

"I am. After this."

Finn looked at her. "You know Katie?"

34

"I'm one of her bridesmaids. We met when she came in to get her hair cut more than a year ago and hit it off."

Shane put down the paintbrush and wiped his hands on a rag. "Katie says you're as good at cutting hair as her sister Cindy, and that's apparently high praise."

"She tells me that all the time. She's too kind."

Finn ran his fingers through his shorter hair. "She made me even handsomer than I already was."

Shane rolled his eyes. "You're uglier than ever."

Chloe covered her mouth but couldn't contain the snort of laughter.

"Tell my girl I said hello when you see her," Shane said.

"I will. This room is beautiful. You guys did such a nice job. I love all the beadboard."

Finn ran a hand over the creamy-white trim that topped the bead-board. "Mac says you have to have it when building on the coast. It's like a rule or something."

"The Rules According to Mac McCarthy, Jr.," Shane said. "It's a thick volume that's always changing."

"In other words," Finn said, "he makes it up as he goes along."

Shane laughed. "Makes it fun to work with him."

It is fun, Finn thought. Mac kept things interesting, and busting balls with his brother and cousins all day was the most fun he'd ever had at work. If only they were having all that fun somewhere other than a tiny island off the coast of Rhode Island where nothing of any consequence happened nine months of the year. The winters were brutal and lonely.

After spending much of the past winter with nothing more than Netflix and an occasional night out with Riley, Nikki and his cousins to keep him entertained as well as some weekends working on the renovations to Nikki's house, Finn couldn't stand the thought of another winter on Gansett. He actually shuddered.

Chloe studied him with her brows furrowed. "You okay?"

"Yeah, I'm good. Let me show you the tiki bars we built into the sand."

35

"That sounds fun. See you later, Shane."

"Bye, Chloe."

Finn led the way downstairs, through the main room where the centerpiece was an enormous mahogany bar with more than one hundred stools around it. "Shane built the bar."

"It's incredible."

"He does great work. He's a master carpenter."

"The whole place is really something. I love how your family came together to make this happen."

"It was my uncle Big Mac's idea. I only have a small stake, but I do love being an owner with the rest of my family. It was a very satisfying project to be part of."

"You have a really amazing family. You know that, don't you?"

"I do. I'm going to miss them."

"How come?"

Finn glanced at her. "I, um, I'm heading back to the mainland after we open the Wayfarer."

"Oh."

Was that disappointment he heard or wishful thinking on his part? "The job is done, and it's time to figure out what's next. I never intended to move here forever."

"I didn't either. Like I said, I came out for a bachelorette party and found out there was no salon. I secured a storefront with affordable rent, and five years later, I'm still here. It's become home."

They walked outside to the wide patio that would soon be covered with tables and chairs for outdoor dining and onto the beach, where two large tiki bars had been built right on the sand.

"You guys are sitting on a gold mine here."

"That's what Mac says, too. We're going to rent umbrellas, chairs and lounges to day-trippers and have live entertainment every day all summer at the outdoor bar over there."

"It's going to be the island's new hot spot. Congratulations on a job well done."

"Mac and Luke get all the credit. They made it happen."

"With a lot of sweat and hard work from the rest of you."

"It was fun." Finn gave the Wayfarer a wistful glance, thinking of the months of work and camaraderie with his family that had made it happen. Work was going to be boring without them around to keep him entertained. "I wish I could offer you a drink or something, but we're not set up for that yet. I thought we would be by now when I invited you for lunch."

"No worries." She checked the time on her phone. "I've got to meet Katie in fifteen minutes anyway. Thanks for the tour."

"You're welcome." He walked her back inside and through the cavernous dining room that would soon be full of people eating, drinking and having fun. It would also be used for wedding receptions and other parties. He would be sorry to miss seeing how the first season went, but he would hear all about it from Riley. "Pick you up at six for the party at Janey's?"

"Sure, that sounds good."

"Great, I'll see you then."

As he stood on the porch, she went down the stairs that led to the pier where charter fishing boats docked during the season. Beyond that was the ferry landing.

At the bottom of the stairs, she turned and looked up at him. "I'm really sorry to hear you're planning to leave." She gave a little wave and was on her way before he could begin to process what she'd said.

She was sorry he was leaving.

What did that mean?

CHAPTER 5

Why had she said that? *I'm really sorry you're planning to leave.* What the hell was wrong with her? She didn't do this stuff. She didn't gnash her teeth over how she'd left things with a guy for days and then spend extra time on her hair, makeup and clothes before she went to casually meet him for a tour of his family's new business. She also didn't send mixed signals or play games when it came to men.

That was not how she rolled.

She didn't get *involved*. Ever. Keeping her dealings with men at the surface level had worked perfectly her entire adult life. She wasn't about to let one stupendously handsome, charming, sweet man upend her existence.

"Are you talking to yourself?" Katie Lawry's amused voice interrupted Chloe's musings as she waited on the sidewalk for her friend.

"Was I?" Talking to herself was another thing she didn't do—not out loud anyway.

"Ah, yeah, but don't worry, I think I was the only one who noticed." Katie linked her arm through Chloe's and escorted her into the South Harbor Diner. "What's got you so wound up?"

Chloe slid into a booth across from Katie. "It's not a what but rather *who*."

"I'm officially intrigued."

Rebecca, the owner of the diner, came by to say hello and dropped menus on their table. "I have minestrone and broccoli cheddar today. Be right back to take your order."

Katie, who wore pink scrubs as her uniform at the clinic and had her blonde hair gathered into a messy bun, leaned in. "Speak."

"Finn McCarthy."

Katie's eyes went wide, and her lips parted in soundless surprise.

Chloe wanted to shoot herself for being so stupid as to confess her crush to the woman who was about to marry his cousin. "Forget I said anything."

"Like that's going to happen. Tell me everything."

"There's not much to tell."

"Tell me anyway."

She told Katie about him coming in for a haircut, how he'd asked her out and she'd said no only to later run into him in the grocery store. "We ended up having dinner together, but I was such a jerk to him that night." Chloe cringed every time she thought about how that evening had ended. "Today, I kept our appointment for him to show me the Wayfarer. I was nervous after the way we'd left things the other night. But he was so cool and friendly and acted like nothing was weird, even though I made everything weird." She dropped her head into her hands. "And then he said he's leaving soon to go back to the mainland, so what does it even matter?"

When Katie had no response, Chloe looked up to find her friend staring at her. "What?"

"I've never seen you like this."

"That's because I don't *do* this. I don't do drama or angst over men. But I felt bad about being such an ass to him the other night when he was so nice, and then I saw him again, and he's so damned sexy and sweet and... You're still staring at me."

"Sorry. It's just that you're the last person I'd ever expect to be so overwrought about a guy, even if he is a nice, sweet, very handsome

McCarthy kind of guy." Katie leaned in closer. "I'm so glad we've become friends over this last year, but I recently said to Shane that sometimes I feel like I don't really know you as well as I could—and I think that's deliberate on your part."

Chloe had her reasons for keeping her relationships closer to the surface, but that had led to a lonely, isolated existence. Maybe it was time to let a few people in, starting with the woman who had been such a good friend to her.

"You're not wrong about that." She fiddled with her napkin, shredding it as she thought about how much she should say. "My childhood was a train wreck. I don't like to dwell on it."

"I know what you mean. Mine was, too."

"It was? Really?" Katie seemed so together, and she was close to her brother Owen and her mother, Sarah, both of whom lived on the island.

"My dad is in prison for abusing my mom. He was finally convicted two years ago, but he was violent with us the whole time we were growing up."

Flabbergasted, Chloe stared at her. "I'm so sorry. I had no idea."

Katie shrugged. "We kept it quiet when the trial was happening because it was right around the time Owen and Laura were getting married. We were so ready to move on. Like you, though, talking about that is the last thing I want to do when I've moved so far past it. Or at least I've tried to."

"You never completely outrun it."

"No, you don't."

When Rebecca returned to take their order, Chloe asked for a cup of the minestrone and a grilled cheese.

"That sounds good," Katie said. "Make it a double."

Chloe grinned at her. "Copycat."

Katie laughed. "My siblings used to call me that. I always think I know what I want until someone else orders, and then I want what they're having."

"You were lucky to have siblings."

"You have no idea. I never would've survived without them, especially Owen. He was the oldest and ran interference for the rest of us."

"Wow. I never would've guessed that he'd been through that. He and Laura brought the kids in for haircuts a couple of weeks ago. He seems so lighthearted and happy."

"He is now, but it was a long road to get there. Having my dad in jail helps. Thank God for Laura. He would tell you that she saved him in so many ways. You know she's Shane's sister, right?"

"I did know that. It's too cute that you and your brother are marrying a brother and sister."

"You'd be amazed how many people think it's got to be illegal."

Chloe laughed. "I love it."

"Listen, you don't have to tell me your shit if you don't want to, but I want you to know that whatever it is, I probably understand."

In all the years she'd lived on Gansett, Chloe had never told anyone on the island about the horror of her past.

Rebecca brought their soup and put it on the table along with crackers.

"Thank you," Katie said for both of them.

Chloe took a sip of the tasty soup but had trouble getting it past the lump in her throat that appeared whenever she allowed the past to overtake the present. Katie had been a good friend to her, and they'd had a lot of fun times together. Hearing what she'd been through made it easier for Chloe to share her past. "My parents fought a lot when I was little. It escalated as I got older. They went from screaming to hitting to him leaving for a while before he worked his way back in. It went on and on like that until she told him she wanted a divorce and full custody of me."

"What happened?"

"He came home with a gun."

"Oh my God… Chloe…"

"I was upstairs, so I didn't see it happen, but he shot her and then himself."

Katie blinked rapidly to hold back tears as she set down her spoon. "God. How old were you?"

"Seven."

"Chloe. I'm so sorry."

Rebecca brought their sandwiches and put them on the table, quickly retreating when she realized she was interrupting something.

Katie dabbed at her eyes with a napkin. "What did you do?"

"I waited for a long time to see if someone would come, but no one did. Eventually, I snuck downstairs hoping to find that everything was fine when I knew it wasn't." Chloe pushed the bowl of soup away, knowing she wouldn't be able to eat. Not now. "All I remember is there was a lot of blood. I ran out the back door and went to a neighbor, who called the police. I don't remember much more about that day or the immediate aftermath. I ended up in the foster system and landed with a nice family. They were good people." She shrugged. "I was one of the lucky ones."

"I'm so sorry you went through such an awful thing."

"You know what I've figured out?"

"What's that?"

"*Everyone* has been through something awful. Some may be worse than others, but no one slides through life unscathed. Take you and what you went through. I've known you more than a year, and I never would've guessed you grew up in an abusive home."

"My siblings and I have often said the victory is in surviving and thriving. That's what we've tried to do. It's our way of showing him that he didn't win."

"I love that." Chloe met Katie's gaze across the table. "I didn't mean to bring down our lunch."

"You didn't. Not at all. I feel like we went from fun girlfriends to true friends in the last half hour."

"I don't mean to make it difficult to get to know me. I just tend to keep to myself. Old habits are hard to break."

"I totally get it. I used to be a crazy introvert until I moved here, fell for Shane and got sucked into the magic of Gansett Island. Now I'm surrounded by people who genuinely care about me, and I've finally let my guard down."

"I'm still working on that."

"I understand that, too."

"You won't…"

Katie reached across the table and rested her hand on top of Chloe's.

Chloe tried not to flinch from the fear of pain that didn't materialize from Katie's gentle touch.

"I won't tell anyone, not even Shane."

"It's not that I'm ashamed or anything."

"I know. But it's not my story to tell. It's yours."

"It helps to talk to someone who gets it."

Katie nudged the plate containing Chloe's sandwich toward her. "This is a good time for comfort food."

Smiling, Chloe took a bite of the delicious grilled cheese. There were other secrets that weighed heavily on her heart, but she'd said enough for now. Protecting herself had been her top priority for so long that it had become second nature. Lifetime habits didn't change overnight.

"There're a lot of people like you and me here," Katie said after a long silence. "Jenny Martinez's fiancé was killed on 9/11, and he was Erin Barton's twin brother. Jenny's sister-in-law Hope's ex-husband is in jail for having sex with minors when he was a high school coach. Stephanie McCarthy waged a fourteen-year battle to get her stepfather out of prison after he was falsely accused of abusing her."

"I know them all, and I had no idea."

"It's like you said, everyone is carrying something. I don't want you to feel alone with your stuff. People around here care about you."

"That's nice to hear."

"And not just because you're the only one who cuts hair on this island."

They shared a laugh that filled Chloe with a sense of belonging that had eluded her for so much of her life. In that moment, she realized that for all the effort she'd put into building her business relationships on the island, she hadn't spent nearly enough time on her personal ties. Perhaps it was time to change that.

"So Finn…" Katie raised her brows.

"Is the sexiest thing on two legs I've seen in quite some time."

"I'd agree with you, but I happen to think his cousin is the sexiest thing on two legs."

"You have to think that. You're marrying the guy in a couple of weeks."

"It's also true."

Chloe laughed. "Spoken like a loyal fiancée."

"I call it like I see it."

"I saw Shane at the Wayfarer, and he said to tell his girl hello."

"He's so sweet." Resting her arms on the table, Katie leaned in. "And for what it's worth, Finn is a good guy. They all are. They were raised by three of the finest men I've ever known, and they sure know how to treat the women in their lives. Shane makes me feel like a queen on a daily basis, and I know the other McCarthy spouses and girlfriends feel the same. They're amazing men."

The thought of being treated like a queen by Finn McCarthy filled Chloe with yearning to know what that might be like. But she no sooner had those thoughts than she shook them off, remembering that he planned to leave the island soon and nothing good could come from indulging the attraction she'd experienced with him. She had another reason for remaining unattached, and she couldn't forget that either. "That's good to know, but he's a short-timer. I don't need to get excited about him and then have him leave."

"I hate that he's leaving. Shane will be so bummed. He loves having all his cousins here. Did he say why he was going?"

"Not to me."

"Well, that's too bad. I like the idea of you seeing him."

"Eh, it was over before it began. No biggie." Though Chloe projected an aura of indifference, the disappointment stayed with her for the rest of the day.

FINN FINISHED his workday and rushed home to shower and shave. He had a date. An actual date with a woman who interested him, a woman who'd said she was sorry to hear he was leaving the island. That simple statement had him rethinking everything. If he stayed, would she be in the picture? If so, she would be enough to change his plans.

"Stop." He spoke to his reflection in the mirror as he shaved. "You already made your decision, and you aren't going to change your plans for a woman you only just met." *Except...* "No. Tonight is just another night with the family and nothing more. Stick to the script." Maybe if he kept telling himself it was just another night, he might start to believe his own bullshit.

His reaction to her defied explanation or reason. All he knew was that the minute he walked into the salon and saw her, the air around him had felt different, charged with something bigger than anything he'd felt before. He felt stupid explaining it to himself that way, so he couldn't imagine trying to explain it to anyone else.

Over the weekend that he'd spent partially with Riley and Nik and partially alone, he'd decided the reaction to her had been an anomaly. A one-off. The result of meeting a sexy woman he found attractive. By the time Monday had rolled around, he'd written off the entire experience as irrelevant. She'd said she wasn't interested. His father had taught him from an early age how to accept no as an answer from a woman.

And then she'd shown up at the Wayfarer earlier, and it was game back on. The same feeling of electricity in the air had accompanied her into his space, leaving him feeling amped the way he did when he drank too much coffee.

I wish you weren't leaving.

God, how many times had he relived that moment in the hours since she left? Hundreds? It wasn't only the words, which had been powerful in their own right. He was haunted by how she'd looked at him as she said them, as if she saw something special in him and was sorry to miss out on whatever they could've been.

With his hands on either side of the pedestal sink, he dropped his head, hoping to alleviate the tension that'd gathered in his neck. He'd turned this date into a big deal when he knew it couldn't be.

His phone buzzed with a text that snapped him out of his thoughts.

Hey baby! Counting down the days until you get home. Can't wait to see you. Love you!

The text from Missy reminded him of the unfinished business he had with her. He replied to her text with a smile emoji, his stomach aching from the odd sense of dismay that had come over him when he read her text. He didn't want to hear from her. He wanted to hear from Chloe, which was bonkers considering he'd known Missy for years and Chloe for days.

As he got dressed in a clean button-down and jeans, he thought about what his dad and Riley would have to say about him "going home to Missy." Even if that wasn't exactly what he was doing. He was going home to work and figure out his life. If Missy was part of that life, that would be his call to make and no one else's. He refused to allow his dad or brother to get so far inside his head that they made major life decisions for him.

Missy had made it clear she wanted to be on-again, texting and calling frequently to tell him she missed him, she loved him and wanted to start over, this time as adults and not the stupid kids they'd been way back when. They'd both changed and matured and held on to their friendship for all the time they'd been apart. That had to count for something.

He wanted to be fair to her, to judge her on the person she was today, not who she'd been in the past when their relationship had bordered on toxic at times. That was what his dad and brother remembered. They hadn't been privy to the good times—and there'd been a lot of them. Enough to keep him in touch with her for the two years he'd been gone.

But tonight wasn't about her, he thought as he got into his truck. Tonight was for Chloe and his family. There'd be plenty of time later to figure out what he was going to do about Missy and the unfinished business he had with her.

CHAPTER 6

hen he pulled into Chloe's driveway, his skin began to tingle with anticipation. He had no idea what that meant as it had never happened before simply from knowing he was going to see someone. He'd known a lot of women, had done his share of dating, had slept with an even dozen of them, but had never once experienced anything like what happened to him when he merely thought about Chloe.

And then she appeared in the doorway, acknowledging his arrival with a wave before she bent to kiss Ranger goodbye.

The tingling became a waterfall of sensation traveling the full length of him, as if his body had been plugged into an outlet. He'd intended to get out of the truck, to greet her properly, but he found he couldn't move as he watched her come toward him. How could he possibly describe the feeling of being almost outside himself, watching the scene play out from a neutral vantage point?

She opened the passenger door and got in, bringing the distinctive scent that belonged only to her, and smiled at him.

He felt like he'd been punched.

"Finn? Are you all right?"

"I... I don't know."

Her brows furrowed with concern. "What's wrong?"

"Nothing." He studied her beautiful face, the violet eyes that held him in her thrall and the lips he desperately wanted to kiss.

"You're sure?"

"Why did you say you're sorry I'm leaving?"

"Because I am."

"Why?"

"I'm not sure exactly."

"I feel something when I see you." He released a huff of laughter. He'd had absolutely no intention of beginning their evening with true confessions, but there was no stopping him now. "Hell, I feel it when I *think* about you, and I don't understand it. It's never happened to me before."

"I feel it, too." She spoke so softly, he almost didn't hear her.

As he turned in his seat to face her, his heart beat fast with desire that left him breathless and lightheaded. "Chloe, I need you to explain this to me."

"I wish I could."

Drawn to her in ways he'd never been to anyone else, he caressed her cheek with a light touch.

She trembled, and her lips parted.

"Why can I not stop thinking about you?"

Her nervous laughter went a long way toward calming the nerves that had seized him at the first sight of her coming out the door to him. To know she felt similarly undone helped. "Probably for the same reasons I can't stop thinking about you."

"It doesn't make any sense."

She looked down at her hands. "It really doesn't." And then she turned those expressive eyes up to meet his gaze, and again, he felt like he'd been struck by something powerful. "I don't do this stuff."

"What stuff?" He continued to caress her face because he couldn't bear to stop touching her.

"This." She gestured between them.

"Why?"

"Many reasons."

"Tell me." He let the silk of her dark hair with the colorful accents run through his fingers, noting the way she leaned toward him while telling him she didn't do these things.

"I don't take risks."

"Why not?"

"I... Um, well, because. What does it matter? You're leaving. This isn't happening."

"It's happening right now. You said you feel it the same way I do. Tell me why you don't take risks."

"They don't usually end well for me." She reached for the hand that had been caressing her hair and placed it on the seat between them.

Finn immediately mourned the loss and then wondered what in the ever-loving fuck he was doing having such a thought. How could you lose something you'd never had in the first place?

"Maybe we should skip tonight," she said, her expression grim.

"Is that what you want?"

"No, but..."

Finn had no idea why, but he knew he'd regret not spending tonight with her. "Let's go to Janey's and have some fun. There's no risk in that, right?"

The look she gave him told him otherwise.

"Is that okay?"

"I'd love to go, but after that..."

"I get it." Disappointment overwhelmed him as he backed the truck out of her driveway and headed for his cousin's home. They rode in silence for the ten minutes it took to get to Janey's, but the feelings she aroused in him continued to cascade through him, his awareness of her ever-present, distracting, unprecedented.

Still reeling, he escorted Chloe into Janey's house, made sure she had a drink and friends to talk to before he stepped outside, looking for Riley. As usual these days, Riley had an arm around Nikki as they talked to Shane and Janey's husband, Joe.

Riley released Nikki to give Finn a side handshake. "Hey, bro."

Finn forced himself to greet the others, to go through the motions with his family, to eat the delicious steak dinner Janey and Joe had prepared, to make small talk, to try to act normal when he felt anything but. The first chance he got after dinner, he asked Riley if he could talk to him by tipping his head toward the yard beyond the patio where everyone was gathered. His brother said something to Nikki, kissed her forehead and joined Finn.

"What's up?"

"I don't know." How to explain the unexplainable? Finn ran his hand over his mouth, more nervous than he recalled ever being. "There's something weird going on with Chloe."

"What happened?"

He looked at his brother, the person who knew him better than anyone and who loved to bust his balls—and vice versa. Was he making a mistake confiding in Riley? Probably, but he needed someone to explain this to him. "The minute I saw her…" Shaking his head, he couldn't articulate the thoughts circling through his mind.

"What?"

Finn tried to find the words he needed while praying his brother wouldn't make light of something that was so important to him, perhaps the most important thing that'd ever happened to him. "It was like someone had electrified the air. That sounds so stupid, but that's what happened."

Riley eyes widened. "What else?"

"I had this, like, tingling thing here." Finn raised a hand to the back of his neck. "And elsewhere."

"Oh. My. *God.*"

"What?" Finn asked, alarmed.

"You've met *her.*"

"Who?"

"The *one.* Your Nikki."

Finn shook his head. "It's not like that."

"Isn't it? What you described? It's exactly what happened to me the first time I saw Nik. I still feel electrified every time I lay eyes on her, and when I touch her…" Riley looked dazed. "There're no words to describe what that's like."

Finn was thankful that Riley didn't have those words, because he certainly didn't want to hear the dirty details. He was too busy reeling from what Riley had said about Chloe being his "one."

"You need to pursue this, Finn."

"She doesn't want that."

"How do you know?"

"She said so. She said she doesn't take risks." Once again, he experienced a sinking feeling inside, as if he'd lost something precious, something he'd never had in the first place.

"Ask her why."

"I don't know…"

"Finn, listen to me. Do you remember how I was after I met Nikki and then she left?"

"Ah, yeah. We all remember the months before she came back."

"I've never been more unhappy or miserable than I was after realizing I'd let something special slip through my fingers. It was the worst feeling I've ever had. I wouldn't wish that on anyone, let alone you. If you don't at least *try* with her, you'll regret it. That much I know for sure."

Nikki walked over to join them, eyeing them with curiosity. "Everything okay, boys?"

Riley put his arm around her and drew her into his embrace, kissing the top of her head. "Yeah, babe."

Not for the first time, Finn noted how Nikki melted into Riley and the way they fit together, like two halves of a whole. He wanted that. He wanted what they had, what his dad had found with Chelsea. And he hadn't even realized that was what he wanted until Chloe electrified his world. He glanced toward the deck where she was talking to Katie and Laura, laughing and using her hands to make a point.

She was so fucking gorgeous.

"Oh damn," Nikki said. "What's going on with our Finnbar?"

"He's met a woman who makes him tingle."

Finn gave Riley the fiercest look he owned. "Shut *up*, Riley."

Nikki gasped and then hugged him. "Oh, Finn! Really? This is so exciting! Is it Chloe? She's been looking at you the whole time you were over here talking to Riley. That's why I came over. After she came by today, I wanted to know what was up with you guys."

"Nothing is up." But hearing Chloe had been watching him filled him with hope.

When Finn would've walked away, Riley stopped him with a hand to his shoulder. "Finn... Wait. I swear to God, I'm not going to be a dick about this. It's too important."

"No, it's not. She's not into it. Just forget I said anything."

"Finn—"

"Seriously, Ri. Leave it alone." Finn was on his way to a clean escape, but Mac came over to talk to them, holding three beers in one hand.

He gave each of them a beer. "Just the cousins I needed to see. We landed a big job this afternoon. You know the Curtis place out on Westview Road?"

"Can't say that I do," Riley said.

"It's that huge old Victorian with the awesome gables? Looks like a haunted mansion?"

"I know that place," Nikki said. "One of my summer friends lived there back in the day. The place was creepier than hell."

Mac nodded. "That's the one. We were all scared shitless of that house when we were kids. Anyway, the Curtis family has hired us to renovate and modernize it over the next few months, and I'm counting on you guys to help us get it done. They're hoping to host a family wedding there in October and wanted my assurances that we could get it finished in time."

"I'm in," Riley said. "Sounds awesome. I can't wait to check it out."

"Excellent." Mac touched his beer bottle to Riley's. "You, too, Finn?"

"Ah, I don't think so. I'm still planning to head home after Shane's wedding and the Wayfarer opening." As he said the words, his gaze connected with Chloe's, and he felt the impact like a punch to the gut that left him stunned.

"You sure about that?" Riley asked, raising a brow.

"Yeah, I am." She wasn't interested. She didn't take risks. Finn couldn't upend his plans for a woman he'd seen four times who didn't want what he did. He wasn't getting any younger, and it was time to find someone who had the same goals he did—marriage, children, dogs, a house in the suburbs and perhaps a business they could run together. That'd be fun.

Mac groaned. "Come on, Finn. You're killing me here. I need you."

"Thank you so much for everything you've done for me and the things you've taught me. I appreciate the opportunity to work with and for you more than you'll ever know. But I'm going home."

"We'll miss you," Mac said, sighing with resignation. "It won't be the same without you."

"I'm sorry to let you down."

"Oh, stop. You're not. We'll figure something out. I just hope you find what you're looking for on the mainland. Funny how I had to come back here to find everything I ever wanted." He glanced at Maddie. "Sometimes what you're looking for is right under your nose. And on that note, I need to check on my wife."

After Mac left them, Riley said, "He's right, you know. What if she's the one for you and you walk away without ever knowing what could've been?"

Riley's question only made Finn feel worse.

I wish you weren't leaving. As her words came to mind, her gaze collided with his, and she smiled at him. In that moment, he questioned everything, especially his plan to leave.

CHAPTER 7

$\mathcal{M}$ ac wandered over to check on Maddie, who had her swollen feet up on one of the coolers. Her obvious fatigue worried him, but then, everything worried him when she was pregnant. After they'd lost their third child, Connor, in utero, they lived in a perpetual state of dread the entire time she was pregnant. Whenever he thought about being stranded on a remote island and how she might need something he couldn't get her, he could feel his blood pressure spike from the anxiety. He squatted next to her. "How you doing, hon?"

"Just ducky."

He smiled and brought her hand to his lips. "Can I get you anything?"

"I'm good, but thanks. Laura asked if I'm having triplets."

"What did you tell her?"

"I deflected, but we're going to have to share the news before long. I'm getting really big."

"I'm still in complete denial that there're two of them in there."

Maddie's smile lit up her gorgeous face. "Two *girls*."

He put his hands over his ears. "I can't hear you. Lalalalalalalalala."

She tugged at his arm to uncover one ear. "We have to tell people."

"Don't wanna."

"Keeping it secret isn't going to change the story."

"Can't hear you."

"*Mac...*"

"*Maddie...*"

"We have to tell our families that we're having twins."

"Are you *sure* we have to tell them?"

"I'm positive."

"And we have to do this now?"

"Well, everyone is here..."

He whimpered.

She patted his head. "It's going to be all right."

"How is it going to be all right? There're going to be five of them and two of us. They're going to overthrow the management and take over the house."

"Mac."

In her golden-brown eyes, he usually found his center, but lately he'd had trouble finding anything but turbulence no matter where he looked.

"Breathe."

He took a deep breath.

"Take another."

Holding her gaze, he continued to breathe until his heart stopped pounding and the roar in his ears lessened somewhat. But the roar had been there since the doctor in Providence had told them there were two babies in there. He still couldn't believe that the baby they hadn't planned to have was actually *two* babies.

Five.

Five children.

Breathe.

His parents had done it and survived, and they would, too. At least he hoped so. He could survive anything as long as he had Maddie by his side. "You really want to tell people?"

"I really do. Or everyone is going to think I swallowed an elephant."

"We can't have that."

Her lips curled into the smile she saved just for him. That smile made his world go round. "Let's get it over with."

"If you insist."

"I insist."

Reluctantly, Mac stood, took another deep breath and then issued a sharp whistle that got everyone's attention. "So, um, Maddie says I have to tell you guys that she didn't actually swallow an elephant."

"Honestly, Mac." He could hear the amusement in her tone.

"The truth is, she's having twins. Girls. *Two* of them."

Janey was the first to snort with laughter that took everyone else down with her. Such a brat.

"Pay up," Janey said to Joe.

Joe scowled at Mac. "You cost me fifty bucks."

"You *bet* on what we were having?"

Joe used his thumb to point to his wife. "She called it weeks ago, and when I said no way you were capable of keeping a secret like that, she bet me fifty bucks, and here we are."

Janey smiled smugly and held out her hand to Joe. "I'll take a fifty-dollar bill, please."

Mac's mom, Linda, pushed her way through the family members. "Move it." The group parted to let her through. She hugged Mac and then bent to hug Maddie, too. "I knew it. I told your father that Maddie is too round to be carrying one baby."

Mac shook his head in amusement. "We never could keep secrets from Voodoo Mama."

"Don't call me that."

"If the Voodoo fits…"

"Your mother did suggest that twins were possible," Big Mac said. "I told her she was seeing things that weren't there."

Mac looked down at his mom. "You'd think by now he'd know better than to question you."

"You would think."

Big Mac extended his hand to his son. "Congratulations, Dad. Well done."

Mac puffed his chest out. "It was rather exceptionally well done of me."

"Shut up, Mac."

Maddie's comment made everyone laugh.

"Telling him to shut up is like telling the tide not to come in tomorrow," Joe said.

As the others cracked up, Mac turned to Maddie. "Well, now they're mocking me. Are you satisfied?"

"My work here is finished." She rubbed her hands together gleefully.

Mac scowled at her. "It's a good thing I love you so much."

Big Mac took his son aside for a private word. "When will you be leaving for the mainland?" Big Mac asked, his expression sober and thoughtful now that the laughter had passed.

"Late August," Mac said. "We're not taking any chances."

"Glad to hear it. We've had enough high-drama deliveries on this island to last me a lifetime."

"You and me both."

"Heard today that Paul and Hope Martinez are on the mainland," Big Mac said. "Their baby is due any time now."

"That's exciting news."

"I'm just glad they've gone over ahead of the arrival."

"For sure."

"I was over at the Wayfarer today, and it looks fantastic. I can't say enough about how happy I am with the job you guys did there."

"I'm glad you're happy with it. I can't believe we're done. A few little things here and there, but mostly done."

"Another job very well done by my son."

"Thanks, Dad. It was fun to work on something the family did together."

"What's next for you?"

"Landed the reno of the Curtis house today."

"That place gives me the creeps."

"You and me both, but they want a full reno, so it'll be a nice job to keep the guys busy for the summer. Although, Finn told me he's heading home after Shane's wedding and the Wayfarer opening."

"Is he? Well, that's a damned shame. I love having all you kids out here with us."

"I know you do, but he says it's time to go home and get a life."

Big Mac's brows furrowed. "Did he now? I rather thought that's what he was doing here."

"Me, too, but I certainly know how this island can start to feel confining at times. He's a young guy with his whole life ahead of him. I understand the need to go figure that out. Maybe after he does, he'll come back."

"You had to come back to find the answers."

Mac glanced at Maddie, who was talking to his mom and Janey. "True."

"Your brothers and cousins, too. Everything you wanted and needed was right here. All you had to do was open your eyes to the possibilities."

"Maybe you need to tell him that."

"Maybe I will."

FINN HAD NEVER FELT MORE off-balance. His brother's words ran around in his mind, tormenting him with the possibility that Chloe could be the "one" for him. What did that even mean? He'd never bought into the belief that there was only one person for everyone, and even after watching Riley find his "one," he still didn't believe there was no one else in the entire world his brother could've been happy with for a lifetime.

Not to say that Finn wasn't thrilled for Riley and Nikki, because he was. He thought they were great together, but that didn't mean his path had to follow theirs. Even as he had that thought, he sought out Chloe in the crowd. As much as he tried to pretend it was no big deal that she was there, he couldn't control the need to find her, to see her, to talk to her, to be near her.

Giving in to the pull that was bigger than anything had ever been, he moved through the group of family and friends until he stood by her side.

She looked up at him, and the turmoil within seemed to calm somewhat.

How did she do that? How did she wind him up and then calm him without saying a word?

"Are you okay?" she asked, her brows knitting with concern.

"No, I'm not."

"What's wrong?"

"Everything is wrong." And this wasn't the time or the place to discuss it further, not surrounded by his loving but overly involved family. "Can we leave?"

"You're not having fun?"

Finn shook his head. He was far too charged up to sit still, let alone endure hours with his family, when all he wanted was to find a way to understand what the hell was happening to him. "I'm going to tell them I'm not feeling well. Go along with me?"

"Sure."

Finn went to make their excuses to Janey.

She eyed him suspiciously. "You don't look sick."

"I've been feeling off all day."

"If you want to be alone with your new lady friend, all you have to do is say so."

"New lady friend? How old are you?"

"Don't deny that you've been playing eye hockey with her since the minute you got here."

Finn suppressed a groan. He should've known an easy escape would be too much to hope for in this family. "Don't make a thing of it. It's not going to happen."

"Why not?"

"She doesn't want it, and I'm leaving soon anyway. It's nothing." Even as he told himself that, the tingles running up and down his spine made a liar out of him. It was definitely *something*.

"May I offer an opinion?"

"Can I stop you?" He loved Janey, who was more like a sister to him than a cousin. The two of them had always been close, and despite how it might seem, he valued her opinion.

She grasped his arm. "Listen to me, Finn. I've known her since she came to the island and opened the salon. She's a really, really great person. If you like her, and I think you do even if you're trying to deny it to yourself and to me, don't be a fool. The good things, the *important* things, they don't come along every day, and when they do, you have to at least *try*, or spend the rest of your life wondering what if."

"Is that right?"

She smacked him upside the head, which she had to do on tiptoes because he towered over her. "I'm serious. I think all the time about what I would've missed out on if I hadn't taken a chance with Joe at the worst possible time for such a chance." She had gotten together with Joe the same night she caught her fiancé in bed with another woman.

"I hear you." He kissed her forehead. "And I appreciate you —always."

"Call me tomorrow?"

"Yeah, I will. Thanks for having us."

"Thanks for all you did at the Wayfarer."

"It was a labor of love."

She hugged him. "You'd better call me."

"I will."

Finn went to collect Chloe and was on his way to a clean escape when they ran into his dad and Chelsea coming in the front door as they went out. Finn introduced them to Chloe.

"We know Chloe," Chelsea said. "She cuts our hair."

Of course she did. He was realizing she knew everyone on the island except him, or so it seemed.

"Where're you going?" Kevin asked.

"We're calling it a night. I'm not feeling great." Finn could tell his father saw right through the white lie. He and Riley used to joke that Kevin had a built-in, finely calibrated lie-o-meter.

"Sorry to hear that."

"I'll check in tomorrow."

"Talk to you then."

With his hand on Chloe's lower back, Finn ushered her out of the house and into the cool evening air. He felt a tremendous sense of relief at having escaped from the loving cloister of his tight-knit family. God knows they meant well, but sometimes he wished they didn't have to be up in each other's business the way they were. Of course, that didn't apply to when Riley was falling for Nikki. Finn had been up in his brother's grill the whole time. That'd been fun. Trying to explain the way he felt about Chloe, even to Riley, wasn't fun. It was pure torture.

"You're so tense."

Chloe's words interrupted his musings as he got into the truck.

He decided to be honest with her. "I'm trying to understand why meeting you has turned my whole life upside down."

"Has it?"

"Completely. And I don't get why."

"If it makes you feel any better, I'm equally confused."

Her confession buoyed his flagging spirits, and then he paused to ask himself why it mattered so much that she was confused, too. She'd already told him this wasn't going to happen. He looked down at the floor, wishing for answers he didn't have.

His phone vibrated with a text, probably from Missy, who'd sent a countdown image earlier that showed fourteen days until June first. But when he thought of her, of returning to her and the relationship he'd had with her, he felt dead inside, as if that was the worst possible thing he could do.

Inspiration struck with sudden clarity. "I'm here for a couple more weeks. Spend that time with me. No promises, no commitments, just two people who enjoy each other hanging out together."

She rolled her bottom lip between her teeth and eyed him with hesitation. "I'm not sure I can do that."

"How come?"

"I'm afraid I'll get attached and be heartbroken when you leave."

Her honesty gutted him. "I already know I'm going to be heartbroken if I never get the chance to know you better. I'll be careful with you. I promise."

"I... I need to think about it. I'm sorry... It's just that there are so many reasons why this isn't a good idea for me."

He wanted to know all her reasons. He wanted to know everything there was to know about her, and that was unprecedented for him. Even after all the years he'd spent with Missy, he'd never wanted to know everything about her. Their relationship had been lighter, more surface-level than what he wanted with Chloe, which flew in the face of his plans to leave the island and return to the life he'd been living before he came here.

None of it made the first bit of sense to him, but he'd meant what he'd said about wanting the chance to know her. "Let me see your phone."

After unlocking it, she handed it over.

Finn punched in his number and then sent himself a text before returning the phone to her. "Text me, call me, FaceTime me—any time you want. I'll be waiting to hear from you, okay?"

"Okay."

He covered her hand with his. "And if it's a no, that's okay, too."

She turned her hand and curled her fingers around his, sending the charge of electricity through him once again. "Thank you."

"Don't thank me for being a gentleman. My father and uncles wouldn't have it any other way. The first thing they taught all their sons was the meaning of the word no."

"The world could use more fathers like them."

"I agree, even if at times I chafed against their 'guidance.'"

"I'm sure you did, but they had the right idea. They raised an incredible group of men."

"That's nice of you to say."

Finn hated to lose the connection to Chloe by releasing her hand, but he had to in order to start the truck and drive her home. He wanted to ask what she was thinking but refrained, trying to show some restraint. One thing he already understood was that if he asked for too much too soon, he'd push her away. That was the last thing he wanted to do.

He pulled into her driveway and left the truck running when he got out to walk her to the door.

"Thanks for a great time. Your family is amazing, but you know that."

"They are fun to be around."

"That's putting it mildly. They're like a reality TV show—the good kind."

Finn laughed. "The stories I could tell you..."

"I'm sure they're epic."

"They are, and if you decide to call me or text me, I'll tell you all about them."

"You're very tempting, Finn McCarthy."

If he'd ever received a more meaningful compliment, he couldn't recall it. "Am I?"

"You know you are."

"I don't know any such thing."

She looked up at him, her expression vulnerable. "You could have anyone. Why me?"

Finn caressed her face and moved closer to her as she took a step toward him. "Why not you, beautiful, sexy, mysterious Chloe?" Before he realized what was happening, his lips were touching hers in the gentlest possible kiss, and the sheer power of that kiss nearly brought him to his knees. "Say no if you don't want this." He waited, breathlessly, to see what she would do, and then she raised a hand, curled it around his neck and drew him into another kiss.

Everything—and everyone—ceased to exist for him the second she kissed him. He had experienced desire, but nothing like the heat that blasted through him when her tongue brushed against his as her hand grasped a handful of his hair.

Finn whimpered. He actually fucking *whimpered*. She was ruining him for any other woman one sensual stroke of her tongue at a time. It took everything he had to slow down, to pull back, to stop this before it became something more, something she had told him she didn't want.

His brain swirled with the confusion that had been present since he met her. The push-pull of what he wanted, what she wanted, his plans to leave... Leaning his forehead against hers, he was content for the moment to breathe the same air as she was, to let her distinctive scent surround and comfort him.

"Finn..."

"Hmm?"

"This is crazy. I don't do these things."

"What things?"

"Tell someone I can't and then kiss his face off."

He chuckled. "If it's any consolation, I'm as confused as you are by what's happening here. I thought I had a plan, and then I got my hair cut. And now, I don't know whether I'm coming or going." Framing her face with his hands, he compelled her to look at him. "All I know is I want more time with you. I just want more."

"I want that, too."

Never had four little words meant more to him. "You do?"

She nodded. "Two weeks?"

"That's all I can promise for now. My lease is up at the end of May, and I told my former boss in Connecticut I'd be back to work for him in early June." His heart sank when he thought about Missy and the countdown she'd sent earlier. Before he did anything else, he needed to talk to her. His reaction to meeting Chloe was a sign he couldn't ignore. No matter what happened with Chloe, his relationship with Missy needed to be over once and for all. They had run their course a long time ago and had held on to each other more out of a sense of nostalgia than anything. But he could worry about that later. Right now, he had Chloe in his arms, and he never wanted to let her go.

"I'm afraid of getting attached." Chloe's words, softly spoken, touched him deeply.

"We'll keep it low-key." Even as he said that, he wondered if he could do it. Would they both end up crushed in the end? "And we'll proceed with caution."

"Thank you for understanding and for a fun evening."

"Thanks for braving the McCarthys to come with me. What time are you off tomorrow?"

"I close at seven."

"I'll make you dinner." He gave her his address. "Come whenever you're free."

"Okay."

Finn kissed her again, lightly, holding back the unexplainable craving for *more* that overtook him whenever she was near. "I'll wait until you're locked in." He forced himself to let her go, to hold the door for her and to walk away when he heard the click of the lock. On the ride home, he thought it through from every angle, trying to make sense of the powerful emotions he was experiencing for the first time.

This was why Riley had made a fool of himself over Nikki, why Mac had ditched his life in Miami for Maddie, why Shane smiled all the time since meeting Katie. This was why Luke rushed home to Sydney and their daughter, Lily, every night after work. If they felt even a fraction of the things he experienced when he was with Chloe or even when he thought of her, then it was no wonder they were so happy.

He wanted that. A year ago, he would've said he wasn't ready, but he felt differently now. Maybe it was the time with his cousins who were settling into marriages and families, or maybe it was having a front-row seat when Riley fell so hard for Nikki. But he felt ready for something more significant now.

Funny how he'd thought he needed to go home to find it.

His stomach actually hurt at the thought of upending his plans, of calling Clint to say he'd changed his mind, of putting down roots on Gansett Island. He'd come for a freaking wedding and ended up staying for a few months that turned into two years. That's not how a mature adult made life decisions.

Big Mac liked to say that life was what happened when you were busy making other plans.

Driving into town on dark, winding roads, Finn laughed to himself. If that wasn't the truth. His phone vibrated in his pocket, and his euphoria dissipated when he thought about how he was going to have to disappoint Missy. He felt like a total asshole for letting it go on as long as it had and for raising her hopes when he didn't feel the slightest bit of excitement about getting back together with her. He'd been indulging the convenient rather than seeking something more meaningful, and he just couldn't do that to either of them.

When he got home, he opened a beer, took it to the sofa and pulled out his phone, determined to take care of this now before it went on any longer.

She answered on the first ring. "Hey. This is a nice surprise."

"How're you doing?"

"I'll be better when you get back."

"So, Missy... About that. We need to talk. I don't want to give you the wrong idea."

"About what?"

Finn cringed. He was bungling the fuck out of this. "I don't want you to think we're going to pick up where we left off."

Total silence.

"A lot of time has gone by, and we've both changed. *I've* changed. I want different things."

"What *things* do you want?" she asked, her tone frigid.

"I don't know yet, but I don't want to go backward. We both need to move forward, and we can't do that if we're holding on to the past."

"Where the hell is this coming from, Finn? Did you meet someone else? Is that it?"

"Yes—and no. I did meet someone, but nothing has happened with her." Nothing except everything. "It's not about her. It's about moving on. We've been apart for two years and have barely seen each other in all that time. Don't you think if we were meant to be, we would've wanted more than that?"

"I *did* want more than that. Every time I suggested coming there to see you, you had some sort of excuse. Have you had someone else all this time you were stringing me along?"

"No, I haven't, and I never strung you along. We weren't together while I was here. You know that as well as I do. Don't pretend otherwise."

"All I know is you went to your cousin's wedding and never came back, and the whole time you've been there, you've continued to talk to me and to give me just enough to keep me hoping you'd eventually come back to me."

"I talked to you because we're *friends*. We've always been friends."

"I don't want to be your *fucking friend*, Finn."

Her outburst shocked him. "Missy—"

"Save it. I've got to go, but know this—we are *not* over. Not by a long shot."

The line went dead before he could reply. For a long time afterward, he replayed the conversation in his mind, going over everything she'd said and trying to understand how he'd misled her. They were not together. They hadn't been a couple in almost two years. Yes, they still talked frequently, texted and had planned to see each other when he got home. But he hadn't made her any promises. That much he knew for certain.

"Fuck," he muttered, taking a long draw from the beer bottle. Her final words echoed through his mind, filling him with dread. What had she meant by that? And what did she plan to do?

CHAPTER 8

*C*hloe floated through the next day in a weird state of anticipation and excitement, two things that weren't usually part of her routine. She'd learned from an early age to keep her expectations reasonable so she wouldn't be disappointed when things didn't work out. Because things rarely worked out for her.

That's why she needed to be very careful with the handsome, sexy devil known as Finn McCarthy. He kissed like a dream and had awakened yearnings in her that had her reeling. At twenty-nine, she'd already had multiple lifetimes, or so it seemed. She had worked long and hard to put her difficult childhood behind her and to build a life for herself that was so far removed from that trauma that it might as well have happened to someone else.

But it *had* happened to her, and she carried it with her everywhere she went. She barely remembered her parents but would never forget the day they died. The images from that event were indelibly etched into her hard drive, never to be removed. A long time ago, she'd accepted that she would always remember things she'd much rather forget. As a result, she went out of her way to avoid any more painful things that would have to be added to the baggage she carried with her.

Thus her reluctance to become involved with a man who'd told her he was leaving soon and who had the power to break her heart. She had realized that the first night she spent with him, when they made dinner at her house. That's why she'd told him she wasn't interested, when that certainly wasn't true. It was more that she wasn't interested in the kind of pain a man like him could cause her.

Every time she closed her eyes, she saw his perfect face, that smile, the wavy dark hair, the piercing blue eyes. He was obscenely handsome, the sort of man women flocked to, which was all the more reason to keep her distance. But damned if she could. She was drawn to him in ways she'd never been to anyone else. That was the simple fact of the matter, despite how she'd tried to deny it.

"Chloe, honey, don't cut it too short."

Chloe snapped out of her thoughts to realize she was giving Tiffany Taylor one hell of a haircut. "Oh crap, sorry. Is it too much?"

"Nah, it looks cute. I love it." She caught Chloe's eye in the mirror. "What's up with you today? You seem distracted."

Chloe started to deny it but couldn't. "Maybe a little."

"Do tell. In my line of work, people tell me their troubles all the time." Tiffany owned Naughty & Nice, which sold lingerie and other intimate items.

Many of her clients—including Tiffany—had become friends over the years, and she desperately needed to air it out with someone.

"I met a guy."

"Ohhh, who is it?"

"Someone you know."

"Duh. Of course I know him. We live on an island. I know everyone."

"Sometimes I hate that part of island life."

Tiffany waved her hand. "We all go through that when we start dating someone. You remember what it was like when I started seeing Blaine, and the mayor was telling him to do something about the traffic menace I was causing outside my store, and he refused. Then the town council got involved." She shuddered. "That was so stressful.

69

Anyway, enough about me and my sexy police chief. Who is this guy that has your eyes sparkling?"

"Are they?" Chloe glanced around Tiffany to the mirror, trying to see what she saw, but to Chloe, her eyes looked the same as they always did.

"Definitely."

Though it was not usually her inclination to dish about her personal life with other women, all bets were off when it came to Finn. She needed perspective. "Finn McCarthy."

Tiffany let out a sound that was half shriek, half squeal. "I *love* him! And he is some kind of sexy, with that hair and those blue eyes. And have you seen him without a shirt?" Tiffany fanned her face. "The man has an *eight*-pack." Tiffany laughed. "That's not to say he's got anything on my husband, of course."

"Of course," Chloe said, amused and flushed. "So there's an eight-pack, huh?"

"Oh yeah."

The information left Chloe feeling lightheaded. The man was too sexy for his own good—and hers. "It's the strangest thing, but when I see him, it's like… I can't even describe it."

"That's attraction for you. It makes no sense whatsoever. Like why do you look at him and feel the buzz of attraction, but when you look at his brother—who is equally handsome—you feel nothing?"

"Yes! That. Exactly. It's so weird. Why him? Why now?"

"I wish I had those answers for you—and everyone else. I remember so vividly the first time I ever saw Blaine. I was at the clinic with Maddie after that awful day at the marina when Mr. McCarthy and Mac were injured."

"Ugh, I remember that day all too well. Linda was in my chair when she got the word, and I drove her to the clinic. It was so scary."

"It was—and Maddie ended up being admitted for observation because she was pregnant with Hailey. I'm sitting there with my sister, minding my own business, and in walks the new police chief, looking for Mac, and my world just tilted on its axis. I was still married to Jim then. I had no business going stupid in the head over anyone else."

"If it was anything like what happened to me when Finn walked in for a haircut the other day, it's not like you could've helped it."

"Exactly. I liken it to a chemical reaction. My whole body reacted to him in a visceral way that had never happened before."

"Same." Chloe was relieved to hear someone else describe what'd happened to her. "Did you start something with him then?"

"Oh God, no. It was a long time, and several extremely arousing encounters, before anything came of it. And when we finally got together... Good Lord." Tiffany fanned her face. "We were so hot for each other by the time it actually happened, that first time was thermonuclear."

"That hot, huh?" Hearing Tiffany describe her relationship with Blaine had Chloe wondering what it might be like to have that kind of connection with someone?

"So hot. Still is."

"Now you're just bragging."

Tiffany laughed. "Sorry about that, but I only speak the truth. My husband is a stud, and he does it for me."

"You're lucky to have that."

"I really am, and I know it. I used to watch my sister with her husband and be so green with envy because I wanted what she had, but I didn't think it would ever happen for me. I was stuck in a dead marriage with a man who belittled me and took me for granted. All I can tell you is the kind of thing I have with Blaine is so rare and special. If you have a chance of having that, I hope you grab it with both hands and never let it go."

"I'd love to grab Finn McCarthy with both hands, but I will let go. I don't do forever. That's not how I'm wired."

When Tiffany's dismay registered in her expression, Chloe realized she'd said more than she'd intended to.

"Besides, he's not looking for forever. He's probably a total player anyway."

"I don't think he is. That's not how any of them are. Their fathers would kill them if they were anything other than respectful to women."

"He can be respectful and still be a player."

"True, but I haven't picked up that vibe from him. Mac says he and his brother are hard workers. I think you might be selling him short."

"Maybe so, but it doesn't matter. He's moving back to the mainland at the end of the month, so it's not like anything can come of it."

"Plans can be changed, Chloe. If there's one thing I know from seeing my sister blissfully married to his cousin, it's that McCarthy men know how to treat the women they love."

Chloe snorted at the mention of love. "I'm glad your sister is happy with Mac, but no one's talking about love here."

"Aren't we? I thought that's what we were talking about. I know I was when I was talking about Blaine. I love him so much, I can't see straight half the time—and I can't walk straight either because the man is a beast in bed. In the best possible way, of course."

When Chloe would've begun to blow-dry Tiffany's hair, the other woman stopped her with a hand on her arm. "Just because it hasn't happened yet for you doesn't mean it can't. If you feel something for him and sense it works both ways, don't be cavalier about what could be the most important thing that could ever happen to both of you."

As Chloe dried Tiffany's hair, she thought about everything Tiffany had said. What might it be like to have someone else to lean on, someone to come home to after a long day—

Stop. It's not possible. You know that, so why are you bothering to entertain the fantasy?

The constant ache in her hands, hips, knees and ankles was a reminder of why she'd chosen to be alone. She glanced at the clock and saw she wasn't due for meds for another two hours. When the pain set in, two hours could seem like forever.

She powered through it the way she always did and would continue to do so for as long as she could. And when she no longer could? She didn't know what she would do, and that scared her more than anything. The fear had become crippling since receiving an official diagnosis. That fear and that diagnosis was another reason to keep her distance from Finn.

Tiffany hugged Chloe on her way out the door. "When you decide to take sexy Finn McCarthy for a ride, come by the shop for something slinky to wear."

"I'll do that." She never would, but Tiffany didn't need to know that. "Don't say anything, okay?"

"Of course not, but you think about what I said."

"I will." How would she think of anything else? As she swept up the hair clippings and prepared for her next client, Chloe ached everywhere, including her heart, which mourned the loss of something she'd never had in the first place.

"You're being ridiculous. You can't let one sexy, charming man turn you into a lunatic. You know your limitations, and you know why it wouldn't be fair to get involved with anyone long term."

"Ahh, Chloe?"

She looked up to see her next client had arrived and was mortified to realize she'd been caught talking to herself.

"Hi there, Mrs. Miller. That's what happens when you work alone."

"Oh, honey, don't worry about it. I talk to myself all the time. Sometimes I even answer myself."

Chloe laughed and gestured for Mrs. Miller to have a seat in her chair. "I do that, too."

As she discussed Mrs. Miller's desire to cut her hair shorter, Chloe tried not to think about Finn or the fears that kept her awake at night. She gave her last client of the day her full attention for the next forty-five minutes. After she locked the door behind Mrs. Miller, Chloe sank gratefully into the chair behind the desk to tend to the administrative tasks of running a business—answering voicemail messages, sending out reminder emails for tomorrow's clients, reconciling the bank statement in her bookkeeping program and paying the rent on her storefront.

She updated her Facebook page to welcome Race Week participants with a twenty-percent-off coupon that she hoped would bring some walk-in business to her door. The demands never ended, and most of the time she loved everything about running her own business, but aching in more ways than one, she was ready to call it a day.

Chloe was on her way out the door when a young man carrying a bouquet of wildflowers appeared on the sidewalk.

"Chloe Dennis?"

"That's me.

"These are for you." He handed over the bouquet, told her to have a nice day and jumped on his bike to head back to the florist at the other end of town.

Chloe carried the flowers to her car, the envelope tucked into the colorful blooms taunting her until she was in the car and could open it.

Thanks for being my two-week girlfriend. I can't wait to see you tonight. Finn.

"Oh, Finn McCarthy." She teared up as she re-read the message. "You don't fight fair."

On the ride home, she gritted her teeth against the pain and fatigue that gripped her after every long day at work. She refused to acknowledge that the pain was getting worse or that she seemed to be having more bad days than good lately—and the timing couldn't be worse with her busiest season at the salon getting underway. If she allowed herself to think about those realities, she would curl up into a ball and give up.

That wasn't an option. She was a survivor. She had always been a survivor and always would be. That her own body was rebelling against her made Chloe more determined to fight back and press on, pretending like everything was fine when it wasn't. It wasn't fine at all.

Her phone dinged with a text from Finn. *Your dinner is almost ready. What time are you heading over?*

Tell him you can't make it. Tell him this was a mistake, that you never should've agreed to be his two-week girlfriend or anything else.

She stared at the phone for a long time before typing her response.

Will be there in fifteen minutes. She'd thank him for the flowers in person. Despite what her better judgment would have her do, Chloe wanted this interlude with him. She wanted something that made her feel happy and alive and separate from the fear she lived with every day. Being with Finn was the most exciting thing to ever happen to her, and she simply didn't have the wherewithal to walk away, even if she knew she should.

Two weeks. She would take this time with him and enjoy it fully and remember it always when it was done.

Before she left the house, she took her meds, fed Ranger and let him out, changed her clothes, brushed her hair and teeth and refreshed her makeup. As she let Ranger in from the backyard, she received another text from Finn. *Bring Ranger if he likes steak.*

"You definitely don't fight fair." She typed her response. *Ranger loves steak, and he said thanks for inviting him.*

Finn replied with the dog emoji and a thumbs-up.

You need me to grab anything?

Nope. Just need you and Ranger to make it a party.

We're coming.

She couldn't wait to see him, and none of the reasons why she shouldn't be going mattered as she clipped a leash onto Ranger and led him out the door.

CHAPTER 9

Finn had been on pins and needles all day, trying to get
through a boring workday of last-minute nitpicks at the
Wayfarer. They had a malfunctioning drain in the kitchen, a door that
wouldn't close properly in the hotel and paint that needed to be
touched up throughout the facility. They'd also helped to haul in a ton
of tables, chairs and patio furniture.

The day had dragged until Mac told them to go home at four
thirty, an hour earlier than usual, which was more than fine with
Finn.

He hadn't stuck around to see what everyone had planned for the
evening, not when he had his own plans to see to. After a stop at the
grocery store, he'd come home to put baked potatoes and brownies in
the oven, while giving thanks to his mom for teaching him the basics.

Next, he chopped lettuce and vegetables for a salad and then put
out bowls of salsa and corn chips. When everything was ready, he ran
for the bathroom for a quick shower and shave before Chloe arrived.
She hadn't mentioned the flowers. He hoped she'd gotten them after
he'd gone round and round most of the day about whether he should
send them and what kind of message to send with them.

At lunchtime, he'd said screw it and had walked up the hill to the florist to place his order. He'd gone with wildflowers because he'd seen the flowers she'd included in her sleeve tattoo and figured she must love them to permanently adorn her body with them. He hoped he'd gotten it right. It had never been more important to him that he get it right.

She was reserved, cautious, almost timid. Though she projected an aura of confidence and toughness, he'd seen her softer center. She fascinated him in a way no other woman ever had. It had taken meeting Chloe to fully realize that his relationship with Missy had been superficial—they went out, had some fun, went home, had sex and that was that. Maybe that made him shallow, but that had worked for him for a long time. Until it didn't.

It alarmed him to realize if he hadn't come to Gansett for Laura's wedding and stayed afterward to keep his dad company after his parents' difficult breakup, Finn might've been stupid enough to marry Missy by now.

He shuddered to think of how easily he could've settled for what was right in front of him rather than looking beyond the obvious. Missy was a good person and he cared about her and wished her the best, but he certainly wanted more out of a life companion than someone who was satisfied with pizza and sex.

He wanted what Riley had found with Nikki, the soul-deep connection that was obvious to anyone who spent time with them. If he hadn't witnessed his brother falling in love firsthand, if he hadn't met Chloe and felt the difference for himself, he wouldn't have known what was missing with Missy. Now he knew, and he could never go back to who he'd been before.

He went out to the deck to put the steak on the grill, and as he went back inside to finish the salad, his phone began vibrating. Finn made the mistake of glancing at it to find Missy blowing it up with a furious series of texts, telling him how awful he was, how he'd made promises to her that she expected him to keep, how she'd been planning their wedding and had even reserved a venue for next summer.

"*What?*" Finn read the texts with a growing sense of alarm and disbelief. She'd booked a *wedding venue*? What the actual fuck? They had never once talked about getting married. He'd been very careful not to go there with her, knowing he wasn't even remotely close to being ready for anything permanent with her or anyone.

The texts kept coming, faster than he could read them, the gist being he was going to be sorry for embarrassing her this way.

In a state of disbelief over the things she'd said, he shut off the phone and put it on the charger. How could she possibly think it was appropriate to book a wedding venue when they'd never so much as had a conversation about marriage? Finn wished he had time to call Riley to tell him about this but didn't want to be in the middle of that conversation when Chloe arrived. So that would have to wait until later. In the meantime, he tried to shake off the unsettling texts. But that was easier said than done.

She'd booked a wedding venue. Dear God! His dad and Riley had warned him that they had concerns about Missy, but he'd never bought into that. Until now.

He thought about every conversation they'd had recently and couldn't come up with a single thing he'd said that would lead her to believe she should book a wedding venue. The most he'd promised her was that they'd get together when he got home. That was it. So how did she go from getting together to planning a wedding?

Before he could process that question, a knock on the front door jolted him out of the past and into the present. He wanted Chloe to have a great time tonight and had gone all out to ensure that she would. This was no time to be thinking about Missy, weird texts or wedding venues.

He shook it off, rolling his shoulders to relieve the tension as he went to get the door. And then there she was, wearing a hot-pink floral top that left her arms bare, black pants and boots with studs. So fucking sexy. He wanted to kiss her but didn't. Not until he was sure that was what she wanted, too. But God, he wanted to. "Come in."

Ranger walked in ahead of her.

She followed the dog, bringing that same electrified feeling Finn had experienced every time he'd been in her presence. How did she do that just by walking in the door?

78

"Geez, Ranger. Make yourself right at home, why don't you?"

Finn grinned at her. "He's more than welcome to make himself right at home, as are you." He led her into the kitchen. "What can I get you to drink?"

"Ice water would be perfect."

"Coming right up." He poured her ice water and opened a beer for himself, wondering if there was a reason she didn't drink alcohol, not that it mattered to him. Chalk up the curiosity to his desire to know everything about her. "Let's go outside. It's nice out." Tucking his beer under his arm, he carried the chips and salsa while she got the doors.

After struggling down the two stairs, Ranger went into the yard and seemed to check out every blade of grass before lifting his leg.

Finn laughed at how particular he was. "He's funny."

"He keeps me entertained." She glanced at Finn. "The flowers were gorgeous. Thank you."

"I'm glad you liked them. They reminded me of your ink."

"Wildflowers are my favorite. I love the way they flourish outside the lines."

"That's an interesting way of putting it."

She offered a small, sly smile that had his full attention. "Life is more interesting outside the lines."

He loaded a chip with salsa and handed it to her.

When she took it from him, he noticed the knuckles on her right hand were red and swollen.

"What did you do to your hand?"

She ate the chip and dropped her hand to her lap as if ashamed that he'd noticed. "It's nothing. Happens sometimes after a long day at work."

Finn couldn't say why, but he sensed there was far more to it than that, but he chose not to push her. "Looks like it hurts."

"Not too bad. How was your day?"

So she doesn't want to talk about her sore hand. Okay, then. "It was fine. Kinda boring with last-minute stuff at the Wayfarer." And some insanity with an ex, not that he wanted to tell her that.

"This is a nice yard."

"My dad gets all the credit. He did the landscaping and bought the deck furniture."

"How did you all end up living together?"

He loaded another chip and handed it to her, noting that her left hand was swollen, too, but not as bad as the right. "We came out for my cousin Laura's wedding."

"I love her—and Owen. And their kids are adorable."

"They really are. They're a great couple. My parents had just split up, and it was kind of awful, especially for my dad, who was sort of blindsided by it."

"Ugh, that's too bad."

"I guess things between them had been not so great for a while, but she left him for another guy, and it really threw him. When he decided to stay for a while after the wedding to spend some time with his brothers, Riley and I stuck around to keep him company. Mac offered us jobs with his company, one month rolled into another, and here we are almost two years later. Dad is remarried and expecting a baby, and Riley is crazy about Nikki. Worked out well for everyone."

"Yourself included?"

Finn shrugged. "Sure. It's been great to have this time with my family and to learn from my cousin, who is an incredible businessman and knows his shit when it comes to construction."

"But?"

"No buts. It's been great."

"And yet you're leaving."

"Well, I never intended to move here permanently."

"Your dad and Riley didn't either, did they?"

"Not at first, but things changed for them. I get that. The lease is up here at the end of the month, and I had to decide what I wanted to do, so I told my old boss I'd be home." What had seemed like such a good plan only two weeks ago didn't look quite as good to him after meeting her.

"It's time to figure out what's next. I've been there. I get it."

"Where are you from originally?"

"Outside of Boston."

"Did you grow up there?"

"I grew up in western Massachusetts. My parents… They passed away when I was young."

"I'm so sorry to hear that."

"It was a long time ago."

Despite what she said, he ached for her. "Where did you go after that?"

"A foster home. They were nice people, and I was brought up along with their kids. After high school, I went to cosmetology school and have been doing hair ever since. By the time I moved here, I was ready for a change. It feels like home."

"I love the name of the salon."

"Thank you. Other than the obvious meaning, it's also a reminder that you have to keep going even when the worst thing happens. Curling up and dying isn't an option."

"You're amazing, but you probably already know that."

"No, I'm not."

"You really are. What happened to your parents?"

Chloe took a deep breath and let it out.

Finn immediately regretted the question. "I'm sorry. I shouldn't have asked."

"It's okay that you asked. They fought a lot. Always did. My dad, he had a drug problem and it had gotten really bad in the last few months before they died. He came home one night with a gun."

"Oh my God, Chloe." Instinctively, he reached for her hand, jolting when she winced. He pulled his hand back. "Sorry."

"He shot her and then himself."

Horrified, Finn could barely breathe. "Where were you?"

"Upstairs. At first, I didn't know what had happened, but when I came down and saw the blood, I ran out of there. Someone told me later that the neighbors called the cops. I don't remember much about what happened after I left the house. A big chunk of my memory is just blank."

"How old were you?"

"Seven."

81

He winced as his heart broke for her. "I'm so sorry you had such an awful thing happen to you."

She smiled, but her glorious eyes were sad. "What is it about you that has me telling you something I rarely tell anyone?"

Her sadness gutted him. "I don't know, but I'm really glad you trusted me enough to share that with me."

"I told Katie about it the other day. You're the first two people here who I've told."

Because he needed it and thought she might, too, he moved his chair closer to hers and held out his arms to her.

She hesitated, but only for a second before leaning into his embrace.

As Finn put his arms around her and felt the silk of her hair brush against his face, he closed his eyes and breathed in her unique scent. He couldn't identify the various elements that made up the scent, but he would forever associate it with her. "I'm supposed to be feeding you, but I can't seem to let go."

She exhaled and relaxed against him. "This is okay for now."

Later, Finn wouldn't be able to say how long they sat there, wrapped up in each other as daylight waned into dusk. Time ceased to matter. The only thing he cared about was offering comfort after hearing her heartbreaking story. He couldn't imagine living through such a tragedy, especially at such a young age. His had been a charmed, blessed existence with two parents who'd adored him and the brother who had been by his side from the beginning. Compared to what she'd endured, he'd never had a problem in his life.

"What're you thinking?" she asked after a long silence.

"How lucky I am to be here with you, and to have had such an easy life compared to what you've been through."

"I don't want you to pity me."

"I don't. I admire all you've accomplished on your own. You opened a business in your twenties and have made a success of it."

"I wouldn't go that far. It pays the bills, but that's about it."

"You support yourself through a business you own. I think that's incredible. I dream about owning my own business, and you already do. It's a huge accomplishment that most people never achieve."

"Well, when you put it that way…"

Her husky laugh made his skin tingle with awareness and, yes, desire. He wanted her, and not just physically. He wanted all of her, and that was truly a first for him. After being with Chloe, he got why Riley had gone over the bend with Nikki. Once you've experienced something so magical, you'd do anything you could to keep it in your life.

"You're making a freaking mess of me. I hope you know that."

She raised her head to look at him, her brows furrowed. "How so?"

He caressed her face, and when her lips parted, he could think of nothing else but how badly he wanted to kiss her.

"Finn?"

"I think about you all the time. I count the hours until I can see you. I've never done that."

"No?"

He shook his head. "Never."

"I… We said we were going to keep this casual."

"I know."

"That doesn't sound casual."

"It's not."

She drew back from him. "Finn. Please. I can't do this. Not if you're leaving. It wouldn't be fair to either of us."

Though it was the last thing he wanted to do, he let her go, then took a deep breath and ran his fingers through his hair, wishing that was all it would take to get his head back on straight. "I promised you dinner. It's all ready."

He got up and went into the house, intent on serving dinner and trying to keep things casual with her, even as he was forced to acknowledge that his feelings for her were anything but. After hearing about what she'd been through, he better understood her aversion to risk. And the last thing he wanted was to hurt her.

He couldn't upend his plans for a woman he'd met less than a week ago. Who did that?

Riley did, and look at where it got him.

Shut up.

Now he was having arguments with himself. Awesome.

He put steak and baked potatoes on plates and walked them out to the patio.

She greeted him with a warm smile that made him want to say to hell with his plans or anything that didn't include her. "That looks so good!"

"Glad you think so. Be right back with the salad."

His hands were actually shaking. What the fuck was happening to him? Back in the kitchen, he took a minute to get himself together, to take a deep breath, to settle himself. With his hands propped on the counter, he took another deep breath.

"Finn? What's wrong?"

CHAPTER 10

$\mathcal{H}$e seemed upset, and Chloe wanted to know why. "Are you okay?"

Finn straightened and looked at her for the longest time while she wondered what he was thinking. Had something happened in the minute he was inside?

She went over to him. "What is it?"

He placed his hands on her hips. "It's you."

"What did I do?"

"You exist, and knowing that is messing with my head—and my plans."

"I don't understand."

He kissed her forehead.

Though she already knew, he told her again, and she already sensed she'd never grow tired of hearing their story. "I was all set to go home at the end of the month. Then I walked into your salon and my whole world got tipped upside down, and now…"

"What?" she asked, sounding and feeling breathless from the way he looked at her.

"Now I don't know whether I'm coming or going, and it's all your fault."

"*My* fault?"

"Uh-huh. One hundred percent your fault."

Then he kissed her, tentatively at first, waiting for her to join him —or not. She knew without question that he would stop if she asked him to. She didn't ask him to. Rather, she wrapped her arms around his neck and opened her mouth to his tongue, losing herself one second at a time to the wild desire that flared between them.

He drew her in closer to him, until their bodies were pressed together as the kiss grew urgent and desperate. No kiss had ever been like this. And when his hand ventured under her top to rest on her lower back, his skin touching hers, she shuddered with need that had her knees going weak under her.

"Easy." He tightened his hold on her. "I've got you."

"We... I..." She looked up at him, comforted to see he was every bit as astounded by their kiss. "We were going to eat."

"Right." He released her in stages, making sure she was steady before he let go completely. The second his hand left her back, she wanted to beg him to put it back.

"The salad. You came in to get it."

"Thank you for the reminder. I got a little sidetracked."

That smile of his would be the absolute death of her. When he looked at her like that, smiled just for her... Potent.

He pulled two bottles of salad dressing from the fridge and handed them to her. "Check the dates. Things like that don't get done the way they did when my dad lived here."

"Neither is expired."

"Excellent. After you."

He carried the salad to the patio, where they encountered a disaster. While they had been making out in the kitchen, Ranger had helped himself to the steak on Finn's plate, and he didn't even have the decency to act guilty.

Chloe was mortified. "Ranger! *Oh my God.*"

The dog burped—loudly.

Finn lost it laughing.

"It's not funny! He's never done anything like that. For God's sake, he can barely walk most of the time!"

"It *is* funny, and it's not his fault. We left him alone with steak for quite a few minutes. What was he supposed to do?"

"He could've been a good boy and not eaten it!"

Ranger was defiant as he licked his chops and then settled on the patio for a full-belly nap.

"Come on." Finn held her chair until she was settled. "You have to admit it's kind of funny."

"I refuse to admit anything of the kind since I believe he understands every word I say and will take that as permission to do it again."

Finn stuck his lip out and made himself even more adorable, if that was possible. "Are you going to share yours with me?"

"Not if you're going to laugh at his bad behavior."

"I'm very sorry I laughed." To Ranger, he said, "Bad boy. Don't steal steak."

If the dog could've rolled his eyes, he would have.

"That wasn't very convincing." She cut a quarter of her steak for herself and gave the rest to him.

"You didn't keep enough."

"I've got what I need." She served salad to both of them and cut open the steaming baked potato to add butter and sour cream. "I haven't had a baked potato in ages."

"I love potatoes of any kind. My parents used to tease me about being Irish through and through because of my love of potatoes."

"That's funny."

"As soon as I said that, I wondered if maybe I shouldn't have shared that."

"Why?"

"After what you told me, I don't want to be insensitive about growing up with parents who teased me about things when you didn't have that."

"Don't be silly. Of course you should talk about them. You're not being insensitive."

"Are you sure?"

"Positive. Remember, this is new information to you, but I've already lived with it for twenty-two years."

He put down his fork, took a sip of his beer and stared at her.

"Do I have sour cream on my face?"

"No."

"Then why are you staring?"

"I'm so awed by everything about you."

"Stop it. You're making my ego swell."

"I mean it. You're wise beyond your years and possibly the most beautiful woman I've ever met."

Chloe's body heated with embarrassment—and arousal. "How much beer did you drink before I got here?"

"I mean it, Chloe. I'd never say something like that unless I meant it."

"Well, thank you. You're not so bad yourself, but you certainly know that."

"Anything that happened before the day I met you no longer matters to me."

"That doesn't sound casual, Finn."

"This doesn't feel casual, Chloe."

The air between them crackled with expectation and awareness. And then she remembered his plans to leave the island in less than two weeks and all the reasons why this wasn't possible for her and had to bring herself back to reality. "What are you doing tomorrow night?" she asked.

"I don't know. Why?"

"I'm the chairperson of the board for the island food bank, and we're having a fundraiser at Stephanie's Bistro. Drinks and appetizers, silent auction and entertainment by Owen Lawry. I have to be there, but I can get you a ticket if you'd like to come." Talking about the fundraiser bought them both time to think about something other than the not so casual thing happening between them.

"I'd like to come, but I'll pay for a ticket." He crossed his arms on the table. "What does it say about me that I didn't know the island has a food bank?"

"It says you should be thankful you've never needed it. In a service economy, a lot of the year-round residents struggle to make ends meet in the off-season. I'm involved in several efforts to help them get by during the winter."

"I'm ashamed to say I've never given much thought to what happens to the seasonal employees in the winter."

"Don't be ashamed. It's not something people broadcast, but there's a fine line between the haves and the have-nots on this island. Maddie has been very involved in several of the organizations I work with and so has your aunt Linda. She and Maddie host a free Thanksgiving dinner at the marina every year."

"I volunteered at the dinner last year. Our whole family was there. It was a great day."

"Yes, it was."

"You were there? Why do I not remember that?"

"I was only there for a few minutes. I dropped off pies before heading to a friend's house for dinner."

"I can't believe I missed the chance to meet you sooner."

"Think about how many times we've probably crossed paths on this tiny island without noticing each other."

"Trust me. If I'd crossed paths with you before the other day, I would've noticed, and I would remember."

"You're very charming."

"I'm not just saying that. I would have remembered you."

Unnerved by his intensity, she looked down at the remains of her dinner, trying to find the wherewithal she needed to keep this situation from spiraling completely out of control. With every minute she spent with him, she wanted more.

"I made brownies."

"You baked?"

"Yes, I baked."

His indignant tone made her laugh.

"What's so funny? My mom taught us how to bake when we were little kids."

Chloe rolled her lips together so she wouldn't laugh again.

"I can tell you're trying not to laugh. We'll see who gets the last laugh when you try my brownies."

He got up, took their plates and went inside.

Chloe turned to watch him go, appreciating the way faded denim hugged his ass. Did he have to be so freaking sexy and sweet and sincere and perfect? Sometimes life really wasn't fair. He'd been here almost two years and she didn't meet him until he was days away from leaving. How was that fair?

Her chest ached with a sense of loss. She had no business allowing herself to get sucked into this crazy attraction to him. Not only was he leaving, but there was a very good chance she could end up disabled in the next few years, and the last thing she wanted was to saddle him—or anyone—with her situation. Speaking of not fair...

She would eat the brownies he'd baked, thank him for dinner, collect Ranger and head home. After the benefit tomorrow night, she would tell him she couldn't continue whatever this was between them. It hurt to think about what might've been, but she needed to be realistic. He was leaving the island, and she was plagued with a condition that was getting worse, even if she wanted to pretend otherwise.

When he returned with a plate of brownies, she tried to push her troubling thoughts to the side to enjoy a few more minutes inside the fantasy. That's all this was. A fantasy. A what-if. A diversion.

Naturally, the brownies were to die for. "Your mother taught you well."

"I'll let her know you think so."

"Are you close to her?"

"Not like I used to be before everything happened between her and my dad. Riley and I have had a hard time with *how* she handled it. I mean, if you want out, get a divorce. Don't run off with someone else when you've been married thirty years. My dad deserved better than that."

"No kidding. Is she still with the other guy?"

"Nope. That didn't last long, and she has since expressed regret for what happened with Dad. He's moved on with Chelsea, so it worked out for him."

"Do you live near her at home?"

"About three miles away. Riley and I own a condo together."

"It's so sweet how close you guys are."

"I don't know about that," he said with a laugh. "We used to fight like tomcats, according to my dad. But once we hit high school, we were over that crap. Truth be told, I had a hard time when he fell for Nikki and moved out. Felt like the end of an era."

"I'm sure it was a big adjustment for you."

"It was, even if I'm a little ashamed to admit it. I really love her. She's great and perfect for him in every way. But still..."

"It was hard for you to let him go."

"Yeah. And that's one of many reasons why it felt like a good time to move home."

"Past tense?"

He looked at her with those ice-blue eyes that seemed to see right through to the heart of her. "Past tense. Now I don't know what the hell I'm doing."

"Finn..."

"I want this to be real, Chloe. I want all these things that I feel when you're around—hell, even when you aren't... I want it to be real."

"I can't."

"Tell me why. Make me understand."

"You are wonderful, and tonight was so great. It's just that I'm not in a place where I can accommodate something like this. Trust me when I tell you that I wish I was. I really do." Her heart broke as she said the words, which told her it was the right thing to stop this now. It wouldn't get easier later. "Come on, Ranger. It's time to go home. Say thank you to Finn for the steak you stole from him."

Ranger got up, stretched and came over to see them.

Finn scratched him behind the ears. "I hope you enjoyed every bite, buddy."

Chloe made herself get up, carry items inside, put the leash on Ranger and turn to say goodbye to Finn. "Thank you for a lovely evening."

"You're welcome."

"I'm sorry, Finn."

"So am I. You have no idea how sorry I am."

"I think I do."

"Then don't go. Stay."

Chloe kissed his cheek. "Thank you again for dinner." Before she could give in to the temptation to take him up on his offer, she shooed Ranger out the door and followed him to the car.

She cried all the way home.

CHAPTER 11

$\mathcal{M}$ ac bathed three kids, read stories, tucked them in and tiptoed out of baby Mac's room, hoping he was down for the count after being fussy earlier. Maddie said he was teething and that if we remembered the pain of getting teeth, we'd be permanently traumatized. She always knew what was wrong with their babies when they weren't themselves.

He felt like a fumbling fool next to her, and soon there would be two more of them.

They were already outnumbered, and it was about to get worse.

It had taken him months to get his head around the fact that he and Maddie were expecting twin girls. She had been so freaked out by the possibility of losing them, she'd refused to tell anyone the news.

Last night, she conked out right after they got home, and today he hadn't gotten a chance to talk to her about anything other than staying on top of the demands of three little kids. He needed some time with her, and he hoped she was still awake.

In case she wasn't, he tiptoed into the master bedroom where she sat up in bed, her hair in a messy bun on top of her head. She wore one of the sexy nightgowns he regularly bought for her at her sister's shop. Tiffany liked to tell him that he was one of her best customers.

"In case I forget to tell you, I'm nominating you for husband and father of the year."

Mac unbuttoned his shirt and pulled it off. "How come?"

"You got all three of them in bed and presumably asleep in forty-five minutes. That has to be a new record."

"They were tired after playing with Ashleigh and Addie." Tiffany, Blaine and the girls had come over for dinner.

"Still, you are my hero."

He stopped short, slayed by her words and the love behind them. They'd been together for years now, and she still managed to stop his heart at least once a day.

She patted the bed. "Hurry up."

"I'm hurrying." He went into the bathroom, brushed his teeth and pulled off his jeans, returning wearing only boxers. Curling up to her in bed at the end of a long day was his favorite thing, and tonight was no exception. "Mmmm, you smell good."

"I put on that lotion you like after my bath."

"Are you trying to get in my pants?"

She snorted with laughter and gave him a playful shove.

"Because I'm rather easy where you're concerned."

"Even when I'm bigger than a beached whale?"

He scowled at her, hating when she talked down about herself. "A. You are not a beached whale. And B. I want you all the time. Twenty-four-seven-three-hundred-sixty-five."

"That's a whole lotta want."

"And it's all for you."

To his horror, her eyes filled with tears that appeared out of nowhere when she was pregnant. Even knowing it was the hormones causing them, every one of them broke him. She quickly swept them away. "Sorry."

"For what?"

"I know how girl tears freak you out."

"Not just any girl tears. *Your* tears freak me out. I never want you to be sad or upset about anything."

"These are happy tears."

"There ought to be a manual that comes with all wives so we know the difference between good tears and bad tears."

She laughed even as tears spilled down her cheeks.

Mac wiped them away. "Why the happy tears?"

"The things you say to me, the way you love me, even after all this time. It amazes me."

"I know that deep inside, the little girl who watched her father walk away keeps thinking that's going to happen to you."

"I don't think that."

"Maybe not consciously, but you know it's possible, so you worry."

"You would never do that to me or our kids."

"Never, ever, *ever*."

"I know that, Mac."

He took her hand and linked their fingers. "And I know it was a big deal for you to tell everyone about the babies."

"I'm still waiting for disaster to strike."

"Me, too."

She rested her head on his chest, and he put his arm around her, holding her close where he wanted her most.

"What the hell am I going to do with three girls?" he asked with a dramatic sigh.

"You'll be their bitch."

"Seriously. They'll lock me in a closet and go out with boys who drive fast cars and drink beer. And if they look anything like their mother... Dear God, I won't survive it."

She rocked with silent laughter. "I'm picturing them pushing you in a closet and locking you in."

"It's not funny."

"Yes, it really is."

"Will you rescue me from the closet, or will you team up with my three daughters against me?"

"I will always rescue you the same way you rescued me the day we met."

"After I walked into your bike and turned you into a bloody disaster?"

"Not that so much as how you loved me—and Thomas—from the beginning and have never wavered in your devotion to us. No one has ever been more devoted to me than you are."

She had a way of bringing him to his knees even when he was lying down. "It's a good thing I married you, then."

"A very good thing. Mac?"

"Hmm?"

"Tell me again that the babies are going to be fine."

"Our babies are going to be perfect—healthy, beautiful like their mother, sassy like their sister and will have their daddy wrapped around their little fingers from the minute they are born."

"Will you keep telling me?"

"Any time you need to hear it."

"I might need to hear it a lot."

"I'm available on a moment's notice." He massaged her lower back, which often ached when she was pregnant. "What're we going to name these angels of ours?"

"Francine and Linda?"

"For middle names, maybe. One should be Madeline, since we have another Mac."

"We only did that to keep up the tradition. One Madeline is enough for this family."

"She is more than enough for me."

"You're stacking up the points tonight."

"I'm sure I'll need them before too long."

"Probably. You do have a way of getting yourself into trouble without trying very hard."

"It's my special gift."

"Back to names. Do we want them to have the same first initial?"

"I wouldn't be opposed to that."

"My grandmother's name was Evelyn. What do you think of that?"

"I like it. Would we call her Evie?"

"We could."

"My grandmothers were Jane—and we've already got one of them —and Emma."

"Two E names! Emma Linda McCarthy and Evelyn Francine McCarthy. What do you think?"

"Works for me. I love that we're naming them after their grandmothers and great-grandmothers."

"It's perfect."

"And they will be, too. I promise."

"I think about Connor every day—how old he'd be and what he'd be doing and how much he'd love having a baby brother and new baby sisters coming."

"I think about him, too. How there should be four of them."

"Except we wouldn't have Mac if he had lived."

"True. And it's already impossible to imagine life without him." Their happy, sunny baby boy was the spitting image of his daddy, and they adored him.

"Another Mac McCarthy. I hope the world is ready for him."

"With you as his mom, he's going to be the best Mac McCarthy yet."

"It's going to be hard for him to top his father and grandfather."

"We'll see about that. You need to close your eyes and get some rest. The natives will be restless in the morning."

"Love you, Mac."

"Love you more, Madeline."

"Not possible."

Mac fell asleep with a smile on his face. With her in his arms and their babies sleeping soundly, everything was right in his world.

CHLOE WAS KEEPING something from him. Something other than the fact he planned to leave was stopping her from giving them a chance. Finn puzzled it through from every angle as he cleaned up after their dinner, opened another beer and took it outside to the backyard that now felt lonely and bereft without her and Ranger to keep him company.

He turned on his phone, which went wild with text messages and voicemails. Seventy-eight of the former and twenty-two of the latter.

What the fuck?

Finn made the mistake of reading the first couple of messages before deleting the rest along with the voicemails.

Missy had clearly lost her mind.

He responded with one text: *I'm sorry you got the wrong impression about us but behaving this way won't change anything. Please don't contact me again.* After sending that message, he blocked her number. Then he realized his hands were shaking.

The phone rang, startling him until he realized it was Riley.

He took the call. "What's up?"

"That's what I called to ask you after you barely said a word to anyone at work today."

"We were busy."

"Cut the shit, Finn. What's going on with you?"

"Nothing." *Everything. Tell him.* "I… I told Missy we were done, and she freaked out. She said she'd booked a wedding venue for next year. Can you believe that?" When Riley had no reply, Finn said, "Ri?"

Riley's deep sigh said it all. "Yeah, man, I believe it. That chick is crazy. Dad and I have been telling you that for years, but you never wanted to hear it."

"Well, you were right. She blew up my phone, and I blocked her."

"I'm surprised you actually told her it was over. What brought that on?"

"After seeing you with Nicholas and Dad with Chelsea, I realized a lot of things are missing in my relationship with Missy, things I don't want to live the rest of my life without."

"Hallelujah, you've seen the light! Dad and I have been hoping you'd figure that out before you did something foolish like marry her. She's not a bad person. She's just not the one for you."

"After tonight's performance, I feel like I've dodged a bullet."

"You have for sure. I just hope you've seen the last of her."

Finn's stomach dropped at the thought of having to see her again. "I hope so, too."

"On a lighter note, how's Chloe?"

"She's amazing, but I don't think anything's going to come of it.

98

She's not really interested in something serious, and I'm a short-timer anyway."

"Are you listening to yourself right now?"

"What're you talking about?"

"You've possibly met *the one*, and you're still talking about leaving? What the fuck is wrong with you?"

Before Finn could begin to process that, Riley continued. "You were there when I met Nikki and after she left. You saw what torture that was for me, *for months*, not knowing if I'd ever see her again. You really want to go through hell like I did before you pull your head out of your ass and figure out that everything you want and need is *right here*? How long do you think you're going to be back in Connecticut before you realize you've made the biggest mistake of your life?"

Finn held the phone away from his ear, waiting for Riley to finish his tirade.

"Finn!"

"Oh, are you finished?"

"Did you hear anything I said?"

"I heard every word."

"So you're staying, and that's it."

"I never said that."

"I don't get it, Finn. You say you want to get a life. You have a life— a damned good one right here, and now there's this possibility with Chloe, and you're going to just chuck that without even trying to see what it might be? I never regretted anything more in my entire life than letting Nikki leave before I had a chance to know her. It took about two seconds after I realized she was gone to know that I had missed out on something important. If you leave without pursuing this thing with Chloe, I promise you won't even be clear of the break-water before you want to come back."

"She says it's not what she wants."

"Bullshit. Nikki and I both saw the way she looked at you at Janey's, as if she wanted something she couldn't have. You have to earn her trust so she'll feel safe to give you a chance."

"What if it's not about trust? What if she genuinely doesn't want the same things I do?"

"If that's the case, then at least you'll know you tried. If you don't try, you'll regret it. I promise you that."

Finn already knew that, but Riley's words had stirred something in him and lit a fire that couldn't be contained. "Should I go over there?"

"Hell yes."

"What if she tells me to get lost?"

"Then leave. But if you don't go…"

"I'll never know."

"Exactly. Go for it, Finn."

"Okay." The fire became an inferno of need and want and desire to feel the way he did with her. Only with her. "Crap. I had three beers. Can't drive."

"I'll call Ned. He'll come get you."

"You're sure this is the right thing to do, Ri?"

"I'm positive. I'll call Ned now. Keep an eye out for him."

"Should I text her?"

"Text her when you're there. Tell her you're outside, and it's totally her call whether she wants to see you or not. Leave it up to her. Say you'll leave if she says no."

"Okay. I'm kind of nervous."

"Because she *matters*, Finn. That's what makes her different from everyone else. If you weren't nervous, I wouldn't tell you to go to her. I'm calling Ned now. Text me later and let me know how it went."

"I will. Thanks, Ri."

"No problem."

For a long time after Riley ended the call, Finn stared at the phone in his hand, trying to get his head around what he'd just agreed to do. He was going to her house. He would see her again soon. The tingling began at the back of his neck and danced down his spine, replacing his nervousness with excitement.

Finn went inside to splash water on his face, comb his hair and brush his teeth. Then he put on a small dab of cologne and immediately felt silly for doing that. What did he think was going to happen? She'd probably tell him to get lost. Hell, she might even be asleep already after a long day at work and another one on tap for tomorrow.

This was stupid.

He shouldn't go over there.

Except the tingling continued unabated, just from the thought of seeing her again. And then a toot from outside let him know Ned had arrived. Finn stared at his reflection in the mirror. "Here goes nothing."

Or maybe everything.

Riley was right. If he didn't try, he'd never know for sure.

Finn walked out of the house and got into the woody station wagon driven by Big Mac's best friend, Ned Saunders. "Hope I didn't get you out of bed."

"Nah. I was out and about seein' as my wife is sitting with Tiffany's kids while she does inventory at the store. Blaine had ta go ta the mainland. Somethin' about his brother being in trouble. Gotta pick up the missus in half an hour. Where we goin'? Yer brother didn't say when he called me."

Finn gave him the address.

"That's where Chloe lives."

"I know."

Ned glanced over at him. "You been keepin' things from us?" Ned was like an uncle to all the McCarthy kids and was usually in the know about everything in their lives.

"Nope."

"Hmmm. Chloe's a nice girl."

"I agree."

They rode in silence along the island's dark, winding roads, stopping at the end of Chloe's driveway a few minutes later. "No need to pull in."

"How ya gettin' home?"

"I'll walk. No worries."

"Don't be ridiculous. You'll get yerself killed walking out here in the middle of the night. Call me. I'll come getcha." He handed Finn a business card. "Don't matter what time 'tis."

"Thank you."

"That girl… She's tough on the outside, but there's somethin' almost fragile 'bout her. Can't put my finger on what, but there's somethin'." Ned looked over at him. "Be careful with her, ya hear?"

"I hear you, and I will. I promise."

Ned seemed satisfied with Finn's assurances.

He got out of the car and waved to Ned as he drove away, leaving Finn alone in the dark. And dark on Gansett Island was a whole other level of *dark*. With every nerve ending in his body alive with need, Finn withdrew his phone and sent a text to Chloe.

Are you still up?

Yes…

I'm outside. Can I see you?

For a long, agonizing minute, there was nothing, and then the bubbles appeared that indicated she was replying. He held his breath.

You're here?!?

Yes, but not in a weird stalker way. I promise. I just want to talk to you. The minute you and Ranger left my house, I missed you. He pressed Send before he could talk himself out of saying something so revealing.

From his vantage point at the end of her driveway, he saw a light go on over her door.

Where are you? I don't see your truck.

Ned dropped me. I had too many beers to drive.

She opened the door and called to him. "Are you really out there?"

He walked down the driveway toward the light. "I really am."

"What're you doing here, Finn?"

"I don't know, Chloe." The uncertainty he'd heard in her voice had him wondering if this was the worst idea Riley had ever had. Finn took a step back, regretting that he'd allowed his brother to talk him into this ill-fated mission. "I'll go if you want me to. I shouldn't have come."

"Don't go."

He stopped.

She'd removed her makeup, which left her seeming far more vulnerable than usual, as if she'd lost her armor. Then she rolled her bottom lip between her teeth, and the vulnerability was all he saw.

"Chloe…"

She opened the door and held it open, inviting him into her home.

CHAPTER 12

*D*rawn by the powerful pull he'd experienced from the beginning, he moved toward her, fully aware that crossing the threshold into her home would give this thing that had been simmering between them new meaning. It would change everything, perhaps forever.

He went anyway.

As he stood in front of her, neither of them seemed to breathe.

"I've never done anything even remotely like this."

"Like what?"

"Showing up at someone's house in the middle of the night because I can't bear to stay away."

"I've never done anything like this either."

"Like what?" Emotion had reduced his voice to a gruff whisper.

"Like this." She took a step to close the distance between them, and Finn stopped breathing when she flattened her hands on his chest and slid them up to curl around his neck. Then she went up on tiptoes to press her lips to his, and he nearly passed out from the flood of adrenaline and desire that surged through him like a tsunami.

Want. Need. Desire. *Yearning.* It seemed like everything he could possibly feel came over him at the same instant, leaving him astounded and wanting more. So much more. For the longest time, they stood in her doorway, arms wrapped around each other, tongues tangling in a desperate dance. How could this be called *kissing*? The word was too simple to describe what the stroke of her tongue against his did to him. And that she seemed to want him every bit as much as he wanted her…

Overwhelming.

The kiss became urgent as they each tried to get closer to each other.

Finn tightened his hold on her and lifted her to walk them the short distance to her sofa, where he lowered her and came down on top of her—without breaking the kiss.

She made a hungry, needy-sounding noise that traveled straight to his cock, which was so hard, it ached.

Christ have mercy.

The last thing he wanted to do was slow down, but he needed to be sure she wanted what he did, which was everything. He wanted every single thing he could have with her—and only her, which was an amazing realization for a guy who'd never wanted that with any woman before her.

"Chloe…"

She tightened her hold on his hair, and the slight pinch of pain only ramped up the desire that pounded through him like an extra heartbeat.

"Sweetheart, wait."

She raised her hips, pressing the heat of her body against his straining erection. "Don't want to wait."

Finn's brain went completely blank. Was she saying she wanted… Then he said something he had never before said when a woman was making it very clear that she wanted to get naked with him. "We should talk about this."

"No, we really shouldn't."

"But…" He thought about what she'd said to him earlier, about not being able to get involved and the sense he'd gotten that she had been keeping something important from him, something that would keep her from doing exactly what they were now on the verge of doing.

"Finn." She touched her finger to his lips. "Stop talking."

He wanted what she wanted. He wanted it more than he'd ever wanted anything, but he wasn't looking for a one-night stand. Not with her. She was already too important for one night to ever be enough. So even though every part of him wanted to take her directive to shut up and press on, his better judgment screamed louder than all the other parts of him that were demanding instant gratification.

"Wait." It pained him to draw back from her, to put the brakes on something that felt so damned good. But before this went any further, they *were* going to talk about it. He sat back, ran his fingers through his hair and tried to calm down.

She closed her eyes and sighed—deeply.

A long, charged silence lingered between them.

Ranger wandered out from the bedroom, took a look at Finn and then turned around and went back to bed, seeming satisfied that his mom was with a friend who provided steak.

"What're we doing here, Chloe?"

"Do you need me to explain the birds and the bees to you, Finn?"

Under normal circumstances, he'd find the comment funny. Under these circumstances, he was not amused. "A couple of hours ago, you left my house after telling me you simply couldn't do this. And now you want to… Well, you're sending me mixed messages, and I'm having a little trouble keeping up. Despite how it might seem with the way I showed up here, I want to respect your wishes, but I also want to understand. I'm very confused."

"I'm sorry to do that to you."

"Don't be sorry." He reached for her hand, careful not to go near her swollen knuckles.

Tears flooded her eyes.

"Tell me what's wrong." Her tears gutted him. "Make me understand."

"I'm not looking for a serious relationship."

"So what was this going to be, then? A one-night stand?"

She sat up, withdrew her hand from his light grip, wrapped her arms around herself and diverted her gaze. "That's all I'm capable of. I wish it could be more—"

"If you wish it could be more, why *can't* it be more?"

"Other than the fact that you're not going to live here anymore in a few days?"

"Other than that. If you give me a chance, if you give *us* a chance, I'll stay."

Chloe shook her head. "Don't say what you think I want to hear."

"I already told you I never say anything I don't mean. If you're willing to make a go of this, I *would* stay."

She rested her head on the back of the sofa and gazed at him with the stunning eyes that had held him in her thrall from the beginning. "You can't change your plans for me, Finn."

"Yes, I can."

"No, you really can't."

"Tell me why not."

"I'm dealing with some things. It's just…" Glancing down, she took a deep breath. "It's not the right time for something like this. It's not you, so please don't think that. You're amazing and wonderful, and if things were different…"

He wondered if she heard the way her voice wavered as she tried to let him down easy. The landing had never hurt more. "I hear what you're saying, and even though I don't understand it, I'll respect your wishes. But I want you to know…" His throat closed, and for a terrifying second, he feared he would lose his composure. "I want you to know that I've never felt for anyone else what I do for you. And if you change your mind, call me, text me, come to me. I'll always want to see you."

Finn kissed her forehead and then forced himself to get up, to walk away from her when every fiber of his being was telling him to stay. But she'd made her wishes clear—more than once—and it was time to cut his losses as painful as that would be.

As he walked down the long, dark driveway that led to the road, he felt shredded. He should've cut his own damned hair the way he had many times in the past. If only he'd done that, he wouldn't now have to live with knowing she existed, so close and yet so far from him. It's not that he expected women to fall at his feet in gratitude for having gained his attention. But these things weren't usually all that complicated for him. He liked women, women liked him. Everyone had fun. It was that simple.

So how had everything gotten so bloody complicated? Between Missy's meltdown and Chloe's rejection, Finn's head was spinning.

He thought about calling Ned, but decided to walk home, mindful to keep an eye out for cars coming in either direction on the dark road. As he walked, he relived every second with Chloe, trying to make sense of it. But nothing added up. He knew she wanted him every bit as much as he wanted her, so why wouldn't she give him a chance?

It's not you, so please don't think that. You are amazing and wonderful, and if things were different...

If things were different. *What things?* He wanted to scream from the frustration and confusion.

Though it was late, and his brother was probably asleep, Finn called him anyway.

Riley answered on the first ring. "How'd it go?"

"The next time you get a big idea, keep it to yourself."

"Oh damn. She wasn't glad to see you?"

"It's not that."

"Then what?"

"I don't know! *I don't fucking know!* She's as into me as I am with her, but she says the timing isn't right, that she's dealing with some stuff and it's not me. I'm wonderful and amazing. What the fuck does that even mean, Ri?"

Finn heard a rustling sound and then Nikki came on the line. "Tell me exactly what she said."

Finn went through the entire conversation, Chloe's words permanently seared into his memory. He told her how Chloe had wanted to fool around—once—but that was all she'd wanted. When he stopped talking, he waited for Nikki to say something. "Nik?"

"I'm sorry, Finnbar. I don't know what to say."

"That's great. Just great."

"Do you want to come over? You shouldn't be alone when you're upset."

"No, I don't want to come over, but thanks for asking. Go to bed. I'll talk to you guys tomorrow."

Finn ended the call feeling more dejected than he had before he called them. If Nikki, one of the wisest, coolest women he'd ever known, couldn't explain this to him, who could?

NIKKI HANDED Riley's phone back to him. "We should go over there."

"It's almost midnight, and we all have to work in the morning."

"He's really upset."

"He said he doesn't want company."

"Because he doesn't want to inconvenience us. We can stay there tonight so he doesn't have to be alone."

Riley moaned. He'd been asleep when Finn called, and now he had Nikki imploring him with those eyes that could bring him to his knees. Riley sat up, rubbed his face and ran his fingers through his hair. "Let's go."

Ten minutes later, they left Eastward Look, which they had spent the winter renovating, and headed out on the dark winding road that led to town.

"Go that way," Nikki said when they reached a three-way inter-section.

"Why?"

"A hunch."

Riley took the right-hand turn that would take them into town the long way, around the island's north end.

Nikki sat up straight, her eyes peeled.

"What're you looking for?"

"Your brother. Ned took him there, but how much you want to bet he's walking home?"

"At this hour? He'll get himself killed."

"Not if we get there first. Hurry up."

Riley pressed down on the gas and made quick time getting to the west side.

"That's where Chloe lives." Nikki pointed to a driveway. "Start looking for him and slow down so you aren't the one to run him over."

They went another mile before Nikki said, "There!"

Riley brought the truck to a stop next to his brother, who was dressed in dark clothes. He leaned forward so he could see around Nikki. "Do you have a death wish?"

"Nope."

"Get in the truck, Finn."

"I told you not to come."

"This is all Nikki's doing, so make it easy on us both and *get in the truck*."

Finn got in and slammed the door.

Riley directed the truck toward town, pulling up to Finn's house ten tense, quiet minutes later.

"You guys can go. I'm okay."

Nikki got out of the truck. "We're not leaving."

Resigned to losing more sleep, Riley followed them inside.

Finn flopped on the sofa.

Nikki went into the kitchen, got a beer out of the fridge, opened it and brought it to Finn. Then she sat in front of him on the coffee table. "What can I do?"

"Nothing. I'm fine. It was a thing. It's not going to happen. I'll get over it."

Riley thought about the merciless way Finn had busted his balls when he was first with Nikki, and how he'd wanted to punch him half the time. Now he'd give anything to see his brother happy. Funny how that worked. Even when Finn was driving him crazy, Riley wanted only the best for his lifelong best friend.

"Maybe I could talk to her," Nikki said.

"Please don't. That's not going to help. But I appreciate the offer."

"I hate to see you hurting."

Finn's face lifted into a small smile. "Thanks, Nicholas. But I'll survive. In other news, Missy has been blowing up my phone like a crazy stalker since I told her we're not getting back together." Finn looked at his phone. "We're up to two hundred texts and sixteen voicemail messages. So far."

"Why don't you block her?" Riley asked.

"I did. She's using other people's phones. I keep blocking the numbers and then a new one pops us."

Nikki gasped. "Holy crap! Who does that?"

"People who can't take no for an answer," Riley said. "Do you think you need to get the cops involved?"

"God, no. No cops. She'll give up when she realizes she's not getting anywhere. She's the least of my concerns."

Having seen her in action in the past, Riley didn't agree that Missy would give up on Finn without a fight, but he kept the thought to himself. For now anyway.

"You guys can go home. I'm really fine. I swear."

Nikki patted Finn's knee. "We can stay here tonight."

"No need for that."

"Are you sure?"

"Positive. Means a lot that you guys came looking for me."

Nikki hugged him. "We'll check on you in the morning."

"Sounds good."

Riley tried to think of something he could say to make Finn feel better. "I know it seems hopeless now, but don't give up."

"I am giving up. She's made her feelings clear. I have no choice but to respect them."

"I'm sorry it worked out this way."

Finn shrugged, projecting indifference that Riley saw right through. "I'll get over it."

"Get some sleep."

"Thanks again, you guys."

As Riley ushered her out the door, Nikki said, "Call if you need us."

"I will."

Riley held the passenger door for her, and when she was settled, he leaned in to kiss her. "Thanks."

"For what?"

"Taking such good care of my brother."

"I love him."

Riley smiled, his heart full to overflowing with love for the incredible woman who would be his wife before much longer, not that she knew that. Not yet anyway. "And I love you."

"I want this to work out for him so badly. I want him to be as happy as we are."

"He'll get there, babe. In his own time."

"I wish he wasn't leaving us."

"I do, too. Maybe if he can convince Chloe to give him a chance, he'll stick around."

"Wouldn't that be awesome? I'm overdue for a haircut…"

"Nikki, don't get involved."

"Who said I was getting involved?"

Riley eyed her shrewdly. "I know that mulish look of yours."

"Are you calling your girlfriend a mule?"

"Don't change the subject, and stay out of Finn's business. I mean it."

She smiled sweetly and batted her eyelashes at him. "Yes, dear."

Riley closed the door and walked around to the driver's side, hoping she listened to him and stayed out of it. But even as he had the thought, he knew she would do anything she could for Finn. While he appreciated and enjoyed the friendship between her and his brother, he hoped she didn't do anything to make things worse for Finn.

That would truly suck.

CHAPTER 13

*I*n the morning, Chloe dragged her aching body out of bed an hour earlier than usual to shower and prepare for an appointment with Dr. Lawrence at the clinic. In addition to the usual aches and pains, her chest hurt today, too. Who knew that broken hearts actually ached? As she showered, did her hair and makeup and consumed the first of two cups of coffee required to jumpstart her day, Chloe kept reliving the scene with Finn last night. She hated that she'd hurt him and left him confused. However, she hadn't yet figured out how to talk about the diagnosis she'd recently received after a frustrating yearlong dance with doctors and specialists and blood tests and baffling symptoms that hadn't added up until they finally did.

Rheumatoid arthritis, an often debilitating, horribly painful condition that would eventually leave her if not completely disabled, then partially. It had been just her luck that the condition had first appeared in her hands, which immediately put her livelihood in jeopardy.

Three weeks ago, she'd finally received a definitive diagnosis and had spent just about every minute since then reeling as anxiety and fear took over. How would she work if her hands didn't work the way they were supposed to? How would she support herself if she couldn't cut hair? How would she afford the health insurance that she desperately needed if she couldn't keep the salon open? Though she did well enough on her own, she didn't make enough to hire someone to cover the winter months when business dropped off significantly.

And then there was the possibility that RA was just the start of it as autoimmune disorders tended to pile on. In an online forum, she'd read about a woman who had fourteen different autoimmune conditions in addition to RA.

The info had left her so freaked out, she'd stayed offline ever since.

For her entire adult life, since she aged out of the foster system at eighteen, Chloe had relied on no one but herself to get by. Unlike other young people she had befriended over the years, she had no family support system to fall back on. Her foster family had been kind to her and they were great about keeping in touch, but they lived in Alaska now, so she didn't see them very often. She didn't have a family support network like other people had and had tried not to dwell on that reality too much as she made her way in an often unkind and unforgiving world.

Coming to Gansett, becoming a business owner and finding the home of her heart had been the best thing to ever happen to her. She had found a life that satisfied her. But now that, too, was in jeopardy, as her illness would require specialists and possibly care that couldn't be provided on a remote island.

She was twenty-nine years old and staring down a terrifying and uncertain future.

Which was why she'd told Finn that they couldn't happen, even if she wanted him more than she'd wanted any man. Ever. It wouldn't be fair to start something with him now, when everything was topsy-turvy in her world. In addition to her fears about her livelihood, the thought of no longer being able to draw, something she'd enjoyed since childhood, broke her heart.

Chloe fed Ranger and let him out in the backyard to do his business, watching as he struggled down the little ramp on legs that didn't work the way they used to. The two of them were quite a pair. When he was safely on the grass, she went into the bathroom to add another coat of mascara to complete the pulled-together look she showed the rest of the world. Cool, competent, stylish, even if she crumbled on the inside. No one needed to know that, least of all the adorable guy who'd set her heart to fluttering the minute he stepped into her world.

Was that only a couple of days ago? It seemed she'd known him so much longer. Sending him away had been the most painful thing that'd happened since she lost her parents. She'd lived long enough by now to know the kind of connection she'd had with him didn't come along every day, especially when you lived on a tiny island in the middle of the ocean.

A sob erupted from her throat, startling her.

"No. I'm not going to cry over him. I've already got enough to contend with. I don't need a self-inflicted wound on top of everything else. That's *enough*."

Despite what she told herself, tears filled her eyes anyway. She blotted them away with a tissue while giving thanks for waterproof mascara. She had a feeling she was going to need it again before today was over. She'd gotten through worse things than losing a man who'd never been hers to start with, and she would survive this, too.

Determined to face the day without allowing her emotions to get the better of her, she let Ranger in, got him settled and headed out for her appointment.

David Lawrence had been an absolute godsend in the year since her hands had first started giving her trouble last summer. At first it had been a twinge of discomfort in her wrists and then her fingers. Within a couple of months, her hips, knees and ankles were protesting the long days on her feet at work, and her hands were swelling and aching fiercely.

When anti-inflammatory medication hadn't alleviated the pain and swelling, David had referred her to a rheumatologist on the mainland who'd put her through more tests than she could count, all of them coming back inconclusive. Her RA factor had been negative, which had prolonged the mystery, but she'd learned that could happen even when you had the disorder.

In the end, the diagnosis had devastated her. The medication prescribed to alleviate the symptoms was also a chemotherapy drug and left her feeling sick to her stomach most of the time. Fiona, the local pharmacist, knew about Chloe's diagnosis due to the medications she needed, but she and David were the only ones on the island who knew. Wanting to protect her business for as long as she could, Chloe had decided to tell no one else until she had to.

That plan had been working out well until Finn McCarthy came strolling into the salon, setting off an intense yearning for something —and *someone*—she couldn't have.

As she drove to the clinic, she knew that sending him away had been the right thing to do. He had his whole life ahead of him and could have any woman he wanted. He didn't need to be saddled with someone who might end up disabled within a decade, if it took that long.

David and the rheumatologist had painted a rosier picture—new drugs and treatments were making RA much more manageable than it had been in the past, which was great news, but that didn't change the reality for her. If her hands didn't cooperate, she couldn't work, and if she couldn't work, she ran the risk of losing her livelihood and her health insurance. Unfortunately, her hands had been getting worse instead of better, even with the powerful drugs.

She walked into the clinic and gave her name at reception. After taking a seat in the waiting area, she tried to look at a magazine, but it didn't hold her attention. In the weeks since she'd gotten the diagnosis, she'd had trouble concentrating on anything other than work. She hadn't read a book or watched a TV show or movie, all things she usually enjoyed. It was like her brain refused to focus on anything other than fear, anxiety and pain. At the same time, she tried very hard not to think at all about the illness, dwelling in a state of denial that kept her from taking to her bed and curling into the fetal position.

Since that wasn't an option, denial had been working pretty well. But meeting Finn had made denial impossible. How could she justify starting something new with a great guy when she had a massive cloud of uncertainty hanging over her?

Chloe prided herself on being truthful and open in her dealings with people. Keeping such a thing from Finn while getting more involved with him would be like lying to his face.

"Chloe."

Katie Lawry's cheerful voice roused Chloe from her unsettled thoughts. Though Katie must've wondered about Chloe's regular appointments at the clinic, she'd never asked if everything was okay, and Chloe hadn't shared her diagnosis. With Katie's wedding coming up soon, she had enough going on.

Besides, keeping her business to herself was second nature to Chloe after being on her own for so long.

Katie led her into an exam room. "David is running a few minutes late, but he'll be right with you."

"Thanks, Katie. How're things in wedding central?"

"We're down to seating charts and final fittings. Home stretch. All I can say is thank God for my mom and Laura. They've been keeping me sane."

"The big day will be here before you know it."

"I can't wait. My brothers and sisters will be here soon, and there's just so much to look forward to."

"It's very exciting." Chloe felt dead inside. What did she have to look forward to? Nothing after last night.

"Thanks for being part of it."

"I'm delighted to have been asked."

"I'll catch up with you later."

"Sounds good."

Katie closed the exam room door, leaving Chloe alone again with the merry-go-round of thoughts that kept her awake at night, churning with fears and scenarios that fueled nightmares when she did finally fall asleep.

David came in a few minutes later, the epitome of tall, dark and handsome—and ridiculously in love with his fiancée, Daisy, who would become his wife in September. They'd postponed their wedding for a year after David's dad had a massive heart attack last summer. Fortunately, his father was doing much better now, and the happy couple was counting down to their big day. Sometimes it felt like everyone Chloe encountered was happy and in love. She'd never been in love with anyone, which had been fine with her until recently. Now she felt lonely for the first time in a very long time.

David took a seat and gave her his undivided attention, the way he always did, as if she were the only patient he had. "How's it going?"

"My hands have been pretty bad."

Wheeling his stool across the exam room, he held out his hands to her. "Let's see."

Chloe put her hands in his and tried not to wince as he gently examined them.

"They do seem more swollen than they've been before."

"And the meds are doing a job on my stomach."

"That's an unfortunate side effect. I want to start you on a steroid that will help. It might make you a little puffy and bloated, but it should help with the swelling. You're apt to feel cured on this stuff, but just a heads-up that it doesn't work forever. As we've discussed, we'll be adjusting and tweaking as we go. It's a continuous process."

"I'm willing to try whatever you think might help so I can keep working."

David wrote the script and handed it to her. "Fiona might have to order it."

"Such is life on an island."

"Exactly." He sat back, crossed his arms and studied her. "How's your mental health?"

Unprepared for the question, she wasn't sure how to reply.

"Have you told anyone about the diagnosis?"

"No."

"It might help to confide in a friend."

"I need to protect my business. I don't want people not coming in because they're afraid that cutting their hair will cause me pain."

"Fair enough. Have you checked out the online support communities I gave you?"

"Briefly. They gave me new things to worry about."

"Well, that's not good. How about a professional? I can write you a referral to Dr. McCarthy. He's a very well-regarded psychiatrist, and we're lucky to have him in our community."

Chloe's brain had frozen on the word "McCarthy." As in Finn's father. "I, um… I don't know about that."

"I think it would help. Despite how it seems to you right now, RA isn't a death sentence in most cases. It's a difficult disorder that requires intensive management, so it's a big adjustment for patients to make after being diagnosed. There's no shame in admitting you need some help wrapping your head around it." He wrote something else on his prescription pad and tore off the page, handing it to her. "Kevin's number. I'll put through the referral for your insurance in case you decide to give him a call."

Chloe took the paper from him. "I'll think about it."

"Go once. Do it for me." His warm, caring smile had her smiling back at him.

"That's very manipulative, Doc."

"I know. I'm sorry, but I really think it will help you to find some acceptance and peace."

Two things that had been in short order for her over the last three weeks. Denial wasn't working, so why not try something new? "I'll definitely think about it."

"Excellent."

"You're very good at what you do, David."

"Thank you. I don't like to see anyone suffer needlessly, and I know you've been suffering these last few weeks."

Chloe couldn't deny that, so she didn't try. "I'm very afraid of what the future will bring."

"Which is understandable. Kevin can help. So can your friends. People care about you, Chloe. Don't feel like you have to do this on your own."

"I also feel guilty for freaking out about this when I know people get much worse diagnoses every day."

"Don't feel guilty. This is a tough one for you. It's painful, and it threatens your livelihood. I totally understand the freak-out."

His kind words had her fighting back tears for the second time in as many hours. "Your kindness and support mean so much to me."

"I wish there was more I could do."

Left unspoken between them was the reality that she might one day require far more specialized care than he could provide on their little island. She refused to think about that on top of everything else weighing on her.

"Knowing you're close by helps."

David walked her out. "Call me any time—day or night. You have my number. If you need me, call me."

"I will. Thank you again." Clutching the prescription and the paper David had given her with Dr. McCarthy's number written on it, Chloe left the clinic and drove to Ryan's Pharmacy.

Fiona, a stunning redhead with a porcelain complexion, was working alone at the pharmacy counter in the back and smiled when she saw Chloe coming. "Hi there."

"How's it going?"

"Getting busy again. I'll be glad when Grace gets home to help." Grace Ryan McCarthy, the owner of the pharmacy, was married to Evan McCarthy. They had been touring during the winter, in support of his music career.

"When do they get home?"

"In time for his cousin's wedding next weekend."

"Right. That makes sense." Chloe handed over the prescription.

Fiona scanned it quickly. "I'll have to order this from the mainland. Should be here tomorrow. I'll call you when it comes in?"

"That'd be great. Thank you."

"My pleasure."

Chloe left the pharmacy and went next door to the grocery store to buy a salad for lunch. Lost in her own thoughts, she didn't see the man coming toward her until she'd crashed into him, causing both of them to stumble and fall. She landed hard on her right hip, grunting from the pain of impact.

The scent of coffee had her staring at the coffee-soaked, faded denim crotch of the man she'd collided with.

"We really need to stop meeting this way."

That voice. She looked up, and her gaze met Finn's. He smiled, but it wasn't the usual big smile that engaged his startling blue eyes. This one was sad, and it killed her to know she'd done that to him.

He stood and reached out to help her up. "You okay?"

She ignored his offer, but only because it would hurt her to have him pull on her hand. Not because she didn't want to touch him. That wasn't it at all. To her dismay, the hip she'd landed on didn't want to cooperate and buckled.

Finn moved quickly to catch her before she fell again, holding her until she had her legs under her. "Are you hurt?"

"No." His nearness had her heart beating so hard, she saw stars. Then she remembered to breathe. Her hip throbbed, letting her know she would pay for the fall all day.

"Are you sure?"

Chloe nodded and forced herself to let go of him, to step back, to let him go when that was the last thing she wanted to do. If she could've done anything she wanted, she would have rested her head on his chest and let him hold her for as long as he was willing. But that wasn't an option.

An employee from the grocery store arrived with a mop and made quick work of cleaning up the coffee that had spilled on the floor.

"Let me get you another coffee," Chloe said. "That was my fault. I wasn't watching where I was going."

"No worries. I'll grab another. Can I buy you one?"

Wanting to prolong the encounter, even though she knew that wasn't wise, Chloe nodded. "Sure. Thanks."

"Right this way."

She stepped gingerly on her right foot, trying not to limp as she followed him to the coffee bar where he poured cups for both of them, handing her one. Chloe stirred cream and a dash of sugar into hers. "You drink yours black?"

"Yep."

"That's kinda gross."

His face lifted into half a grin. "So is all that crap you put into yours."

Even in the midst of the busy store as they stood there making fun of the way they drank their coffee, Chloe felt the undeniable connection, the electricity in the air that sizzled between them any time he was close by—and even when he wasn't. All she had to do was think about him to feel the zing.

"I'm sorry about last night," she said softly.

"No need to apologize. But I do want you to know..." He glanced around them. "Not here. Let's go outside."

"I'm going to grab a salad for lunch."

"Lead the way."

He stayed with her as she visited the salad bar and then insisted on paying for her coffee and salad when they got to the checkout counter.

"You didn't have to do that."

"I wanted to." He walked her to her car. "What I wanted to say in there is that I feel like there's something bigger than this happening." He waved a hand between them. "I know we just met and it's none of my business, but I want you to know that if you need a friend—and only a friend—I'm here, and I want to help."

His kind words filled her with the now-familiar yearning he inspired in her. What would it be like to have someone like him by her side to help her navigate the new reality? He would be incredible and supportive and caring. She'd known him a matter of days and already knew that he'd be someone she could count on. She was so very tempted to unburden herself, but she couldn't do that to him. Once again, it came back to fairness.

Chloe forced herself to look at him, not that looking at him was any kind of hardship. "Thank you. That's very sweet of you, and I appreciate it." The words she wanted to say were right on the tip of her tongue, burning to get out. If the truth was all it would take to keep him close to her... She realized she was staring at him, drowning in the blue of his gorgeous eyes, and looked away. "I, um, I have to go. I have a customer at ten."

His disappointment was palpable. "I guess I'll see you around."

"I hope so."

He held the car door for her, waited for her to get settled and then waved as she drove away.

She hoped he didn't see the tears running down her face.

CHAPTER 14

ere those tears he'd seen on her face as she left? The question plagued him as he went home to change his coffee-soaked pants before driving to the Curtis house to meet Mac and the others. Finn wouldn't be sticking around to work on that job, but he was curious about it nonetheless. Or he had been until he ran into Chloe—again—and took another wild ride on the emotional roller coaster.

How was it that they had lived on the same tiny island for two years and never saw each other, and now she was everywhere he looked, or so it seemed. He felt like he'd known her forever. Had it really been only a few days since the guys talked him into getting his hair cut at her salon? Was it possible for a life to change so dramatically in the span of a few days?

He wouldn't have thought so until it happened to him.

The others were already there when Finn arrived, and he tried to shake off his dour mood as he joined them.

"Thought you weren't sticking around for this one," Shane said.

"I'm not, but I'm still curious."

"Wish we could change your mind." Luke sounded forlorn. "Won't be the same without you and Riley busting each other's balls all day long."

"But it will be quieter," Mac said, making them laugh.

"It's good to know I'll be missed." Finn would miss them and their camaraderie. They did good work together and had fun, too. Thinking about not seeing them every day only added to the glum mood he'd fallen into after the latest encounter with Chloe.

Mac led them through the Gothic-style, three-story house that sat back from the craggy bluffs of the island's west side. The inside was dark and dreary and badly in need of an update.

"Please tell me we're doing a full gut," Riley said, echoing Finn's thoughts.

"Yep, but we're going to try to preserve some of the original details, such as the stained-glass windows on the stairway and the molding."

"The woodwork is incredible," Luke said.

"It really is." Mac pointed to built-in bookcases in what must've been a library. "They want to restore the woodwork in here."

Finn ran a hand over one of the bookshelves. He loved doing restoration work that brought a building that had fallen into disrepair back to life. This one had a story to tell, and he couldn't wait to see what the guys would do with it.

His cell phone rang, and he withdrew it from his pocket to see a call from a Connecticut number he didn't recognize. "Hello?"

"Nice of you to finally answer your phone."

Missy. Fuck. "I'm at work, and I asked you to leave me alone."

"I don't care where you are! You're going to talk to me right now or—"

Finn ended the call, turned off the phone and put it back in his pocket.

"What the hell was that?" Riley asked.

"Nothing." Finn realized his hands were shaking, so he stuffed them into the front pocket of his pullover sweatshirt.

Riley's eyes narrowed as he looked at Finn. "Was that Missy again?"

"Maybe."

"Bro, you need to call the cops."

"I'm not calling the cops." She'd give up when she figured out he wasn't going to change his mind.

Mac came over to them. "What's going on?"

"Tell him, Finn."

Sighing, Finn said, "My ex is hassling me. It's nothing I can't handle."

"Hassling you how?"

Riley answered for him. "She's blowing up his phone and screaming at him. I just heard the latest call."

"Did you block her?" Mac asked.

"Yeah, but she's calling me from other people's phones. I thought it might be Clint calling about work, so I took the call."

"Maybe you ought to mention it to Blaine," Mac said. "Just in case."

"In case of what?"

"In case it escalates."

"It won't. She's pissed, but she'll get over it."

Riley crossed his arms and stared him down. "She booked *a wedding venue*, Finn. She's not going to just get over it."

Mac's eyes bugged. "She did *what*?"

"She booked a wedding venue for next year," Riley said.

"Jesus. Had you talked about getting married?"

"Not once, ever."

"Sorry, man, but that's fucked up."

By now, Shane and Luke had joined them, the four men forming a circle around Finn.

"Sane people don't book weddings when the other half of the relationship doesn't know he's getting married," Luke said. "I don't think you should just blow this off like it's no big deal."

"I agree," Shane said. "You need to show your phone to Blaine, tell him what she did and said. See what he thinks."

"I thought I heard Blaine was off-island." Finn felt sick at the thought of reporting Missy to the cops. Had it really come to that?

"He's back with his brother Deacon, who's apparently going to be

Gansett's new harbor master," Mac said. "I'll go with you to talk to him."

"Oh. Um. Okay."

"Let's do it."

"Like right now?"

Mac stared at him without a hint of the usual humor he was known for. "Right fucking now."

Finn swallowed hard and allowed his cousin to lead him out of the house. Everything about this felt wrong. He and Missy had been friends since high school, had dated on and off for five years before he moved to Gansett. Was he really about to turn her in to the cops for harassing him?

Mac gave him a gentle shove toward the passenger seat of his truck, and Finn got in, ceding to the cousin who'd never steered him wrong and who'd always had his back, from the time Finn had been a little kid hungry for the attention of the older cousins he'd adored. If Mac said he needed to report it, he would report it.

As Mac started the truck, Riley jumped into the backseat, settling awkwardly between the car seats belonging to Mac's kids.

They drove to the public safety building in tense silence.

"Turn your phone back on," Mac said right before they pulled into the parking lot where Blaine's department-issued SUV sat in the spot reserved for the chief.

Finn turned on the phone, and it went wild, beeping with texts and messages.

"She's persistent," Riley said. "You gotta give her that."

"She's harassing him," Mac said. "Plain and simple. If a guy was doing that to a woman, it would be a big deal. It's no less of a big deal because a woman is doing it to a guy. Harassment is harassment, and it's *not* okay."

After Mac parked, Finn got out of the truck and followed him inside, hoping he didn't actually throw up.

Riley squeezed his shoulder, letting him know he was there, which Finn appreciated. This totally sucked, and he wanted nothing to do with it, but his cousin was right. Her behavior was not okay.

"It's Mac and his identical twin baby cousins," Blaine said, grinning when he saw them coming.

All their lives, Riley and Finn had heard about their startling resemblance to Mac and his brother Adam, so Blaine's comment was nothing new.

"What's up, boys?" Blaine stood next to a younger man who shared his sun-streaked brown hair, golden-brown eyes and muscular build but not his friendly disposition. The other guy, who Finn assumed was his brother, glowered at Blaine behind his back. Finn wondered what his deal was.

"Tell him, Finn," Mac said in that no-nonsense tone that had put Finn on edge earlier. Usually, Mac was all about the nonsense.

"I told my ex at home that we were over for good, and she kind of lost it a little."

"Not a little," Riley said. "A *lot*. Show him the phone."

Finn unlocked the phone and showed Blaine the texts and voice-mails he'd received from Missy. "I haven't read them all—"

"You probably should have." Blaine's expression grew serious as he scrolled through them. "'If you've got someone else, you'd better let her know to watch her back. I'll fucking stab her.' That was the most recent one."

Alarmed, Finn immediately thought of Chloe. "I've been seeing Chloe Dennis."

"I'll have patrol keep an eye on things at the salon, and I'll give your friend a call and let her know what kinds of charges she might be looking at if she keeps up this behavior. Is this her number?"

"No, she borrowed someone's phone to call me after I blocked her." He found the number in his contacts. "This is her number."

"Unblock the number. Let's give her a call."

"Right now?"

"You busy doing something else?"

Finn wished he was anywhere else on earth than about to sic a cop on Missy, but she'd brought this on herself. Maybe if he kept telling himself that, he could beat back the nausea. He unblocked her number, put through the call and handed the phone to Blaine, who put it on speaker.

"It's about fucking time you called me back."

"It's not Finn."

"Who is this?"

"Chief Blaine Taylor, Gansett Island Police Department. I'm here with Finn, who showed me the texts and messages you've left for him, and you may not be aware that the things you've said in your texts could result in charges. Felony charges."

"Did he tell you what he did? Leading me on for years and then trying to dump me right before he comes home *after I waited all this time for him?*"

"Ma'am, we're not talking about what he did. We're talking about the threats you've made against him in texts and voicemails that would be admissible in court should Mr. McCarthy choose to press charges."

"Mr. McCarthy *can go fuck himself!*"

"Shall I take that to mean he won't hear from you again? Because if he does, I'm sure my friends at the Connecticut state police would be happy to pick you up and take you into custody as the kinds of threats you've made are taken very seriously by law enforcement."

A loud click served as her answer.

"Nice young lady," Blaine said, handing Finn's phone back to him.

"Yeah," Riley said, "she's a real prize."

"If you hear from her again," Blaine said, "I want you to let me know right away. I'll make good on calling in Connecticut state police."

"I will. Thanks, Blaine."

"Thanks a lot," Mac added. "I appreciate the assist."

"Happy to help any time. This is my brother, Deacon." Pointing to them, he said, "Deacon, you know Mac. These are his cousins, Riley and Finn."

Deacon shook hands with them. "How you doing?"

"Better now that my brother reported his crazy ex," Riley said.

"So you're taking the harbor master job?" Mac asked Deacon.

"That's his big idea. I haven't agreed to anything."

Blaine glared at his brother, who glared right back at him. "He's taking the job."

"We'll leave you to fight that out." Mac led Riley and Finn out of the police station. "You hear from her again, you call Blaine, you hear me?"

"Yeah, I will. Thanks, Mac."

"I know it's hard to go to the cops about someone who has been a friend, but you did the right thing."

Finn knew that was true, but it still made him sick to have to do it. "Don't tell the dads, okay? I don't need mine up my ass about this."

"I won't say anything," Mac said.

"I won't either," Riley said.

Mac checked his watch. "This day is getting away from me. Maddie and I are going to the food bank fundraiser tonight, so I need to get back to the Curtis place to do some measuring so I can get the materials ordered." They got into Mac's truck and drove back to the Curtis house, where Finn had left his truck.

"I'll give you a hand with the measuring," Riley said.

"I'll see you at the fundraiser." Knowing his cousin would also be there cemented Finn's determination to keep the "date" he'd made last night with Chloe. "I've got to get the house packed up and do a few other things this afternoon."

"Nik and I are going to the fundraiser, too," Riley said. "I'll see you there."

Finn wondered if Riley had just now decided to go so he and Nikki could keep an eye on him. "Sounds good."

After he parted with Riley and Mac, he drove home with the window down, letting in some of the warm spring breeze blowing in off the sound, where the faint outline of sailboats competing in Race Week could be seen on the horizon.

Finn tried not to think about the ugliness with Missy, the despair over Chloe or anything other than going through the motions to prepare for the move back to Connecticut. Although, with Missy losing her mind, he had reason now to wonder if moving home was still a good idea. One thing he knew for sure was that after meeting Chloe, he couldn't stay on Gansett and continue to run into her everywhere he went. That was just too painful to endure long term.

For the first time in his adult life, Finn had no idea where he belonged.

CHAPTER 15

"You're taking the job," Blaine said to Deacon after the McCarthys left his office.

"Why? So you can keep tabs on my every move? You'd love that, wouldn't you?"

"Someone needs to keep tabs on you so you don't end up back in jail."

Deacon rolled his eyes. "You say that like I'm a jailhouse regular."

"For all I know, you could be. I haven't heard a word from you in months, and then you call in the middle of the night, needing me to pull some strings for you with cops."

"Sorry to bother you."

"You didn't bother me! But what the fuck is going on with you, Deac? Aren't we a little past the age of bar fights?"

"Maybe you are now that you're all domesticated."

"Happened long before I got married. In case you've forgotten, I've been a cop for a while now."

"Like you'd ever let any of us forget."

Blaine had to resist the urge to punch the smug smile off his younger brother's face. "Don't turn this around on me. What're you doing fighting in a bar?"

"I told you. Some dude was hassling a woman. I asked him to knock it off. He didn't want to, and we got into it."

"Who was the woman?"

"One of the waitresses."

"Someone you know?"

Deacon shrugged. "We've hung out."

"In other words, you've slept with her and didn't want any other guy talking to her."

"It wasn't like that. She's a nice girl. A hardworking single mom."

"The kid isn't yours, is it?"

"For fuck's sake, Blaine. The kid is not mine. I like her, and I didn't like the way that douche was talking to her. It was that simple."

"Did they arrest him, too?"

"Nope."

"How come?"

"Everyone said I jumped him. They didn't hear what he said to her."

Hands on hips, Blaine studied the face that had always been far too handsome. Deacon had had women throwing themselves at him from the time he was a teenager, including the mother of one of his friends. Deacon had left the island the day after his eighteenth birthday and had rarely returned, not even for Blaine's wedding.

Deacon was the Taylor family's black sheep, or so their mother liked to say. Blaine didn't think the label was fair. Deacon had marched to the beat of his own drum, for sure, but to Blaine's knowledge, he'd never been in any trouble—until now. The chief of police in the town where his brother had been arrested had agreed to drop the charges if Blaine personally took custody of him and removed him from the area for the time being.

That was how Deacon had landed in Blaine's office on Gansett Island.

Deacon picked up a framed photo of Tiffany and the girls from Blaine's desk. "Now that you have me here, brother dear, whatever will you do with me?"

Blaine snatched the photo from him and put it back where it

belonged. "I told you—you're going to be Gansett's new harbor master for the season, and when the summer is over, we'll see." His brother had worked as the harbor master for one of the towns in Cape Cod the previous year, and his certifications were up-to-date. Having him here would solve one of Blaine's pressing concerns. The mayor had been on him about filling the position, and with Race Week signifying the unofficial start to boating season on Gansett, Deacon's arrival was very well timed, even if his brother was probably going to be a huge pain in his ass.

"So you plan to hold me hostage here for the summer, keep me out of trouble and let me go after Labor Day, if I behave?"

"Something like that."

"And where am I going to live during my captivity?"

"In the garage apartment at my place."

"Oh, awesome. So you'll be able to keep tabs on me round the clock. This is like the summer camp from hell."

"Cut the crap, Deacon. I have no desire to keep tabs on you, but unless you want an assault charge and possible conviction on your record, you're here to stay for the summer."

"Does that stick up your ass ever get uncomfortable? I'd imagine it would start to hurt after a while."

Again, Blaine wanted to punch him, but he resisted the urge. "Feel free to take the next ferry back to the mainland. I'll give Chief Over-meyer a call and let him know you're no longer in my custody."

"You'd just love that, wouldn't you?"

"What I'd love is to go home to my wife and daughters, who I haven't seen in more than twenty-four hours, thanks to your shenanigans."

"You're such a family man. It's touching."

"You might want to try it one of these days."

"Eww, gross." Deacon shuddered dramatically. "No way. You can't put a collar on me." He tugged on the neck of his shirt. "It would kill me."

Blaine rolled his eyes. "Marriage is the single best thing to ever happen to me. I highly recommend it."

"One woman in your bed for the rest of your life? No way, Jose. That's not for me."

"If it's the *right* woman, you won't ever want anyone else."

Deacon waggled his brows. "Variety is the spice of my life."

"If you cause one second of trouble on my island this summer, I'll send you back to face the music, you hear me?"

"Yes, sir," Deacon said sarcastically. "I hear you loud and clear. I think they heard you on Martha's Vineyard."

"Let's go."

Blaine drove them home in his department-issued SUV, dodging traffic and pedestrians as they went through a town that came back to life during Race Week each spring. It wouldn't slow down again until after Labor Day. Summer was Blaine's favorite and least favorite time of year—his favorite because of the warm weather and outdoor time with family and friends. It was his least favorite because the huge influx of tourists that came to the island to party often took him away from his family at the best time of the year.

"How do you stand being stuck here year-round? When we were kids, all we talked about was getting the hell out of here."

"It's different now."

"How so?"

Tiffany. Ashleigh. Addie. That was how, but he wasn't about to say that to Deacon after the way he'd disparaged marriage and commitment. "It just is. You might see it after you're here awhile."

"Doubtful. I'm already counting the days until I can go back to my real life."

Blaine ignored him and focused on driving, dying to see his girls after one day without them. And yes, he knew that was ridiculous, but so be it. He loved them madly and had missed them. He pulled into the long driveway that led to home and tooted the horn the way he did every night. How old would Ashleigh be, he wondered, before she no longer ran out to greet him after work?

He got out of the driver's side just in time to catch the five-year-old when she launched off the stairs and into his arms. "Hey, bug." Hugging her tightly, he breathed in the fresh strawberry scent of her hair that came from the same shampoo her mother used. "How you doing?"

"Good. Where ya been?"

"You know where I've been." She knew everything that went on. He and Tiff joked that she'd been born with the soul of a thirty-year-old. And even though he was "only" her stepfather, he adored every precocious inch of her.

"Did you find your brother?"

"I sure did. That's him over there." He turned her so she could see Deacon. "Ashleigh, meet Deacon. Deacon, this is Ashleigh."

She burrowed her face into Blaine's neck, going shy as she always did with new people. "He looks like you."

"I do not," Deacon said. "He is way uglier than I am."

Before Blaine could chastise him, Ashleigh giggled.

"Hey." Blaine gave her a playful shake. "He's not funny."

"Yes, he is."

"Yes, I am," Deacon said.

Tiffany came out with Addie on her hip, and Blaine's heart melted at the sight of them. All three of his girls had dark hair and exquisite faces. The girls were the image of their mother, who was the sexiest, smartest, sassiest, funniest, most adorable woman he'd ever met. That he was married to her still amazed him. Forgetting all about his pain-in-the-ass brother, Blaine carried Ashleigh up the stairs to hug and kiss his wife and baby girl.

Addie bounced in her mother's arms as she tried to get to him. "Dadadadada."

"Someone missed her daddy," Blaine said, taking her from Tiffany and holding both girls.

"We all missed Daddy." Tiffany looked up at him with the green eyes that had slayed him from the first time he ever saw her. Back then, she'd still been married to that asshole Jim Sturgil. Blaine had thought he would die of impatience waiting for her to be divorced. And now that she was his… How many hours until bedtime? Too many.

He kissed her quickly. "Daddy missed you, too."

Deacon cleared his throat. "Don't let me interrupt."

Blaine was going to kill him before this summer was up. No question about it. "Tiffany, meet my brother, Deacon. Deacon, my wife, Tiffany, and our daughter Adeline. We call her Addie."

Tiffany leaned around Blaine so she could see Deacon. "Nice to finally meet you. I've heard a lot about you."

Deacon came up the stairs. "I'm sure you have. All good, I hope?"

"Ummm."

Deacon laughed. "Believe half of what you hear."

Though it was the last thing he wanted to do, Blaine released Tiffany, kissed both girls, put Ashleigh down, handed Addie to her mom and took Deacon by the arm. "Let me show you where you're staying."

"I guess I'll be seeing you around," Deacon said to Tiffany.

"I made dinner. You're welcome to join us."

"No, he isn't," Blaine said.

"Yes, he is. Come over in half an hour, Deacon."

Blaine perp-walked his brother down the stairs and across the driveway to the apartment over the garage that also doubled as Tiffany's dance studio. Since opening the Naughty & Nice boutique, she didn't give lessons anymore, but she and Ashleigh still used the space to practice from time to time.

He threw open the door to the apartment, and the fresh scent that greeted them indicated that Tiffany had cleaned it ahead of their arrival. "You can thank my wife for cleaning the place for you."

"That was nice of her."

"The bedroom is back there. Bathroom over there. Hopefully, a free place to stay here will make it so you can keep your apartment on the mainland."

"You've thought of everything, haven't you?"

"Would you rather I left you to rot in jail?"

"Is that a rhetorical question?"

Blaine reached his limit. "I'm going to see my family. Come to dinner if you want. Don't come if you don't want to. Show up for work at eight in the morning. Stay out of trouble. Or I'll send you back to face the charges."

Before Deacon could respond, Blaine was out the door and down the stairs. He crossed the yard and stepped into the cool comfort of his own home, leaned against the door, closed his eyes and released a deep breath.

He smelled her sweet strawberry scent before he felt or heard her.

"That bad?" Tiffany asked as she wrapped her arms around him and rested her head on his chest.

That was all it took to make everything better. He held her tight against him, breathing her in and letting go of the stress of the last two days. He'd done what he could for his brother. "He likes to push my buttons."

"Sounds like a sibling."

"He's exceptionally good at it."

Tiffany laughed.

"You can't find him funny and sleep with me, too. You got me?"

"Yeah, babe. I got you. Don't leave again, though, okay? I hate sleeping alone."

Blaine groaned and pressed his erection against her soft belly. "How many hours until bedtime?"

"Way too many."

"I'm not going to make it. What're the girls doing?"

"Watching Dora."

"Oh, I *love* Dora." They had joked that their girls would sit through a nuclear bomb if Dora was on the TV. Blaine grabbed Tiffany's hand and led her to the half-bath off the kitchen.

"Um, what're you doing?"

"This." Leaving the door cracked open so they could hear the kids, he turned and pulled her into a hot kiss that made his head spin with desire. His hands moved over her, wanting to touch all of her, as if he hadn't seen her in weeks rather than just a day.

She broke the kiss, breathing hard. "Blaine."

"I need you."

"Later."

"Now."

"We can't." Her nervous laughter thrilled him. Everything about her thrilled him.

"Yes, we can." He pulled her shorts and panties down.

"Blaine!"

"Shh. They're watching Dora. It's fine."

"Close the door."

He wanted to fist-bump the air when he realized she was on board. Ashleigh wouldn't let anything happen to Addie in the two minutes this was going to take. He was so primed, he'd be surprised if it took that long.

Tiffany tugged at the button to his uniform pants, growling with frustration when it didn't come loose.

"Easy, baby. I got it." He freed himself from his pants, wrapped an arm around her waist, lifted her and pushed into her heat, his head falling back as he tried not to lose control too quickly. Every damned time was like the first time all over again. "God, I love you."

She tightened her arms around his neck. "I love you, too."

After that, there were no more words, just the desperate pleasure he'd found only with her. Deacon could have his variety. Blaine wanted her—and only her—for the rest of his life.

"Blaine," she said, gasping.

He knew that sound. It meant she was close. Reaching between them, he pressed his fingers to her clit and pushed her over the edge into an orgasm that took him with her. *Holy fuck.*

She laughed as she kissed him. "You're crazy."

"About you, baby."

"Mommy! Addie is poopy!"

"Duty calls. Let me go."

"Only because I have to." He lifted her off him and set her gently on her feet.

Tiffany opened the door an inch. "I'll be right there."

They cleaned up quickly and got dressed.

"This reminds me of the early days," she said. "Remember that time against the wall in the store?"

"I remember everything." He gave her a lingering kiss. "Every single thing. And in case I forget to tell you, thanks for putting up with my asshole brother for the summer."

"I'm sure he'll be fine."

"I wish I could be so sure." Blaine had a feeling that having Deacon around for the summer was going to be anything but smooth sailing.

CHAPTER 16

*W*hen he got home, Finn did some laundry and packing and ended up on the sofa watching an early-season Red Sox game. He had two hours before he needed to shower and get dressed for the benefit and was thinking about cutting the grass when his phone rang with a call from his cousin Adam.

"Hey, what's up?"

"What's this I hear about you leaving?"

"It's time, and my lease is up at the end of the month."

"Who says it's time, and did you ask about extending?"

In the background, Finn could hear Adam's son, Liam, crying.

"Hang on a sec." Adam was gone for a minute before he came back. "Liam says hi."

"Hi, Liam. How's he doing?"

"He's phenomenal. Smartest baby I've ever known."

Finn laughed. "Doesn't every new dad say that?"

"Maybe so, but in my case, it's true. My son is wise beyond his years. But that's not why I called. You can't leave us, Finny. It won't be the same around here without you. You'll miss Liam growing up."

"*Whoa.* Way to lay down a guilt trip."

"Well, it's true. It's so great having everyone here, and you're also going to miss all the fun with the Wayfarer."

"I've had plenty of fun at the Wayfarer."

"I mean the good fun—beaches, bars, bikinis."

"Um, hello, you're married."

"I'm talking about *you*, dipshit. Not me."

A week ago, a summer like the one Adam described would've appealed to him. Now? Nothing did.

"What're you doing?" Adam asked.

"Right now? Nothing."

"Come over. I'm hanging with Liam while Abby does some work at the store."

"Let me grab a shower, and I'll come by before the food bank benefit tonight."

"I used to go to benefits. Now I'm a dad who barely leaves his house because he doesn't want to miss anything his incredibly bright son does."

"You're a mess. You know that, don't you?"

"I'm a very happy mess. See you soon?"

"I'll be there."

As Finn showered, shaved and changed into khakis and a button-down shirt that he had to iron, he thought about Adam and his wife, Abby, who had adopted their baby boy last winter and had been happier than two pigs in shit ever since Liam arrived. They had been open about their struggles to conceive a child of their own, and now it was like those struggles had never happened. They'd all breathed a huge sigh of relief when Adam and Abby passed the point in which the biological parents could no longer change their minds about the adoption, which would be final any time now.

Funny how one little bundle of joy could fix everything that had been wrong before he arrived.

He drove over to Adam's, gave a quick knock on the mudroom door and let himself in, staying quiet in case Liam had fallen asleep.

"In here, Finn!" Adam was in the family room, stretched out on the floor with the baby who was playing with something above his head.

"We're hanging in the baby gym."

"That looks like fun."

Adam gazed at his son. "Most fun I've ever had in my entire life."

The baby really was adorable, with dark hair like both his parents as well as alert gray eyes. When he started to fuss, Adam picked him up and handed him over to Finn. "Go see your cousin Finny and tell him he can't leave right when things are getting interesting around here."

Finn held the baby carefully, awestruck by the responsibility. "Your daddy is very good at guilt-tripping me, buddy. Don't let him pull that crap with you."

"Don't say crap in front of the baby."

Finn gave his cousin a withering look. "Seriously?"

"Abby says it's never too soon to start behaving ourselves around him."

"Let's see how long that lasts in this family. He'll be playing Naked Boy-Naked Girl with his cousins in no time."

Adam laughed. "We're all hoping that game was a one-time thing."

None of them would ever forget five-year-old Thomas and Ashleigh running through the McCarthy family Christmas Day festivities naked as jaybirds, playing the game they called Naked Boy-Naked Girl.

"I'm sure the next wave of McCarthy cousins will get up to all kinds of no-good, the same way we did," Finn said.

"My son will have nothing to do with his cousins."

Finn snorted with laughter. "Right... You're delusional. They'll be his best friends, the same way ours were and are."

"You hear what you just said? You really want to leave your best friends?"

"Not as much as I did a week ago."

"How come?"

"I met someone."

Adam's blue eyes, so similar to his, Riley's and Mac's, nearly popped out of his head. "*Who?*"

"Chloe."

"As in Curl Up and Dye Chloe?"

"Yeah." Finn kept his focus on Liam but could feel Adam staring at him.

"When did this happen?"

"Last week when I went in for a haircut. It was the craziest thing. I just took one look at her and… It was… I don't even know how to describe it. Like someone had electrified the air or something, and I'm well aware of how stupid that sounds."

"Not stupid at all. I know that feeling. I remember the first time I saw Abby in a whole new light. She'd been my brother's girlfriend for ten years and completely off-limits to me. I never thought of her as anything other than a friend. And then there she was, half-drunk and spouting off on the ferry about how she was done with men, and it was like I was meeting her all over again as someone completely new."

"Was it weird with Grant when you started seeing his ex?" Finn had always wondered but had never asked.

"He and Abby had been over for years by then, and he was happy with Steph, so we talked about it and agreed not to make it into something when everyone was happy."

"That's very evolved of you."

"The last thing either of us wanted was trouble with each other. We've always been close, and we still are. It's all good. He knows I wasn't lusting after his girlfriend when they were together. That would've been a totally different ballgame."

"True." Finn stood Liam up and let him bounce on rubbery legs. "Could I ask you something?"

"Anything you want."

"Do you believe there's only one person for everyone?"

"No. I don't believe that. But I do believe that when you find someone who really does it for you, who gets you on every level and who you can't imagine living without, that you should do everything you can to keep that person in your life."

"What if that's not what she wants?"

Adam blew out a deep breath. "That's a tough one."

"Yeah, it really is, especially because I can tell the attraction is entirely mutual. But she says she can't get involved."

"And she didn't say why?"

"No, just that she has her reasons."

Adam thought about that for a minute. "Maybe you could ask her to tell you about the things that are keeping you guys from being together."

"I've tried. She's not talking about it. Not to me anyway."

"I'm sorry, Finn."

"It really sucks. I've never felt anything like what happens to me when she's around. I even told her I would stay on Gansett if she'd just give me a chance. But she said it's not the right time for her." Finn sighed. "If it wasn't for Shane's wedding, I'd be out of here now. I keep running into her around town. It's torture."

"Damn, that does suck. I wish I had some words of wisdom for you, but if she's not into it, there's not much you can do."

"I know. I'm working on accepting that."

Liam spit up a little, and Finn, being a coward when it came to spit-up, handed him over to his dad. Adam cleaned him up like an expert and settled the baby into the crook of his arm, where Liam seemed right at home.

"I've never really wanted the wife and kids and picket fence, but after meeting Chloe, I can see why you guys would chuck it all for that life if it meant you got to be with *her* every day."

"I can't imagine life without Abby. When we found out she might not be able to have kids, she wanted to set me free, so I could find someone else who could have babies."

Finn had never heard that. "Really? What'd you say?"

"I said I'd rather be childless with her than have six kids with someone else. I wanted *her*, not just anyone."

"I'm so glad it worked out for you guys."

"I am, too, and it'll work out for you, Finn. Maybe not with Chloe, but you'll find your Abby."

A loud crash startled them. Abby ran into the house, her big brown eyes wide and her face pale. She made a mad dash for the bathroom off the kitchen. The sound of retching echoed through the big house.

"Yikes," Finn said.

Adam handed the baby over to Finn and got up to check on her.

ADAM KNOCKED on the bathroom door. "Babe? Are you okay?"

"Don't come in here."

"I've seen you puke before."

"I mean it, Adam. Do not come in here."

He went in anyway and found her sprawled on the floor in a pool of vomit. Dear God... "What happened, honey?"

"I was driving home and started to feel sick, and the next thing I knew..." She broke down into sobs. "I told you not to come in here! And where is Liam?"

"With Finn. He's fine. Let's get you up and into the shower."

"I can't move."

"I'll do everything."

"Please." The single word was barely more than a whimper. "Just leave me alone. I'll be fine."

"Not going to happen, so we can either work together to get you cleaned up or hang out in here until Liam poops himself and Finn freaks out."

"Adam."

"I'm right here, sweetheart. What can I do?"

"I'm gonna be sick again."

He grabbed the trash can and got it to her in the nick of time.

She heaved violently, until there was nothing left but dry heaves.

"You're kind of freaking me out, Abs. How long have you felt lousy?"

"Twenty minutes. Came on out of nowhere when I was leaving the shop."

"Let's get you into the shower."

"Go check on Liam first." Her voice was barely a whisper, her face so pale, it scared him. What the hell was this? Adam opened the bathroom door. "You okay, Finn?"

"We're good."

Adam returned his attention to Abby. "They're fine. Come on. Let me help you up."

She was like a rag doll, but he was able to get her into the shower, where he got completely soaked washing the vomit out of her hair while also holding her up. He left her wet clothes in the bottom of the shower and wrapped her in a towel so he could carry her up to bed.

"Adam... Put me down. You'll break your back."

"Hush. I've got you. Hold on to me." He went up the stairs and set her down on their bed. She closed her eyes and was asleep before he finished covering her. Just to be safe, he got the trash can from the master bathroom and put it on the bedside table before going back down to rescue Finn.

"Is she okay?"

"Seems to be for the moment, but you'd better get out of here in case it's contagious."

Finn handed the baby back to Adam.

"Thanks for the assist."

"Happy to help. I hope she's okay."

"I hope so, too." She had to be okay. Adam would make sure of it.

CHAPTER 17

$\mathcal{F}$inn left Adam and Abby's, hoping that Adam and the baby wouldn't get whatever Abby had—and that he wouldn't either. That'd be just what he needed as he prepared to move home. For a minute, he thought about skipping the fundraiser, but the opportunity to see Chloe had him pointing his truck toward the Sand & Surf Hotel, home to Stephanie's Bistro.

He was nothing if not a glutton for punishment.

Soon enough, he wouldn't have to see her anymore. In the meantime, he was hungry for whatever he could get of her. As he pulled into the parking lot at the hotel, Riley was helping Nikki out of his truck. They waited for Finn to park and walked in with him as he donned the navy blue blazer he'd brought.

"Looking dapper, Finnbar."

"Thank you, Nicholas. You two clean up rather nicely."

"We actually made an effort." She laughed as she glanced up at Riley. "I told him we don't go out very often and we ought to at least *try* to be presentable."

"That's what happens when you spend an entire winter renovating a house," Riley said.

"Not sure what we'll do for entertainment when we finish it."

Riley barked out a dirty laugh. "I have a few ideas."

Nikki elbowed him in the gut, drawing an oomph from her beloved.

Riley rubbed his belly. "That wasn't nice."

"Hey, I was just at Adam's, and Abby is really sick. Puking her guts up."

"Aww, poor thing," Nikki said. "I was at the clinic today, and Katie said they've had a few people in with whatever's going around."

"I hope the baby doesn't get it," Finn said.

"That would truly suck," Riley said.

"Yeah." A pang of fear struck Finn. If anything ever happened to that baby… No. Just no. He couldn't even bear to think about it. Absorbed in his thoughts of Adam's family, he almost missed his first glimpse of Chloe, who was surrounded by a group of people. But she was the only one he saw. Resplendent in a black dress with huge red flowers on it, her hair up and her makeup flawless, she looked like she'd just stepped off the pages of *Vogue*.

"Our Finnbar is gobsmacked," Nikki said, breaking the spell.

Finn tore his gaze off Chloe to look at Nikki. "What'd you say?"

"I said you're gobsmacked."

"What does that mean?"

"It's British slang for astounded."

He couldn't deny that and found himself looking at her again, unable to look away, afraid that if he did, she might disappear. With a sudden, painful urgency, he realized that if she disappeared, if he didn't see her again, he'd never forget her.

Nikki wrapped her hands around his arm. "You want me to talk to her, Finn?"

"No." The single word came out more harshly than he'd intended. He knew she meant well, so he softened his tone. "Please don't."

"I hate this for you," she said in the same soft tone.

"I'll be okay."

"You should ask her to dance later."

"Why? So I can make everything worse?"

"Maybe it will make everything better somehow."

Finn gave her a one-armed hug. "Thanks for caring."

"I do care. I've never had a brother until I had you."

He kissed her forehead. "You're incredibly sweet, and I'm thrilled to have a sister to look out for me."

Riley came over bearing drinks for all of them. Finn had been so focused on Chloe that he hadn't seen him walk away. "Get your filthy paws off my woman."

Nikki grasped Finn's arm. "Ask her to dance. I promise you won't regret it."

"Leave him alone, Nik," Riley said, putting his arm around her.

Finn winked at her. "She's helping me."

"*No one* can help you."

Leave it to his brother to sum things up. No one had ever amused or aggravated him—sometimes in the same second—the way Riley did.

Their dad and Chelsea joined them a few minutes later. "My sons are looking rather handsome tonight, aren't they, Chels?"

Chelsea indulged him, as she always did. "Very much so."

"We're not twelve anymore, Dad," Riley said disdainfully.

"And yet you'll always be my little boys."

"Dear God," Finn said. "I need another beer." Luckily, he could walk home from the Surf if it came to that, and he had a feeling it might with the way this night was going.

HE'D COME. Even after she'd sent him away, he'd still come to her event. The minute he walked into the room, looking sinfully handsome, everyone else had disappeared from view. He was all she could see, and dear God, she wanted him. Despite all the reasons she knew she should keep her distance, she wanted him with her whole heart and soul. She saw him, and she *wanted*. It was that simple.

Except it was anything but simple. She rubbed her aching hands together, trying to remember the many reasons she had resisted him up to now. But all he'd had to do to shatter her defenses was walk into the room wearing a navy blue blazer. As she greeted guests, she felt him watching her every move, which made her body tingle with the awareness that only he had ever made happen. Why him? Why now?

She had no idea, but her resistance had crumbled to the point of nonexistence by the time he actually spoke to her.

"You got a hell of a turnout."

Stephanie's was completely full, with people spilling into the lobby of the Surf.

Chloe forced herself to look up at him, to make eye contact, while trying not to let on how powerfully affected she was by his mere presence. "We did. I'm thrilled."

"You look beautiful."

She'd received compliments from other men, but none greater than those three simple words from him. "You look rather beautiful yourself."

He unleashed that potent smile, the one that made her knees go weak from the flood of desire that rippled through her. "I ironed and everything."

God, he was adorable. And sexy. So damned sexy. And sweet. Her thoughts were focused exclusively on him at a time when she had other things to be concerned with. One of the volunteers came over to tell her she needed to start the program. "Off I go. I'll see you later?" *Please, yes. Please see me later.*

He nodded. "I'll be right here when you're finished. Come find me?"

"I will."

The brief encounter left her lightheaded and off her game as she stepped up to the microphone on the stage where Owen Lawry would perform after the official part of the evening had concluded. "If I could have your attention for just a minute." Chloe hated being the center of attention, but it was for a good cause, so she soldiered through the ordeal of public speaking. "I want to welcome you, thank you for being here and extend a huge thank-you to our sponsors, Stephanie's Bistro, McCarthy's Gansett Island Marina and Hotel, the Beachcomber Hotel, the Sand & Surf Hotel, the Gansett Island Ferry Company, Naughty & Nice, Ryan's Pharmacy, Island Breeze Records, the Oar Bar, the Lobster Pot, Domenic's, Abby's Attic, McCarthy's Wayfarer, McCarthy Construction and my own Curl Up & Dye Salon."

She reviewed the silent auction items and asked everyone to be as generous as possible to help the seasonal workers get through the off-season. "And on that note, I encourage everyone to have fun and enjoy the music provided by our own Owen Lawry."

The attendees gave Owen a rousing round of applause as he took the stage, strummed his guitar and launched into "Tequila Sunrise."

Chloe stepped off the stage, determined to make her way back to Finn as quickly as she could. Just for tonight, she would try not to think about the many reasons it was a bad idea to be so wildly attracted to a man she couldn't have.

AN ARM CAME around Finn from behind, and he turned to find his cousin Laura attached to him.

"Hi there. Your husband sounds fantastic, as always."

"He's the best."

"You look happy tonight."

"I have a night off from baths and bedtime for three kids under the age of three. You'd be happy, too."

Amused by her glee, Finn cuffed her on the chin. "Who's with the little animals?"

"Sarah and Charlie," she said, referring to Owen's mom and her fiancé. "They're thrilled to do baths and bedtime."

"My mom used to say thank goodness for grandparents."

"How is Auntie Deb doing?"

"Okay, I guess. She doesn't say much about what's going on. Last I heard, she's doing online dating and having some misadventures with that."

"Not sure I could handle that after what happened with Justin. I wouldn't trust my judgment."

"That had nothing to do with you and everything to do with him being a douche." Laura's first husband had continued to troll for online dates after they were married until he'd been found out by two of her friends. "And besides, your second husband has redeemed you and your judgment."

She directed a loving gaze at Owen. "Yes, he certainly has."

Chloe made her way through the crowd, coming toward him.

Finn's heart skipped a beat, and he all but stopped breathing as he waited for her.

"What's this I see?" Laura asked.

Finn realized he hadn't been subtle about the way he stared at Chloe.

"Are you and Chloe…"

"No, we're not."

"But you'd like to be?"

He shrugged, feigning nonchalance even as every part of him stood up for a better look at her.

Shane, Katie, Mac, Maddie, Janey and Joe joined them, and for a second, Finn lost track of Chloe in a sea of cousins and their spouses.

"Excuse me." He ducked between Joe and Mac on his way to meet Chloe, who was flustered and sexier than ever with her cheeks pink from excitement and heat from the room full of people. Oblivious to the fact that half his family was watching, Finn put an arm around her, as if he had the right to, and drew her into his protective embrace. "I'd say you have a huge hit on your hands."

"Seems like it."

"Want to get some air?"

"I'd love that."

He guided her toward the Surf's lobby, ignoring the prying eyes of his family members, and gave her his full attention. If this was all they were ever going to have, he planned to enjoy every single second of his time with her. With his hand on her lower back, he directed her through the lobby to the back porch. They stepped outside into a cool breeze blowing in off the ocean.

Finn removed his blazer and draped it over her shoulders.

She snuggled into it, taking a deep sniff.

"Are you smelling my jacket?"

153

"It smells really good, and you did a great job of warming it up for me."

"I aim to please you."

"You do."

Raising a brow, he said, "I do what?"

"You please me. Greatly."

"Chloe…"

"Will you hold me, Finn?"

"You don't ever, ever have to ask." He put his arms around her, sliding one of them under the coat of his that she wore, and drew her into his embrace, resting his chin on the top of her head and breathing in her appealing scent. Everything about her just did it for him. They stood there, wrapped up in each other for a long time. Behind him, he heard voices he recognized—Slim Jackson, Alex Martinez, Tiffany Taylor.

He tuned out everything and everyone to focus exclusively on the woman who'd somehow become the center of his universe in a few short days. As always, the air around them pulsed with possibility.

"Come home with me tonight," he whispered, his lips close to her ear so he wouldn't be overheard.

"I can't. I have Ranger." She drew back and looked up at him. "You could come home with me."

A lump in his throat made it impossible to speak, so he only nodded and then brought her back in close to him where he wanted to keep her forever. He didn't know what had changed, but he wasn't about to ask. Not when he had an entire night with her to look forward to. Whereas last night he'd turned down her offer of one night, tonight he wouldn't say no. He couldn't say no.

"Chloe?"

Finn released her so she could answer the woman who had called her.

"What's up?"

"Sorry to interrupt. We're getting ready to close the silent auction. Do you want to make an announcement?"

"Sure, I'll be right in." To Finn, she said, "I've got to go."

"Dance with me when you're done?"

"Okay." She removed his blazer and handed it back to him. "Thanks for the loan."

"My pleasure." He watched her walk away, wishing he could make the next couple of hours pass in a blink so he could be alone with her. This was actually happening. After taking a few minutes to get himself together, he went back inside to rejoin his family, which now included his uncle Mac and aunt Linda as well as his uncle Frank and his fiancée, Betsy.

"What's this I hear about you leaving us?" Big Mac asked, handing Finn a fresh beer.

"It's time to head back to my real life, which has been on pause the last couple of years." As he said the words, his gaze locked on Chloe across the room.

"Seems to me you have a real life here."

"I do, but I never intended to move here forever."

"Neither did I when I first came here. I heard about a marina property for sale for dirt cheap, came to check it out and the rest, as they say, is history."

"You didn't ever feel like you were missing out by living on an island all this time?"

"Missing out on what?"

"I don't know. A bigger life, I guess?"

"If my life on Gansett were any bigger, it would be too much. I have everything I need right here. Look, I'm not exactly unbiased in this situation. I love having you and your brother and cousins here. I love that the whole family has ended up on my island, but I also get that this life isn't for everyone. I was just sorta hoping it would suit you long term the way it has the others."

"I haven't been unhappy here. I wouldn't want you to think that."

"I know you haven't been. I pay attention, and I can see how much you love being with your brother and your cousins and us old guys, too."

"I really do love being around the family. There's no shortage of entertainment."

Big Mac laughed. "That is for sure." He placed his huge hand on Finn's shoulder and gave a gentle squeeze. "All I'm going to say is that sometimes everything you want and need is right under your nose."

At that moment, Chloe stepped up to the microphone and asked for everyone's attention.

She already had his full attention. As she went down the list of silent auction items and winners, Finn never took his eyes off her, drinking in every detail. He never wanted to forget the way she looked tonight.

Sometimes everything you want and need is right under your nose.

He had tonight with her to look forward to. But what would tomorrow bring?

CHAPTER 18

*C*hloe went through the motions of running the fundraiser while ignoring the persistent aching in her hips, knees and ankles from too much time on her feet—the last three hours in heels she had no business wearing anymore.

Everyone in attendance wanted to talk to her about something, or so it seemed. The only one she wanted to talk to was the dark-haired man in the back of the room who watched her intently even as he talked and laughed with various family members and friends.

Every time her gaze collided with his, her body reacted the same way it did when he touched her. How did he do that with merely a look? And what was she doing agreeing to spend the night with him? She had no idea, but she could no longer bear to resist the overpowering attraction.

Other women did one-night stands all the time. Why couldn't she?

Even as she had the thought, she knew that one night would never be enough. But it was all she had to offer.

Owen returned to the stage and, propped on a stool, began strumming his guitar. "I used to live a vagabond life, traveling from one gig to another. Until I met the stunningly beautiful Laura McCarthy and wanted to put down roots for the first time ever, right here in this hotel my grandparents ran for fifty years. This is 'Better Together' by Jack Johnson, for my wife, Laura, the mother of my three beautiful children and the love of my life. I am so much better when we're together, baby."

With a hand over her heart, Laura pretended to swoon and then blew a kiss to her adorable husband. Chloe could only imagine what it must be like to have such a connection with a man. She'd never come close to what Laura had with Owen.

"You promised me a dance."

Finn's breath against her ear sent goose bumps skittering down her arms and made her nipples tighten.

"So I did."

He led her to the dance floor, drew her into his arms, and she wrapped hers around his waist, inside the blazer.

They were making a rather public declaration that would be the talk of Gansett Island, but she couldn't bring herself to care. Not when she had him and the delicious scent of him to focus on.

"I like this song." She tried to ignore her out-of-control hormones. "I've never heard it."

"I like it, too. How long do you have to stay?" His gruffly stated question had her hormones on full alert.

"I can leave any time now. The silent auction announcement was my last official duty."

"You want to go?"

"Right now?"

"I'm dying to be alone with you."

No man had ever said anything remotely like that to her, and it was all she could do to continue to breathe.

"After this song."

"Not sure I can wait that long." A full-body shiver rattled her and drew a tortured groan from him. "Let's go."

"Don't you have to say goodbye to your family?"

"If I do that, we'll be here another hour, and that's not an option. It's okay. They won't care." He took a gentle hold of her hand, always mindful of her swollen knuckles, and led her out of Stephanie's. They were on their way to a clean escape when Riley emerged from the men's room in the lobby and spotted them.

"Leaving so soon, kids?"

Finn grimaced. "Chloe has to work early."

"Is that your story, and you're sticking to it?"

"Bye, Riley." Placing his hand on her lower back, he guided Chloe out the hotel's front door, placing his coat over her shoulders once again.

"Thank you. I forgot to bring a sweater."

"Did I tell you how incredible you look tonight?"

Chloe's face flushed with heat. "You might've mentioned something about that earlier."

"Well, it bears repeating."

"Thank you."

"It's really not fair," he said.

"What isn't?"

"You being so stunningly beautiful when I'm trying to honor your wishes and keep my distance." He put his arm around her shoulders and matched his stride to her much slower one. "You've got me turned upside down and inside out, Chloe."

"I'm sorry. I don't mean to do that to you."

"I've never been in a situation like this one before."

"What's different about it?"

"*Everything* is different. Everything." In the parking lot, he steered her toward his truck. "I'll bring you back to get your car in the morning." He opened the passenger door, helped her in and studied her in that intent, all-consuming way of his. Leaning in, he said, "The way I want you is different. The way I think about you is different. The way I feel when I'm with you is different. Even the way I feel when I'm *not* with you is different."

Chloe's heart beat so fast, she feared it might burst from her chest. She raised a hand, placed it on his face and drew him into a kiss.

The needy sound that came from the back of his throat was like a shot of gas on the already out-of-control wildfire that burned between them. Their kiss escalated so quickly, she forgot where she was or that anyone might see them kissing. She turned her head to break the kiss. "It's different for me, too."

He took a shuddering deep breath. "Let's go."

As he drove them to her house, he reached across the center console, palm up, inviting her to hold his hand. Chloe appreciated that he did that, rather than taking hold of her sore hand and hurting her. She rested hers on top of his, palm to palm, which was somehow more erotic than full-on sex with other men had been.

This man was different. She wanted to trust him with the truth of her diagnosis but wouldn't because she didn't feel comfortable telling anyone, even him. Protecting her business was her top priority. She couldn't afford to take any risks that would endanger the flimsy security net beneath her.

If her condition got to the point where she couldn't work at all, she would have to apply for disability.

And why was she falling into that rabbit hole when she was headed home to spend the night with the sexiest man in the universe? She had far better things to do tonight than dread her uncertain future.

"You okay?" he asked after a long silence.

"Uh-huh."

"If you've changed your mind about tonight, it's okay to say so."

"I haven't."

"Oh good," he said, exhaling dramatically.

She rubbed her hand against his. "Does that mean you haven't changed your mind either?"

"Um, no. I haven't changed my mind."

Chloe laughed at his quick reply.

He looked over at her. "I like that."

"What?"

"The sound of your laughter. It makes me happy to hear it."

"I haven't had a lot to laugh about lately. Thanks for giving me reason to."

After another period of silence, he said, "You know... I've been told I'm a pretty good listener. If you want to talk about whatever's weighing on you, I'm right here."

160

God, she was tempted. It would be so easy to spill her guts to the sweet, sexy guy who made it so easy to trust him. He wouldn't tell anyone. She knew that for sure, but she didn't want him to know either. She didn't want his pity or even his empathy, and she sure as hell didn't want him feeling obligated to her in any way. "That's very sweet of you, but it's the last thing in the world I want to talk about."

"The offer is on the table. No expiration date."

"Thank you." Crushing disappointment overtook Chloe as she realized that not only was he the sexiest man she'd ever met, but that he'd also make one hell of a friend. She wanted him in every way she could have him—as a lover, a friend, a confidant and a partner.

But the persistent ache in her hands and joints was a reminder of why she couldn't go there with him. He could have anyone. Chloe couldn't bear the idea of making her problems his problems. She shouldn't even be taking him home with her and cursed the weakness that had led to their plans for the evening.

She couldn't have him long term, but she could have him tonight, and with everything else so tentative, she planned to fully enjoy this one night with him. A nagging worry crept into her mind… What did he think would happen after they spent tonight together?

"Finn…"

"Hmm?"

"You know this is only tonight, right?"

He didn't say anything at first, making her wonder what he was thinking.

"I don't understand why it has to be that way, Chloe. There's something between us. You feel it every bit as much as I do."

"I'm not denying that. It's just that there are things…"

"What things? There's nothing you could tell me that would make me not want this or you. *Nothing.*"

Her laugh had a bitter edge to it. That wasn't true. He was twenty-seven years old with his entire life ahead of him. The last thing he needed was to be saddled with what was ahead for her.

"Make me understand, Chloe." He gave her hand a gentle squeeze. "I have never once felt for any woman what I do for you, and I barely know you. When I tell you there's nothing you could say that would change that for me, I mean it. I truly mean it."

"I know you do."

"And still you won't tell me."

"It's not that I don't want to. It's just…" She was still coming to grips with it herself and had no idea how to bring other people into it. Perhaps it was time to take David's advice and seek out professional help in dealing with her diagnosis, because she was doing a piss-poor job of dealing with it on her own. If only the island's shrink wasn't Finn's father. However, she was becoming desperate enough for some coping skills that she might have to reach out to Dr. McCarthy. Doctor-patient confidentiality would force him to keep her secrets, even if his own son was involved. "I'm not able to talk about it. I'm just not."

He sighed. "Okay."

"I'm sorry that it can't be more, and I'll understand if you'd rather not hang out tonight."

"Unless you're sending me away, I'm staying."

"I'm not sending you away."

FINN HAD NEVER BEEN MORE TORN between what he wanted and what was best for him. Spending tonight with her was what he wanted more than he'd ever wanted anything, but he knew it wasn't in his best interest to get more involved with a woman who continued to hold him at arm's length even as she invited him into her bed.

For the first time in his charmed life, he ran the risk of heartbreak, and even knowing that, he couldn't stay away from her.

They arrived at her house, and as he followed her inside, he reminded himself of what this was—and what it wasn't. One night. That was all she'd offered, and he needed to keep reminding himself of that. He would take his lead from her.

Ranger came shuffling out to greet them, and Chloe bent at the waist to give her baby a kiss on the top of his head.

Finn's gaze was drawn to her ass until she straightened, turned and caught him looking. He smiled sheepishly. "The view was too great to pass up."

Smiling, she let the dog out into the backyard and returned to where Finn stood in the middle of her kitchen. "You sure do know how to make a girl feel good about herself."

Resting his hands on her hips, he dropped his forehead to lean against hers. "If you're judging by how I see you, you should feel *spectacular* about yourself. You are, hands down, the sexiest, most beautiful woman I've ever met." He kissed her softly, lingering against the cushion of blueberry-flavored lips. "From the purple streaks in your hair to the ink on your arm to this little gem." He kissed the glittering stud in her nose. "Everything about you does it for me. You're so fucking sexy, you take my breath away. And just so you know, I love talking to you as much as I love looking at you." *So much for keeping things in check*, he thought, as he bared his soul to her.

She curled her arms around his neck and drew him into a sizzling, frantic kiss, fueled by the pent-up need that had been building between them since the day they met. Her mouth opened to his tongue, and the brush of hers against his combined to create the single most erotic moment of his life thus far. One kiss had him hard and ready for more.

Ranger barked outside the door, and still the kiss went on until he barked again, more sharply this time, and they pulled apart, laughing and breathless.

"Hold that thought," she said as she went to let in the dog and lock the door.

"It's the only thought in my head at the moment."

As she returned to him, she eyed the erection he couldn't hide, licked her lips and looked up at him with violet eyes full of vulnerability that made him ache with wanting her—all of her. Not just her body, but her heart and soul, too. That was most certainly a first for him.

She took his hand, led him from the kitchen and shut off the light on the way out of the room.

Finn followed her down the hallway to her bedroom, still not entirely sure he believed this was really going to happen. It was like a dream in some ways. Despite all the reasons why he knew it couldn't be, it felt like the most significant thing that had ever happened to him. If he shared that thought with her, she'd surely tell him to leave. So he kept it to himself and waited for her to show him what she wanted.

She turned so her back was to him. "Will you unzip me?"

His fingers were all thumbs as he dragged the zipper down her back while trying to remember to breathe. She made him feel like a teenager about to get laid for the first time—a thought that made him chuckle as he skimmed his lips over the curve of her neck.

"What's so funny?"

"I'm actually nervous. Reminds me of the time Mary Jane O'Connor took me down to the basement of her parents' house and made a man out of me. I had no idea what I was doing then, and I feel the same way now."

Holding the dress up with a hand to her chest, she turned to him. "Do I need to be concerned about this Mary Jane O'Connor?" She raised a brow to go with the teasing tone of her question.

"Baby, you don't need to be concerned about anyone." His gaze dropped to the hand that held up her dress, noting the swollen knuckles that caused her such pain. He hated that for her. Then she removed her hand, and the dress fell to the floor, leaving her bare except for a strapless bra and what looked to be a thong.

On her chest, a tattoo of a fairy with a wand sprinkled hearts down over the plump crests of her breasts.

His mouth went dry as he kissed each one of the tiny hearts that he could reach.

She reached up to push the coat off his shoulders and began unbuttoning his dress shirt.

When he noticed her fingers weren't working the way she wanted them to, he pulled the shirt and T-shirt he wore under it over his head and tossed them aside.

Her eyes widened as she took in the sight of his bare chest. "Holy moly," she whispered as she dragged her fingertips over the hills and valleys of his chest and abdomen. "I'd heard something about an eight-pack."

Hard physical labor kept him in excellent shape, and her obvious appreciation made him even harder than he already was. Not to mention, she'd been gathering info about him.

She tugged on his belt, groaning in frustration when it didn't come loose for her.

Finn took over, releasing the belt and the button and unzipping, which gave him some badly needed room to breathe.

She stared at him in awe that made him feel like Superman. "I don't know where to touch you first."

"I can give you some pointers, if that would help."

She giggled, and the lighthearted sound of it made him smile. He wanted to hear more of that giggle.

With her hands flat on his back, she dragged them down and into the back of his pants to cup his ass. When she gave a little squeeze, he nearly passed out as half the blood in his body headed south in one massive wave of need. Then she pushed his pants down, laughing again when they got caught on his hard cock.

"This is no time for laughter," he said in a teasingly stern tone. Being undressed by her trumped the kiss in the kitchen to become the most erotic experience of his life. "You've got me on the verge of losing it, and you're laughing."

"I haven't done anything."

"You're here, you're breathing, you're touching me, and you're mostly naked."

She looked up at him. "That's all it takes?"

"With you, it takes even less than that. All you have to do is be in the room, and I'm a goner."

"Finn…"

"I know." He kissed her, released the clasp on her bra and looked down in time to watch it fall away, revealing her gorgeous breasts to him. "One night. I heard you. But that doesn't mean I don't want so much more than one night." Before she could respond or object, he kissed her again, this time with more serious intent while allowing his hands to roam over her delicious curves. He cupped her firm ass and pulled her in tighter against the hard length of his erection, moving against her as he kissed her.

The press of her breasts against his chest had him gasping. If being around her had left him feeling electrified, being naked with her had him completely captivated.

Finn needed to slow things down, to find some semblance of control, so he put his arms around her and held on tight for a few critical minutes, focusing on breathing.

"Are you okay?"

"I'm so much better than okay." Lowering her to the bed, Finn hovered over her, taking in the sight of gorgeous skin, the ink, the tight nipples and flat belly. "You're a fucking goddess, Chloe." He wanted to kiss her everywhere, but started with her collarbones, moving to the deep valley between her breasts and down to her belly.

Her hands tunneled into his hair, and her hips came off the bed, seeking him.

Cupping her breasts, he skimmed his tongue over her left nipple before drawing it deep into his mouth.

Her sharp cry of pleasure made him crazy for more.

Before this, he would've said of course he'd experienced real desire, but he would've been wrong. *This* was the real thing, and it was nothing like anything that had happened to him before. He focused exclusively on her, moving to her right nipple and then kissing his way down the front of her until he hovered over her core. All he could think about was giving her so much pleasure that she pleaded with him for more than just tonight. A pipe dream, maybe, but it was worth trying. He already knew that if this was all they ever had, the memories of this night would haunt him forever.

Tugging on the silk that covered her, he finally bared her completely. His heart jolted in a way that would've concerned him at any other time. He arranged her feet on the edge of the mattress and gently pushed them apart. As he leaned in, he noticed yet another small tattoo, a tiny flower right above the small patch of hair between her legs. He kissed the flower and then dropped to his knees to kiss the rest of her.

"Finn..." She sounded nervous, hesitant.

He couldn't have that. "Relax, sweetheart. Let me love you." Opening her to his tongue, he set out to ruin her for all other men. Nothing had ever been more important to him than what would happen tonight in this bed. If she still walked away, at least he would know he'd done everything he could to show her how incredible they could be together.

With his fingers and tongue, he stroked, caressed and sucked, keeping it up until she screamed her way through the first of what he hoped would be many orgasms. Moving quickly, he found a condom in his wallet, rolled it on and pushed into her, riding the last waves of her release.

Oh God... Oh my God. Hot, wet, tight. This has to be what heaven feels like.

Her hands on his ass pulling him deeper into her body were nearly his undoing.

With one deep thrust, he buried himself inside her and then froze when she cried out in pain. He immediately recognized the difference and withdrew. "What hurts?"

"My hip." Her face flushed with embarrassment. "Sorry."

"Don't be. Should we try it another way?"

"No, it's okay this way. Just go slow."

"I can do that." He moved into her again, watching her closely for any signs of distress and, not seeing any, held still, waiting for her to catch up to him. "Is this okay?"

"It's so good."

"Stop me if it hurts?"

She nodded, and when her lips parted, he leaned in to kiss her, wanting to be connected to her in every possible way. If only he could stay connected to her in every possible way—forever—he would never want for anything or anyone else. One minute inside her, and he got why his brother had lost his mind over Nikki, why his cousins were so slavishly devoted to their wives. If it was like this for them, he understood it now. He would do anything, anything at all, to hold on to her forever now that he'd found her.

"Chloe," he said, sounding as breathless as he felt, "you feel so good."

"So do you."

They moved together like they'd been doing this for years, but all the while, he watched for signs of discomfort. He wanted this to be as perfect for her as it was for him. He wanted it to go on forever, but when he felt her internal muscles clamp down on him, he reached between them to give her the push she needed.

She exploded, crying out and clawing at his back as he rode the waves of her climax straight into his own, the pleasure so sharp and all-consuming, he nearly passed out.

Holy. Shit.

As he came down on top of her, careful not to crush her, his mind raced with plans, scenarios, possibilities. He would do whatever it took to keep her right here in his arms where she belonged. If he lost her now, he'd never survive it.

CHAPTER 19

*H*aving sex with Finn had been the biggest mistake she'd ever made. In fact, the minute he'd removed his shirt and revealed his magnificent chest and abdomen, she'd known this was going to be a huge mistake. She'd courted crushing heartbreak by allowing this to happen.

Here in her arms was the man of her dreams—handsome, sweet, funny, thoughtful, sexy as all get-out and tied to a family that anyone would want to be part of. He was the full package, and not for nothing, he had a rather full package.

The thought would've made her laugh if she hadn't been trying so hard not to cry.

How could she have been so stupid as to think she could do this once, get him out of her system and move on with her life?

Instead, she'd allowed him so far inside her, she'd never again be free of him.

She ran her fingers through his hair, over and over again, because she could. Soon enough, this evening would be a distant memory to treasure when he had moved back to the mainland and she had gone on with her life, richer for having known him but always sad because she hadn't been able to keep him.

"Am I crushing you?"

"Nope." She would pay for this tomorrow, with aches and pains that would be exacerbated by the physical activity. As her condition had worsened, she'd had to give up her workouts at the gym and the nature hikes she had enjoyed in order to conserve her stamina for the long days at the salon.

"Do you want me to go?"

"Not unless you want to."

"I don't want to."

He wasn't leaving yet, but he would leave in the morning, and that would be that. The ache in her chest was the most concerning of her many aches and pains.

She had survived worse, or so she told herself. It took effort not to become bitter at the various backhands life continued to hit her with. Hadn't it been enough to lose her parents the way she had? Why did she have to keep being dealt such shitty cards to play? Too bad she wasn't a selfish bitch. If she had been, then she could've gone all in with Finn by saying to hell with the consequences for both of them. So what if she ended up being a burden to him?

But that wasn't how she was wired. Never had been. She had been looking out for herself for far too long to change now. No, her problems were her own, and she'd never inflict them on a sweet guy like Finn.

He stirred, brushing his lips against her neck. "I've got to get some water. You want anything?"

"Water sounds good. Glasses are to the right of the sink."

He raised himself up on his arms, kissed her and withdrew.

Chloe watched him go first into the bathroom, noting that the rear view of him was almost as good as the front. Nothing was better than that face, those eyes, that thick dark hair... She shivered. He was the hottest guy she'd ever slept with, that was for damned sure.

The toilet flushed in the bathroom. As the light went on in the kitchen, she remembered that her medication was sitting on the windowsill where he was sure to see it.

"Damn it."

. . .

AS HE DOWNED a glass of water, Finn tried not to look, but curiosity
got the best of him.

Methotrexate.

Prednisone.

He'd never heard of either of them, but they sounded serious.
Staring at the prescription bottles, he began to understand what she
wasn't telling him. The situation with her hands was something more
than aches and pains. And her hip, just now, when they'd been
having sex...

Finn wished there was a way he could look up the meds on his
phone, but his phone was in his pants pocket on the floor of her
bedroom where she waited for him to bring water. He refilled the
glass and brought it with him when he turned off the light and
returned to her, forcing a smile for her.

He didn't want her to know that he'd seen the meds. He wanted
her to trust him enough to share the truth with him. Maybe that
wouldn't happen tonight, but now, at least, he had an inkling of what
was standing between them.

Although why she thought her health problem would stand in
their way was beyond him. When he'd told her there was nothing she
could say that would make him not want her, he'd meant it. That
included health concerns.

Chloe seemed tense when he got into bed with her, handed her the
glass of water and pulled the covers up over both of them.

"Thanks."

Was it his imagination or was she having trouble looking at him?
Had she realized what he would see after she let him go into the
kitchen?

Finn decided to address the elephant in the room. "Chloe..."

She yawned. "God, I'm so tired, and it's getting late. I've got to get
some sleep, or I'll be a zombie tomorrow."

Okay, so the conversation wasn't going to happen tonight. Finn
could be patient and let her get around to telling him when she was

ready—or not. He couldn't force her to tell him anything, nor would he ever push her to do something that made her uncomfortable. No, he could only hope that she would level with him so he'd know what he was up against.

And if she didn't? He had no answer to that question. "Come here." Raising an arm, he waited and hoped she would snuggle up to him.

After a brief hesitation, she turned toward him and rested her head on his chest.

Finn wrapped an arm around her. "Get some rest." He made small, smoothing circles on her back, hoping she would relax enough to sleep. "And just so you know, there is nothing I wouldn't do for more with you. Nothing at all. So if you think there's something I can't handle or wouldn't want to handle, you're wrong. I want to be with you, any way I can have you."

CHLOE SQUEEZED HER EYES CLOSED, hoping to contain the tears that wanted out after his sweet words. Did he have any idea what those words meant to her? To know he cared enough to put that out there, to perfectly summarize everything she had been thinking and feeling since they met? He couldn't possibly know what the medications were for, but he'd put two plus two together to understand that she was dealing with a serious health problem.

Tell him.

Her inner voice registered its vote even as her better judgment voted to refrain from sharing. It was too much to unload into a brand-new relationship that wasn't even really a relationship at all. Rather, it was more like a flirtation that had gotten out of hand.

If she kept telling herself that, maybe she'd begin to believe her own lies.

This had been way more than a *flirtation* from the beginning. And as she breathed in the fresh, clean scent of him while his chest hair tickled her face and his hand made soft circles on her back, she began to accept that she was well and truly screwed when it came to him—in more ways than one.

The sex had been astonishing, not that she should be surprised. He could practically make her come just by being in the same room. For the rest of her life, she'd never forget the sexy way he'd pulled his dress shirt over his head to reveal the beautiful chest that now served as her pillow.

Thinking about the sex made her want more of it, but she couldn't have that. Not now anyway. She wasn't kidding when she said she'd be a mess in the morning after being on her feet all day into the evening at the fundraiser and then giving her body an aggressive workout in bed with him.

Tell him.

The words sat on the tip of her tongue. *I have rheumatoid arthritis. Over the next few years, it's likely that I'll become unable to work, among other possible challenges. I'm terrified of what the future holds, and the last thing I want to do is drag a sweet guy like you down with me.*

He would argue with her, tell her that it didn't matter when they both knew it did matter. It mattered greatly. If they'd been dating a couple of years when she got the diagnosis, that would be another story. But they'd only just met, and while the attraction was intense—and mutual—it couldn't be more than that. It just couldn't.

Chloe needed to talk to someone about this, and as much as she wished she could unload on a professional, she couldn't bring herself to take this particular issue to Finn's father. It wouldn't be fair to Finn or his dad. In the morning, she would ask Katie to meet her for a drink after work, and Chloe would ask for her friend's take on it. She trusted Katie to keep the information about her condition confidential, but more than that, Katie was engaged to Finn's cousin, which would give her the kind of insight she desperately needed to figure out what to do about the man who had upended her well-ordered life the second his head smacked into hers.

Satisfied that she had a plan, Chloe closed her eyes, released the deep breath she'd been holding and drifted off to sleep.

· · ·

AT MIDNIGHT, Adam tiptoed up the stairs to check on Abby, who'd been asleep for two hours following another bout of vomiting. Hearing that others on the island had the same flu made him feel slightly better, but he was still concerned about how lethargic she had been earlier. She hadn't even had the energy to hold Liam, which meant she had to be truly sick. Under normal circumstances, she rarely put the baby down, going so far as to strap him to her chest while she worked at the store.

Liam was fast asleep after taking his last bottle from Daddy, who had also bathed and dressed him in the cute little footie pajamas that had become part of Adam's daily life, along with the many other things that had come with having a baby.

The little guy had utterly transformed their lives, and they wouldn't have it any other way. Adam had cut way back on work so he could spend most of his time with Liam, and Abby had even hired someone to help out a few hours a week at the store so she could be home more during the busy summer season.

Life had never been better for either of them. What did it say about how much he loved his wife that one afternoon and evening without her had left him craving her company? He brushed his teeth and changed into lightweight pajama pants, checked the baby one more time and then slid into bed next to his sleeping wife.

Adam gently rested a hand on her forehead, which was thankfully cool. At least she didn't have a fever. He hoped Liam wouldn't get whatever had felled her.

Abby stirred with a moan.

"Are you okay?" Adam whispered.

"Feel sick again."

Adam turned on the light, jumped out of bed, got the bowl he'd put on the bedside table and held it for her with one hand while containing her hair with the other hand while she suffered through more dry heaves. "If you still feel shitty in the morning, I want to take you to the clinic."

She groaned. "Can't go anywhere like this."

"Then I'll call David and ask him to come here. You're scaring me, sweetheart."

"Sorry."

He kissed her forehead. "Don't be sorry."

"I think it passed. For now."

Adam settled her back into bed, smoothing the dark hair back from her pale face. He would text David first thing and ask him to stop by on the way to the clinic.

She was up twice during the night with dry heaves, and Adam was up another time with Liam. Exhausted after a rough night, he texted David at ten after six, asking him if he could possibly swing by to check on Abby on his way to work.

David wrote right back. *Happy to. The annual stomach bug arrived with Race Week. Will be by around seven thirty.*

Thanks so much.

The man who would've been his brother-in-law once upon a time had redeemed himself for cheating on Janey by saving Mac's daughter Hailey and then, later, saving Janey and her son, PJ, who would've died without David performing an emergency C-section. The McCarthy family owed David a debt of gratitude that could never be repaid.

Adam brewed a smaller than usual pot of coffee and sat by himself in the kitchen, waiting for the telltale squeak from the nursery that began every new day. He'd never been a morning person until he became a dad. Now the early mornings, sleepless nights and shorter workdays were a small price to pay for the boundless joy that Liam had brought them.

He yawned and ran his fingers through his hair, anticipating a long day on baby duty since Abby was sick.

Right on schedule, Liam began his morning chatter, bringing a smile to his father's face. Adam downed his second cup of coffee and went upstairs to tend to his little man.

Forty minutes later, a light knock on the mudroom door announced David's arrival.

Carrying the baby, Adam went downstairs to let him in. "Morning."

"How's it going?" David offered a finger to Liam, who wrapped his little fist around it.

"We've been better. Mommy isn't feeling good, right, buddy?"

"Yayayayaya."

"I swear he's going to talk early."

David rolled his eyes. "All parents think they've got the next Albert Einstein."

"You'll be singing that tune before much longer."

"Hope so. We're certainly enjoying the trying."

"Spare me the details, Doc."

David laughed.

"Let me go tell Abby you're here and give her a minute to wake up. Help yourself to some coffee."

"Don't mind if I do."

Still holding Liam, Adam went upstairs. "Let's wake up Mommy and tell her Doctor David is here to see her."

Liam managed to grab a fistful of Adam's hair and give it a good yank.

"Yow, buddy. That hurts."

Liam's belly laugh had Adam on the verge of laughing, too, but he was trying not to laugh at every naughty thing the baby did. "No, no. That hurts. Use gentle hands."

Liam patted his face, which turned Adam to putty.

"Yeah, buddy. Just like that." He sat on the edge of the bed and was alarmed once again by how pale Abby was. "Hey, hon. David is here to see you." Giving her a gentle shake, he waited for her gorgeous eyes to open. But on this morning, not even the sight of Liam could bring a spark of life to them.

"David is *here?*"

"I texted him, and he agreed to stop by on his way to the clinic. Is it okay if I let him come up?"

"Let me at least brush my teeth first."

He got up so she could and ended up having to grab her to keep her from falling. What the hell was going on? "Easy, babe."

She held on to him until the dizziness passed. "I'm okay."

Adam stayed close as she walked to the bathroom and then back to bed. The small bit of activity seemed to have left her completely drained. He was more concerned than ever. "Let me get David." He called down for David to come upstairs and showed him into the master bedroom.

Liam picked that moment to loudly fill his diaper and begin howling.

"I'll let you guys talk while I take care of him." Adam wanted to be there to hear what David had to say, but Liam needed to be changed and fed. In that order.

Twenty minutes later, he had the baby in his high chair chowing down on oatmeal and applesauce when David came downstairs.

Adam's heart was in his throat. "Is she... Is she okay?" That was the only thing that truly mattered to him—that she and Liam and the rest of his family were okay.

"She's going to be fine. I'll let her fill you in. I've got to get to the clinic."

Adam stood to shake his hand. "Thank you for coming by. I really appreciate it."

"No problem at all. Have a good day, Adam."

"You, too."

On fire with curiosity, Adam quickly got Liam cleaned up and out of the high chair over the baby's strenuous objections. "Give me five minutes with Mommy, pal, and I'll fill your tray with Cheerios." Sometimes Adam was certain that Liam understood every word he said. This was one of those times, because the promise of Cheerios calmed him right down.

Adam headed up the stairs, taking them two at a time. He went into the bedroom and stopped short at the sight of Abby, propped up in bed, her face awash in tears. "Abby... What's wrong?" He was almost afraid to ask.

She held out a hand to him. "Come here."

177

Adam forced himself to take the steps to the bed, to reach for her hand, to sit on the edge of the mattress while his heart hammered with anxiety and dread. "If you don't tell me what's wrong right now, you may be visiting me in the hospital."

Abby reached for Liam.

Adam handed him over and wiped his sweaty palms on his pajama pants.

"David thinks it's possible I might be…" She took a deep breath. Released it.

Adam died ten thousand deaths.

"Pregnant."

It took a second for the word to register, and when it did, he tipped his head, hoping he had heard her correctly. "You… You're… *How* is that possible?"

She laughed even as tears spilled down her cheeks. "I can't explain *how* it's possible in front of Liam, but Adam, he thinks that's what it is."

And then he was sobbing as he reached for her and wrapped them both up in a tight hug that had Liam squeaking in protest.

"Are you happy?" she asked in a soft voice.

"Abby, honey, if I was any happier, my heart would explode. I can't believe this."

"I've heard of it happening to people—they adopt and stop trying and then bingo. It happens."

"You hear that, Liam? You were the secret weapon."

Abby cleared her throat. "Um, well… I think you might be in possession of the secret weapon, actually."

They laughed through their tears, and then he kissed her and rested his forehead against hers. "Is this real?"

"We won't know for sure until they confirm it at the clinic, but he said my uterus felt enlarged. And until he asked when my last period was, I hadn't even realized I'd missed one. Remember when we used to know down to the hour when I was going to get it?" She swiped at the tears that continued to slide down her cheeks. "Now we don't even pay attention."

"Because we have what we wanted, so we quit worrying about it," he said, amazed and thankful. So incredibly thankful. "How soon can we go to the clinic?"

"I have an appointment with Victoria at eleven."

"Do we have any tests left from before?"

She gasped. "Oh my God! Yes!" Handing the baby back to him, she bounded out of bed, stopping when the dizziness caught up to her again.

Adam was right there to hold her up with an arm around her waist. "Slow down, sweetheart."

"I'm so excited, I can barely breathe."

"I know. I am, too, but we don't want you to fall. Especially not now."

"No, that wouldn't be good."

"You need to breathe."

She took a series of deep breaths and squeezed his arm. "I'm good."

"Go slow."

He stood outside the bathroom door, focused on entertaining Liam so he wouldn't go crazy waiting. Time slowed to a crawl, or so it seemed anyway.

"Adam. Come in."

As he took the first step, he felt like he might faint, so he took his own advice. He took a deep breath and then another as he joined Abby in the bathroom, where her huge, tearful smile told him what he wanted to know. "Yes?"

She nodded. "We did it, Adam. We really did it."

He put his arm around her and kissed her. "We certainly did, and now…"

"Another baby." Gasping, she looked up at him. "We're going to have *two babies* in *one* year. Adam!"

Damn, he hadn't thought of that. He tightened his hold on her. "It's going to be awesome. I promise." He only hoped that was a promise he could keep.

CHAPTER 20

*F*inn woke before Chloe and got to enjoy the sight of her sleeping as the sun streamed into her colorfully decorated room. The walls were an intriguing shade of dark pink, with the wall behind the bed boasting a white pattern that had been painted over the pink base. He wondered if she had done that herself or had it done. Like the woman who slept here, the room was funky and original and eclectic.

His phone buzzed with a text, so he got out of bed to retrieve it and read the text from Mac. *Can you help me with something at the Wayfarer around eleven?*

Finn wrote back. *Yep, no problem.*

Thanks!

With the Wayfarer all but finished and work not set to begin on the Curtis place until after the grand opening at the Wayfarer, Mac had told his construction team to enjoy a little downtime while he and Luke saw to getting the marina up and running for the season. Finn had no idea how Mac kept so many balls in the air and made it look so effortless when it had to be anything but. And now that he had twins on the way and would have five children, he'd be busier than ever.

Bringing the phone with him, Finn stretched back out on the bed, careful not to disturb Chloe. She didn't have to be at work until ten, and it was only seven thirty. Maybe he could entice her into going out for breakfast before work. Anything to spend more time with her.

After making sure she was still asleep, he opened the browser on his phone and did a search for methotrexate, his heart nearly stopping at the word chemotherapy, which was the first thing he saw in the description of the drug.

Oh my God. Did she have *cancer?*

As he skimmed the information about the drug, he became more despondent. Having seen more than enough, he closed the browser.

Was this why she didn't want to get involved with him? Because she was sick and scared? Did she think that would matter to him? It wouldn't. But how could he express that to her without letting on that he had invaded her privacy by looking up the medication she was taking?

What a dilemma.

"Hey."

How could one word become the sexiest thing he'd ever heard? Jesus, he had a bad case for this woman, and it was getting worse all the time. Worse had never felt so good. "Morning. Did you sleep well?" Finn tried to keep his voice normal, to mask his panic over what he'd discovered about the medication.

"Better than I have in ages, thanks to your bedtime remedy."

He grinned. "My remedy is available on demand." Only because he was gazing at her gorgeous face did he see the exact moment when she remembered all the reasons why this couldn't be anything more than it had already been.

To hell with that. Did she think he couldn't see the way she looked at him? As if she wanted something she couldn't have. Well, she could have him. She could have all of him, and he was going to find a way to convince her to take what was right in front of her. Whatever was wrong, they would deal with it together.

"Let's go out to breakfast."

"I, um, I need to get to work."

"The salon opens at ten. It's not even eight. We have plenty of time, and besides, I have to take you back to get your car anyway." He rubbed his belly. "I'm a growing boy, and you wore me out last night. I need my protein."

She looked at him in a way that told him everything he needed to know. Last night hadn't been enough for her, either. He could work with that.

"Come on…" He stuck out his lip. "You don't want to send me off hungry to face the day, do you?"

She rolled her eyes. "Does this nonsense work for you?"

"Every time."

That made her laugh, which had been his goal. He loved her laugh.

"All right. Fine. Breakfast. But that's it. After that…"

"One step at a time, sweetheart. One step at a time." He bounded out of bed, stretched dramatically and opened his eyes to find her staring at him. "See something you like?"

She looked away, wrapped the sheet around her body and dragged it with her into the bathroom, closing the door behind her.

"Take your time, babe," he said, loud enough for her to hear through the closed door. "I'll let Ranger out and feed him." Looking down at the dog, who eyed him warily from his bed on the floor, Finn said, "I think that went very well. Don't you?"

WHAT THE HELL was she thinking agreeing to go to breakfast with him? Why was she prolonging the agony? This was supposed to have been one and done. She'd had her one night and had been well and truly done. Going to breakfast with him just made her greedy.

It was his fault for being so ridiculously hot and sweet and nice. He was so damned *nice*. She found that quality more attractive than all the other attractive things about him. Unlike other guys she'd dated, he didn't play games or have trouble taking no for an answer. He approached her with the kind of respect and understanding that she'd craved in a partner and had never found until him.

Figured, right? At a time when she had no business getting involved with anyone, she met the man of her dreams.

"You can't have him." Chloe looked at herself in the mirror as she said the words. "You. Cannot. Have. Him. So knock it off. Right now." She turned on the shower and let the heat soothe her aching joints. A warm shower had become critical to getting her day started. As she moved through her morning routine, she tried to ignore the pervasive aches and pains that were, as she knew they'd be, worse today than usual. The shower had barely made a dent on the pain.

Every inch of her body hurt, but she wouldn't have traded her night with Finn for a pain-free day. Not for all the money in the world. It had been everything she'd known it would be, which made it that much harder to do what needed to be done today.

After breakfast, she would thank him for a great night and say goodbye. It would hurt like hell, but it was the right thing to do for both of them.

It's not the right thing for you. He's the right thing for you.

Damn that voice inside her that just had to be contrary. She rinsed conditioner out of her hair and got out of the shower, grimacing at the pain in her hips. It'd been worth it. So incredibly worth it. She'd agreed to allow herself one night with him. She'd had that and now it was time to move on.

At this point, she'd started over so many times in her life that it ought to be as easy as breathing.

This time, though… This time, it wouldn't be easy. It wouldn't be easy at all.

When she thought of never seeing him again, she ached deep inside, the pain reminding her far too much of how she'd felt after losing her parents so suddenly. If she had her way, she'd never feel like that again, and if it was this painful after one night with him, she was doing the right thing by ending it now.

The pain wouldn't get better with more time with him. No, it would become excruciating, and she had enough pain to deal with as it was.

She rushed through drying and styling her hair and applying the makeup she wore every day to work, wanting to "look the part" of a together, stylish woman who could make other women look beautiful.

At least her exterior would look put together. Her customers wouldn't know that she was crumbling on the inside.

Opening the bathroom door, she saw that she had her bedroom to herself and got dressed in one of the many black-pants-and-sleeve-less-top combinations she wore to work. She liked having her gorgeous ink on full display. It had started many a conversation with clients, who always commented on it. Some were disapproving, but none could deny the beauty of it.

Rather than fully straighten her hair, she put it up with a few strategically placed pins that would keep it out of her way for work.

She grabbed her phone off the charger and headed for the kitchen, stopping short at the sight of the six-foot-something man sprawled on the floor wrestling with Ranger, who had never looked happier.

Ranger liked to wrestle? Who knew? He was nothing but sweet and gentle with her, but with Finn, he growled and pounced playfully as if having the time of his life, despite *his* usual aches and pains.

Chloe glanced at her meds on the windowsill and moved to the sink to grab them and drop them into her work bag to take after breakfast. They wrecked her stomach, so she never took them without food. Even then, sometimes they still made her sick. But that was a small price to pay for the relief they offered.

"I'm ready when you are," she said to Finn.

He patted Ranger and got up off the floor. "I'll let you win next time."

Ranger barked, clearly not ready to end the game.

Finn laughed. "You're a devil."

"Not usually. You bring it out in him."

"Aww, that's so sweet of you to say. I've always been a bit of a devil myself."

"That might be the understatement of the decade. You're the devil himself."

"You flatterer."

"You would take that as a compliment."

"My brother and I always say we'll be in good company down there." With the blazer he'd worn last night flipped over his shoulder, he held open the door to his truck and helped her up and into the passenger seat.

She appreciated his manners and the way he subtly helped her without making a big deal out of the fact that she needed the help in the first place. Who was she kidding? She liked everything about him.

"You're kind of doing the walk of shame going out to breakfast in the same clothes you wore last night."

"I'm not at all ashamed of my walk of shame. I got to spend last night with you. Best night of my life."

"Finn..."

"What?"

"You shouldn't say things like that."

"Why not? It's the truth."

"This was a mistake."

"No, it wasn't."

"Yes, it really was. I still can't—"

"Because you're sick?"

If someone had punched her in the gut, Chloe wouldn't have been more surprised or knocked breathless than she was by his question.

"It's none of my business. I know that. But I saw the meds, and I was curious. I'm sorry, but I want to understand, and if that's the reason you think this can't happen, it doesn't matter to me."

"How can you say that without even knowing what it is?"

"The only thing that matters to me is that we do whatever we can to beat it, so we can spend as much time together as possible."

Do whatever we can. We. As in the two of them. Together. Was he for real?

"I'm not going to beat it."

"Why not?"

"Because it's not something I'll ever get rid of. It's something I'm learning to live with."

"What is it exactly?"

"Rheumatoid arthritis."

"Oh." He released a deep breath. "That's a relief. I thought it was cancer."

185

"It's not cancer, but it's going to eventually be an even bigger deal than it is now."

"Okay."

"Okay what?"

"Okay, we'll deal with that when it happens."

"Finn, you need to hear me when I tell you that's not how this is going to go. We had a nice time last night, but that's all it's ever going to be."

"Why are you lying to both of us?"

"I'm not lying."

"Yeah, you are. What happened between us last night wasn't a one-night stand, Chloe. It was the start of something much more significant."

"No, it wasn't!"

"Yes, it was!"

They didn't say another word to each other until he parked outside of Rebecca's diner. He shut off the engine but made no move to get out. After a long, charged moment of silence, he said, "I have never felt this way about anyone. Ever." He looked over at her. "If you don't feel the same way, I can live with that. But don't lie to me, Chloe. Please don't lie to me. I was there last night. I know you feel the same things."

"I do, but—"

"No buts. We will deal with this together, and we'll figure it out together."

She shook her head. "I can't do that to you."

"What are you doing to me besides giving me what I most want? A chance to be with you."

"You don't know what you'd be taking on."

"Then tell me." He released his seat belt and turned in his seat to face her. "Tell me what you're so worried about."

"For one, there will come a time, possibly sooner rather than later, when I can't work anymore."

"Okay."

"It's not okay! If I don't work, I don't have insurance. If I don't have insurance, I'm totally screwed."

"I'll put you on my insurance. What's your next concern?"

She stared at him, incredulous. "It's not that simple."

"It can absolutely be that simple. What else have you got for me?"

Returning his mulish look with one of her own, she said, "RA could just be the start. I could end up with other conditions."

"Okay. What else?"

"I could have fertility issues."

"Okay. And?"

"The meds that work so well right now could stop working."

"Okay."

"My hips hurt all the time. That could make sex difficult at best, impossible at times."

"We'll work around it. Anything else?"

"I may need care that can't be provided here. Infusions and stuff they can't do at the clinic."

"So we'll go to the mainland or move there if that's where you need to be."

"Finn, honestly, you're very sweet, but—"

He leaned across the console to kiss her and then, keeping his face very close to hers, looked her dead in the eyes. "I haven't heard one thing that has changed my mind about what I want. I'm all in with you, Chloe Dennis, and with Ranger. I want you. I want him. I want us."

"You could have anyone, Finn. Why in the world would you want to take this on?"

"Because I'm crazy about you, and I have been from the second you smacked your head into mine."

It was all she could do to hold it together when she wanted to bawl her head off. Was he for real? "Um, *you* smacked your head into *mine*."

Finn dragged a finger over her cheek. "It was all you." He kissed her again. "Are we all straight now?"

"No, we are not straight."

"I want you to know—it means a lot to me that you talked to me about this. At least I understand now why you thought we couldn't happen."

"You're moving back to the mainland," she reminded him.

He took her by the chin. "Sweetheart, as long as you're here, I'm not going anywhere."

CHLOE FELT like she was dreaming. He had systematically dismissed every reason she had given him for why they shouldn't be together. Her emotions were all over the place as she tried to process the last ten minutes.

Sweetheart, as long as you're here, I'm not going anywhere.

Hearing those words out of his sexy mouth as he looked at her with affection and desire had been among the greatest moments of her life. Hell, it had been *the* greatest moment. It would take a lot to top that.

He guided her into the diner with his hand on her lower back. She loved the way he touched her, as if he couldn't be near her and not touch her.

When they were seated across from each other in a booth, he continued to study her in that particular way of his that made her feel more seen than she'd ever been by anyone. "What're you thinking?" he asked as they studied their menus.

"So many things."

"Such as do I want an omelet or French toast? Those kinds of things?"

Could he be any cuter? "Among other things."

He tossed his menu aside and leaned in, giving her his full attention. "Like what? I want to hear *all* the thoughts."

Finn McCarthy's full attention would overwhelm the strongest of women. Chloe was off her game after the emotional conversation in his truck and definitely not at her strongest.

"I want you to know... I appreciate everything you said."

"Don't you dare add a 'but' to that statement."

Rebecca came over holding two coffee mugs in one hand and a pot of coffee in the other. "Morning. Coffee for both?"

"Please," Chloe said.

Finn nodded. "Me, too. Thanks."

Rebecca put the pot on the table and pulled out her pad and pen. "Take your order?"

He gestured for Chloe to go first.

"I'll have the egg white veggie omelet with an English muffin, please."

"I'll do the bacon and cheddar omelet with white toast, please."

"Coming right up."

Chloe turned up her nose. "*White* toast? I knew there had to be something about you that wasn't perfect."

"What can I say? I'm a Wonder Bread kind of guy. Don't change the subject. You were saying you appreciated what I said in the truck." He rolled his hand to encourage her to continue.

"One thing I need to ask of you…"

"You could ask me for anything."

"Please don't tell anyone about the RA. I'm afraid it will hurt my business if the word gets out. People might stay away."

"I won't say a word. What else are you worried about?"

She sat back against the booth, sighing. "It's just that it's a lot, Finn. *A lot* a lot. I really do appreciate that you said all the right things—"

"I meant every word I said. I wasn't just saying what you wanted to hear."

"I know, and that means so much to me. But you should really take some time to think about this, to look into it and to fully understand it before you decide anything."

"Before I decide anything about you? Too late. I've already decided."

"Finn—"

"You son of a bitch!" The shrieking female voice came from Chloe's left, and the woman was upon them before she could begin to process what was happening. The blonde was punching Finn and tearing at his shirt.

189

Acting without thinking, Chloe stood to pull the woman off Finn and fell backward, landing hard on the same hip she'd landed on in the grocery store and then gasping when the woman came down on top of her and began smacking the shit out of her.

Chloe held up her arm to ward off the blows. What the fuck was happening?

Then Finn was there, lifting the woman off her. "Missy! What the hell is wrong with you?"

"You're such a *liar*! You said you didn't have someone else. You promised me things, and this is what you're doing? *Having breakfast and God knows what else with this whore?*"

By now, the diner had come to a halt and everyone was looking at them.

Who in the hell was this woman who'd left Finn with a bloody lip and a rapidly swelling eye *and* was calling her a whore?

"I'll take it from here." Blaine Taylor pulled handcuffs from his back pocket and slapped them on the woman so quickly, she never saw it coming. "This is Missy, I presume?"

Missy continued to scream and flail against the restraints, but she was no match for Blaine.

"Yeah." Finn bent to help Chloe off the floor. "That's her."

When Chloe was standing, he kept his arms around her as if he feared she would run away from him if he let go of her. Maybe she ought to. This was so not her scene.

Blaine effortlessly contained Missy, who struggled the entire time. "I'll need you both to come in and make a statement."

Missy shrieked all the way out of the diner.

Rebecca came over with a bag and two coffees in to-go containers. "Breakfast is on me."

"I'm so sorry that happened here, Rebecca," Finn said.

"You didn't do anything. You were minding your own business."

"Still. I'm sorry it happened."

"No worries. I'm just glad you're both okay."

Finn took the to-go bag from her while Chloe accepted the coffees.

Ignoring the stares of everyone in the diner, they left and walked to his truck, every step causing Chloe new aches after the skirmish and fall. He helped her in and put the bag of food on the floor in front of her. "I'm really sorry about that."

"Who is she?"

"My ex-girlfriend, who was apparently making plans for me in my absence that I knew nothing about."

"What kind of plans?"

"She booked a wedding venue when we have never once talked about getting married."

"Holy crap. How long has she been your ex?"

"Since before I moved out here. We kept in touch, but I never gave her hope that we'd get back together. I swear."

"I believe you."

"And when I told her the wedding she had planned was never going to happen and that we were over for good, she lost her shit and started blowing up my phone. Mac made me report the harassment to Blaine, who called her and told her to knock it off. I thought I'd seen the last of her. I never imagined she'd attack me—or you. Tell me you're okay. If she hurt you..."

"I'm okay." Chloe pulled a tissue from her purse and reached up to dab at the blood on his lip. "You'll have a shiner."

"She cold-cocked me before I realized what was happening."

"You're going to press charges, I hope."

"Hell yes. If it was just me, I wouldn't care, but she could've hurt you, and that is *not* okay."

"It's not okay with me that she hurt you."

He cocked an eyebrow. So ridiculously sexy. "No?"

Chloe shook her head.

Finn leaned in and kissed her, wincing when his cut lip protested. "I wonder if Blaine can charge her for messing up kissing for me right when things were getting *very* interesting."

She placed her hand on his face, rubbing the stubble on his jaw. "We can work around it." Chloe used his words from earlier and loved the way his brilliant blue eyes went dark with desire.

"Chloe—"

"Not now. First, we go to the police station, then we eat our break-fast, and then I go to work. After work, we'll talk more."

"You promise?"

"Yes, Finn, I promise."

CHAPTER 21

Chloe floated through her workday, laughing more than she had in ages and feeling unburdened after having shared the truth with Finn.

And the things he had said...

She would never forget those minutes in his truck or the way he'd looked at her. With every minute she spent with him, she fell further into what was happening between them. How could she not? Despite her best intentions to resist him, he was proving rather irresistible.

"You're awfully perky today," Janey Cantrell said as Chloe trimmed Janey's long blonde hair. "After the day you put in yesterday, I'd be a zombie."

"It was a good day." A great day, not that she could tell Finn's cousin that. "We made more than twenty-five thousand dollars for the food bank. That'll get us through next winter."

"That's fantastic. Such a great cause."

"We appreciate the donation from the ferry company."

"That's all Joe and Carolina," Janey said of her husband and mother-in-law, who owned the ferry company.

"They're very generous."

"This island has been very good to their family—and mine. We're happy to give back." Janey cleared her throat dramatically. "But enough of all that. What's up with you and our Finny?"

Chloe had known Janey since shortly after she arrived on the island, had cut her hair for years and knew her well. Still, Chloe's face heated with embarrassment at the question about her and Finn.

"And don't say nothing," Janey added. "Because I definitely saw *something* last night and the other night at my house."

"We've been spending time together."

"Tell me everything. Don't leave out a single detail except for those that might scar me for life."

Chloe laughed. "We met when he came in for a haircut, and, funny enough, we ended up smacking our heads together when we both reached for something he'd dropped on the floor."

"That's so cute! Like when Mac knocked Maddie off her bike by accident and fell madly in love."

"Not like that at all, actually."

Janey caught Chloe's gaze in the mirror. "But it could be?"

"I'm not sure yet." *Liar, liar, pants on fire.* Sometimes her inner voice could be a royal pain in the ass.

"Can I tell you something and will you listen to me?"

Chloe combed out a length of Janey's hair and cut two inches off the end. "Of course."

"Finn is a great guy, and I'm not just saying that because he's my beloved baby cousin. I'm saying it because it's true."

"I already know that."

"But do you know that he was the one who lived with my grandmother for an entire summer after she broke her hip? He kept her from having to go to a nursing home by moving in with her. He was seventeen."

"No, he hadn't told me that."

"We were so amazed when he offered to do it. I mean, what seventeen-year-old boy gives up an entire summer with his friends and girlfriend to take care of his seventy-five-year-old grandmother?"

"Not many."

"That's for sure. He may be the baby of our family, but he's grown up to be one hell of a man."

"I agree."

"And he's not hard on the eyes either, is he?"

"Um, no." Chloe laughed. "Not at all."

"The men in my family are far too good-looking. It drives me insane how every girlfriend I ever had went stupid at the sight of my brothers and cousins."

"It couldn't have been easy being you."

"It wasn't! Imagine having four ridiculously handsome older brothers and three cousins who were equally handsome. It was a lot of work for me and Laura back in the day."

Chloe giggled at the faces Janey made to go along with her tirade.

"Finn and I have always been close, and I promise you—cousin or not—if he wasn't the best of the best, I'd tell you so."

"I appreciate that."

"So… Are you guys officially dating?"

"I'm not sure I'd say that." She didn't know what to call the events of this morning.

"I really hope something comes of it, because that would keep him here where we all want him to stay."

Sweetheart, as long as you're here, I'm not going anywhere.

Just thinking about him saying that was enough to make her heart flutter. "What do you know about his ex-girlfriend?"

"Missy?" Janey snorted. "She's nothing to worry about. We've never liked her or thought she was right for him."

"Did you hear what happened this morning at the diner?"

"No! What?"

Chloe filled her in.

"Are you freaking *kidding* me? She came here and *attacked* him?"

"Yep."

"Is he okay?"

"Other than a split lip and a black eye, he's fine. She also knocked me down when I tried to help him and took a few swings at me, too. Luckily, only my hip is bruised."

"Oh my God! Did you call the cops?"

"Didn't have to. Blaine was there and took her into custody. Apparently, she'd reserved a wedding venue for her and Finn when they'd never once talked about getting married—or at least that's what he says."

"If he says that, it's true. Like I told you, we're tight, and he hasn't said one word to me about marrying her. If he was thinking about that, he would've told me. She's clearly off her rocker if she's making wedding plans without even being engaged."

"I didn't know what to make of it."

"Please don't think poorly of him because of her. They've been broken up the entire time he was here. Other than a few quick visits to see his mom, he hasn't left here, and to my knowledge, she hasn't come out here, either. She's no threat to you, Chloe."

"Ugh, I hate to even have conversations like this about a guy. I don't do drama."

"Just remind yourself that he didn't cause the drama. Someone else did."

"True."

As she blow-dried Janey's hair, Chloe thought about the things Janey had said about Finn. None of it surprised her. She could easily picture him giving up a summer to take care of his grandmother. A strange fluttering sensation overtook her, as if a thousand butterflies had been set loose inside her. It took a few minutes to understand what the butterflies signified—that she was falling hard for him.

He had given her hope, and that had been in short supply recently.

Chloe thought she was imagining him when his face appeared at the door to the salon.

The bells on the door jingled when he opened it and stepped inside, carrying a brown shopping bag.

Ridiculously happy to see him, Chloe shut off the blow-dryer just as Janey caught sight of her cousin.

"Finny! Ouch, your eye! Chloe told me what happened."

"Oh, hey, Janey. Didn't realize you'd be here."

"I'm enjoying every second of the break from my two precious darlings." Janey checked her watch. "In fact, Cinderella is about to turn into a pumpkin if she doesn't get home to feed her daughter before nap time. My mom can handle a lot of things, but that's not one of them." She pressed some bills into Chloe's hand, kissed Finn's cheek and was out the door two seconds after Chloe removed the smock.

"Was it something I said?" Finn asked when they were alone.

"I believe that was Janey encouraging my *friendship* with you by leaving us alone."

Finn took three big steps that brought him to where she stood. Looking down at her with his glorious eyes dancing with delight, he said, "Is that what we are? *Friends?*" The bruise around his left eye only added to his gorgeousness.

"Good friends?"

He put down the bag and looped his arms around her, bending to nuzzle her neck. "Very, *very* good friends. Possibly best friends."

"I take it your lip is feeling better."

"Much better."

Chloe sighed, closed her eyes and tipped her head to give him better access to her neck.

His lips traveled up to her ear. "I brought you lunch."

She shivered as goose bumps erupted on her arms. "I just ate breakfast."

"That was hours ago. You need to eat to stay strong, so I will feed you."

Chloe flattened her hand on his chest, trying to regain some control. "I don't need you to feed me, Finn."

"I know you don't need it. I *want* to feed you. Big difference."

"You're making it very difficult for me to resist you."

"Excellent." He kissed her softly, wincing.

"Still hurts?"

"Only a little. I can't believe Missy came here and made such a scene. I'm really sorry you had to see that and that you were hurt."

"It's okay. I'm fine."

"It's not okay. Blaine said it's up to me as to whether I wish to press charges. If it'd only been me, I might've let it go, but she hurt you and called you an awful name. I don't want her to get away with either of those things."

"Don't have her charged on my account. If you want to drop it, then drop it. It's up to you."

"Maybe I will. I want it to be over with her for good, and if there're charges pending, then that drags it out indefinitely. I'll have Blaine give her a good warning and send her home."

"You might want to consider a restraining order, too."

Finn shrugged. "I'll see what Blaine says. But I don't want to talk about her anymore."

"No?"

"Nope."

"Why are you really here?"

"I told you. I brought you lunch."

"You're aware that I'm twenty-nine and fully able to get my own lunch, right?"

"I didn't know you were twenty-nine, but now I do. I'm just a baby compared to you."

"Haha." She crooked an eyebrow, hoping he would tell her what else had brought him there during her workday.

"I also wanted to make sure that the progress we'd made earlier wasn't undone by Missy's unfortunate arrival."

"It wasn't."

"You're sure?"

"Uh-huh."

"That's good, because I'd be super bummed if you retreated from me because of what she did. I keep thinking about what you told me and how worried you've been about so many things, and I want to help. I want to be there for you." He reached for her hand and brought it to his lips, placing a gentle kiss on her swollen knuckles. "There has to be some way for you to continue to run the business without having to do the work yourself."

"If there is, I haven't figured it out yet. And while I appreciate the concern—and I really, really appreciate it—I don't want it to be your problem."

He turned her hand and kissed the sensitive skin on the inside of her wrist. "Why not?"

"Because! We just met, and you're not responsible for me or my problems."

"What if I wanted to be?"

She shook her head. "It's too much too soon, Finn."

"Is it? I'm in way over my head here. I have no idea what I'm doing. Everything about this is new to me."

"Everything?"

"Every single thing."

"You're incredibly sweet."

"That's not all I am." He rubbed against her suggestively. "What time are you done today?"

"Six."

Finn groaned dramatically. "That's a lot of hours from now."

"Yes, it is," she said, amused by him.

"Come to my place. I'll make you dinner."

"You brought me lunch. I should make *you* dinner."

"You're working. I'm off for the rest of the day. I'll cook for you." He kissed her neck, her cheek and then her lips. "Oh, and I told Mac he could count on me at the job they're starting out at the Curtis place, and I accepted Nikki's offer to squat in her garage apartment for the summer. In case you're wondering, everyone is thrilled that I'm sticking around."

"You already did all that?"

"Uh-huh."

"Because of me?"

"Because of *us*."

"Finn, you can't change your plans for someone you've known for *a few days*."

"Why not? My uncle did when he met my aunt Linda. Mac did when he met Maddie. Adam did after he started seeing Abby. Grant did when he met Steph. Evan—"

Chloe squished his lips together, careful to avoid the side with the cut.

He kept talking anyway, his words muffled. "Riley did it for Nikki."

"Are you for real?"

Finn nibbled his way free of her fingers. "I'm absolutely for real, and your next customer is here." He kissed her, bent to pick up the bag from the floor and handed it to her. "Eat your lunch." Then, as if he couldn't resist, he kissed her again. "See you after work. Bring Ranger." As he went out the door, he greeted Jenny Martinez, who came in with brows raised.

"Hope I'm not interrupting anything."

Mortified, Chloe waved off her comment. "Don't be silly."

"Finn McCarthy, huh? You go, girl."

Chloe planned to tell Finn he wasn't allowed to stop by during her workday and scramble her brains while giving her clients too much to talk about.

"He's a good one," Jenny said. "All those McCarthy guys are the real deal."

"So I hear. How's your little guy doing?"

"My little George is so sweet. Looks just like his daddy." Jenny pulled out her phone and showed off pictures of her husband and son.

"He really does. He's adorable."

"I think so, too. Alex says I have to stop telling everyone he's perfect."

"Nah, you're his mom. You get to say that to anyone who will listen."

"My feeling exactly!" Jenny gazed at the photos. "I waited such a long time for what I have now. I don't care who thinks I'm a loon."

"That's the attitude." Jenny had met Alex Martinez when she came to Gansett to be the lighthouse keeper. "How is Hope doing?" Hope was married to Alex's brother, Paul.

"She's about to pop. Any day now. I'm glad they're on the mainland for the delivery. She had a C-section with her son, so they wanted her to deliver in a hospital."

"Do they know what they're having?"

"They don't, but I think it's a girl. Just a feeling I have. Oh! Did you hear that Alex and Paul are moving their mom back to the island after the baby arrives?"

"I hadn't heard, but that's awesome. I've missed Marion."

"We all have. It's going to be so great to have her back on the island. We're just hoping it's a smooth transition. She's done well in the memory-care facility she's in now, but the guys hate not being able to see her whenever they want to."

"Quinn and Mallory will take good care of her." Finn's nurse cousin Mallory and her doctor fiancé, Quinn James, ran the new elder care facility that had opened the previous fall on the island.

"I know how much they appreciated your house calls to do Marion's hair when she lived here."

"It was a pleasure to be able to do something for them. I so admired the way her sons took such good care of her."

"They really did. That was a big reason why I fell for Alex."

"Among other reasons," Chloe said, chuckling.

"Well, of course he's smoking hot, makes me laugh till I cry and treats me like a queen."

"I'm happy for you, Jenny. You deserve all the good things."

"Aww, thanks. Speaking of good things… Nice deflection away from your good things onto mine. What's up with Finn?"

"We're hanging out."

"Um, I only saw you together for thirty seconds, but that looked like more than hanging out to me."

"Maybe." Chloe shrugged, afraid to jinx it by saying too much too soon. "It's new."

"I remember that stage with Alex," Jenny said with a smile and a sigh. "It was so exciting, even if I felt like I went days without sleeping. Did you ever hear how we met?"

"I don't know if I did."

"I was living at the lighthouse and had been complaining to the town about the grass not getting cut out there. He showed up at dawn with the biggest monster lawn mower I've ever seen, and after he woke me up, I threw tomatoes from my garden at him."

"You did not!"

"I did! Hit him square in the back." She laughed. "I wish I'd gotten a picture of his face when he turned around, boiling with outrage, to catch me in my skimpiest nightgown. It was during that heat wave we had a few years back." Jenny fanned her face. "It was hot from the start with him."

"Sounds like it."

"We were up against it, though." Her expression sobered. "He and Paul were contending with their mom's worsening health, and I was, well, still pretty much a mess after losing Toby."

"I can't imagine what you've been through, Jenny. You and Erin are my heroes." Toby's twin sister, Erin, had fallen for the island's favorite pilot, Slim Jackson, after she replaced Jenny as the lighthouse keeper.

"That's nice of you to say, but everyone is dealing with something, you know?"

"I do know." She knew all too well.

"The one thing I've learned is that when true love comes along, you have to grab it with and never let it go. It's the greatest thing there is. After I lost Toby, I never expected to feel that way again, but then along came Alex with his monster lawn mower, and there it was."

"I love that story. Thanks for sharing it with me."

"Maybe Finn is your Alex, hmmm?"

Chloe laughed at Jenny's shamelessness. "I guess we'll see."

CHAPTER 22

*H*ours later, Chloe lay on her side, staring at Finn on the pillow next to hers while trying to decide how she'd completely lost control of this situation—in the best possible way. She'd arrived at his house with the best of intentions to slow things down. Her intentions had flown out the window when he greeted her in a towel, still dripping from the shower.

She'd taken one look at that perfect man chest and her intentions had evaporated.

He caressed her arm, outlining her ink with his fingertip. "What're you thinking about?"

"About you coming to the door in a towel and reducing my brain to pudding."

His laughter lit up his beautiful face. "Did I do that?"

"You know you did. In fact, I think you did it on purpose."

"That would be awfully conniving of me."

"I wouldn't put it past you."

Finn slid his leg between hers, drawing her in closer to him. He touched her with gentle reverence, making sure to never hurt her. "Are you feeling okay?"

"I'm feeling quite good, thank you."

"I'm glad to hear that, but you have to tell me if anything ever hurts. I couldn't bear to hurt you."

"Thank you for that, but I'm okay."

"You'll tell me if you aren't? Any time?"

"I will."

With his hand on her face, he kissed her. "I promised you dinner."

"I'm a big fan of dessert before dinner."

He laughed, his thumb caressing her cheek. "I'm completely hooked on you. I hope you know that."

As she was unprepared for him to say that, Chloe's throat tightened with emotion.

"Is that okay?"

She nodded because that was all she could do.

"You're still not convinced this is a good idea, are you?"

"I want to be, but I still think it's not the best idea for you."

"Is it okay if I decide that for myself?"

"Of course, but—"

He kissed the words off her lips. "No buts. I'm exactly where I want to be with the person I want to be with. I heard everything you said this morning, and I respect your concerns. In fact, I read up on RA this afternoon."

"You did?"

"Yep. I wanted to know what we're dealing with."

Her eyes filled with tears.

"What?" he asked, alarmed.

"It's very sweet of you to care."

"I do care. I care deeply, and I want to understand it. After reading about it, I feel so bad that you've had to deal with this on your own. It must've been so scary to get that diagnosis."

"It was. It took a long time to get a definitive diagnosis because I tested negative for the RA factor, which happens sometimes. So in some ways, it was a relief to know what it was, but the relief was quickly eclipsed by the panic about how it will affect my livelihood."

"I have an idea about that."

"What idea do you have?"

"I'm not sure if I should share it until I know if it's feasible."

"You can't dangle that and not tell me!"

Smiling, he said, "I'm sorry. This afternoon, I was thinking about whether we might incorporate a salon and spa into the Wayfarer that you could manage. After the spa that opened a few years ago went out of business when the owner got arrested for tax fraud last winter, I've been thinking someone needed to open a new one. Why not you? If you were the boss, you wouldn't have to do the actual haircutting anymore."

Chloe stared at him, incredulous. "You can't just come swooping into my life and try to solve all my problems."

"Why not?"

"Because! It doesn't work like that."

"Why can't it work like that?"

Chloe had never met anyone like him.

He kissed away her tears. "It's a McCarthy family trait. We see a problem, we want to fix it. It's not my fault. Blame the DNA." His lips slid over hers, seductive and persuasive. The cut on the right side of his lower lip hadn't kept him from kissing her passionately earlier or from doing it again now.

Chloe was powerless to resist him. She wrapped her arms around him and buried her fingers in the soft silk of his hair, lost to him and the desire that simmered between them all the time. Being naked with him ranked right up there as the most thrilling thing she'd ever experienced.

"Finn."

"Hmm."

"Let me this time." She wanted to show him that despite her challenges, she was more than capable of holding her own when it came to sex. At least for now.

He lay back on the pillows, watching her with those sexy blue eyes that slayed her, waiting to see what she would do.

On her knees, Chloe leaned in to kiss the prominent jut of his collarbone, taking little nips that made him gasp.

His fingers combed through her hair, and his breathing became choppy. Knowing he wanted her so fiercely empowered her to make this good for him. She wanted to give something back to him, to find a way to let him know how much his care and concern meant to her.

Skimming her lips over the finely honed muscles of his chest and abdomen, Chloe smiled at his sharp inhale and the way his fingers tightened their hold on her hair.

Her mouth watered when his hard cock strained for her attention, which she was happy to give, starting at the base with her tongue on his balls.

"Fuck… Chloe." He spoke through gritted teeth. "*Babe.*"

She heard the desperation in his tone and fed it by wrapping her lips around the broad tip and sucking gently.

"God. *Chloe.* So good. Don't stop." His hips came off the bed, and his grip on her hair tightened until her scalp tingled. That only added to the pleasure for her.

Fueled by his enthusiasm, she slid her lips down farther, taking as much of him as she could.

He made a desperate noise that was a cross between a moan and a groan.

Chloe added some tongue action.

"*Stop.* Christ… *Chloe.*"

She didn't stop.

His hips came off the bed in the second before he exploded.

Chloe stayed with him until he sagged into the mattress, panting, arms over his head. She released him slowly and then looked up to find him watching her with sizzling eyes that were so full of affection that she could barely process everything she felt coming from him in that hyper-charged moment. "Are you okay?"

"I've never been better." He crooked his finger. "Come here."

She grimaced when all her joints protested the movement.

Finn sat up to meet her halfway, wrapping his arms around her and cuddling her into his chest. "You're hurting."

"Just a twinge when I moved. I'm okay."

"That was… You wrecked me."

"Did I?"

"You did." He rolled on a condom and then tipped her chin up to receive his kiss. "Sexiest fucking thing *ever*."

"How's your lip?"

"It's fine." Moving carefully, he arranged her so she straddled him. "Is this okay?"

"Yes." Chloe moaned when his reawakened cock nudged against her clit. She would be sore tomorrow, but she would worry about that then. For now, she would chase the pleasure.

"Is that a good moan?"

"Mmm-hmmm." She hated that he had to ask, that he watched her with concern when he should be losing himself in the moment. Now that he knew about her condition, he would always ask. Her heart sank a bit at that realization.

"What's wrong?"

He paid attention, he cared, he saw the very heart of her, and that scared her.

Eager to get his attention back where it belonged, she kissed his neck. "Nothing."

"You'd tell me if something hurts?"

"I will. Don't worry about me."

"Can't help it." His hands slid down her back to cup her ass, lifting her. He entered her slowly, carefully, stretching her to the absolute limit as he brought her down in increments. "So good," he said on a long exhale. "So, so good."

Everything about this was good, except the part where he treated her like she was made of glass and might shatter if he moved the way he had the night before when he hadn't known about the RA. She would never see that version of him again, and that made her sad for them both.

FINN HAD NEVER UNDERSTOOD the expression "on top of the world" until he had been there, and after two nights in bed with Chloe, he was still floating somewhere well above the top of the world. Tonight, they were meeting Riley and Nikki for dinner at the Wayfarer, where

Anthony and the waitstaff would be doing final tests of the house specials and working out any kinks in the service ahead of the grand opening to the public.

He arrived at Chloe's fifteen minutes after she closed the salon and waited for her to get home while Ranger barked inside. Finn wished he could go inside to feed him for her, but he didn't have a key and didn't think they were "there" yet.

He was *there*. He'd happily give her the keys to his entire life, but he didn't want to freak her out by letting her see how excited he was about her.

While he waited, he pulled out his cell phone to make a call that he couldn't put off any longer. He found the number he needed and pressed Send, holding his breath while he waited for Clint to answer. Finn hoped he didn't have to leave a message.

"Hey, Finn. What's up?" Clint sounded rushed and stressed.

Finn grimaced. He hated this. "So, um…"

Clint let out a loud groan. "Don't do this to me, Finn."

"I'm sorry."

"Ugh, you and your brother are going to be the death of me."

"I feel so bad, but some things have changed, and I'm staying on Gansett for now."

"What is it about that place that makes it so hard for you guys to leave it?"

"So many things." Especially the realization that if he got to be with Chloe, he'd never want to leave. "Our entire family is here, and we're opening a new business, and there's just a lot happening. I'm really sorry to be flaky with you, and I know Riley feels the same way. We both intended to come back, but then life happened."

"I get it. I don't like it, but I do get it."

"I hope we haven't completely burned our bridges with you."

"Nah. I'm always in need of good people who do the job without the drama, so if you get tired of being marooned out there, call me before you call anyone else."

"I'll do that. Thank you again for being so great to us. Riley and I both appreciate it."

"Yeah, yeah. Keep in touch and call me if you need me to send a rescue boat to pick you up."

Finn ended the call laughing. Clint wasn't the first to say that to Finn or Riley since they moved to the island. Their college friends, who came out to visit for a weekend the previous summer, had wanted to kidnap them and bring them home. Their mom had repeatedly asked what was so great about a remote island and when were they coming home.

He dreaded having to tell his mom that his plans had changed and would have to let her know soon.

Chloe drove into the driveway, parked next to him, smiled and waved, and Finn was reminded of why his plans had changed. He got out of his truck to greet her.

"Sorry. Were you waiting long? My last client was late arriving."

"I just got here. No worries. But Ranger is ready for his dinner."

"So I hear."

Finn followed her to the door, noting the slight limp that came from a long day on her feet. He wanted to help her find a way to simplify her life so she could make a living without having to be on her feet using her hands all day. In the morning, he was having breakfast with his uncle Mac to pitch the idea of a spa and salon at the Wayfarer. He hoped the others could be convinced and that they'd want Chloe to manage it for them.

After she fed Ranger and let him out, she headed for her bedroom. "I'll be just a minute."

"Take your time." Finn wondered if he'd asked too much of her by making plans for the evening after she'd had such a long day at work. His stomach churned with nerves as he tried to navigate her situation with the proper amount of empathy that didn't stray into the area of pity, which she did not want.

He'd never confronted a situation quite like this one and wanted to do the right things. If only he knew for sure what the right things were. As much as it pained him to admit it, he needed advice from his dad the shrink, who always had advice to give—so much so that his sons often begged him to let up.

But he was flying blind with Chloe, and he didn't like the feeling that he might screw up this incredibly important relationship at any second by saying or doing the wrong thing.

Perilous. That's how this felt, and he hated that. Even though she'd come around somewhat, he still wasn't sure of where he stood with her.

They enjoyed being around each other, were incredible in bed and had chemistry to spare, but would that be enough to build on, or would it take more to make a go of this? Finn didn't know, and he hated not knowing. He'd been waiting his whole life to feel the way he did about her, and to be so uncertain about so many things had his emotions in an uproar.

Chloe came out of the back room wearing a clingy blue dress that tied at the waist and carrying a faded denim jacket. "Is this okay? Not sure of the dress code at the Wayfarer."

"You look beautiful, as always." He admired the effortless way she combined clothes and makeup and accessories to look stylish and put together.

"Thank you."

"Hey."

She looked over at him.

Finn held out his arms to her.

After an initial hesitation, she came to him and stepped into his embrace.

He held her close, breathing in the scent that was so uniquely hers, the disquiet within him settling when her arms slid around his waist. "That's better." He kissed the top of her head. "Was today a really, really long day, or was it just me?"

"It was just you." Then she laughed. "Sorry, I couldn't resist."

He loved that she'd teased him. "That's not nice. I'm hanging by a thread here, and you're being mean to me."

She looked up at him. "Why are you hanging by a thread?"

"It's you. You're all I can think about. I count the hours until I can see you again. I want to spend every minute with you that I can, and I have never, ever, *ever* felt like this before."

"Finn…"

He didn't wait to hear what she was going to say, preferring to kiss her before she could tell him he needed to take it down a notch or be less honest and forthcoming or whatever she might say. When it came to her, he didn't know how to be less forthcoming. Their kiss quickly spiraled from sweet and undemanding to sensual and needy, making him wish he hadn't made plans with Riley.

Finn withdrew slowly, placing soft kisses on her lips, nose and forehead. "We messed up your lipstick."

She reached up to rub her thumb on his lip. "You're wearing most of it."

He puckered up. "Is it a good look on me?"

"Yeah, it is."

"Are you okay?"

The look she gave him made him wonder if he shouldn't have asked that—again. But how was he going to know if he didn't ask?

She gave a brief nod, patted Ranger on the head and led the way out the door.

Finn followed her, bringing the desperate feeling that he was messing this up with him as he walked to the truck.

CHAPTER 23

*C*hloe had looked forward to seeing him all day, had been thrilled to find him waiting for her outside her home and had loved the way he'd held and kissed her as well as the things he'd said about never having felt the way he did about her.

But...

Always a *but*.

Was she doing the right thing becoming more involved with him by the day? Was it the right thing to have dinner with his brother and his brother's girlfriend, as if she and Finn were a couple? Was it the right thing to let him propose a salon and spa at the Wayfarer to help solve her most pressing concern? She had prided herself on being completely independent since she'd aged out of the foster system, so allowing someone else to step in and try to help her went against everything she had believed in prior to her diagnosis.

But now... Now, she'd be a fool to not at least consider the idea, and that had her thoughts spinning.

The only thing she knew for certain was how much she loved being with him. If only her worries about the future weren't weighing so heavily on her mind, this would be the happiest time in her life. He was a truly great guy in every possible way, and the way he looked at her made her swoon on the inside.

Part of her wanted to say to hell with the worries and go all in with him. But something was holding her back from making that leap, and she suspected it was tied up in her concerns about what was ahead for her—and him if they were going to be a couple going forward.

Riley and Nikki were waiting for them on the porch of the Wayfarer, seated next to each other in rockers, holding hands as they swayed back and forth, the picture of contentment and commitment.

Once again, a powerful sense of yearning overtook her. She wanted what they had, and she wanted it with the man holding her hand, the man who'd changed his plans after meeting her, who made her feel safe and desired, who knew about her diagnosis and didn't care. The information hadn't changed anything for him. He would, however, continue to be careful with her, but only out of fear of hurting her. She could live with that.

In the time it took to come to those conclusions, she realized it was already too late to turn back, not that she wanted to. That didn't mean she was no longer worried about becoming a burden to him, but that didn't seem as important as it had before she'd told him about the RA. His immediate acceptance of her situation had been nothing short of remarkable.

Chloe took a deep breath and released it, trying to get her emotions in check so she wouldn't ruin their evening by losing her composure. She was surprised when both Riley and Nikki hugged her like they were old friends.

"So glad you guys could come tonight." Nikki led them into the Wayfarer. "Anthony has prepared a feast that Riley and I could never do justice to on our own. We're supposed to act like regular customers from the second we walk in the door."

They were greeted by a hostess, who showed them to the only table in the vast dining room that was set for guests. She handed them each a menu and told them that their server, Carlo, would be over in just a minute.

"So far so good," Nikki said.

"If they can't get that part right, you're in trouble, babe," Riley said.

Finn and Chloe laughed at the face Nikki made at him.

As the four of them studied the menus that were so new, they still smelled freshly printed, Carlo came over to offer them drinks.

"Where in the hell did you find him?" Riley asked, scowling after the young man had gone to get their drinks.

Nikki's brows knitted with confusion. "Why? What's wrong with him?"

"Absolutely nothing," Chloe said, fanning her face.

"That!" Riley pointed to Chloe. "Exactly."

"Oh my God, will you please shut it?" Nikki rolled her eyes. "He's a college student in need of a summer job."

"He looks like he could be an underwear model," Chloe said.

Finn glanced at her, seeming amused. "Is that right?"

"Uh-huh."

"How many male underwear models did you hire, anyway?" Riley asked.

"Wouldn't you like to know?"

Riley put both elbows on the table and glared at her. "Yes, I would."

"Down, boy. I'm too busy to ogle the waiters at work, and besides, why would I want to when I have my own underwear model waiting for me at home?"

While Riley grinned widely, Finn made puking noises.

"I've lost my appetite," Finn said. "I still have nightmares about Riley in his underwear. I saw far too much of that shit growing up."

"I'll never see enough of it," Nikki said, waggling her brows at Finn.

Smug with satisfaction, Riley sat back in his chair with a dopey smile on his face. "You see why I love her so much?"

"I don't," Finn said. "I don't get it at all."

Chloe busted up laughing. They were too funny—and very cute.

"Sorry to subject you to their nonsense, Chloe, but welcome to my life with these two. They're a handful."

"I'm much more than a handful," Riley said, "as you well know."

"Stop talking," Nikki said to her boyfriend.

Chloe tried to smother her laughter behind her hand, but it snuck out anyway.

"Sorry my brother is so disgusting," Finn said with a pointed look for Riley.

"How is speaking the truth disgusting?"

"Shut *up*," Finn said.

Chloe laughed so hard, tears ran down her face.

"Chloe thinks I'm funny," Riley said.

"She's still new," Nikki replied. "Give her time. Your charm wears off after a while."

"That's not what you said last night when I was—"

Nikki's hand over his mouth ended that sentence prematurely, which was probably for the best.

Carlo returned with wine for Nikki, beers for the guys and ice water with lemon for Chloe. She missed having a glass of wine after work.

Finn moved closer to her and slid his arm around the back of her chair.

Riley's brows lifted. "Things are getting cozy over there."

"Mind your own business."

Riley howled with laughter. "Like you did when I was first seeing Nik? Sorry, Chloe, but there's no way in hell I'm going to mind my own business."

Finn scowled at his brother.

"No problem," Chloe said. "Something tells me he probably deserves whatever he gets."

"Oh, you have *no* idea!"

"Tell her about the night we were out plowing snow," Nikki said.

"Do we have to tell her about that?" Finn asked.

"Hell yes, we do," Riley said. "So Nik and I are out at the bluffs minding our own business—"

"Which means having sex in the truck when he was supposed to be plowing snow," Finn said.

"We were not having sex!" Nikki said.

"*Yet*," Riley said. "Anyway, we're minding our own business when

215

he showed up, lit us up with his high beams and started in on the horn."

"And then he broadcast what we were doing to everyone else on the radio," Nikki said.

"I was just making sure you guys were okay. It was cold out there, and if you were having engine trouble…"

Riley lost it laughing. "*Whatever.* You're the same pain in the ass you've always been. Mom and Dad should've quit with perfection. Instead, they ruined everything when they had you."

Finn scoffed. "You would've been so bored without me around."

Their "argument" ended when Carlo approached the table to offer the chef's list of specials. They gave him their full attention as he recited the details from memory.

Chloe settled on the baked cod, while Nikki ordered one of the shrimp specials. Finn went with lobster and Riley with the filet mignon.

Nikki also ordered the charcuterie for the table.

"What the hell is charcuterie?" Riley asked.

"It's a meat and cheese board," Finn said. "You heathen."

"Why can't you just call it that, then?"

"Because," Nikki said, "charcuterie is a much better word."

"It's stupid," Riley said.

"*You're* stupid," Finn retorted.

Riley laughed. "Damn, that was a softball."

Finn pretended to swing a bat. "That I knocked right out of the park."

"Is it always like this?" Chloe asked Nikki.

"Pretty much."

"How do you stand them?"

"Small doses," Nikki said in a stage whisper.

"Oh, stop it," Finn said. "Don't listen to Nicholas. She loves us. We renovated her entire house this winter."

"They did do that," Nikki said. "They have their uses."

Riley snorted.

"Do not say it," Nikki said, "or you'll never get it again."

"Yes, dear."

Finn hooted with laughter. "She's got you by the short hairs, bro."

"Pipe down," Chloe said to Finn, "or you'll be feeling the pain in your short hairs. *Bro.*"

"Oh, I like her," Riley said. "I like her *so* much."

Finn smiled at her as he twirled a strand of her hair around his finger. "So do I."

"WHAT A FUN EVENING," Chloe said as they walked to his truck after being fed to within an inch of their lives. "They are so cute together."

"They really are. In case it wasn't obvious in there, I adore them both."

"It was very obvious—and they adore you right back."

"I hope you know the BS between me and Riley is all in good fun. He's my best friend."

"I totally got that. You're really lucky to have each other. I always wanted a sibling."

"You're more than welcome to Riley. He's a lot of work."

Chloe laughed. "He would say that you are, too."

"Of course he would. That's how we roll."

"I loved the story about the snowplowing. I can't believe you did that to them!"

"Oh please. That had to be done. They were right out there *begging* to be caught."

"You know that payback is going to be a bitch, right?"

"He's nowhere near as clever as I am."

"Sure, he isn't."

Finn held the passenger door open, helped her into the truck and stole a kiss. "You fit right in with us."

"Did I?"

"Uh-huh. It was awesome. They like you almost as much as I do."

She cupped his cheek, sending a shiver through his body. Her touch set him on fire, and seeing her interact so effortlessly with Riley and Nikki had only made him want her more than he already did.

"I hope it was okay that Nikki asked about your hand." She'd explained away the swelling by calling it an infection.

"It was fine. I know my hands are unsightly."

"No, they're not."

"Yes, they really are. No need to sugarcoat it."

Finn took the hand that was on his face and placed a gentle kiss on her inflamed knuckles. "I'm meeting with my uncle in the morning to ask him about the feasibility of a salon and spa at the Wayfarer."

"I told you that you don't have to do that, Finn. It's not your problem."

"I know it isn't. I think it would be a brilliant addition to our business or I wouldn't ask. If it also helps you out, all the better."

"You've got this all figured out, don't you?"

"Not entirely, but I'm working on it." Finn kissed her again, put her seat belt on her and closed the door. He ran around to the driver's side and hopped in to drive her home, hoping she'd invite him in because he was dying to be alone with her. Tonight had been awesome—the food, the company, the laughs. Finn had meant it when he said she fit right in with the three of them. She'd more than held her own in a tough crowd, and that pleased him tremendously.

She pleased him tremendously.

Every minute with her only confirmed his initial reaction to her had been spot-on and his decision to stay on Gansett with her for the summer had been the right move. After spending time with her these last few days, he couldn't imagine moving away from her. The implications that came with such a realization weren't lost on him. He had fallen in love with her, and it had been the best fall of his life.

If only he could be certain she was right there with him, everything in his world would be perfect. But he wasn't sure, and he couldn't come right out and ask her. Not yet anyway.

After lunch with his uncle, he was meeting Riley to shop for a ring for Nikki. He would take the opportunity to talk to Riley about it. And if necessary, he'd consult with his dad, too. He needed all the advice he could get to successfully navigate this relationship.

When his cell phone rang, Finn pulled it from his pocket and took the call without checking the caller ID.

"You son of a bitch!" Missy's shrill scream startled him.

Keeping his eyes on the road, he pressed the button to turn off his phone. "Sorry about that."

"She doesn't give up."

"I never knew she was like this." *Yes, you did. You knew she had a hint of crazy in her, and you liked that about her.* "Well, that's not entirely true. She was always a little much, but not like this."

"I'm worried that we haven't seen the last of her."

"You have nothing to worry about where she's concerned."

"I have *you* to worry about."

Had six words ever packed a greater punch? Not that Finn could recall. "That's very sweet of you to say, but I can take care of myself. And besides, after what she pulled yesterday, she wouldn't dare step foot on this island again. Blaine told her to go and stay gone."

"Doesn't mean she will. You need to be vigilant."

"I will. Don't worry about me."

"Too late. I'm already worried."

"Why does that make me so damned happy?"

"Because you're sick and twisted?"

Finn laughed. "If being happy that you care about me is sick and twisted, then so be it."

"I do care."

He took hold of her hand—carefully—and raised it to his lips. "I care, too. Far more than I should after what? A week?"

"Is it even that?"

"I've lost track. I never believed in things like this."

"Things like what?"

"Lightning striking when you lay eyes on a total stranger and see everything you've ever wanted."

"Finn…"

"Too much, too soon. I know that, but it's true." So much for staying cool and not driving her away by wanting her too much. He kept his mouth shut the rest of the way to her house. When he pulled into her driveway and killed the engine, he looked over at her. "I'm sorry if I'm too honest, but I can't seem to be any other way with you. That day in the salon? Total lightning strike."

Her small smile went a long way toward alleviating his fear that he'd freaked her out. "It was for me, too."

Finn leaned across the center console.

She met him halfway, her lips connecting with his and setting him on fire with a craving for more of her.

"Invite me in."

"I have to get some sleep tonight."

"I'll let you sleep. I promise."

The look she gave him was full of skepticism.

"I will. I promise." In a whisper, he added, "After."

Chloe laughed and opened the passenger door. "Come on, then."

Finn felt like a kid on Christmas as he got out of the truck and followed her inside.

CHAPTER 24

"*M*ac." He surfaced from deep sleep to realize Maddie was shaking him awake.

"What's wrong?"

"I don't know. I feel weird."

That quickly, he was wide awake. He sat up, turned on the bedside light and was startled to find her wide-eyed and pale. She'd been fine at bedtime. They'd both been worn out, so they'd gone to bed right after they got the kids down. "Weird how?"

"My heart is racing, and I feel sweaty."

"How long?"

"About an hour now."

"An *hour*? Why didn't you wake me up sooner?"

"You've been so tired lately. I didn't want to bother you."

"Madeline, you know better. If you need me, wake me up."

"Maybe we can have this fight later?"

Mac nodded and picked up the phone to call Janey since she was the closest.

"Mmm, what?"

"Maddie isn't feeling well. I need to take her to the clinic. Can you come stay with the kids?"

"What's wrong with her?"

"I don't know. Can you come?"

"I'm on the way."

Mac ended that call and made another to Victoria, who'd given them her personal cell phone number ages ago.

"This is Victoria." She sounded alert and wide awake.

"It's Mac McCarthy. Maddie is feeling strange—her heart is racing and she's sweaty."

"Can you meet me at the clinic?"

"We'll be there in fifteen minutes. I'm sorry to wake you."

"I'm already there with another patient. I'll see you shortly."

To Maddie, Mac said, "Vic is at the clinic and will be watching for us. Let's get you dressed, honey."

Maddie's big eyes filled with tears. "Is it happening again, Mac?"

"No." It couldn't happen again. He wouldn't let it. "Everything is fine. I'm sure of it. Let's get you to the clinic so Victoria can confirm it."

She nodded, but he could see that she didn't completely believe his assurances.

Hell, he didn't either, but assurances were all he had.

Mac helped her into yoga pants and a sweatshirt of his that she'd "borrowed" from him while pregnant with Hailey and had never given back, which was fine with him. He loved the way his zip-up sweatshirt looked on her. After he zipped it over her bountiful breasts, he drew her into his arms. "Breathe, baby. Everything's okay."

"How do you know that?"

"I just have a very strong feeling that I'm meant to be the father of three little girls who will drive me mad the same way their gorgeous, incredible mother does."

"You feel that? You really do?"

"I really do." He gazed down at the stunning face of the woman who had changed his life. "Breathe."

She took a shaky breath and let it out.

"Keep doing that." Light flickered into the room from headlights in the driveway. "There's Janey. Let's go." He took Maddie's hand and led her down the stairs as Janey came pounding up the outside stairs. Mac released Maddie's hand to admit his sister, who was wild-eyed and sporting bed head that would've amused him at any other time. "Thanks for coming."

Janey hugged Maddie. "What can I do?"

"Mac might need a bottle around four." Maddie's voice sounded shaky.

"I'll take care of it. Don't worry about a thing."

"Thanks for coming, brat." Mac led Maddie out the door and helped her into her SUV because it was more comfortable than his truck. As he drove them through the darkness to the clinic in town, he realized his hands were shaking. At times like this, island life totally fucking sucked. He wanted a top-level hospital and had to make do with an island clinic. Not that Victoria and David weren't the best at what they did, but what if Maddie needed something they couldn't provide? Like the day that Janey had needed an emergency C-section in a clinic not equipped for surgery… Mac's own heart began to feel like it might explode inside his chest, which of course his perceptive wife picked up on.

"Take your own advice, Mac. Breathe."

He tightened his grip on the wheel and focused on breathing. The last thing she needed from him was stress. She needed him to be calm and focused on her, not filled with dread over the thing that was *not* happening. It couldn't be. Not when he'd finally gotten his head around the idea of twin girls.

Driving a little faster than he should have, Mac got them to the clinic in ten minutes. In the parking lot were two other cars—Victoria's and Adam's white BMW SUV. "What's he doing here?"

"I was just about to ask you that. I hope Liam is okay."

Mac hoped so, too. He couldn't bear to think of anything being wrong with the baby who had made Adam and Abby so happy. After helping Maddie out of the car, he walked her inside with an arm around her shoulders. They encountered Adam walking a squalling Liam in the waiting room.

"What's wrong?" Mac asked his brother.

"Abby is crazy sick. Can't stop puking. She's dehydrated, so Vic put her on an IV. Liam doesn't appreciate the middle-of-the-night outing. What're you guys doing here?"

"Maddie is feeling weird, so we came in to get her checked."

"I hope everything is okay," Adam said.

"You and me both, brother. Come on, Maddie. Let's go find Vic." He led her through the swinging doors that led to the cubicle area, where they were greeted by the sound of violent retching.

"Oh God," Maddie whispered. "Poor Abby."

Victoria came out of a cubicle, saw them and directed them to the room on their right. "I'll be there in one minute."

"I hope you don't get whatever she has." Mac felt like a caged tiger in the small room. He wanted Victoria to come in there and tell them they had nothing to worry about. Until she said those words, he wouldn't be able to relax.

From her perch on the exam table, Maddie held out a hand to him. "Come here."

He went to her, took her hand and let her tug him into her embrace.

She ran her fingers through his hair. "You're not breathing."

"Yes, I am."

"No, you're not."

"How's your ticker?"

"It's not racing like it was, but it still feels faster than it should be."

Mac rested his head against her chest, listening to the rapid beat of her heart and wishing he knew what it meant.

Victoria came in five long minutes later. "So sorry to keep you waiting."

"Is Abby okay?" Maddie asked.

"She will be." Victoria waved her hand under the sanitizer dispenser and rubbed the liquid gel into her skin. "Now what's going on with you?"

"My heart has been racing, and every time it happens, I break into a sweat and my chest feels tight."

"How many times has it happened?" Mac asked, alarmed.

"This is the third time."

"Maddie! Why didn't you tell me?"

"I didn't think anything of it at first, but this time was worse than the others."

Victoria reached for a stethoscope. "Let me have a listen." She closed her eyes and listened intently, moving the device around on Maddie's chest until Mac was certain he was going to lose his mind if she didn't say something soon.

Another minute passed before Victoria opened her eyes. "I don't hear anything unusual, but I'd like to put you on a monitor for a couple of hours, just to be sure."

"What about the babies?" Mac asked.

"I'll put a monitor on them, too."

"You don't think…" The fear was so intense, he couldn't find the words to articulate it.

"We'll know much more in an hour."

He would lose his shit by then.

Victoria left the room, saying she'd be right back.

"Mac."

Raising his gaze from the floor, he found his wife watching him in that knowing way of hers. "Come here."

"I'm here."

"Closer."

He did as directed.

She grabbed a handful of his T-shirt and brought him in close enough to kiss. "Relax, would you?"

"How am I supposed to do that?"

"Go get your nephew so Adam can be with his wife."

Mac stared at her until she poked him in the chest to get his attention.

"We need the distraction, and Adam needs to be with Abby."

"I don't want you to catch what she has."

"I was with them yesterday. If the baby is carrying it, I've already been exposed. Go get him."

Mac went to the waiting room, where Adam continued to pace

back and forth with Liam, who was now quiet and sleepy-eyed. "Maddie says to bring Liam to her so you can go to Abby."

"She doesn't need to do that."

"I told her that, but she's insisting. If you guys have cooties, I don't want her getting it."

Adam snorted out a laugh. "Cooties? What're you, eight?"

"She doesn't need the stomach flu, Adam."

"Abby doesn't have the stomach flu, Mac."

"Then what's wrong with her?"

"She's pregnant."

At first, Mac thought he'd heard him wrong. "She's…"

"Pregnant. By now, you should know what that word means."

"But, I thought she couldn't."

"So did we." Adam blinked and swallowed hard. "Turns out we were wrong. Victoria confirmed it earlier and put her on an IV for dehydration."

"That is the best news I've heard in, well, ever. Congratulations."

"Thank you." Adam's jaw clenched with tension as he glanced at the doors to the treatment areas. "I just hope she's not going to be sick like this the entire time."

"Some people are. Laura was."

"I know, but hasn't Abby been through enough already? She's due for a break."

"I'm sure Vic will have her feeling better in no time." Mac reached out to take Liam from his father. "Go see her. Maddie and I will keep an eye on him."

"Are you sure?"

"Positive. She's on the monitor for the time being, and it was her idea to come get Liam so you could go to Abby."

"Thanks, Mac."

Mac snuggled the now-sleeping baby into the crook of his neck and shoulder. "No problem. Go take care of your wife. We've got your little man."

. . .

ADAM WENT through the double doors to the room where he'd been forced to leave Abby alone when Liam started fussing. He'd never felt so torn between the two people he loved best, but when Abby had told him to take Liam for a walk, he'd taken Liam for a walk.

He stepped into the exam room to find her dozing, her face so pale as to be alarming. Standing at her bedside, he reached over to brush the dark hair off her forehead.

Her eyes popped open. "Where's Liam?"

"With Mac."

"What's Mac doing here?"

"Maddie's not feeling well either."

Abby closed her eyes and licked her dry lips.

"How're you doing, honey?"

"Awful."

"What can I do?"

"Nothing. Vic said I'll feel better in a few hours when the IV does its thing."

"I sure hope so."

She offered a feeble smile. "Be careful what you wish for, huh?"

"No kidding." He continued to stroke her hair, wishing there was more he could do to comfort her.

"It'll be worth it, though. Whatever we have to go through."

"I'm glad to hear you say that."

"Of course I feel that way. I wanted this my whole life." Her eyes filled. "Everything I have now... It's what I've always wanted."

He leaned over the bed to kiss her.

She made a face and turned away from him. "You can't kiss me when I have puke breath."

"Yes, I can."

"No, you can't. You're never going to want to kiss me again."

"Now that is just not true, and you know it." He touched his finger to her lips. "These are my favorite lips to kiss."

"When they don't stink like puke."

"Any time. All the time. For better or worse."

227

"You're the best husband I've ever had," she said, her eyes heavy with exhaustion.

"I'm the only husband you're ever going to have." He kissed her forehead. "Get some rest, love. I'm right here, and I'm not going anywhere."

"Take care of my son."

"I will. Don't worry about a thing. Just rest."

MAC CARRIED Liam into the exam room, where Victoria was attaching Maddie to the various monitors. Nerves fluttered through him as he stressed out about what they'd reveal.

Maddie held out her arms for Liam, and Mac carefully transferred him to her.

"Your heart rate just slowed considerably." Victoria glanced at one of the screens. "That's the cure. You need more babies in your life."

"Two more babies and that's it," Mac said. For Maddie's benefit, he added, "Here's a newsflash. Abby isn't sick. She's pregnant."

Maddie gasped. *"What?"*

"You heard it here first."

"That's incredible! They stopped trying and boom! I'm so excited for them."

"I am, too. I just hope she's not going to be sick like this the entire time."

"Some moms are," Victoria said. "It's awful, but they get through it."

"Like Laura." Maddie shuddered. "I don't know how she went through that twice."

"Luckily, she got three kids out of two pregnancies," Mac said.

"True."

"And she would probably tell you that she's so busy with three little ones that she rarely thinks about how sick she was having them," Victoria said.

"For sure." Maddie stroked Liam's downy soft dark hair. "It's a good thing babies are so cute. They make it easy for us to forget pregnancy and delivery."

"The fathers never forget." Mac shuddered at the memory of Maddie delivering Hailey in the midst of a tropical storm with the island's only doctor on the mainland. Thank God David Lawrence had been home for a visit and had come when Janey called him.

Maddie reached out to him. "Don't think about the bad stuff."

"Kind of hard not to when you're in the clinic, attached to monitors in the middle of the night."

"An abundance of caution," Vic said. "I don't see anything to be worried about so far."

"Well, that's a relief," Maddie said.

"I'm wondering if what you're feeling is caused by anxiety and not pregnancy."

"How do you mean?"

"After what you went through with losing Connor, it's only natural that you would be concerned about it happening again. That fear can manifest itself in physical symptoms like the ones you're describing."

"But she didn't have this when she was pregnant with baby Mac," Mac said.

"True, but this time around is more complicated due to the multiples and the fact that it's her fifth pregnancy."

Mac looked to Maddie for answers. "Do you think it could be stress, hon?"

"Possibly. I think all the time about losing Connor and how there was no sign of trouble before he was just…gone."

Victoria patted her arm. "I understand that fear. I truly do. But you've had three successful pregnancies, which puts the odds very firmly in your favor."

"I know."

"Try to get some rest while you can. I'll be back to check on you after a while."

After Victoria left the room, Mac stood at the side of the bed looking down at Maddie and Liam and wondering if he'd missed the signs that she was unusually stressed out. "Did I miss this?"

"Miss what?"

"That you've been so worried about losing the babies that you've given yourself heart palpitations?"

"I haven't been sitting around stewing about it, but sometimes I wake up in the middle of the night in a cold sweat with my heart pounding because I dreamed about it happening again."

"Why didn't you wake me up when that happened?"

"Because. It was just a dream, and you work so hard. I don't want to disturb you."

"Madeline…" He shook his head in disbelief. "After all this time, how can you think I wouldn't want to be disturbed if you're upset or worried or freaking out or *anything*?"

"I knew you'd want me to wake you up."

"So why didn't you?"

"Do you think I can't see how exhausted you are after working a million hours a week to get the Wayfarer done in time for the season? And now you've got the marina to deal with, too. I don't know how you do it all."

"Look at me."

She looked at him with those caramel-colored eyes, and as always, his heart fluttered.

"If you are scared, lonely, anxious, horny—middle of the night or middle of the day—you wake me up or call me, and I'll come running."

She laughed even as her eyes went shiny with tears. "Leave it to you to toss horny in there."

"I mean it, Maddie. It kills me to think I slept through you having a panic attack about losing these babies. Don't let that happen again, you hear me?"

"I think the whole island can hear you."

"Maddie!"

Liam let out an indignant squeak and then settled once again into sleep.

"Hush," she whispered. "I hear you, and it won't happen again. I'm sorry."

"Don't apologize to me."

"Don't scowl at me."

"I'm not scowling."

"Yes, you are. Knock it off and kiss me."

"I'll do you one better." He walked around to the other side of the hospital bed, kicked off his shoes and climbed in next to her, wrapping an arm around her and Liam.

"Much better," she said, smiling at him.

That smile rendered him powerless to resist her—not that he ever wanted to resist. With a hand on her face to turn her in his direction, he kissed her sweet lips. "I want to hear about every worry, every fear, every concern."

"Those words all mean the same thing."

"Don't edit me. I'm being serious here."

"I know you are."

"Share the load with me, Madeline. That's what I'm here for." He kissed her again, more intently this time, tossing in some tongue as his fingers tangled in her hair.

"Um, excuse me, but are you actually making out in front of my son?" Adam asked from the doorway.

"He's asleep," Mac growled. "Go away."

"I'll just collect my impressionable child before you can corrupt him." Adam lifted Liam out of Maddie's arms. "Thanks for keeping an eye on him. Looks like you're feeling better."

"I am, thanks. How's Abby?"

"She's sleeping."

"You've got your son," Mac said to his brother. "Now go away."

"How can you stand him?" Adam asked Maddie.

"It's not easy, but someone's got to do it."

"We're all very thankful that you manage him for us." With the baby snuggled into his chest, Adam left the room, laughing at his own joke.

"You're supposed to be on my side at all times, especially when my siblings are taking jabs at me."

"Where is that written in the marriage doctrine?"

"Under 'thou shalt not team up against your husband with his siblings.'"

"I never would've agreed to that clause. Ganging up on you with your siblings accounts for half the entertainment in my life."

"You think you're so funny."

"I know I'm funny. Now shut up and kiss me some more."

Since there was nothing he'd rather do, he wrapped both arms around her, slid one leg between hers and kissed her with the kind of gusto he usually saved for the privacy of their own bedroom. But after hearing she'd been stressed out and enduring it alone, he wanted to remind her of how very much he loved her.

He kissed her until his lips were numb and his cock hard and throbbing between them, only stopping when alarms sounded on one of the monitors.

Victoria came running into the room, saw them wrapped up in each other and started laughing. "Well, that's one way to get your heart rate up."

Maddie buried her face in Mac's neck. "This is mortifying."

Mac laughed so hard, he shook with it. He loved her so damned much, and he'd never had more fun doing anything than he did getting her heart rate up.

CHAPTER 25

*W*ith Ranger settled into his bed for the night, Chloe
went into the bathroom to take the last of the pills that
got her through the day. When she came out of the bathroom, she
found Finn on the sofa waiting for her.

"Come sit with me for a minute."

She went to him and sat next to him, snuggling up to him when he
put his arm around her.

"I had the best time tonight."

"I did, too."

"I'm so glad you like Riley and Nikki."

"They're great. I love the way you and Riley razz each other."

"We've made that into a blood sport since just about the day I
could talk. All kidding aside, I'd take a bullet for him, and vice versa."

"Please don't do that."

Finn grimaced. "I'm sorry. It was incredibly insensitive of me to
put it that way."

"No need to apologize. It's a common saying."

"Still, I could've said it another way."

"Honestly, it's fine. Don't walk on eggshells around me. I promise
it's not necessary."

He held her closer, kissed the top of her head and caressed her back.

"What's this top-secret errand you and Riley are doing tomorrow?"

"I'm going with him to pick out a ring for Nikki. He's going to pop the question as soon as he has a ring—if we can even find one on the island. He might have to buy it online."

"Good for them."

"I'm thrilled for him and can't wait to have her join our family. She's the best. She fits right in with us."

"I can see that."

"You do, too."

"You really think so?"

"Absolutely, and so do they."

She raised her head and smiled at him. "That's nice of you to say."

He kissed her. "I'm not just saying it." His lips slid over hers, gentle and persuasive, making her forget that she'd intended to go right to bed, to get the sleep she desperately needed to function the next day. "You want me to go?"

She shook her head.

"You need to sleep."

"I need you more." For the rest of her life, she'd never forget the look on his face when her words registered with him.

"Chloe, I'm falling so hard for you, and I don't know if that's what you want."

"I'm falling just as hard. But..."

Finn groaned. "No buts."

"Just one, and it's something you need to know before you decide anything."

"I've already decided." He drew in a deep breath and exhaled dramatically. "Lay it on me anyway."

She looked him dead in the eyes. "I know you're excited for Riley and Nikki, but you should know that I'm never getting married."

Judging by the flat, shocked expression on his face, he hadn't expected her to say that.

"Why?"

"I decided a long time ago that it isn't something I want. After seeing what my mom went through in a marriage she felt trapped in and how it cost her everything, I made up my mind that I'd never put myself in that position. Since we were talking about falling for each other and your brother getting married, I thought it was only fair to tell you this."

"Okay…"

Chloe tried to figure out what that "okay" meant, but his expression and body language gave nothing away. Was her line in the sand truly okay, or was it a deal breaker? She waited for him to break the silence, and when he did, he looked at her with heartbreak in his eyes.

"Here's the thing, Chloe. I want to get married someday. I want to stand up in front of all the people I love and make that commitment to someone I can't live without. I want to have a family with her and dogs and a house that's all ours. I want to take vacations with her and see the world together. I want to live and work and play and *love* with her, every day for the rest of my life. The woman I love, the woman I marry will be treated like a queen because that's how I was raised by my dad and my uncles. It's how my cousins treat their wives. I don't know any other way but the McCarthy way."

The life he described sounded so perfect as to be right out of a fairy tale. Life had taught her not to believe in fairy tales.

"So while I respect your line in the sand and understand the reason why you feel you need that line, if you were to give me a chance, I would show you a whole other way than what you knew growing up." Finn kissed her forehead and stood. "I'll go so you can get some sleep."

Chloe's heart slowed to a crawl as she watched him pat Ranger on the top of his head. She wanted to call out to him not to go, not to leave it like this. And how, exactly, had they left it? Did it have to be all or nothing?

She didn't know, and as she forced herself to get up, to lock the door, to get ready for bed, to brush her teeth, she wondered if she'd made a huge mistake by drawing that line with him.

. . .

235

FINN SLEPT like shit and was about to get up for work when he got a group text from Mac. *Spent the night at the clinic with Maddie. Everything's fine, but it was a long night. We all need some time off after finishing the Wayfarer on time and on budget. Take a paid week off. Meet me at the Curtis place next Wed morning, bright and early. Enjoy!*

A week off! Jeez, how awesome was that? Finn could use the time to finish packing up the house and getting ready to move to Nikki's garage apartment for the summer.

Although, had his reason for staying evaporated last night? He didn't know and had spent a sleepless night tossing and turning while going over it in his mind.

I'm never getting married.

When she'd mentioned a "but," he'd never imagined she'd say that. Granted, in the new millennium, lots of people were choosing to forgo marriage for domestic partnership, and Finn totally respected that choice for others. He'd just always pictured himself married someday. Not any time soon—or at least he'd thought that before he met a woman he could see himself spending a lifetime with. Now that he knew Chloe was out there, how would he settle for less than what he felt for her? What if he never again felt for anyone what he did for her?

"There's a depressing thought."

His phone chimed with a text from Chloe that made his heart skip a beat. How bad of a case did he have if all it took to make him light-headed with desire was seeing her name on his screen?

I feel like we ended our evening on an odd note last night. Can we talk more later?

Finn stared at her text for a long time, trying to figure out how to respond. She could see that he'd read the text, so he needed to say something.

Sure. Call me when you're done at work.

OK.

He blew out a deep breath and then took a call from his uncle Mac. "Morning."

"Hey there. Are we still on for lunch? South Harbor at noon?"

Finn had almost forgotten about the lunch he'd scheduled with his uncle to talk about the possibility of a salon and spa at the Wayfarer. "Sounds good."

"You mind if I ask your dad and Frank to come, too?"

"Not at all."

"Excellent. See you soon, son."

The phone went dead, leaving Finn grinning at how Big Mac called them all "son," even his nephews. His dad and uncles had raised a tribe together, and each of the McCarthy kids had always known they had three dads they could count on, no matter what. Finn realized that the three of them would know how he should proceed with Chloe, and suddenly, he couldn't wait for lunch because he needed some answers.

The McCarthy brain trust was a good place to start.

FINN ARRIVED at the South Harbor Diner at noon and wasn't surprised to see the three brothers already in a booth, talking and laughing as they did whenever they were together. Ever since his dad and Frank had moved to the island, the three of them had been inseparable. His brothers had helped to put Kevin back together after his marriage ended and were two of the reasons why his dad had been so happy here. Of course, Chelsea was the biggest reason his dad walked around with a dopey grin on his face these days, but Finn was happy he'd found her.

Usually, Big Mac's best friend, Ned, was with them, the honorary fourth McCarthy brother, as they referred to him, but Ned and his wife, Francine, had left the day before on a trip to Italy and weren't due back until right before Shane's wedding.

Finn walked over to the booth, feeling as if he was interrupting something even if he was the one who'd invited Big Mac to lunch. "Can anyone join this party?"

"Hey, son." Smiling, Kevin slid in to make room for Finn. "Good to see you."

Since they'd been living on the island, his dad always acted as if they hadn't seen each other in ages, when in most cases, it had barely been a day. "You, too." Finn took the menu Big Mac handed him. "What're you boys up to?"

"We're still talking about the fishing trip in which your father nearly landed the biggest tuna any of us has ever seen," Frank said.

"The one where he couldn't use his arms for two weeks because he was so sore?" Finn asked, glancing at his dad in time to catch the scowl.

"Yep," Big Mac said. "That's the one. The poor guy was useless."

"And I didn't even have the tuna to show for it," Kevin said glumly.

"Poor baby," Big Mac said. "That mean old fish got the better of you."

"Kev put up one hell of a fight," Frank said.

"Thank you, Frankie. At least one of my brothers realizes that."

Finn laughed at their back-and-forth, which was always entertaining.

"Enough about Kevin getting beat up by a tuna," Big Mac said, his eyes glittering with mirth as they so often did. The man was pure fun and one of Finn's favorite people in the world. "Finny called this meeting, so what's on your mind, son?"

"First of all, I'm twenty-seven years old. Maybe we can dispense with the Finny business?"

Big Mac looked at him like he had two heads, then glanced at Frank and Kevin. In a chorus, the three of them said, "*Nah.*" And then proceeded to high-five each other like they were teenagers. Idiots.

Finn rolled his eyes.

"What's next on our agenda?" Big Mac asked.

"I have an idea for the Wayfarer."

"Let's hear it."

"Have you considered adding a salon and spa there?"

"I hadn't but what're you thinking?"

"I just wondered if it might be an added draw, to bring people in, especially in the off-season. Since the other spa was shut down last year, there's been nothing to take its place. I asked around town, and people said the place was almost always busy, even in the off-season. It was taken down by bad management, not a lack of interest."

"Wouldn't it compete with Chloe's salon?" Kevin asked.

"My idea includes hiring Chloe as the manager."

"Very interesting." Kevin looked at Finn with those all-seeing shrink eyes, as he and Riley called them. Those eyes that had made it impossible for them to get anything past Kevin as kids. He always seemed to know what they were up to before they did.

Big Mac sat back and appeared to give the idea some thought. "I'm not sure it would be a good fit at the Wayfarer, which is more of a day-trip sort of crowd, coming for the beach and the bar."

Finn's heart sank. He'd so hoped Big Mac would jump on the idea.

"But it might be perfect at the hotel," Big Mac said. "Auntie Linda and I have been talking about ways to ramp up the off-season business there, and we've got buildings on the property that could be converted. We could market it for women looking for a mid-winter getaway with their friends, complete with breakfast and spa packages."

"That'd be awesome," Frank said.

Finn couldn't agree more.

"Let me run it past the boss," Big Mac said, "and see what she thinks, but I really love your initiative, Finny. You're thinking outside the box, and I like that."

"I think he's actually looking for a way to help out Chloe more than anything," Kevin said. "Am I wrong about that?"

Finn shook his head. "You're not wrong."

"She's a great lady," Frank said.

"Yes, she is." Truer words had never been spoken, Finn thought. "She could really use something like this that would give her a safety net she doesn't have now."

"I thought her business did really well," Big Mac said. "After all, she's the only hair game in town."

"She does well." Finn didn't want to say too much. She'd told him about the RA in confidence, and he wouldn't betray her, not even with three of the men he trusted most. It wasn't his story to tell. "But being the owner of a small business can be tough, as you know." This he directed at Big Mac, who'd made something from nothing, first at the marina, then at the hotel and now at the Wayfarer.

"That's a fact," Big Mac said, nodding.

As they ate lunch, they talked more about what it would take to turn one of the buildings at the hotel into a spa.

"We could fold it into the reno we're doing of the hotel over the winter," Big Mac said. "I think Lin will love the idea."

"That's great," Finn said, impressed by the way Big Mac got things done. "And you think she'd be in favor of hiring Chloe to run it?"

"That part would be a no-brainer. Linda adores Chloe, gives her full credit for keeping her looking so young. Which means I adore her, too, because my wife is the prettiest girl in town."

"Now, wait just a minute," Frank said as Kevin began to register his objection.

Finn cracked up laughing. "Y'all are nuts."

"What about you?" Big Mac gave him the shrewd look that Finn remembered from childhood. "What's going on with you and our Chloe?"

"We've been hanging out." Recalling their conversation from the night before, Finn felt despondent.

"Riley said the four of you had a great time last night," Kevin said.

"We did." Finn let his knife dangle between his fingers, needing something to focus on besides the grinding fear that had him wondering if they could get past the roadblock they'd encountered last night.

"What's wrong?" Frank asked. "And don't say it's nothing. You're talking to professional fathers here. We know *something* when we see it."

"Things were going pretty well between us. Really well, in fact."
Kevin leaned on the table. "Until?"

"Until she told me she doesn't want to get married. Ever."

"Whoa," Big Mac said. "Like to anyone?"

"Right."

"How come?" Frank asked.

"She has her reasons—and they're good reasons. Things that happened when she was a kid. I'm not opposed to making a life with someone without getting married, but I always thought I'd get married. Someday."

"That is a tough one." Kevin scratched at the stubble on his jaw. He seemed to shave a lot less often since he'd been with Chelsea. "I suppose it comes down to what do you want more—her or a future marriage with someone else?"

Leave it to his dad to cut straight to the heart of the matter. "Since I met her, I seriously can't imagine ever wanting anyone else ever again." Saying the words out loud, knowing they could never be unsaid, would've made Finn itchy and nervous a couple of weeks ago. But everything had changed since he met Chloe, and there was no going back to who he'd been before her.

"This is big news," Frank said to his brothers. "We were just talking about how there was only one left."

"Huh?"

"That your brother and cousins have found their true loves. You were the last one left."

"And we were super bummed that you were leaving," Big Mac added. "So it's great that you're going to stay now."

"If I can figure things out with her," Finn said. "I won't want to be here if that doesn't work out."

"Figure it out," Big Mac said, "or spend the rest of your life wondering what if."

Frank pointed to Big Mac. "What he said. Regrets are a bitch. None of us want to see you eating your heart out because you let something great slip through your fingers."

"Don't let that happen, son," Kevin said.

"There are concerns," Finn said haltingly. "Significant concerns."

"Then come into the office and air them out," Kevin said. "That's what I do. I help people figure out their shit."

And he was, Finn had to acknowledge, extremely good at helping people to figure out their shit. But would Chloe go for that?

There was only one way to find out.

"Thanks, you guys. I appreciate the advice."

"As Ned would say, that's one thing we've got plenty of," Big Mac said, cracking up his brothers.

"And we're not afraid to share it," Frank said to more laughter.

Thank goodness for that, Finn thought, thankful for their wisdom in a way he never had been before. But then again, he'd never needed the benefit of their combined wisdom as much as he did now.

CHAPTER 26

*A*fter lunch, Finn met Riley at the island's only jewelry store. His brother was already inside, perusing the inventory.

"Hey," Finn said when he joined him. "See anything you like?"

"A couple." Riley pointed to a diamond ring in a platinum setting. "What do you think of that one?"

"I like it." Lowering his voice so the shopkeeper wouldn't hear him, he added, "But you're going to pay way more for it here than you would on the mainland. We could go over for a day this weekend and buy it there."

Riley shook his head. "I can't leave right now. Nik is up against a deadline at the Wayfarer, and I've been helping her after work."

"So wait until after the opening?"

"I can't wait that long."

"It's a week, Riley."

"Too long."

"You're insane. You know that, right?"

"I'm aware of that, but the time is right, and I don't want to wait. Her sister is coming for the opening, and she'll be staying with us. I want to do it before Jordan gets here."

Riley gestured to the sales clerk. "Could we see a couple of these rings?"

"Of course." He came over to unlock the case and withdrew a tray of rings that he placed on the glass countertop. "Let me know if you'd like more information about any of them."

"I will. Thanks."

The clerk went to help another customer while Riley picked up the ring he had pointed to initially. "I like this. It's not so big that it'll get in her way, but it's not puny either."

"It's really nice. She'd love it. But she'd probably love anything you gave her."

"She's easy to please. That's one of many things I love about her."

"I'm really happy for you guys, Ri."

"Thanks. You know she loves you almost as much as she loves me."

Finn smiled. "The feeling is mutual. Let's face it, you couldn't marry her if she didn't love me."

"No, I really couldn't." Riley laughed. "I can't believe I'm actually about to buy an *engagement* ring."

"I know. It's crazy."

Riley looked over at him. "I really, really love her, Finn."

"I know you do. You guys are perfect for each other."

Riley continued to study the ring from all angles. "What's up with you and Chloe?"

"I'm not sure yet. We're hanging out, having fun." Finn shrugged, playing it cool even as he continued to churn over their conversation from the night before.

"I like her a lot, and Nik does, too."

"Glad to hear it."

"After we left you guys last night, Nik said something that's been bugging me all day."

"What's that?"

"She thinks you might be more into it than Chloe is. Nik is worried about you getting hurt."

"I can understand why she might've picked that up. Chloe is cautious and more reserved than I am. She has good reasons to be."

"What kind of reasons?"

"Stuff I can't really talk about, but it's part of who she is."

"Does it have to do with why her hands are so swollen?"

"Partially." He should've known Riley would wonder about that.

"You're being careful, right?"

"Trying to be, but I'm totally into her. Like you were when you first met Nik."

"Whoa, really?"

Finn nodded. "You were right that night at Janey's. She's my Nik, Riley."

"You already know that?"

"I knew it the minute I met her. Everything about her is different."

"Wow, that's awesome. Does that mean you're sticking around after the lease is up?"

"Yeah. I was going to text Nik today to ask her if I can still have the garage apartment."

"She'll tell you it's all yours. She fixed it up for you, hoping you'd take it."

"That's really nice of her."

"For some reason that I can't fathom, she *really* loves you."

"I'm a lovable kind of guy."

Riley snorted. "Whatever." He held up the ring to capture the light coming in through a window. "I think this is the one."

"I approve—of the ring and the girl."

"Thanks, man." He signaled for the clerk. "I'll take this one."

"Very good. I'll ring it up for you."

Riley handed over his credit card and exhaled. "Here goes nothing."

"Here goes *everything*."

"Yeah, true. What about you? Are we going to be ring shopping again before long?"

"I don't think so. Chloe said she doesn't want to get married."

Riley's brows lifted. "Seriously? Like *ever*?"

"Yeah, and again, she has good reason to feel the way she does."

"What about what you want?"

"I want her. I've never felt this way before." There, in two brief sentences, was the heart of the matter as far as he was concerned. "When I'm with her, it's just... It's like lightning in a bottle."

"I know that feeling. There's nothing else quite like it."

"I'm sorry if I was an asshat when you were first seeing Nik."

Riley cracked up. "You were a total asshat, but I'd expect nothing less from you."

"I've grown up since then."

"That was five months ago."

"I'm a changed man."

"Whatever you say, bro. Any more nonsense from Missy?"

"She called me the other day, but I hung up when I realized it was her calling on a borrowed phone."

"I cannot believe she booked a wedding venue and came here to confront you the way she did. That's some crazy shit right there."

"No kidding. I never saw any of that coming. What part of us being *broken up* for two years says I want to get married?"

"Nothing. The girl is a nut job. I've tried to tell you that for years."

"I know, and I should've listened to you and Dad and everyone else."

"Let that be a lesson to you, little brother. I am older and wiser and always know best."

"Jeez, I walked right into that, didn't I?"

Smiling, Riley said, "I'm just glad you've seen the light where Missy is concerned. I always thought you could do better. Not that she's a bad person..."

"Um, hello? She punched me in the face. Twice."

"I've wanted to do that for years. But I digress. She's a little unhinged, but not a bad person. She's not the one for you."

"I get it. I've known that for some time. Why do you think I jumped at the chance to move out here for a while? She was smothering me, and when I told her I wanted to take a break from everything and come here, she lost her shit. That should've been the end of it, but I made the mistake of keeping in touch with her, and that gave her hope that when I came home, we'd pick up where we left off."

"Don't beat yourself up for being a good friend to someone who's been part of your life for a long time. Hopefully, she's gotten the message after a few hours in jail."

"I don't know. She's still calling me."

"Tell Blaine. He can give her another warning. And if that doesn't work, you need a restraining order."

"God, I hope it doesn't come to that."

"I know. That'd suck."

The clerk returned with the charge slip that Riley signed and the small bag he handed over. "Congratulations. I hope you'll both be very happy."

"Thank you," the brothers said.

"He's talking about me and Nik, you idiot."

"I know that, you idiot."

They walked out of the store into warm sunshine and a cool ocean breeze.

Riley pulled the sunglasses from the top of his head down over his eyes. "So what's the plan with Chloe?"

"I don't have a plan."

"You probably ought to get one. Quick."

"Yeah, I'm working on that. What's the plan for popping the question?"

"When she gets home tonight, I'll be ready for her."

"Send me a text and let me know what she says."

"She's gonna say *yes*," Riley said, exasperated. "You don't buy the ring until you're sure of the answer. So much to teach you, little brother, and so little time."

Finn gave him a shove that sent Riley in the direction of his truck. His brother had it all figured out. Finn wished he could say the same.

CHLOE WENT through her day feeling as if she was wading through a muddy swamp. Finn's heartfelt words from the night before played through her mind on automatic rewind, torturing her again and again with the possibilities if only she could find the courage to try.

247

Her hands ached almost as badly as her heart did, and as she dried the hair of her final customer of the day, she looked forward to going home, putting on comfortable clothes and taking to her bed to snuggle with Ranger.

Hopefully she would hear from Finn, but she wouldn't be surprised if she didn't. At what point did someone become more trouble than they were worth?

Chloe cashed out her customer, walked her to the door and was stunned to see Finn standing on the sidewalk. She held the door open for him and waited for him to come up the stairs. As he brushed by her, every nerve ending in her body seemed to go haywire. She fumbled through the locking of the door as well as the turning of the sign from Open to Closed. Taking a deep breath to calm the nerves that had gone bonkers at the sight of him, she turned to face him, preparing herself for whatever he might say.

He picked up the broom and swept up the hair on the floor, scooping it into the dustpan and dumping it in the stainless-steel trash can she'd paid far too much for online because it seemed classier than the plastic options available on the island. And why was she thinking about that now? Because it was better than thinking about the possibility of him having come there to tell her they were over.

She didn't want to hear that. "You don't have to do that."

"I don't mind."

"Thank you."

"No problem."

Ugh, they were so freaking *polite*! Is that what it had come to? Awkward conversation full of platitudes?

"Finn—"

"Chloe—"

Leaning against the broom handle, he flashed that devastating smile that rendered her stupid in the head. "You first."

"I'm sorry about last night and the way I tossed such a big thing into the conversation without any warning. I handled it all wrong, and I'm sorry."

248

"You didn't do anything wrong. You told me how you feel, and I respect that."

"You do?"

"I do." He laughed. "No pun intended."

She laughed, and that simply, the ice was broken. "I've thought about what you said all day, about how it would be with you, and I can see it so clearly."

"I meant every word I said."

"I know you did."

He leaned the broom against the wall and came over to her, placing his hands on her hips and a gentle kiss on her lips. "Can you believe everything that's happened since my head smacked into yours right about here?"

"No, I can't believe any of it. I feel like I've been living a dream ever since then."

"It's a dream come true. Here's what I think we ought to do, and feel free to tell me if this isn't going to work for you. We both seem to want more of this." He kissed her again. "And everything that goes with it, but there're significant challenges standing between us and what we both want. So I'd like to propose something I never in my wildest dreams thought I would suggest to anyone ever."

Breathless with anticipation, Chloe said, *"What?"*

"I want us to spend some time with my dad in a professional capacity. I want us to put all the concerns on the table and pick them apart until there's nothing standing between what we both want and having it. What do you think?"

"You…you want us to go to therapy. Together?"

"Yes."

"With your dad?"

"Since he's the only game in town, yes."

"And we would talk to him about…"

"Everything but the super-personal stuff. That'd be off-limits."

"Would it be a conflict for him to counsel his own son?"

"Yes, so that's why we'd keep it casual and not official. He's the best at cutting through the BS to get to the heart of an issue and finding solutions. Riley and I spent most of our lives resisting that, but the reality is, he's very good at what he does, and with that kind of help available, I can't see a downside to trying it. But if you're not game, then it's off the table."

Chloe bit her bottom lip and tried to get her head around what he was suggesting.

He bent his knees to bring himself lower so he could look into her eyes. "What're you thinking? Air it out with me. There's nothing you can say to me that I wouldn't want to hear." He paused, tipped his head adorably. "No, wait. That's not true. I don't ever, *ever* want to hear the word goodbye from you."

Chloe wrapped her arms around him and held on tight, breathing him in. "I thought maybe I'd driven you away with what I said last night."

"I'm not easily driven."

"I see that." The fact that he'd shown up and had come with a plan to fix what was wrong between them made him ten thousand times *more* than any man she'd ever known. He was a man of substance. She'd known that from the outset, but he'd proven it to her repeatedly since then. "You're extremely special to me, Finn McCarthy. I don't ever want you to think otherwise."

"That makes me very happy to hear, sweet Chloe."

For the longest time, they stood together in the waning daylight, arms around each other in the middle of her shop, where anyone walking by could see them. Chloe didn't care who saw them or who knew that she was falling madly in love with this extraordinary man.

"I'm willing to talk to your dad if you think he can help."

"I really do, or I never would've suggested it."

"Okay."

"I'll talk to him about it tomorrow."

"You haven't already talked to him about it?"

"Not until I ran it by you. If you weren't into it, there would be no point in discussing it with him."

A rare and special man, indeed.

His hand slid down her back to cup her ass, giving a gentle

squeeze. "In the meantime, how about we grab take-out, go home to check on Ranger and hang out?"

"I would love that."

"Then let's get going."

Leaving her car at the salon, they picked up salad and a pizza from Mario's and headed to her house in his truck.

Chloe was relieved that they'd cleared the air and made a plan, although she wasn't completely sure that involving his father would help. But Finn seemed convinced, and she trusted his judgment. After spending most of the day thinking she'd completely blown it with him, knowing there would be more was enough for now.

He followed her into the house, carrying the pizza and the bag with the salad.

While she let Ranger out, Finn filled his water and food bowls.

"Are you starving?" she asked him.

"Not really. Are you?"

She shook her head. "Give me ten minutes, and then come find me." Trailing her finger across his rigid abdomen, she left him in the kitchen with a stunned expression on his face that made her smile.

CHAPTER 27

*H*oly shit. Sexiest woman *ever*. For a few minutes after she walked away, Finn stood there reliving the way she'd left the room, knowing he would never forget what she said or how she'd looked at him as she'd said it.

She scrambled his brain and made him so hard, he was lightheaded from the rapid flow of blood to his cock.

Had it been ten minutes yet? He had no idea how long he'd stood there being stunned by her.

Get yourself under control. Act like you've done this before.

He'd done this before. Lots of times. But it had never meant what it did with her. Why that was, he couldn't say. All he knew was that from the instant his skull had connected with hers, he'd been a goner. Life as he knew it would never be the same, and that was just fine with him if it meant that life would now include her.

Finn took a series of deep breaths to calm himself that had Ranger looking at him as if he thought Finn was crazy. Maybe he was. Squatting, he gave Ranger some attention and was rewarded with a tongue to the cheek. Laughing, Finn used his shirt sleeve to wipe up the dog spit and stood, glancing down the hallway for some sort of clue as to what might be awaiting him. But with the bedroom door closed, he couldn't see anything but darkness.

He took another deep breath and went down the hallway to knock on the door.

"Come in."

If he lived to be a hundred years old, Finn would never forget the sight that greeted him when he opened that door. Chloe, bathed by candlelight, wearing a sexy, silky thing that clung to her curves as she knelt in the middle of the bed.

For the longest time, he could only stare, feasting his eyes on the most magnificent sight he'd ever beheld.

"Finn? Are you okay?"

"I'm completely dazzled."

Her smile lit up her face. "Do you want to come in?"

"I most definitely want to come in." He stepped into the room and closed the door behind him, so Ranger wouldn't interrupt them.

Chloe scooted to the edge of the bed and held out a hand to him.

Finn tried not to notice the swollen knuckles that followed a long day of working with her hands, but his attention was drawn to them anyway. He took her hand and pressed gentle kisses to the sore areas. "You have rendered me speechless, and that's not easy to do."

Her low, sexy laugh traveled through him like a live wire, sending a shiver of need down his spine.

Flattening her hands on his chest, she began unbuttoning his shirt and pushed the two sides apart to place hot, openmouthed kisses on his chest.

Finn sucked in a sharp deep breath and buried his fingers in her hair. "You make me so crazy, Chloe. I never knew it could be like this until I met you."

She twirled her tongue around his nipple, and his brain went completely blank. The only thing he knew was need, pure and simple.

His head fell back in surrender as her lips and tongue spun a magical web of desire, entrapping him completely. "Chloe… Christ, you're killing me."

"I don't want to do that."

Smiling, he said, "In the best possible way." He tipped her chin up so he could kiss her with the pent-up desire that had him ravenous for more of her. Though she fully participated in the kiss, he sensed her discomfort with the position and eased her down onto her back to give her knees some relief. Hovering over her, he studied every detail of her exquisite face before dropping a light kiss on the stud in her nose. "I hope you know you could ask me for anything in this world, and I'd give it to you if I could. I'd give you anything if it meant I got to continue feeling the way I do when I'm with you."

She reached up to caress his cheek. "All I want is you. Just you."

"You have me. I'm all yours."

"I don't want you to feel like you have to be careful with me. Yes, I have aches, but I won't break."

"I'll always be careful with you."

She shook her head. "It's okay to be like you would be with anyone else."

Finn kissed her. "Nothing about this is like it's ever been before. It's all new. It's you and me, and we'll do it our way. I'll always be very careful not to cause you any more pain. You've already had more than enough. If you hurt, you'll tell me, and we'll try something else. Okay?"

"Okay."

"Excellent. Don't worry about anything. Whatever comes up, we'll deal with it."

"You have such faith when you have no idea what might come up."

"I have faith in what I feel when you're in the room. And when you're naked in a bed with me..." He shivered dramatically. "They haven't yet invented the words to adequately describe what that feels like."

She looked up at him with bottomless violet eyes. "You're not going to turn out to be too good to be true, are you?"

"Nope. What you see is what you get. And you, my sweet, sexy, adorable Chloe, haven't seen *anything* yet." He kissed her again while pressing his hard cock against her core. "Now it's time for less talk, more action."

Bending his head, he drew her left nipple into his mouth, sucking and licking until it was tight and hard. Then he moved to the other side, while she squirmed under him, making him crazy as he moved down to worship her toned belly and hip bones.

"Finn," she gasped, "*please*. Hurry."

The urgency he heard in her voice more than matched his own, so he decided to speed up his agenda to get to the main event. "Need a condom."

She tightened her arms around him to keep him from getting away. "I'm safe if you are."

"I'm so safe. I've never…" He swallowed hard. "Not without a condom."

"First time for everything?"

He dropped his head to her chest, summoning control. The thought of being inside her with nothing between them made his head spin.

"Are you okay?" she asked, caressing his hair.

"I just need a minute to prepare myself for this."

That sexy laugh was going to be the death of him.

Raising his head, he gave her his best indignant look. "Are you laughing at me?"

"I'm laughing *with* you. Big difference."

"Except I'm not laughing."

She dissolved into helpless laughter that made him smile at the joyful noise. He loved that sound and was determined to do whatever it took to make her laugh like that every day. She was still laughing when he pushed into her tight, wet heat, his eyes rolling back in his head from the searing pleasure.

Finn wouldn't have thought it would be all that different without a condom.

He would've been very, very wrong. After pushing the rest of the way into her, he had to take a moment to breathe, holding her as close as he could get her. "Is this okay?"

"So, *so* okay." Moving carefully, she raised her legs and wrapped them around his hips.

Finn groaned, his fingers digging into her shoulder and hip. "You're a fucking goddess."

"No, I'm not."

"Yes, you definitely are. My goddess." He began to move while keeping a close eye on her to make sure nothing he did hurt her. But she was right there with him, moving with him like they'd been doing this forever. Maybe they had been. Maybe they'd been together in another life and finding each other in this one had always been fated.

What other explanation could there be for something like this?

"Chloe…" He tried to hold off, waiting for her, but the need overtook him.

When she reached between them to touch herself, she triggered her own release and his. It seemed to come from his soul, the very heart of him, and went on for what felt like forever, leaving him shaken and depleted from the sheer power of it.

He realized he was lying on top of her, possibly crushing her, and started to move.

"Not yet." She held him tighter. "Not yet."

Finn sagged into her, breathing her in and riding the aftershocks that had him hardening again, as if he hadn't just come so hard, he saw stars.

Chloe chuckled. "You're going to break me."

"Never." He was determined to do everything he could to keep her in his life, his arms, his bed—forever.

IT TOOK a few days to juggle schedules and find a time when Finn, Chloe and Kevin were available to chat. Kevin had invited them to come to his house for dinner on a night when Chelsea was working.

Chloe would be lying if she said she wasn't nervous about spending time with Finn's dad in a professional capacity, even if they weren't meeting at his office or becoming official patients of his practice. Of course, she knew Kevin from cutting his hair, but this would be different. Now she was the woman sleeping with his youngest son, and that changed everything.

Finn insisted that his father was thrilled for them both, but would he still be thrilled when he heard about her condition?

Her nerves had stretched to the breaking point by the time Finn picked her up. Naturally, he realized that right away.

"Don't be nervous. He's a pussycat. I swear."

"I'm not nervous."

"Sure you aren't," he said with a laugh as he curled his hand around hers in a light grip. "How're the hands tonight?"

"Aching."

"And the rest of you?"

"Aching in a good way." The last few days and nights with him had been the best time of her life. They were in total sync—inside the bedroom and everywhere else, too. In ten days, he'd become the most important person in her life, and she wanted this to work so badly. In fact, she could honestly say that she'd never wanted anything as much as she wanted him in her life to stay.

That's why the stakes felt so high as they headed for his dad's house.

"What if he freaks out about the RA?"

"He won't."

"You don't know that."

"I know *him*. He won't freak." After stopping the truck at a four-way intersection, Finn glanced over at her. "He won't freak. I promise. The only thing he's ever wanted for me and Riley is to be happy and healthy and productive. He's seen me with you. He knows how happy you've made me. That's *all* that will matter to him."

Though he said what she needed to hear, Chloe still had her doubts. What father would want to see his twenty-seven-year-old son settling down with a woman who could one day, in the not so distant future, be physically disabled?

"Whatever you're thinking, knock it off."

"I'm not thinking anything."

"Oh, yes, you are. You're thinking about all the bad things. Let's think about the good things, shall we? Like last night. That was a good thing, wasn't it?"

"A very good thing."

"And the night before. And the one before that…" He shivered. "I swear to God, I can't even think about it without embarrassing myself."

"Bedtime has become my favorite part of the day."

He brought her hand to his lips and carefully kissed each of her swollen knuckles. "Mine, too. You're all I think about, sweet Chloe, so whatever you're worried about, let it go. No matter what happens with my dad, we'll still be going home together after. Tonight and every night from now on."

"You're so certain."

"You're not?"

"I want to be."

"You can be. It's all good, babe. I swear. It's never been better."

He made her want to believe in rainbows and unicorns and happily ever afters. Even when she told him she would never get married, he'd taken it in stride and continued to dazzle her with his presence—to the point that she could no longer remember what life had been like before him.

Life hadn't been as much fun before him, that's for sure. In the days that she'd spent with him, she'd laughed more than at any time. He made her laugh, he made her think, he made her want things she'd never wanted before, and he made her scream from the pleasure they found together.

"I talked to Big Mac today, and he and my aunt Linda are very interested in the spa idea, but they'd want to put it at the hotel in North Harbor rather than at the Wayfarer. They have plenty of space on the North Harbor property and feel it would be a better fit there. What do you think?"

"I suppose that could work, but I'd lose the walk-in business that I get in town."

"So keep the Curl Up and Dye open. Nothing says the spa has to include a salon. If you keep the place in town devoted to hair and everything else at the spa, then they wouldn't be in competition."

"You've given this a lot of thought," she said, impressed and amazed by the effort he was putting into solving her problems.

"It's important to you, so it's important to me."

"I just hope your aunt and uncle aren't doing this just for me."

"Sweetheart, they're *brilliant* businesspeople, and the only way they'd take on something like this is if they think it's a great idea, too. Aunt Linda is already talking about off-season spa and breakfast packages and marketing them to women as a getaway."

"I'm excited to be involved in this, and I just want to thank you for suggesting it to them. I really appreciate it."

"I'm just glad they went for it and that it gives you one less thing to worry about."

"You have no idea what it means to me that you came up with this idea and sold it to your aunt and uncle."

"I know, sweetheart. I just hope it works out."

They arrived at his dad's home, the small house that had been Chelsea's before they were married.

Finn cut the engine and glanced over at her. "Everything will be fine with my dad, so don't be nervous. Okay?"

Chloe nodded, deciding to trust him even as butterflies stormed around in her belly.

"Wait for me." He insisted on helping her out of his truck every time they went anywhere together. Opening the passenger door, he surprised her when he put his arms around her. "Any time it's too much for you, reach for me. I'll be right there with you."

God, she loved him. How was that possible after only knowing him for ten days? She didn't know the how of it, but there was no question that this was love. She loved him, and judging by the way he looked at her, he felt the same way.

"Come on." Keeping his arms around her, he lifted her out of the truck and let her down easy, holding on until she had her feet under her.

"You're going to throw your back out hauling me around like that."

"*Please...*" His tone dripped with disdain. "You're a feather."

"Sure I am."

He patted her on the ass and directed her to the front door, where his dad waited for them wearing a big smile and an apron that said, "Kiss the Cook."

"Sexy, Dad," Finn said.

"It was a gift from my wife." He hugged his son and then surprised Chloe by hugging her, too. "Welcome to my humble home."

"Thanks for having me." She handed him the bottle of Chardonnay she'd picked up on the way home from the salon.

"It's a pleasure."

"What's for dinner?" Finn asked. "I'm starving."

"I got lobster that was caught today."

"Oh, yum." Finn glanced at Chloe. "You like lobster, right?"

"Ah, *yeah*, I love it." She was immediately concerned about whether she'd have to break open the shells. Even with the tools, that might be a challenge for her.

"I gotcha covered, babe." Finn spoke in a low tone that only she could hear. "Don't worry."

And that, right there, was why she loved him. Because he understood her, he *saw* her so completely, like no one else ever had. She offered him a grateful smile. "Thanks."

"Drinks?" Kevin asked.

"I'll have a beer, and ice water is good for Chloe."

"Coming right up."

They took their drinks to the back porch, where Kevin had a pot simmering on the stove attached to the most elaborate grill Chloe had ever seen.

"That's quite a setup," she said.

"A man and his grill," Kevin said with the same disarming smile his sons had.

"Dad is very serious about his grill. Riley and I used to joke that he liked his grill better than us."

"There were times, especially during the teenage years, when that was actually true."

Chloe laughed at the face Finn made.

"We weren't that bad."

Speaking directly to Chloe, Kevin said, "They *were* that bad. Worse than bad sometimes."

"I believe you."

Kevin cracked up laughing. "I like you, Chloe."

"Thank you."

"You can't think he's funny," Finn said. "That's not allowed."

"Oh, sorry, you should've told me that before we came."

"I did tell you."

"No, you didn't."

Kevin rolled his eyes. "I believe Chloe."

"This is a tough crowd," Finn said, smirking at her.

She appreciated the laughter and the humor that had put her at ease with Kevin. The McCarthys had a unique gift for making everyone feel welcome and included, and she should have known that Kevin would be no different than the rest of his family that way.

"I'm glad we could finally find a night to do this," Kevin said, sipping from his beer.

"We are, too," Finn said. "Chloe and I appreciate you feeding us."

"That's always my pleasure. You know that." Kevin leaned on the table. "I have to confess to being surprised that you were interested in my professional services." To Chloe, he said, "Neither of my sons has *ever* wanted my advice about anything."

Finn sputtered with outrage. "That's not true!"

Kevin laughed. "Trust me, it's true. So, what's going on?" He looked to Finn, then Chloe and back to Finn.

Chloe glanced at Finn. "May I?"

He gestured to give her the floor. "Go for it."

She placed her hands flat on the table. "I was recently diagnosed with rheumatoid arthritis."

"I wondered if that's what it was."

Chloe stared at Kevin, stunned. "What do you mean?"

"I've noticed your hands when you were cutting my hair."

"You already knew."

"I suspected. I didn't know for sure until now."

Chloe sat back in her seat, uncertain of how to proceed.

Finn picked up the slack for her. "Chloe is concerned about the impact of her condition on our relationship, among other things."

"Which is totally understandable."

"It's not going to get better from here," she said. "In fact, it's actually been getting worse."

"From what I understand, it can take a while to settle on a treatment plan. What works for one RA patient does nothing for another."

"Yes, that's what David has told me."

"How long have you been under treatment?"

"About a month. It took a long time to get an actual diagnosis."

"Were you negative for the RA factor?"

"Yes."

"Ah, that does make for a tougher diagnosis. And it's probably too soon to tell for sure if the current meds are going to work for you."

"They've helped somewhat, but my hands are the biggest problem I have."

"And you need them to earn a living."

"Exactly. Becoming disabled is my greatest fear. Without a job, I can't afford health insurance, and without that…"

"I totally understand where you're coming from. What do you think, son?"

Finn turned his formidable gaze on her. "I think Chloe is the most exceptional human being I've ever met, and in case she hasn't already figured it out, I'm madly in love with her, and other than my concerns about her well-being, I don't give a flying fuck about anything other than spending as much time with her as I possibly can, every day for the rest of my life."

Chloe felt like she'd been hit by lightning—again. To hear him say that, out loud, in front of his dad no less… She had no idea what to say. No, wait, that wasn't true. She knew exactly what she needed to say. "I love you, too."

And then he was kissing her as if they were alone rather than at a table with his dad watching their every move.

Kevin's chair scraped on the patio as he got up. "I'll just, um, give you guys a minute."

They came up for air many minutes later, and Chloe could only stare at him. "You're too much."

"Was it too soon?"

She shook her head and blinked back tears as she caressed his face. "It was perfect. I'll never forget it."

"I'll never forget you saying you feel the same way."

"How could I not? You're...everything."

"It's the same for me, sweetheart. Let me ask you something."

"Sure."

"If I went to work one day and fell off a ladder and broke both my legs and couldn't work for months, would that change the way you feel about me?"

"Of course not. I'd take care of you."

Smiling, he tucked a strand of her hair behind her ear. "So why do you think it would matter to me if one day you were unable to work? I'd take care of you, and you'd take care of me when I needed you. That's how it goes when you love someone. You take care of each other."

"You love me."

"Hell yes, I love you. I'm batshit crazy about you."

She leaned her forehead against his, staring into his dazzling blue eyes. "Same."

"And I'm going to want very much to marry you at some point." Before she could protest, he rested a finger over her lips. "And because we might get married, it makes sense for us to have a family health insurance plan."

"You think you're so clever, don't you?" she asked, amused and touched by his logic.

"I'm not being clever. I'm being practical. And I'm being self-serving. I want forever with you, Chloe. I want everything with you—the good, the bad, the healthy, the sick, the ups, the downs. I've never wanted that with anyone, but I knew about two days after I met you that if I let you get away, I'd regret it forever."

"I've never known anyone like you." She flattened her hand on his face, feeling the prickle of his late-day whiskers against her palm.

"You're so certain about what you want."

"I'm sure about you, but I haven't been sure about anything before now. Just ask my boss in Connecticut. I've given him whiplash with my indecision. I kept thinking I had to go home to figure out my life, but it turns out my life was right here, waiting for me to find it. Two years I was on this island, and you were right here all along."

Smiling, she pushed the hair back from his forehead. "I was waiting for you to need a haircut."

He barked out a laugh. "I needed a haircut months before I got one. And P.S., your fingers combing through my hair made me hard in your chair."

"No way."

"Yes way."

A throat clearing reminded them they were not alone. "Sorry to interrupt, but dinner is ready."

"Bring it on, Pops."

Kevin brought out a salad, salad dressing and a bowl with steaming potatoes and corn on the cob. Then he went back for a platter to get the lobsters from the pot on the grill.

"Allow me." Finn took one of the lobsters and cracked open the shells for Chloe, then handed the plate over to her. "There you go."

"Thank you."

"So," Kevin said after a long silence while they ate, "it seems to me that you two may not need my help after all."

"I think we might be good," Finn said, gazing at Chloe.

"I think so, too."

"If I may make one suggestion," Kevin said. "Find out everything you can about RA. Join the online forums, get all the support you can. Things are less frightening when you have all the info and you're well supported."

"She'll be very well supported, but I agree with you, Dad. We need to get all the info we can so we can be prepared for whatever might happen."

"Even with the info, there will be obstacles and difficulties and things you don't see coming. Maintaining communication will be key to getting through it together."

Chloe put down her fork, took a sip of water and summoned the courage she needed before glancing at Kevin. "Could I ask you one thing…"

"Anything."

"Are you okay with Finn being with me, knowing what you do about my condition? I mean, if we stay together, someday in the not too distant future, I may be reliant upon him, and I'd totally understand if you didn't think it was fair for me to get involved with him, knowing that."

Kevin propped his elbows on the table.

Chloe resisted the urge to squirm while she waited to hear what he would say.

"We learned when our Finn was very little that when he sets his mind to something, get the hell out of his way. When he played Little League baseball, he was determined to be an all-star, and damned if he didn't make that happen. He wanted to be class president, ran a professional campaign that would've made the pros weep and was elected class president all four years of high school. If Finn *wants* something, really *wants* it, he finds a way to make it happen. And if there's one thing I knew after the first time I saw the two of you together, it's that Finn wanted you as much as he wanted to be an all-star and as much as he wanted to be president of his class."

"More," Finn said, his eyes sparkling. "I want her much, *much* more than that."

"I know my son, Chloe, and I've never seen him *glow* the way he does when he's with you. So if you're asking for my approval, you have it. You have my approval and my support and my appreciation for making my son so happy. That's all I've ever wanted for him and his brother. And if the time comes when you need additional support because of your condition, you'll have it—from me and our entire family."

Overwhelmed by Kevin's heartfelt words, Chloe used her napkin to dab at her eyes. "I see that you come by your charm naturally, Finn."

Both men laughed.

"It's a McCarthy family trait." Kevin placed a hand on her shoulder. "But I mean every word, Chloe, and I appreciate your concerns about how your condition might impact Finn."

"I don't care how it impacts me. I've spent a lot of time online this week, reading about it, and I have a much better understanding of what we're up against. I firmly believe it's nothing we can't handle. I even joined a support group for partners of people with RA. They talk about *everything*. There's a whole thread about the best ways to have sex with someone who has aching joints." He waggled his brows for effect. "They're very *inventive*."

Flabbergasted, Chloe could only stare at him.

"What?" Finn asked after a long silence.

"Just when I think I've seen the full extent of your fabulousness, you go and top yourself."

Finn flashed a cocky grin. "Like I've said before, you ain't seen nothing yet."

"Is he for real?" Chloe asked Kevin.

Kevin beamed at his son with fatherly pride. "Very much so. In my completely unbiased opinion, he's one of the very best men I've ever known."

Chloe looked at Finn. "I couldn't agree more."

"Aww, shucks, you guys. My head is swelling."

Chloe laughed as she rolled her eyes at his predictable response. "Doesn't take much."

"You know it, baby," he said on a dirty laugh.

Her face burned with mortification as she glowered at him. She couldn't believe he'd said that in front of his dad! Well, yes, maybe she could...

"On that note," Kevin said, his lips quirking with amusement, "who wants dessert?"

CHAPTER 28

*R*iley had planned this evening down to the last dinner roll. Everything had to be perfect, and by seven thirty, he was ready. The dinner he'd picked up at Domenic's was in the oven to stay warm, champagne was chilling in the dining room, where Nikki wouldn't see it until he wanted her to, the kitchen table was set with her grandmother's china, and vases of red roses had been strategically positioned.

He wanted this to be the best night of her life—and his.

And he was so fucking nervous, he was afraid he might puke before he got to the main event.

He checked the time on his phone for the eighteenth time.

She'd be home any minute.

He'd showered, shaved, ironed a shirt and put on the cologne that she said drove her crazy. Driving her crazy had become his favorite thing in life, and if the cologne did it for her, he wore it. Whatever she wanted was what he wanted, too.

And yes, it had occurred to him on more than one occasion over the last few months that she'd made a hot mess of him, and he couldn't bother to care. He loved her madly, passionately. He loved her in a way that he hadn't known existed until he came to fix her roof and ended up losing his heart.

Shortly after they first met, she'd left the island with her troubled identical twin sister, Jordan, leaving Riley to wonder what might've been if only she'd stayed.

Then she came back.

Thank *God* she came back.

Riley looked around at the sparkling new kitchen they'd installed together, working side by side to get it just right. It was gorgeous, if he said so himself. Knowing they'd done it themselves was incredibly satisfying. Eastward Look had been Nikki's grandmother's summer home. She had told them to make it their own, and they were working room by room to update and renovate.

One nail at a time—no pun intended—Nikki had become his partner in every possible way, and he couldn't imagine a single day without her in it. Last month, she'd gone to LA for three endless days to visit her sister, and he'd about gone mad without her. Their reunion had been thermonuclear.

Riley smiled thinking about it. They'd spent an entire day in bed after she returned. He loved everything about their life together and couldn't wait to make it official by asking the most important question of his life.

He checked the time again.

She was officially late for a very important date.

Riley was about to call her when he saw headlights coming down the driveway.

Showtime.

He lit the candles and shut off the lights in the cozy kitchen where they'd spent at least half of their relationship. The other half—perhaps more—had been spent in bed. He kept thinking they would reach a point where they weren't jumping each other every five minutes, but if anything, the longer they were together, the more he wanted her. With other women, he'd gotten bored after a month or two. With Nikki, he became more curious and interested in her with every passing day.

As their time together ran through his mind like the best movie he'd ever seen, he found himself relaxing, the nerves disappearing in a wave of certainty. He had absolutely nothing to worry about where she was concerned.

The front door opened and closed, the distinctive sound familiar to him after months of living here.

"Hello?"

"In here!"

Riley took a deep breath and released it slowly. By the time she appeared in the open doorway to the kitchen, he was ready for her.

"Whoa, this is nice." She took in the candles and the table. "What's the occasion? Did I forget our anniversary or something?"

Riley chuckled at her confused expression. They celebrated every month they'd been together. "You didn't forget anything. Come here, and I'll tell you what the occasion is."

She walked tentatively into the kitchen, which further amused him. His Nikki was never tentative, not with him anyway.

Riley relieved her of the heavy messenger bag she'd brought home almost every night as the Wayfarer opening drew closer. Maybe this wasn't the right time to throw one more thing at her, but he simply couldn't wait another day.

"You're acting weird."

"Am I?"

She nodded. "You're making me nervous."

"We can't have that. I never want you to be nervous around me."

"Usually, I'm not, but I've never come home to candles and china and roses before."

"That's a damned shame. I need to up my game and do this more often."

"If you upped your game any more than it already is, I wouldn't be able to walk, so please don't do that."

Riley laughed as he put his arms around her. "Relax, okay? It's all good. In fact, it's so damned good that I wanted to plan a special night to tell you just *how* good it is for me."

"How good is it?" she asked with the saucy grin he loved so much.

"It's the best thing ever to happen to me. *You* are the best thing to ever happen to me." He'd planned to feed her first, but now that she was here, he couldn't bear to wait. "In fact…" He released her and dropped to one knee, reaching for her left hand as her right hand flew up to cover her mouth. Tears filled her eyes as she finally understood what was happening. "I wanted to be right here in the kitchen we rebuilt together when I told you how you've totally rocked my world and given me things I didn't even know were missing until I had you."

A sob escaped from her sweet lips, and tears ran down her face.

"I love you more than anything in this life, Nicole. I love the life we're building together, one piece of tile at a time. I love every second I get to spend with you, no matter what we're doing. Will you please do me the incredible honor of being my wife?"

"Yes," she said on a hiccup. "Yes, Riley. Yes, yes, yes."

He got up to hug and kiss her. "That's a whole lot of yes."

"Yes times eleventy trillion. I love you, too. So much. I wake up some days, and I still can't believe this has happened. That *you* happened."

"*We* happened, and it's the best thing ever."

"I am so very, very thankful for my leaky roof."

Riley smiled and kissed her again. "So am I. Oh shit! I knew I was forgetting something." He dug into his pocket where he'd stashed the ring earlier and withdrew it, reaching for her left hand. "I stole your emerald ring to check the size, but I put it back in your jewelry box."

"You're very sneaky," she said, sniffing as he settled the gorgeous ring on her finger.

"Do you like it?"

"Oh God, Riley. I *love* it. It's stunning."

"It's got nothing on you, babe." He kissed the back of her hand. "I like the way it looks on you."

"I *love* the way it looks." She hugged him so tightly, she nearly shut off his air supply, but he didn't care. He loved being hugged to death by her. "Holy shit, we're engaged!"

"Yes, we are. I want to make it official as soon as we can. Pull some strings at the Wayfarer and get us on the calendar for the fall."

"Oh jeez, you're kidding me, right?"

"Would I joke about something this important?"

"So while I'm managing a brand-new business for my future husband's family, during the busiest season of the year, you also expect me to plan a wedding?"

"I'll plan it."

She laughed—hard. "No, you won't."

"It's not that funny."

She went weak with laughter. "It's hysterical. We'd end up with beer and pork rinds and bowls of peanuts on every table."

"I don't know what you have against pork rinds."

"They're disgusting, and we're not having them at our wedding."

"Fine. Be that way. We can do it in the late fall, after the season is done, but that's my final offer."

"Or we could elope."

"Really? You'd want to do that?"

"If it meant I didn't have to plan my own wedding on top of the other twenty I'm overseeing this summer at the Wayfarer."

"I'm intrigued."

"Your family would murder us."

"Nah, they wouldn't care. They've been to so many weddings the last couple of years, they'd hardly notice if we didn't have one. But… And I absolutely cannot believe I'm saying this when you offered me an out… *But…* I think I might want that moment when you walk toward me in your stunning white dress and blow my mind."

"I would blow your mind for sure."

Riley growled and nibbled on her neck.

"I have an idea," she said, sounding breathless.

"I'm listening."

"Let's have it at the Chesterfield and let Lizzie plan the whole thing. We'll just show up and get married."

"Yes. Let's do that. Excellent idea."

"That's why I'm the brains of this operation."

"Yes, you are. Let's make an appointment with her tomorrow and see what they have available."

"I'll call her in the morning."

"We have people we need to tell about this development," he said.

"Yes, we do, but first we need to celebrate."

"Oh crap. I forgot the champagne. Hold on."

She grabbed his arm. "I'd love some champagne, but that's not the kind of celebrating I had in mind."

His mind went blank as every blood cell in his body headed south. That tended to happen whenever she looked at him that way.

"Will dinner keep?" she asked.

"Uh-huh."

She took his hand and led him to the sofa, gave him a gentle push to seat him and then crawled on top of him, straddling his lap and framing his face with her soft hands. "Before I forget to tell you, this just became the best day of my life."

Cupping her ass, he pulled her in closer to him, as close as he could get her. "Mine, too, sweetheart. Mine, too."

"YOU REALLY JOINED an online forum for partners of people with RA?" Chloe asked Finn when they were back at her house. She still couldn't believe he'd done that.

"I really did, and I spent hours reading the various threads. It was very informative. And in case you're wondering, I didn't see or hear anything in there that scared me off or made me think twice about what I'm 'getting myself into.'" He used air quotes to make his point and then put his arms around her and kissed her. "My eyes are wide open, and I *love* what I see."

"I'm still trying to figure out what I did to get so lucky to find you."

"You opened a hair salon on an island that didn't have one and made yourself essential to everyone who lives here, including me."

She rolled her bottom lip between her teeth.

"What're you worrying about now?" He recognized the signs by now.

"I'm not worrying for once. I'm excited about renovating and designing the space for the spa."

"I'm glad you're excited. Riley and I will do all the work, and we'll do whatever you want."

"Does he know that yet?"

"He'll find out soon enough. He owes me his left nut after all the time I gave to him and Nikki this past winter."

"That's gross, Finn."

"It's true, Chloe." He walked her backward toward the bedroom, always mindful to be careful with her, to go slow, to let her set the pace.

"So what did you learn about how to have sex with someone who has RA?"

"Um, quite a few things, actually."

She reached up to unbutton his shirt. "What was your favorite?"

His Adam's apple bobbed in his throat. "Like my own *personal* favorite?"

"Uh-huh."

"Um, well, if I'm being entirely honest—"

"I'd never want it any other way."

"It went something like this…" He was like a man possessed removing her clothes and then his own with a frantic haste that made her giggle.

"There is *nothing* funny about this, Chloe."

Making an effort to curb her amusement, she said, "I'm sorry, Finn." She loved saying his name, and apparently, he loved saying hers, too.

"I don't think you're sorry at all."

"How can I make it up to you?"

"Since you asked, you could get on the bed with your head here and your feet over there."

Intrigued, Chloe did as he directed, on fire with curiosity and desire.

"Remember—you asked what my favorite thing was. This was my *most* favorite, but there were many others, too."

"Got it." Did he have any idea how adorable he was?

"Scoot a little bit this way."

She moved closer to the edge of the bed. "Good?"

"A little more."

She looked up to see his big, hard cock hovering over her and began to get where he was going with this. Such a guy.

"Is this okay?"

"Yep."

He got bigger right before her eyes, and his hand trembled as he stroked himself. "You know you don't *have* to do anything if you don't want to, right?"

"I do know that."

"Okay."

She reached up to push his hand away, so she could take over. "Come closer."

He leaned over her, his hands braced on either side of her hips, which made it possible for her to tongue the underside of his balls.

"*Fuuuuuck*," he said on a long exhale.

Chloe smiled. This was going to be fun. She licked her way up the length of his shaft and took the wide head into her mouth, sucking gently and loving the way every muscle in his body seized up with the effort to stay in control, to not thrust into her mouth, to let her take the lead.

He didn't cede control easily. She knew this about him and appreciated the gift he was giving her by allowing her to own him this way. Chloe fully intended to make sure he remembered this forever. For the longest time, she focused on the tip, sucking, licking and tightening her lips around him.

The noises he made ranged from needy to desperate.

"Baby, please… Please."

Chloe took more of him, continuing to caress with her tongue and the lightest bit of teeth, which had him going completely still as he waited to see what she'd do next. With both hands, she squeezed his ass cheeks, drawing another wild-sounding groan from him as he sank deeper into her mouth.

"Chloe, Chloe, *Chloe*."

Emboldened by his reactions, she dragged a finger down to press against the sensitive spot behind his balls, and he erupted into her throat. Even in the throes of his release, he was careful not to give her more than she could handle.

His head landed on her belly, his body heaving and his cock twitching.

Chloe licked him clean and released his cock from her mouth with one final suck that made him tremble. "Was that what you had in mind?"

He laughed and rolled to his back next to her. "That was way more than my fertile imagination could dream up."

She sat up and crawled into his outstretched arms.

"Are you okay?"

He would, she realized, always ask her that. Every time. And that had to be fine with her. He was asking only because he cared. "I'm good. You?"

"I'm wrecked. The guys on the forum said that position was a winner, and they were right."

"What're some of the others they suggested?"

"There's this one from behind where you're on your side and your legs are together that looked particularly interesting."

"Wait, there're *pictures*?"

"Drawings."

"I need to see this."

"I'd rather surprise you with the things I'm learning. I'm a very good student."

She raised her head off his chest so she could see his face. "Thank you."

"Why are you thanking me when you just gave me the best blow job in the history of mankind?"

"I'm thanking you for making my problem your problem."

"That's the way this works, Chloe. Your worries are mine. Mine are yours. We deal with it all together."

"This is really happening."

"It really is." He took her face in his hands and forced her to meet his intense gaze. "I love you. I'm right here, and I'm not going anywhere unless you go with me. It's safe for you to have complete faith in me, because I'll do everything in my power to never let you down."

"You're making a believer out of me."

"Good. Maybe someday I'll even talk you into marrying me."

"Maybe so."

He gasped. "Really?"

"You're incredibly persuasive." Resisting him—any part of him—was futile and unnecessary. Nothing about him reminded her of the volatile, unpredictable man who'd fathered her. She had nothing to fear from Finn McCarthy. That much she already knew for certain.

"I am rather good at persuading you."

She poked his shoulder. "Don't get too full of yourself."

"I'd much rather be full of you. Wanna try that behind thing?"

"I want to try it all, Finn."

"Then that's what we'll do, Chloe."

CHAPTER 29

Over the next week, Chloe discovered that being an unofficial member of the McCarthy family came with a lot of social obligations. Not that she minded, because everything they did with Finn's family was fun, but with Shane and Katie's wedding right around the corner, they were busier than ever.

Tonight was the bachelor and bachelorette parties for the happy couple. The men would be gathering at the marina, which had become their custom, while the women congregated at Maddie's to make it easier for her to participate. Since her anxiety scare, Mac had been insistent that she do as little as possible so she could focus on relaxing and incubating their twin girls.

Chloe couldn't imagine what it would be like for Mac and Maddie to have twins on top of the three kids they already had. Finn had mentioned that Mac was talking about hiring a nanny to help out after the twins arrived. They were going to need all the help they could get.

This would be the first time that Chloe hung out with Finn's family members without him there with her. She knew all the women from the salon, but she'd been close to only Katie before she started dating Finn. Now they all treated her like a long-lost sister, which was just one of many things that had changed for her since his skull connected with hers.

With hindsight, she'd begun to believe that head bump had been the single best moment of her entire life.

He made her deliriously happy, the kind of happy she'd thought existed only in romance novels and sappy movies. When they were apart, she counted the hours until she could see him again. And when they were together... Every minute with him had her craving more. As much as she could get. Fortunately, he felt the same way, and they'd fallen into the habit of spending every night together at her house.

They'd spent time at his place, too, packing up the few things he'd brought with him to the island in anticipation of his move to the garage apartment at Nikki's.

Chloe planned to ask him if he'd rather move into her house. She was waiting for the right time, and with everyone focused on Shane and Katie right now—as well as Riley and Nikki, who'd gotten engaged—now wasn't the right time. But she would ask him soon.

The thought of making it official, of sharing a home with him, filled her belly with butterflies that were more about excitement than anxiety. When it was right, it was right, and everything about Finn McCarthy was right. Nothing had ever been so right.

He'd even gone with her to her last appointment with David, intent on learning everything he could about the RA and how he could be supportive of her.

She'd lived long enough to know that men like him were one in a million, and she still couldn't believe she'd actually found him. When she thought of how close she'd come to not finding him before he left the island for good, she could only count her blessings for the brother and cousins who'd teased him about his man bun and driven him into her salon to shut them up.

Despite the pervasive glow of happiness that filled her days and nights, a niggling worry had her wondering when the other shoe would drop. In her experience, there was always another shoe, something she didn't see coming until it had blown up her world. What would it be this time?

"Chloe!" Finn called for her from the backyard, jarring her out of the disturbing thoughts. "Are you coming?"

"Yes, be right there!" She was dropping him off at the marina on the way to Maddie's and planned to pick him up later so he could have a few beers without having to worry about getting home. He'd been looking forward to the night out with his favorite guys all week, and she wanted him to have fun.

She checked her outfit in the full-length mirror one last time, grabbed her purse off the bed and went to join Finn and Ranger in the yard. Judging by Ranger's tongue hanging from his mouth, they'd either been wrestling or playing fetch. Ranger seemed to forget about his physical limitations when Finn was around to play with. She and Ranger had that in common.

Finn wore dark jeans and a white button-down shirt rolled up to reveal his muscular forearms. She'd never found forearms sexy until she'd had his forearms to look at. His hair had gotten a little longer again, and the late-day scruff on his jaw only added to his over-the-top sexiness.

"Yum," he said, giving her the once-over. "Are you sure we have to go out again tonight?"

"I'm sure."

He came over to her, wrapped an arm around her waist and flattened his hand on her ass. "These jeans are so smoking hot, it's a wonder they don't catch on fire. I'm glad you're going to a bachelorette party, otherwise I might be worried about other guys coming on to my girl."

"From what I hear, bachelorette parties around here may include male strippers."

His eyes nearly bugged out of his head. "*What?*"

"Don't shoot the messenger."

"You're not going if there's gonna be strippers there."

"Ease up, caveman. I can take care of myself."

His scowl spoke volumes about his true thoughts, but thankfully, he didn't push the matter any further or try to forbid her from going. That would've been a problem for her. She was so used to calling her own shots that ceding to someone else didn't come naturally to her. And she never had been good about taking orders from anyone, which was why self-employment suited her so well.

Finn had assured her that his aunt and uncle would give her total autonomy over the spa and would leave her alone to run the business the way she saw fit. She could live with that if it meant steady employment and health insurance. Having both those things alleviated some of her greatest concerns, and for that, she would always be thankful to Finn—and his family.

Chloe drove them to the marina, where the garage doors to the restaurant had been thrown open to allow in the warm spring breeze. Many of the other guys were already there, and when Finn leaned over to kiss her goodbye, they let loose with catcalls and whistles.

"Idiots," he muttered. "Every one of them."

"You'd do the same thing. Don't even try to deny it."

"Okay, I won't," he said, smiling. "At the first sign of strippers, you'll call me to come rescue you, got me?"

"No, Finn, I don't got you, and I won't call you. Get out of my car so I can go have some fun without my ball and chain."

"You're being kinda mean to me, Chloe. I gave you three orgasms last night. I would think that'd buy me some points for a few days. But *no*."

Someone knocked on the passenger-side window.

Finn put down the window. "Look who's back! Chloe, you remember my cousin Grant, right?"

"Of course. Nice to see you again."

"You, too, Chloe. So you're sucking face with Finn, huh? You could do *so* much better."

"Shut the fuck up, Grant. She's not aware that she could do better, and I'd like to keep it that way."

Grant laughed and shook his head. "It's so weird to see the babies kissing girls."

"On that note, I'm outta here." Finn stole one more kiss from Chloe before shoving Grant out of the way with the car door. "Move it." Finn leaned into the open window. "No strippers."

"Bite me."

"I will, and I'll make it hurt."

She rolled her eyes and stuck out her tongue. "Let go of my car, or I'll run over your foot."

Finn stepped back, and she watched him long enough to see him embrace Grant. They walked into the marina with their arms around each other. The McCarthy family gave her all the feels with the way they busted each other's balls nonstop but loved each other so fiercely. Witnessing their dynamic up close the last few weeks had shown her the kind of family she'd seen on TV but had never known personally. It had been a revelation, to say the least.

As she drove to Maddie's house, she contended with a flutter of nerves when she thought about walking into the gathering without Finn there to ease the way for her. Despite the fact that she knew all the women, this was different from cutting their hair and making casual conversation while they were in her chair. She'd been invited to things before, always a "you should join us" kind of thing that she'd said no to most of the time. As a lifelong outsider, she'd felt strange about inserting herself into existing groups and social circles.

Finn had become her ticket into this group, and everyone had been so nice and supportive of her dating him. But this would be her first time alone with the women, and she was nervous. Thank goodness Katie would be there. For whatever reason, Chloe had really bonded with her in a way she hadn't with the others. Not yet anyway. Katie had told her that the more time she spent with the women, the more true friends she would have.

That would take some getting used to. A loner didn't become a social butterfly overnight. Maddie's driveway was packed with cars, so she parked on the street where she wouldn't get blocked in if she decided to leave early. She carried the crab dip she'd made and the bottle of wine she'd brought, even though she wouldn't drink it. Someone else would. Wine and women went together like peanut butter and jelly.

She went up the stairs that led to the back deck, knocked on the sliding glass door, but no one answered, so she poked her head in. "Knock knock?"

"Chloe!" Chelsea came over to her, leading with the baby belly that seemed to get larger by the day. "Come in."

She gratefully accepted the hug from Chelsea.

"Let me help you." Chelsea took the bottle of wine from her. "Pregnant lady with wine, coming through."

In addition to Katie, who wore a big white hat that declared her THE BRIDE, Chloe encountered a sea of familiar faces—Nikki, Janey, Tiffany, Jenny, Sydney Harris, Erin Barton, Carolina O'Grady, Daisy Babson, Mallory Vaughn, Lizzie James, Kara Torrington, Victoria Stevens, Laura Lawry and a bunch of McCarthys—Linda, Stephanie, Grace, Maddie and Abby as well as Frank's girlfriend, Betsy Jacobson.

"Ladies!" Jenny held up her phone. "Big news from the mainland! I'm an auntie! Hope and Paul had Scarlett Marion Martinez at two thirty this afternoon, weighing in at six pounds, nine ounces and eighteen inches. Hope delivered her naturally, and they sent pictures."

Everyone offered their congratulations and passed the phone around to view the photos of the baby.

"She's beautiful," Linda McCarthy declared.

Jenny took back the phone. "I've got to call Alex and make plans to take Ethan over to meet his baby sister. He's been with us since they went to the mainland because he has school. He must be so excited!"

Katie called Chloe over to her. "Come meet my sisters—Julia and Cindy. Julia's my twin, not that you can tell that by looking at us." Katie vibrated with excitement.

"Nice to meet you both." Chloe shook hands with Julia and Cindy. "I've heard so much about you."

"Likewise," Julia said. "Katie talks about you all the time and says you're the coolest chick she's ever met. I try not to be insulted by that."

Chloe laughed. Whereas Katie was a blue-eyed blonde, Julia had dark hair and gray eyes and Cindy had light brown hair and brown eyes. Despite the differences in their coloring, Chloe could see a resemblance among the sisters, and she saw hints of their brother, Owen, in each of them.

"It's true! She's so cool!" Katie burped—loudly, which sent her sisters and Chloe into hysterics. "Sorry. Too much champagne. Show them your ink, Chloe."

"Do I have to?"

"Yes, it's gorgeous! I want ink just like yours."

Julia took the champagne from her sister. "Easy, badass. You need to pace yourself, or you'll be tits up by eight o'clock, and that's when the strippers are coming."

"Wait," Chloe said. "There's really going to be strippers?"

"Hell yes!" Julia fist-pumped. "I came straight from Texas, and I brought 'em with me! They're *cowboy* strippers! Wait till you see their six-packs and tight little asses." She fanned her face. "So hot, you'll *melt*!"

"No way," Maddie said. "Mac is going to kill me."

"You can say you had no idea." Cindy used her thumb to point to Julia. "Blame her. She's the wild child of our family. We never could control her."

"I don't know about this, Jule," Katie said, hiccupping. "I don't think Shane would want me cavorting with strippers right before our wedding."

Julia waved her hand, brushing aside Katie's concerns. "Oh please! It's all in good fun. And it's too late to turn back now." Julia checked her watch. "They're already on the island!"

"Oh God," Katie said, moaning.

Chloe nudged Chelsea. "What're they doing?" Chloe pointed to the center of the living room, where Janey sat on the floor collecting and counting money that was being tossed her way by the other women.

"They're taking bets."

"On?"

"What time the guys will show up and which one of them will be first through the door."

"They're *betting* on that?"

Linda McCarthy joined them, patting Chloe's arm. "It's become tradition. The men are rather predictable, so they make it fun to take wagers."

"You people are insane," Chloe said, astounded and amused.

"We know." Janey looked up from the floor with an expression that could only be called diabolical. "And we own our insanity because it's so damned fun to torment them."

"Although Mac makes it super easy because he's almost always the first one through the door," Laura said.

"Not tonight he won't be," Maddie said. "I had a talk with him and told him it's time to pass the torch to someone else."

"That'll be the day." Linda produced a fifty-dollar bill. "My money is on him."

"*Whoa*," Janey said. "Mama just upped the ante and bet against her own son!"

"I'll put a hundred on Alex," Jenny said. "If he hears there might be strippers, he'll be here so quick, his head—and mine—will spin."

"I'll put a hundred on Luke," Sydney said.

Linda pulled out another fifty. "Not to be outdone, make that a hundred on Mac."

"It's a sad day when your own mother bets against you," Maddie said, feigning sadness on behalf of her husband.

"I'm nothing if not a realist, sweetheart, and I know my son. He'll be the first one through that door or my name isn't Linda McCarthy."

"I wish I could disagree with you," Maddie said, giggling.

"We wouldn't have him any other way, would we?" Linda asked her daughter-in-law.

"Um, well…"

The others cracked up laughing.

"Remember the last time we told them there'd be strippers?" Tiffany said. "Blaine was so mad that we had the hottest makeup sex ever."

"Oh God, Mac was, too," Maddie said.

"We got them *so* good," Jenny said.

"What's going to happen when they find out there really are strippers coming?" Chloe asked.

"The shit's gonna hit the fan," Chelsea said bluntly. "And it'll be epic."

. . .

AFTER HE TOOK a ton of grief for kissing Chloe in front of everyone, Finn tried to settle in and enjoy the evening with his favorite men. The whole crew was there, including Grant and Evan, who'd made it home to Gansett in time for the bachelor party and would be staying for the summer. Dan Torrington and Slim Jackson were also back on the island after wintering in Los Angeles and Palm Beach, respectively.

Those guys had the right idea—party all summer on Gansett and then head for warmer climates in the winter. Grant had come home with the news that Stephanie was expecting and that they'd be staying close to home for the rest of this year.

Blaine introduced Riley and Finn to his brother, Deacon, as Owen walked around handing out bottles of beer to newcomers that included David Lawrence and Seamus O'Grady, who was married to Joe's mom.

"I wasn't going to say anything, and don't tell Grace that I did, but we're knocked up, too," Evan said with a giddy grin.

"So are we," Adam said.

"Wait, *what?*" Grant and Evan said in stereo.

Mac put his arm around Adam's shoulders. "You heard him right. Turns out our boy is going to be a dad—again."

"That is fantastic news." Grant hugged Adam. "I'm thrilled for you guys."

"Thanks. We're pretty thrilled, too. At least we are when Abby isn't puking up her guts."

Owen groaned. "That's the worst. Laura went through that both times. It was brutal."

"How long did it last?" Adam asked.

"Um, I hate to tell you, but she was sick the whole time."

Adam groaned. "Ugh. I can't imagine that. Abby is barely functioning. She even hired someone to run the store for her this summer because she doesn't think she can do it."

"Wow, that's hard-core," Evan said. "We've been lucky so far. Grace has felt great, and she's super-*duper* horny."

"Shut it, Evan," Big Mac said as he came in with Ned, Frank and

Kevin. The fabulous foursome was back together since Ned returned from Italy. "No one wants to hear about your horny wife."

"Um, I do," Evan said, grinning. "That's my favorite subject."

"Ciao," Ned said, as he accepted a beer from Owen, who was Shane's best man. Mac, Riley and Finn were his groomsmen.

"How was your trip?" Finn asked Ned.

"Magnifico," Ned said, kissing his fingertips with dramatic flair.

"You can barely speak English," Big Mac said to him. "And now we've got to put up with you speaking Italian?"

Ned huffed with pretend indignation while the others howled.

"Good one, Dad," Evan said, slapping Big Mac on the back.

"Watch yerself," Ned said to Evan. "Or I'll start becoming an *unsilent* partner in yer studio."

"Oh God," Evan said, recoiling. "I take it back. I take it all back."

Ned chuckled. "Thought ya might say that."

"How's the studio doing?" Adam asked Evan.

"It's great. Josh has done a fantastic job of keeping things moving while I was gone. I'm going to be recording my new album there this summer."

"That's awesome," Grant said. "It's so freaking great to be home. I love the sunshine in the winter, but there's no place like Gansett Island."

"Hear, hear," Evan said, raising his beer bottle. "Now, let's talk about Shane."

Shane groaned. "Let's not and say we did."

"You know better than that, son." Frank squeezed Shane's shoulder. "Let me go first."

"Here it comes, cuz." Adam handed Shane a fresh beer. "Drink up."

"Hush," Frank said. "All of you." When he had their attention, Frank cleared his throat. "I can't think about your wedding to Katie without getting a great big lump right here…" Frank pointed to his neck and cleared his throat again as he battled his emotions. "…because you got it so bloody right with her. The two of you are perfect for each other, and I can't wait to welcome yet another Lawry to our family. Everyone here, we all know what you had to go through to get to where you are now, and I think I speak for all of us when I say that no one deserves the happiness you've found with Katie more than you do, son. I love you, I'm so proud of you, and I can't wait to dance at your wedding. To Shane."

The others raised their bottles. "To Shane!"

"My turn," Big Mac said.

Shane groaned, earning a glare from his uncle.

"I just want to say that your dad is absolutely right," Big Mac said. "You deserve this happiness so very much, and we are thrilled for you and Katie. Love you, Shane."

"What they said." Kevin used his thumb to point to his brothers. "We're all so proud of you and how you've weathered the storm to get to this moment with Katie. She's the best, and we couldn't be happier for both of you. Love you, buddy."

CHAPTER 30

Finn found himself oddly emotional, listening to the tributes to his cousin, who had, indeed, been to hell and back while married to his first wife, Courtney. Quite some time after they were married, Shane had learned that she was a drug addict. He'd gotten her through rehab only to receive divorce papers for his troubles. For a while, they hadn't been sure that Shane would ever get over the way his marriage had ended. But he'd come to Gansett to help Laura with the renovations to the Sand & Surf, had met Katie and had rebuilt his shattered life. And then, over the winter, Courtney had overdosed and died, breaking Shane's heart all over again.

"Thanks, everyone," Shane said, understated as always. He was, by far, the quietest and most contained of the McCarthy cousins.

"We're not finished yet," Owen said. "It's the best man's turn."

"Now you're in trouble," Adam said.

Owen ignored the razzing to focus on Shane. "You guys all know what my family and I went through at the hands of my dad growing up. I never would've survived it without Katie and Julia, who were right there with me through the worst of it as we protected our younger siblings and ran interference for them with our dad. I've always known that someday, I'd have to let them go, and I hoped that when the time came, I'd be able to be somewhat graceful about it and refrain from throat-punching any guy who dared to even look at them."

"Jesus," Mac muttered. "He's worse than I am."

"*No one* is worse than you are," Evan said.

"No one," Grant added.

Mac raised his middle finger and directed it at his brothers.

"As I was saying," Owen continued, giving Mac a pointed look, "the thought of either of them falling in love and getting married was almost too much for me to bear. Until Katie met Shane and showed me that when it's the right guy, there's no need for me to throat-punch him."

"Gee, thanks," Shane said, rubbing his throat while trying not to laugh.

"You're welcome," Owen said, super serious.

Another ripple of laughter went through the group.

"I absolutely love that Laura's little brother is marrying my little sister and that our kids will be double cousins and that the four of us will take this journey together. I love you like a brother, Shane, and I just ask you to take good care of my Katie. She's the absolute best."

Shane's eyes were bright with unshed tears as he hugged Owen and said something that only Owen could hear.

Owen nodded and patted Shane on the back.

"Can we drink now?" Mac asked.

"Don't let me stop you," Shane said. "And, um, thanks, everyone, for coming out tonight and for all the good wishes. Katie and I are excited for the wedding and for everything else."

"Especially the wedding night," Evan said, "which is the whole point of the wedding."

"Dad, will you please do something about him?" Grant said.

"Sorry," Big Mac said, "he's a lost cause."

Evan beamed with pleasure. "Yes, I am. Now, about the wedding night—"

"Shut up, Evan," the others said in a loud chorus.

Joe Cantrell came in through the wide garage doors. "What's he saying now?"

"It's not worth repeating." Mac handed Joe a beer. "Good of you to join us."

"I had the last run from the mainland." As the owner of the Gansett Island Ferry Company, Joe often filled in as needed.

"Thanks for coming," Shane said.

"Wouldn't have missed it. But, um, listen, I think we might have a very small problem."

Everyone gave Joe their full attention.

"What kind of problem?" Big Mac asked.

"The stripper kind."

"Oh *no*," Mac said. "I'm not falling for that nonsense again."

"This could be legit," Joe said. "I saw them. They were on the boat just now."

After a long silence, Blaine spoke first. "You saw actual male strippers on the ferry."

"Yes."

"How do you know they were strippers?" Evan asked.

Joe gave him a withering look.

"What? It's a legit question! I assume you don't have a ton of experience identifying male strippers. Although, I could be wrong about that…"

"Shut the fuck up, will you? I've never seen a male stripper in my life except for on TV and in movies, but there were eight guys on the boat in cowboy hats and chaps and not much else. Caused quite a stir with the women in the office who sold them their tickets. There was actual screaming when they turned to walk away, because their ass cheeks were out and proud."

"Oh my God," Mac said, his face purple with rage. "And they're headed to *my house*. Let's go, boys."

Big Mac stood in the doorway and held up his hand. "Before you run off half-cocked, may I remind you of what happened in Anguilla when you thought it was a good idea to steal their clothes while they were skinny-dipping?"

"That was different, Dad," Mac said through gritted teeth. "That was a *prank*. This is actual half-naked men going to my house where my wife and children live to do God knows what."

"Um, actually," Joe said, "it's more like three-quarters naked."

Mac charged forward.

His father stopped him with his hand on Mac's chest. "Take a minute and think before you act."

"I don't want to take a minute. I want to get to my wife before a band of naked cowboys arrives at my house."

"I agree with him," Blaine said. "This is not happening."

Big Mac kept his gaze fixed on Mac. "Why do you care if a band of naked cowboys is at your house?"

"*Why do I care?* Are you really asking me that?"

"Yeah, I guess I am. Are you afraid your pregnant wife is going to take off with a naked cowboy and leave you and her three other children to fend for yourselves?"

"No."

"Then what's the problem? It's harmless fun."

"And you don't care if your wife is drooling over a naked cowboy?"

"Nope, because at the end of the night, she'll come home to me and tell me all about it." Big Mac's eyes sparkled with delight as he leaned in closer to his son. "And she might even drool a little over me."

"The old man does have a bit of a point," Grant said, "even if the thought of Mom drooling over him is disgusting."

"Nothing disgusting about it, my friend," Big Mac said with a dirty grin.

"He does *not* have a point," Mac replied, seething.

"Ah, yeah, he does," Adam said. "The last time we followed you into battle, I didn't get any for a month. Abby was seriously pissed."

The other guys nodded.

"Maddie was so pissed, she nearly broke your arm marching you off the beach," Grant said to Mac. "You sure you want to go there again?"

"They're probably taking bets on which one of us is going to come busting in first," Shane said. "They're evil that way."

Finn glanced at Riley, wondering what his brother thought.

Riley shrugged, but his eyes were wide with dismay, probably because Nikki was at the party.

Quinn and Jared James approached the garage door, stopping when they seemed to realize they were interrupting something.

"What's going on?" Quinn, who was engaged to Big Mac's daughter Mallory, glanced between the two Macs.

"Word on the street is that there's gonna be strippers at the bachelorette party," Owen said.

"Didn't you guys already fall for that once before?" Jared asked.

"Saw them with my own eyes," Joe said, grimacing. "Need a brain scrub."

"You don't say." Quinn chuckled.

"There is nothing funny about this," Mac said, glaring at Quinn.

Owen stepped forward. "If I know my sister Julia, and I know her as well as I know anyone, the strippers are legit and they're probably as dirty as it gets."

"That's it," Mac said. "No more dicking around. I'm going over there."

Realizing he was fighting a losing battle, Big Mac sighed, dropped his arm and stepped back to clear the way for Mac to leave.

"Who's coming with me?" Mac asked.

"I am," Blaine said.

"No way am I missing this," Deacon said, chasing after Mac and Blaine.

"Mac's apt to get himself killed if he gets between the women and their strippers," Finn said to Riley.

"Yeah, it could get ugly. Let's go keep an eye on him."

"Hold our beers," Finn said to the others. "We've got this."

"Oh Jesus," Kevin said. "The babies are in charge."

He and Riley chased after Mac, Blaine and Deacon, managing to jump into the bed of Mac's truck in the second before he peeled out of the parking lot and gunned it for home.

Riley grasped the side of the bed for something to hold on to. "He's gonna get us killed."

"No shit," Finn said, white-knuckling it.

After a swift and perilous ride to Mac's house, Finn and Riley were more than ready to get the hell out of that truck bed.

"Christ on a stick," Riley said to Mac. "You're a lunatic."

"No one asked you to jump in the back."

"Someone has to keep you guys from doing something stupid," Finn said.

"So the babies decided to be our keepers?" Mac shot the comment over his shoulder as he made for the stairs to the back deck.

Riley, Finn and Deacon followed Mac and Blaine up the stairs. The first thing Finn heard was the music—loud, wild and twangy. Oh shit, they were too late. For the rest of his life, he'd never forget the sight that greeted them in Mac's living room: buff cowboys in chaps, gyrating, and the women who were also gyrating, laughing and screaming. Was Katie getting a *lap dance*? For the first time ever, Finn wished he was blind.

"Oh. My. God." Riley's words summed things up rather well.

"Mom is the winner!" Janey screamed. "Mac was first again!"

Blaine went over to shut off the music, and the stunned silence that followed seemed to get the attention of the women who hadn't noticed the arrival of the men.

Maddie spoke first. "Uh. Oh."

"Show's over, boys." Blaine flashed his badge. "Get out. Right now."

"The show is not over, boys." With her eyes flashing with anger, Tiffany went to her husband, placed her hand on his chest and walked him backward. "Move it, buster. Don't you dare come in here flashing that badge when we are having innocent fun."

"There is nothing innocent about naked men flashing their junk in your face!"

"They are not flashing their *junk*, and if you want me to ever look at your junk again, you will *get out of here! Now!*"

For a long, charged moment, no one moved or even seemed to breathe.

Until Blaine blinked and the fight seemed to go out of him. "Tiffany…"

"Leave, Blaine. Right now."

"I'm not leaving," Mac said. "I live here."

"You won't live here anymore if you don't get the hell out of my party," Maddie said.

Linda snorted and then quickly tried to cover the fact that she was trying not to laugh.

"This is awesome," Deacon said. "And here I thought Gansett would be so boring."

"Shut up and get out," Blaine said to his brother. "We're staying outside until they're gone."

"Knock yourselves out." Tiffany flipped the switch on the wireless speaker the strippers had brought. "Now, where were we, ladies?"

Blaine took Mac by the arm and dragged him along as the guys retreated to the deck.

"She can't kick me out of my own house," Mac said.

"I think she just did," Riley said.

"This is fucked up," Blaine said, pacing the length of the deck as screams of laughter came from inside.

Someone called Finn's name.

He spun around and was shocked to see Missy standing in Mac's yard. What the hell was she doing there?

"You got Mac covered?" he asked Riley.

"Ah, yeah, but what're you doing?"

"Seeing what she wants and getting rid of her—in that order."

"You should let Blaine deal with it." Blaine was so consumed by what was happening inside the house that he hadn't noticed Missy in the yard.

Though Finn agreed with his brother, he decided to see if he could get rid of her without involving cops. After ten years of friendship, he figured he owed her that much, even if she had become unhinged lately. He went down the stairs, took her by the arm and directed her away from the house. "What're you doing here?"

"I wanted to talk to you. People in town said you might be here."

"There's nothing left for us to talk about, Missy. When you came here and basically assaulted me and shoved my girlfriend—"

"I'm your girlfriend! I have been for years!"

"Not anymore. We're over. I told you that two years ago when I moved out here."

"And the whole time, you kept texting me and calling me—"

"Because we were friends! But we were *not* together! You knew that. Don't even pretend like you didn't know."

"I didn't know! You said you were coming home, and I waited for you! All that time, I waited. You're not going to just toss me aside like I meant nothing to you."

"That's not what I did, and you know it. You *know* it."

"This is what I know—you're going to tell that stupid bitch you've been hanging out with that you're done, and you're coming home with me because you said you would. You're going to keep your promises to me, or else."

Finn regretted not taking Riley's advice to call Blaine. "Or else what?"

She shocked the ever-loving fuck out of him when she pulled out a switchblade and flipped it open. "Or someone's going to get hurt."

CHAPTER 31

The strippers were ridiculous and raunchy, and the women were loving every minute of it. Chloe had enjoyed watching Maddie and Tiffany dispose of their irate husbands. The Chester sisters were not messing around. While the others whooped it up with the strippers, Chloe edged closer to the slider, hoping for a word with Finn. But when she looked out, she didn't see him. However, she noticed Riley looked worried.

She stepped outside in time to hear a woman screaming in the yard.

"Oh fuck." Riley took off down the stairs.

Curious, Chloe followed him and was shocked to see Missy with a shiny blade pointed at Finn, who stood before her, his hands raised, trying to talk some sense into her.

Riley moved toward them, trying not to startle Missy, whose full attention was on Finn.

Chloe didn't think. She reacted, racing down the stairs, prepared to throw herself between him and anything that could hurt him. The instinct to protect him was so overwhelming that a surge of adrenaline had her running like she had before the RA had made her joints hurt too badly to run. She didn't feel anything other than the urgent need to get to him.

Riley was ahead of her, and in the second before he would've reached his brother, Missy pounced.

Finn let out an unholy cry of pain that made Chloe see red as she jumped onto Missy's back, pulling her off Finn.

Everything shifted into silent slow motion as Missy reared back, trying to dislodge Chloe and causing them both to fall backward.

Chloe landed hard, and Missy came down on top of her.

Chloe's side burned, and her vision swam as Riley pulled Missy off her. She could tell that Riley was screaming, but Chloe couldn't seem to hear what he was saying.

And then Blaine was there, cuffing Missy.

Riley's words finally permeated the fog. "She fucking stabbed my brother!"

Finn!

Oh God, Finn had been stabbed.

Chloe tried to get up, to get to him, but her legs wouldn't hold her, and she collapsed onto the grass.

Riley's screams grew more frantic. "She got Chloe, too! Somebody call the rescue. Hurry!"

Chloe caught a glimpse of a huge red stain on the front of Finn's shirt before everything faded to black.

FINN CAME TO SLOWLY, trying to figure out where he was and why the lights were so bright. What the hell was going on? He tried to sit up.

A hand on his shoulder stopped him.

David Lawrence? What was he doing there? Oh right, he'd come to the bachelor party. The party. The strippers. Missy. Oh fuck.

"What's wrong?" Finn asked David. Why did his voice feel so weird?

"Your ex-girlfriend stabbed you."

"She *what*?"

"She stabbed you in the chest. Fortunately, she didn't hit anything important. You lost some blood and had forty-two sutures. You'll be sore for a few days, but otherwise, you're going to be okay."

Wait. Missy had *stabbed* him?

He tried to remember what had happened, but it was all a blur.

"She also cut Chloe."

David's words cleared the fog in his brain and filled Finn with rage like he'd never felt before. "Where is she?"

"In the other exam room—"

Finn got up quickly, so quickly that his head swam, and his legs buckled.

Riley materialized, grabbing him before he could fall.

Finn fought back against his brother's tight hold. "Let me go! I need to get to her!"

Riley held firm. "You need to sit the fuck down before you bust open your stitches and bleed to death."

"Take me to her right now, Riley, or I swear to God, you're going to need a doctor."

"Is it okay, Doc?" Riley asked David.

"Take it slow. He lost a lot of blood."

"Get me to her, Riley. *Now.*"

Taking David's directive to heart, Riley moved so slowly that Finn wanted to roar from the minutes it took to walk down the corridor to where Chloe was in a bed with Katie, Julia and Nikki by her side. Her face was pale, her violet eyes huge and tearful when she saw Finn.

"You shouldn't be up!" she said.

"Excuse me, ladies." Finn moved to her side when Nikki and Katie made room for him.

He took a visual inventory. "Where are you hurt?"

"My side. It's just a flesh wound. Ten stitches and a tetanus shot, which was the worst part of it."

Finn couldn't recall any other time in his life when he'd felt this kind of fury. He turned to Riley. "Where is she?"

"Blaine carted her off to jail."

"Call him. Tell him I want her charged with everything. No leniency."

"I'm on it, bro. Why don't you sit before you fall over?"

"Move over," Finn said to Chloe.

She shifted to the left, wincing, and made room for him.

That wince made him feel like he'd been stabbed in the heart. Seeing her hurt broke something in him, especially when she was hurt because of him.

"You should've seen her," Riley said. "She was like Wonder Woman taking Missy down."

"I was not," Chloe said. "I just did what anyone would do."

"You were incredible," Riley said. "You might've saved his life. David said if she'd hit him an inch to the left, he could've bled out before they got him here."

"His life has become very important to me," Chloe said.

To his tremendous mortification, Finn's eyes filled with tears. "I could kill her for hurting you," he said in a gruff whisper.

"I could kill her for hurting *you*."

"What do you say we give them a minute?" Riley said to the others.

Katie kissed Chloe's cheek and hiccupped her way out of the room, followed by Julia, Nikki and Riley.

"Katie has had the hiccups for hours," Chloe said. "She can't handle her champagne."

"Chloe…"

"What if she still has them for the wedding?"

"Chloe." He held her chin, looked into her gorgeous eyes and kissed her. "I don't want to talk about Katie. I want to talk about why you would endanger yourself the way you did."

"She was holding a knife on you. I didn't think. I just acted."

He put his arms around her, wincing when the laceration on his chest made its presence known. "Don't ever, *ever* do that again. You're the most precious thing in the world to me, and I can't bear the idea of you getting hurt because of me."

"It wasn't because of you. It was because of *her*, and I'd do it again in a hot second. Because you're every bit as precious to me, and I'd rather get hurt than let anyone try to take you from me."

"Have I mentioned recently that I love you?"

"It's been a couple of hours, but you were kinda busy being stabbed, so I'll let it go this time."

"I really, *really* love you."

"I love you just as much, but I really hope we've seen the last of Missy."

"God, I hope so, because we've got things to do and plans to make."

"And love to make."

He cupped her cheek, drinking in the details of her exquisite face. "That, too."

The moment was interrupted when Kevin appeared in the doorway, his eyes wild. "She *stabbed* you?"

"Both of us, actually."

"You've got to be kidding me. What the hell was she hoping to accomplish?"

"Who knows? Who cares? Blaine tossed her in jail, where I hope she'll stay for the foreseeable future."

Kevin ran a trembling hand through his hair. "Jesus, Finn. You scared the hell out of me."

"Sorry."

"Not your fault."

"Take a breath, Dad. Everyone's fine."

Kevin took a deep breath and released it. "The entire town is in the waiting room, along with eight mostly naked cowboy strippers."

Chloe glanced at Finn, and when their eyes met, they lost it laughing. The knot of fear that had settled in his chest when he heard she was hurt finally eased. They were both okay, and they had each other.

What else did they need?

Nothing. As long as he had her, he had everything.

EPILOGUE

*S*hane and Katie were married on the beach outside the Surf
at sunset, exchanging vows under an arbor Finn had helped
build as one of the last official tasks on the Wayfarer job site. He and
Riley had brought it over to the Surf the day before so Shane and
Katie could use it to be married in the place where he saved her life.
As he watched his cousin get married, Finn wondered how many
brides and grooms would stand under that arbor in the years to come.
He took pride in what they'd built together. The Wayfarer and that
arbor would provide a lasting legacy to the McCarthy family, which
had rallied around him and Chloe after they were injured.

Riley and Nikki had taken them both home to Eastward Look to
recover, and the others had kept them in food and entertainment for a
week, until they insisted on returning home to Chloe's so they could
have some much-needed time alone.

She'd asked him to move in with her rather than going to the
apartment Nikki had offered, and Finn had jumped at the chance to
live with Chloe. It had taken him two hours to move his stuff from the
rental house to her place, which already felt like home to him. As long
as she and Ranger were there, he had what he needed.

Katie's sister Cindy had filled in for Chloe at the salon and had liked it so much, she'd asked to be considered for a position when the spa opened. Mac had agreed to renovate the building on the hotel property over the winter as part of the hotel renovation, with a goal of opening the spa by next May. After consulting with Big Mac and Linda, it had been decided to offer only a spa at the hotel and keep the Curl Up and Dye salon open in town to attract the walk-in traffic that had been so critical. Cindy had been thrilled to be asked to work there. She'd be moving to the island next spring. Chloe would manage both businesses and would no longer be cutting hair as of the spring. As an official employee of the McCarthy family business, she'd been offered full benefits, relieving another of her most pressing concerns.

With plenty of work lined up over the next year, Finn was eager to get started, to throw himself into life as a full-time island resident.

Next week, he and Chloe were traveling to the mainland to meet with an RA specialist in Boston that David had recommended and planned to attend a conference on the topic in Florida over the winter, taking some vacation time in the sun while they were there.

Finn still hoped to talk Chloe into marrying him at some point, but he wasn't in any rush.

Missy had been charged with multiple felonies after stabbing him and Chloe and had been denied bail. He still couldn't believe that she'd actually stabbed him—and Chloe—or that Chloe had tackled Missy and possibly saved him from a life-threatening injury.

He'd started calling Chloe Wonder Woman. His Wonder Woman. His love. As he watched Shane and Katie commit their lives to each other, he grinned at Chloe, who was standing next to Katie on the other side of the proceedings, to let her know he was thinking of her. Hell, when was he not thinking of her?

She returned his smile, her eyes watery from the emotion of watching two people who'd survived life's storms and come out whole and happy on the other side as they took the next step in their journey together.

After the newly married couple had made their way down the

aisle, Finn offered his arm to Chloe, and whispered in her ear. "Maybe someday?"

She looked at him with her heart in those dazzling violet eyes. "Maybe."

He could live with maybe—as long as he got to live with her.

SHANE HELD Katie in his arms for their first dance as husband and wife, waiting to see what their best man had decided to play for them. They'd left it up to Owen, certain that he'd find the right song for them.

Standing on the stage at the front of the big room at the Wayfarer, with his sleeves rolled up and guitar in hand, Owen barely resembled the sharply dressed man he'd been half an hour ago as he gave away the bride and then stood by Shane's side as the best man.

Now, he looked more like the rumpled Owen they knew and loved.

"I can't wait to hear what he picked," Katie whispered to Shane.

He couldn't stop staring at his new wife. She was the most beautiful bride he'd ever seen.

Owen began to strum his guitar, his gaze fixed on the two of them. "As the best man, it's my job to toast the bride and groom, and I also got assigned the added task of finding the right song for them, something that summed them up as a couple. So first I want to welcome Shane to the Lawry family. My mom, my brothers and sisters and I all agree—we're made better by having you as one of us, Shane. And Katie… What can I say about my sweet sister Katie, who has been right by my side through the best and the worst moments of my life, except that I love you and I'm so happy for you and Shane. Laura and I have been blessed to have a front-row seat to Shane and Katie's love story, which began at our wedding, after Shane saved Katie's life when she got caught in a riptide."

"And right after that," Shane whispered to his wife, "she saved my life."

She beamed up at him, her smile lighting up her entire face. "We saved each other."

"I finally decided on 'Lucky' by Colbie Caillat and Jason Mraz. I think Shane and Katie would agree that the day he saved her life was the same day their luck changed forever. I love you both and wish you the best of everything. To Shane and Katie."

While the other guests raised their glasses in toast, Owen played the opening notes of the song.

Holding Katie in his arms, with the weight of the ring she'd given him on his finger and their whole life ahead of them, Shane was thankful for the second chance he'd gotten with her. He still thought of Courtney often and mourned her premature death. But she was firmly in the past now. His present and his future were with Katie, the best thing to ever happen to him.

"Love you, Mrs. McCarthy," he said as he kissed her.

"Love you, too, Mr. McCarthy."

JULIA STOOD in the back of the room, watching her sister dance with her new husband, trying not to be a jealous cow and failing miserably. Katie had never had a boyfriend until Shane, while Julia had dated every man in Texas. And *Katie* was getting married first?

How was that fair? She'd done the legwork—literally—and had absolutely nothing to show for it but three maxed-out credit cards, an empty bank account, an eviction notice and a newfound reliance on Maker's Mark bourbon. She'd used the last of her savings to bring the cowboy strippers to Gansett, wanting to do something spectacular for Katie, and now she had to figure out how she was going to get home to Texas.

She'd have to hit up Owen for a loan, and the thought of that made her sick.

Julia took a deep drink from her glass of bourbon, straight up, while giving thanks to the inventor of the open bar.

"What's up?"

The voice startled and intrigued her. Deep and scratchy and a bit dirty sounding. Then she made the mistake of looking his way and realized who he was. That guy Deacon from the other night, the police chief's brother, who'd been at the clinic when she arrived with Katie to check on Chloe and Finn.

He'd given her a long, obvious once-over then.

She'd been unimpressed, even if he was hotter than the sun. In her experience, hot guys were most often world-class douchebags, and she'd had more than enough of his type.

"Usually when someone asks you what's up, you would say 'nothing' or 'not much.' It's kinda rude to not respond at all."

"It's also kinda rude to tell someone you've never talked to that they're rude."

"If the shoe fits, baby."

"Go away. I'm watching my sister and her husband dance."

"Weddings are boring. Let's get out of here and go find some trouble."

Julia stared at him as if he was insane. "It's my sister's wedding. My *twin* sister's wedding. I'm not leaving. I'm the maid of honor, for crying out loud."

"You two are twins?" He looked at Katie and then at her. "I don't see the resemblance."

"That's because we're fraternal twins."

"Huh. Interesting. So that's a no to getting out of here?"

"A hard no. I'm sure that's a word you don't hear often, but I'm happy to repeat it for you if you didn't understand the first time."

He flashed a grin that was so sexy, her panties melted, and her ovaries stood up for a better look at him. "You're a feisty little thing, aren't ya?"

"What're you even doing here? You're not friends with Shane or Katie."

Shrugging, he said, "I was bored, so I crashed."

"You did not."

"Did so. Are you going to tattle on me? Are you that kind of girl? The one who was always up the teacher's ass in school?"

"I've never been up a teacher's ass in my life."

His eyes grew very wide in the second before he lost his shit laughing. "Bet you've never said that sentence before."

She leaned in close to him. "Go. Away."

He leaned in closer, so close his nose nearly touched hers. "Make. Me."

Curling her lip in distaste, she backed away from him.

"Tell me this—if she's your twin and you're the maid of whatever, why don't you seem happy for her?"

"Not that it's any of your business, but I *am* happy for her. *No one* is happier for her than I am."

"Coulda fooled me. You were staring at them like you wanted to stab them." He caught himself. "Sorry. Poor choice of words after the recent outbreak of stabbings."

"Will you please leave me alone to enjoy my sister's wedding? You shouldn't even be here."

"I'd be happy to leave you alone if I thought you were actually enjoying your sister's wedding."

Julia wanted to smack him—and she wanted to kiss him, which infuriated her because he was obnoxious and entitled and everything she disliked about men in general. So she decided to ignore him, returning her focus to Shane and Katie, who were gazing into each other's eyes and kissing as Owen sang to them. They were so damned sweet, her teeth ached.

"You really ought to take off with me. I could show you a good time."

God, she was tempted. So bloody tempted. Anything was better than pretending everything was fine when it wasn't. It wasn't fine at all, and it might never be again.

She sighed deeply.

"Darlin'," he said in a softer tone, "I don't know who you think you're fooling, but you're not fooling me. You're miserable. And what I don't understand is why someone who's so beautiful she makes me want to beg would ever want to be miserable if she had a choice not to be?"

He made a good point. In fact, it was an excellent point. She was miserable, and Katie was so happy, she'd never even notice that Julia was gone. And as far as compliments went, he'd quite outdone himself. She stared into the golden-brown eyes of the devil himself, feeling the pull of temptation so great, she couldn't resist. "Let's go."

~

KEEP READING for a sneak peek at *Trouble After Dark,* Deacon and Julia's story!

THANK you for reading *Yours After Dark!* I hope you enjoyed Finn and Chloe's story and the chance to catch up with the Gansett Island crew. Twenty books into this series, and still the most fun I've ever had as a writer is every chance I get to take the ferry to Gansett to find out what's going on with the McCarthys and their friends! There is MUCH more to come for the Gansett Island Series with NO END IN SIGHT!

A huge, profound thank you to my friend, Celeste Hornbeck, who has rheumatoid arthritis and other autoimmune disorders, for helping me to flesh out Chloe's character and her challenges with RA.

After you finish reading, join the Yours After Dark Reading Group *https://www.facebook.com/groups/YoursAfterDark/* to dish on the details of the book with spoilers allowed and encouraged, and make sure you're a member of the Gansett Island Reader Group at *www.facebook.com/groups/McCarthySeries* to never miss news of the series or upcoming books. Have you read ALL my books? If so, you're a Marie Force SUPER Fan! Join the SUPER Fan reader group at *www.facebook.com/groups/MarieForceSUPERFans/.*

As always, thank you to my husband, Dan, and the incredible team that supports me behind the scenes, including Julie Cupp, Lisa Cafferty, Holly Sullivan, Isabel Sullivan, Nikki Colquhoun, Anne Woodall, Kara Conrad, Linda Ingmanson, Joyce Lamb, Jules Bernard and Jessica Estep. I couldn't do what I do without their help and support.

And the biggest thanks of all to the incredibly supportive readers who have given me a dream-come-true career. Love you all.

xoxo

Marie

TROUBLE AFTER DARK

Chapter 1

Deacon didn't wake up that morning planning to crash a wedding and steal a bridesmaid. In fact, he didn't wake up expecting much of anything on his fourth day on the boring remote island where his older brother was holding him hostage for the summer. What the hell was he even doing on Gansett, the island he'd grown up on, where his brother was now the freaking police chief?

Deacon was a grown-ass man and could do whatever the hell he wanted. Why was it that Blaine had such power over him, even now? It was infuriating, but he didn't need to think about that while he had a hot babe holding on tight to him as he drove his motorcycle toward the bluffs on the island's north side.

Since she was wearing his only helmet, he could hear the ends of her sexy red dress whipping in the wind as he accelerated around a curve, dodging a family of four on bicycles who were smack in the middle of the road. He, who didn't have much trouble attracting female companionship, could honestly say it'd been years—perhaps a lifetime—since he'd met a woman as stunningly gorgeous as the one wrapped around him at this moment.

He'd first seen her the other night at the island's clinic after one of the craziest nights in recent memory—when Finn McCarthy's ex had stabbed Finn and his new girlfriend, Chloe Dennis. Half the island had ended up at the clinic, along with the cowboy strippers who'd been performing at Katie Lawry's bachelorette party when the stabbings took place.

Deacon didn't recall Gansett Island being that interesting when he'd lived there as a kid.

His bridesmaid had long, silky dark hair that fell nearly to her spectacular ass, flawless, lightly tanned skin, bluish-gray eyes fringed with extravagant lashes, large breasts that were barely contained by the halter-style dress and lips made for kissing.

The last thing Deacon needed, especially right now, was any more female complications. However, he'd dare any red-blooded man to take one look at the sexy bridesmaid on the back of his bike and not want her riding shotgun. Downshifting, he turned into the lot at the bluffs, pulled into a parking spot and killed the engine on the vintage Harley he'd bought off a buddy on Cape Cod, where he used to live before being banished to freaking Gansett by his goddamned brother.

Despite his displeasure at being back on the island, Deacon had to admit that Gansett had a kind of wild, untamed beauty that he'd forgotten about during his years away. He wanted to hate everything about being there and how Blaine had issued the ultimatum to Deacon, as if he were a recalcitrant teenager—*come home with me or face major charges*. Hell of a choice.

He got off the bike and helped his stolen bridesmaid remove the helmet. First order of business would be finding out the name of the goddess he'd run away with. Wait till Blaine figured out that she'd left with him. He'd pop a nut. Deacon choked back a laugh at the thought of Blaine's nuts popping because of him. It had given him great pleasure all his life to irritate his brother and vice versa. Why? He couldn't say. That's just how it was between them.

Blaine was such a Dudley Do-Right, and Deacon, well, he was a Dudley Do-Whatever-the-Fuck-He-Wanted.

With his passenger free of the helmet, Deacon took another long look at one of the most exquisite female faces he'd ever beheld. It didn't take a rocket scientist to see that while she was stunning, she was also troubled, and he'd had more than his share of troubled females. The most recent one had landed him in jail, which had led to his ex-communication to Gansett, the last place on earth he wanted to be. Although, the godforsaken island was looking pretty damned good to him at the moment.

She ran her fingers through her hair, attempting to straighten the damage done by the helmet. A light breeze ran through it, and he was struck dumb by the sight of her standing on the cliff like a goddess in red.

Deacon Taylor didn't stare at women.

They stared at him.

His unprecedented reaction to her should've been cause for concern in light of his recent troubles, but he wasn't going there today. He opened the compartment on the bike where he'd stashed a six-pack of beer and some ice before leaving the apartment Blaine had assigned him, located behind the house Blaine shared with his wife, Tiffany, and their daughters. Getting to know his nieces was one of the only goals he had for his summer in exile.

After twisting off the cap on one of the beers, he handed it to the goddess.

"Thanks."

"What's your name?"

"Julia."

He touched his bottle to hers. "Nice to meet you, Julia. I'm Deacon."

"I've never met anyone named Deacon before."

"It was my grandmother's maiden name."

"It's cool."

"Thanks. I like it." He took a deep drink from the bottle. Blaine would pop the other nut if he knew Deacon was riding around with a makeshift cooler on the bike. Deacon took pleasure in thinking up new ways to aggravate his brother. "Are you sure it's okay that you left the wedding?"

"It's fine. Katie is so wrapped up in Shane that I doubt she's even noticed I'm gone."

He wondered if she felt as sad as she looked and sounded. "Are you okay?"

"Never better." She forced a smile and then chugged half the beer in one long gulp.

"Do you not like him?"

"Who?"

"Your sister's husband?"

"Oh God, I *love* him. He's great. He saved Katie's life when she got caught in a rip current outside the Surf."

"*Whoa.*"

"Trust me, our whole family will love him forever for saving her. Not to mention, his sister, Laura, is married to our brother Owen."

Deacon took a minute to do that math in his head.

"A brother and sister married a brother and sister," Julia said. "Nothing illegal about it."

He laughed. "If you say so."

"Laura and Shane are awesome. Owen and Katie got lucky. They married into an amazing family. Do you know the McCarthys?"

"Sure. I grew up with them. My sister-in-law's sister is married to Mac McCarthy."

"My family loves your brother. He was good to my mom during a very difficult time in her life."

"That sounds like him. He's a saint."

"You don't like him?"

"He's okay, if you like the holier-than-thou type."

"I take it you're not holier than thou?"

He laughed. "Ah, no, not exactly." Deacon wondered what she'd think of him if she'd known he spent a night in jail five days ago or that his saintly brother had gone to the mainland to bail him out. His alleged "crime" had been for a good cause, but when a woman like Julia heard the word *jail*, she wouldn't stick around to hear the

312

story. She'd be long gone, and he wouldn't blame her. "How about you?"

"I try to do the right thing, for all the good that does me."

"What do you mean?"

"People suck."

"All people, or certain people?"

"Most people, especially the male variety. Present company excluded, of course."

He laughed again. "Of course. What happened?"

They wandered over to a massive log that acted as a curb to keep cars from driving off the cliff and sat next to each other.

"It would be easier to tell you what *hasn't* happened."

"Okay…"

She didn't say anything for a long time as she stared out at the ocean.

Deacon thought she wasn't going to tell him, but then she began to speak.

Why was she about to air out her problems with a total stranger? Not to mention another guy who was so hot, he probably had women throwing their panties at him to get his attention? What was the point of talking about it? How would that fix anything? It wouldn't, but she found herself telling him anyway.

"People take advantage of me."

His brow furrowed, possibly with a touch of outrage that she appreciated. "How so?"

"Guys… They take one look at me and think they have me figured out. I must be easy. I must be a slut. I must be gullible. I attract all the wrong guys, especially the most recent one." Her heart was like a cement block in her chest when she thought about Mike, the promises he made, the things he said to her, the hopes she'd pinned on him, only to find out he was far worse than the others.

"What did he do?"

"He played me for a total fool. Made me fall in love with him. Promised me everything. We were going to have a life together and

313

have babies and a house." To her fierce annoyance, a tear slid down her cheek. She brushed it away angrily. The last thing she wanted was to spend any more tears on him. "Then his mom got sick with breast cancer. He was freaking out because she didn't have insurance and needed treatment. I loaned him money."

Deacon winced. "How much?"

"Fifteen thousand. Almost everything I had."

"Let me guess—his mom's not sick?"

"Ding-ding-ding. You win the grand prize. His mom is fine, but his *girlfriend* is pregnant, and he needed the money to get prenatal care for her because *she's* the one who doesn't have insurance."

"What a scumbag."

"So now she has my money, my man and a bouncing new baby. I heard they're buying a house together. They probably used my money for the down payment." She couldn't help but laugh at the sheer madness of it all. "Ridiculous, right?"

"I'm sorry that happened to you."

"I am, too, because now I'm flat broke and stuck here for God knows how long until I can make some money to get home to Texas and get the stuff I had to move into storage after I got evicted from my apartment. If the storage place doesn't sell it since I missed a payment."

"What's in Texas?"

"A job I used to love until I got a new boss who called me Sugar and asked me to do personal errands for him."

"Seriously?"

"Yep. It was awful, and after I loaned Mike the money and then figured out what he was really about, I called out sick for a few days because I was too upset to leave my house. The boss from hell told me not to bother coming back. That led to me losing my apartment when I couldn't afford to renew the lease."

"I'm sorry. That sucks."

She shrugged. "I brought it on myself by being stupid with Mike and then handing my boss a reason to get rid of me. I tried to find another job, but nothing materialized that would pay me enough to cover my expenses."

"So there's no reason to go rushing back, then?"

"No." Julia kicked at a rock with one toe of the sandals she'd bought with the last of her credit card limit. She'd been sleeping on a coworker's sofa since she got evicted from the apartment she used to share with Katie. She'd been unsuccessful in landing a roommate, thus her basically homeless status. That word *homeless* struck fear in her heart the way few things ever had since she left her violent childhood behind. "Not anymore."

"I'm stuck here for the summer, too."

"How come?"

"Doing a favor for my brother."

"What kind of favor?"

"He needed a harbor master. I'm certified, so he asked me to come do it."

"What about your regular job?"

"I'm between jobs at the moment, so the timing worked out for both of us." The Cape Cod town he'd worked for last year as the harbor master had invited him not to return after he spent a night in their jail.

"What'll you do after the summer?"

"Find something else, I suppose. How about you?"

"Same, I guess. Although the thought of starting over, *again*, is exhausting."

"You've done it before?"

"Too many times to count. My father was in the military. We moved a lot."

"We grew up here on Gansett. I *hated* it."

"My siblings and I spent summers here with our grandparents, who owned the Sand & Surf. It was our favorite place on earth." It was also the only break they got from their abusive father. They'd lived for those blissful summer days on Gansett, where they were safe and loved and away from the monster, as they'd called General Mark Lawry.

"Really? You loved it?"

"We loved everything about it."

"Huh. I couldn't believe when my brother moved back here willingly to become the police chief. He hated it as much as I did when we were kids. But then he met Tiffany, who's now his wife, and he's happier than a pig in shit with her, their kids and a job he loves."

"Do you like his wife?"

"I barely know her, but he sure as hell likes her."

"Some people get lucky. Like my brother and sister." Julia, Katie and Owen had been a team for so long that she wasn't sure how she was supposed to function now that they'd found new lives for themselves. Julia was lost without them, not that she'd ever say as much to them. She'd never do anything to undermine their hard-won happiness.

But God, she missed them. Especially Katie, who'd lived with Julia until Katie had come to Gansett for Owen and Laura's wedding, met Laura's brother, Shane, and decided to stay for a while that turned into forever.

Julia glanced at Deacon, wishing he wasn't hotter than the sun. He had messy dirty-blond hair the color of honey, golden-brown eyes, a muscular body and the perfect amount of scruff on his jaw. But whatever. Who cared if he was hot? She'd had more than enough of good-looking guys who were beautiful on the outside and assholes on the inside. "How old are you?" she asked, to make conversation more than anything.

"Thirty-five. You?"

"Thirty-three."

"I wonder if we ever crossed paths as kids. Although, I'm sure I'd remember you."

Another line from another pretty mouth. Julia had heard such things so many times, they barely registered anymore. Just once, she wished a man would see her for who she was on the inside, but they never got past her packaging to discover what she was really made of.

She looked out at the gorgeous scenery, wishing Gansett could have the usual effect on her. As a kid, she'd come alive the minute she stepped off the ferry. This time, she was just dead inside. "Did you think you'd have it all figured out by now?"

"Have what figured out?"

"Life."

He shrugged. "I never had a timeline for figuring things out. Maybe that's why my brother finds me so annoying. He's a police chief at thirty-seven. Not that he didn't have his rocky times, but he's married with two kids and a dream job. He's got his shit together."

"I thought I'd be married with kids in school by now. I had a definite timeline. But nothing has worked out the way I hoped it would, and now..."

"What?"

"Nothing. It doesn't matter."

"Sure it does. What were you going to say?"

She crossed her arms against her knees and rested her head on her forearms while continuing to look at him. "Maybe it's time to give up on the dream."

"Don't say that. You never know what's coming right around the next corner. Anything can still happen."

She shrugged. "Doesn't matter."

"You know what I'm thinking?"

"What?"

"You're stuck here for a while. I'm stuck here for a while. Maybe we can hang out and make it more fun than it would be otherwise."

Sitting upright, she eyed him with skepticism that was hardwired into her DNA after so many disappointments. "Is 'hang out' a metaphor for sex?"

He laughed. "You don't pull any punches, do you?"

"What's the point of pulling punches? I've had enough of the bullshit. If you're asking me to have sex with you, the answer is no. I'm on a man diet, which also means a dick diet. If you're looking for someone to hang out with and have some fun this summer that doesn't in any way include sex, then sure, why not?"

Deacon sputtered with laughter. "A dick diet?"

"Yes, as in no dick."

317

He shook his head as his gorgeous eyes danced with amusement. "How long have you been on this so-called diet?"

"Four months now."

"Gotcha. Just to be clear—I wasn't coming on to you. I was legitimately looking for a friend to make my summer in exile more bearable."

Julia didn't believe him, but she kept that to herself.

"What's your number?"

She recited it and watched him tap the numbers into his phone and add her name to the contact.

"I'll hit you up."

"Cool." She couldn't care less if she ever heard from him. "I should probably go back to the wedding."

"How come?"

"I'm the maid of honor. I have to give a toast after dinner."

"You want a plus-one?"

"It's kind of late for that at this point since you already crashed."

His wolfish grin revealed a sexy dimple in his left cheek and did wondrous things to his gorgeous face—and she had no doubt he knew that. "I won't eat."

Julia had to admit that soldiering through the rest of this night would be more fun with a companion than it would've been on her own. Besides, Katie was so in love with her new husband that she wouldn't even notice if Julia brought a last-minute guest. "Sure. Let's go."

Trouble After Dark is available in print from *Amazon.com* and other online retailers, or you can purchase a signed copy from Marie's store at *shop.marieforce.com*.

OTHER BOOKS BY MARIE FORCE

Contemporary Romances Available from Marie Force

The Gansett Island Series

Book 1: Maid for Love (*Mac & Maddie*)

Book 2: Fool for Love (*Joe & Janey*)

Book 3: Ready for Love (*Luke & Sydney*)

Book 4: Falling for Love (*Grant & Stephanie*)

Book 5: Hoping for Love (*Evan & Grace*)

Book 6: Season for Love (*Owen & Laura*)

Book 7: Longing for Love (*Blaine & Tiffany*)

Book 8: Waiting for Love (*Adam & Abby*)

Book 9: Time for Love (*David & Daisy*)

Book 10: Meant for Love (*Jenny & Alex*)

Book 10.5: Chance for Love, *A Gansett Island Novella* (*Jared & Lizzie*)

Book 11: Gansett After Dark (*Owen & Laura*)

Book 12: Kisses After Dark (*Shane & Katie*)

Book 13: Love After Dark (*Paul & Hope*)

Book 14: Celebration After Dark (*Big Mac & Linda*)

Book 15: Desire After Dark (*Slim & Erin*)

Book 16: Light After Dark (*Mallory & Quinn*)

Book 17: Victoria & Shannon (Episode 1)

Book 18: Kevin & Chelsea (Episode 2)

A Gansett Island Christmas Novella

Book 19: Mine After Dark (*Riley & Nikki*)

Book 20: Yours After Dark (*Finn & Chloe*)

Book 21: Trouble After Dark (*Deacon & Julia*)

Book 22: Rescue After Dark *(Mason & Jordan)*

Book 23: Blackout After Dark

The Green Mountain Series

Book 1: All You Need Is Love *(Will & Cameron)*

Book 2: I Want to Hold Your Hand *(Nolan & Hannah)*

Book 3: I Saw Her Standing There *(Colton & Lucy)*

Book 4: And I Love Her *(Hunter & Megan)*

Novella: You'll Be Mine *(Will & Cam's Wedding)*

Book 5: It's Only Love *(Gavin & Ella)*

Book 6: Ain't She Sweet *(Tyler & Charlotte)*

The Butler, Vermont Series

(Continuation of Green Mountain)

Book 1: Every Little Thing *(Grayson & Emma)*

Book 2: Can't Buy Me Love *(Mary & Patrick)*

Book 3: Here Comes the Sun *(Wade & Mia)*

Book 4: Till There Was You *(Lucas & Dani)*

Book 5: All My Loving *(Landon & Amanda)*

Book 6: Let It Be *(Lincoln & Molly)*

Book 7: Come Together *(Noah & Brianna)*

The Treading Water Series

Book 1: Treading Water

Book 2: Marking Time

Book 3: Starting Over

Book 4: Coming Home

Book 5: Finding Forever

The Miami Nights Series

Book 1: How Much I Feel (*Carmen & Jason*)

Book 2: How Much I Care (*Maria & Austin*)

Book 3: How Much I Love (*Dee's story*)

Single Titles

Five Years Gone

One Year Home

Sex Machine

Sex God

Georgia on My Mind

True North

The Fall

The Wreck

Love at First Flight

Everyone Loves a Hero

Line of Scrimmage

The Quantum Series

Book 1: Virtuous (*Flynn & Natalie*)

Book 2: Valorous (*Flynn & Natalie*)

Book 3: Victorious (*Flynn & Natalie*)

Book 4: Rapturous (*Addie & Hayden*)

Book 5: Ravenous (*Jasper & Ellie*)

Book 6: Delirious (*Kristian & Aileen*)

Book 7: Outrageous (*Emmett & Leah*)

Book 8: Famous (*Marlowe & Sebastian*)

Romantic Suspense Novels Available from Marie Force

The Fatal Series

One Night With You, *A Fatal Series Prequel Novella*

Book 1: Fatal Affair

Book 2: Fatal Justice

Book 3: Fatal Consequences

Book 3.5: Fatal Destiny, *the Wedding Novella*

Book 4: Fatal Flaw

Book 5: Fatal Deception

Book 6: Fatal Mistake

Book 7: Fatal Jeopardy

Book 8: Fatal Scandal

Book 9: Fatal Frenzy

Book 10: Fatal Identity

Book 11: Fatal Threat

Book 12: Fatal Chaos

Book 13: Fatal Invasion

Book 14: Fatal Reckoning

Book 15: Fatal Accusation

Book 16: Fatal Fraud

Historical Romance Available from Marie Force

The Gilded Series

Book 1: Duchess by Deception

Book 2: Deceived by Desire

ABOUT THE AUTHOR

Marie Force is the *New York Times* bestselling author of contemporary romance, romantic suspense and erotic romance. Her series include Gansett Island, Fatal, Treading Water, Butler Vermont and Quantum.

Her books have sold nearly 10 million copies worldwide, have been translated into more than a dozen languages and have appeared on the *New York Times* bestseller more than 30 times. She is also a *USA Today* and *Wall Street Journal* bestseller, as well as a Speigel bestseller in Germany.

Her goals in life are simple—to finish raising two happy, healthy, productive young adults, to keep writing books for as long as she possibly can and to never be on a flight that makes the news.

Join Marie's mailing list on her website at marieforce.com for news about new books and upcoming appearances in your area. Follow her on Facebook at www.Facebook.com/MarieForceAuthor and on Instagram at www.instagram.com/marieforceauthor/. Contact Marie at marie@marieforce.com.